PRAISE FOR

THE MUSE

"Burton's latest historical novel will carry you to 1967 London and 1937 Spain to follow two women and a mystery about a lost painting that ties them together. The masterpiece links their stories over decades as the writing rotates between time periods. Love, war, desire, and art—it's all here."   — *Elle*

"*The Muse* asks a lot of its readers, in the best of ways. It asks us to pay close attention, given the unexpected paths that wander variously through time, race, global politics and art history. . . . [A] well-crafted tale that draws you in, and in the end, respects you as a reader."   — *Star Tribune* (Minneapolis)

"Like its predecessor, this is a tale with a refreshingly feminist slant, interested in the slipperiness of meaning"
                                                   — *Daily Mail* (UK)

"In *The Muse* Burton has once again done the hard yards of research to reimagine not one but two distinct eras of the 20th century, and fused them to an intricate story of imposture. . . . Burton, juggling the two narratives, sets off chimes and resonances in her double portrait of hidden creativity. . . . Emotional and sensual."
                                                   —*The Guardian* (UK)

"*The Muse* is a brilliantly realised story, and the parallel narratives are perfectly balanced, propelling the story forward at break-neck speed. Both tales conclude with their own shocking climaxes, which tie the whole story neatly together. An exhilarating read, Jessie Burton can expect more awards to soon be coming her way."   — *Sunday Herald* (Scotland)

"Those who loved *The Miniaturist* will find here all the cliffhangers, twists and heart-stopping revelations they expected, and in two evocative settings: sweaty, stuffy London and the bohemian Spanish finca. . . . As a study of female creativity, it triumphs. . . . Burton's muse, in whatever form it may take, is clearly in fine fettle."
—*The Telegraph* (UK)

"Burton's second, equally ambitious work, *The Muse*, continues [the] theme of 'parallel possibilities,' dual selves and our ability—or lack thereof—to claim ownership of people, places, language and art. . . . Burton emerges as the architect of a well-structured and intricate plot with tremendous scope, and a stylist with a talent for recreating life's ordinary and extraordinary moments alike in great splashes of colour. . . . [A] riveting and deeply intimate exploration of inspiration, personal freedom and the many selves that make up a life."
—*Financial Times* (UK)

"[A] rich palette of ideas and emotions. . . . The novel excellently explores the writing process itself."
— *The Independent* (UK)

"Burton's second novel is a complex, vividly drawn tale. . . . Striking. . . . The intricate way in which Burton pulls the two plots together is unexpected and impressive, a most original story about creative freedom, finding one's voice, and the quest for artistic redemption."
—*Publishers Weekly*

"Like her best-selling *The Miniaturist* (2014), Burton's second novel is a smart blend of literary and commercial fiction with intriguing characters and a compelling mystery at its center. . . . Both historical settings are deftly evoked, and the alternating story lines enhance the charged atmosphere. Burton creatively infuses historical fiction with mystery in her exploration of the far-reaching consequences of deception, the relationship between art and artist, and the complex trajectory of women's desires.
—*Booklist*

"*The Muse* is a tale of love, obsession, and rejection, as well as a compelling mystery. . . . Burton interweaves the two stories skillfully. . . . You will remember Burton's characters long after you finish *The Muse*; and her prose is magical. Highly recommended."

—*Historical Novels Review*

"Historical fiction lovers as well as fans of B.A. Shapiro's *The Muralist* and *The Art Forger* will appreciate the intriguing characters, skillful writing, and evocative atmosphere of two very different eras."   —*Library Journal*

"Each portion of her story is carefully and entertainingly patterned and possessed of propulsive narrative force, and the interweaving of narrative threads—when it comes—is inventive, intricate, surprising and attentively handled. . . . Burton is also adept at generating atmosphere and a sense of place (both Spain and London are vividly realised), and she brings to her characters' lives a degree of commitment, imaginative compassion and detail that brings them palpably and affectingly to life. Olive and Odelle in particular feel fully faceted, carefully imagined, memorable."

—*The National* (UAE)

"Jessie Burton meticulously reconstructs two different worlds connected by a thread of lies and ruminates on the nature of truth in art. Each seemingly disparate story is told with remarkable care and evident research, and draws the reader in to a serpentine tale about art, truth and artistic ambition. Fans of *All the Light We Cannot See, The Nightingale* and *The Goldfinch* will be equally enthralled by this beautifully constructed story of art, ambition and the sacrifices one makes in the pursuit of both."

— Bookreporter.com

THE MUSE

ALSO BY JESSIE BURTON

The Miniaturist

The

MUSE

JESSIE BURTON

ecco

An Imprint of HarperCollinsPublishers

THE MUSE. Copyright © 2016 by Peebo & Pilgrim Limited. All rights reserved. Printed in the United States of America. No part of this book may be used or reproduced in any manner whatsoever without written permission except in the case of brief quotations embodied in critical articles and reviews. For information address HarperCollins Publishers, 195 Broadway, New York, NY 10007.

HarperCollins books may be purchased for educational, business, or sales promotional use. For information please e-mail the Special Markets department at SPsales@harpercollins.com.

A hardcover edition of this book was published in 2016 by Ecco, an imprint of HarperCollins Publishers.

FIRST ECCO PAPERBACK EDITION PUBLISHED 2017.

Designed by Shannon Nicole Plunkett
Background art by GreenArt Photography/Shutterstock, Inc.

Library of Congress Cataloging-in-Publication Data has been applied for.

ISBN 978-0-06-240993-5

17 18 19 20 21 OV/LSC 10 9 8 7 6 5 4 3 2 1

For
Alice, Teasel
& Pip

Never again will a single story be told as though it were the only one.

—JOHN BERGER

CONTENTS

PART V – RUFINA AND THE LION

PART VI – THE STICKING PLACE

AFTERWORD

THE MUSE

PART I

Cabbages and Kings

JUNE 1967

1

*N*ot all of us receive the ends that we deserve. Many moments that change a life's course – a conversation with a stranger on a ship, for example – are pure luck. And yet no one writes you a letter, or chooses you as their confessor, without good reason. This is what she taught me: you have to be ready in order to be lucky. You have to put your pieces into play.

When my day came, it was so hot that my armpits had made moons on the blouse the shoe shop supplied to every employee. 'It don't matter what size,' the woman said, dabbing herself with a handkerchief. My shoulders were aching, my fingertips chafing. I stared; sweat had turned the pale hair at her brow the colour of a wet mouse. London heat; it never has anywhere to go. I didn't know it, but this woman was the last customer I would ever have to serve.

'I'm sorry?'

'Just *said*,' the woman sighed. 'Any size'll do.'

It was nearing closing time, which meant all the crumbs of dry skin – toe jam, as we called it – would have to be hoovered out of the carpet. Cynth always said we could have moulded a whole foot out of those scrapings, a monster to dance a jig of its own. She liked her job at Dolcis Shoes, and she'd got me mine – but within an hour of our shift, I craved the cool of my room, my cheap note-books, my pencil waiting by the narrow bed. 'Girl, you got to pick your face *up*,' Cynth would whisper. 'Or you working in the funeral parlour next door?'

I backed away to the stock cupboard, a place where I would often escape, immune as I was by now to its noxious smell of rubbered soles. I thought I might go in and scream silently at the wall of boxes.

'Wait! Oi, wait,' the woman called after me. When she was sure she had my attention, she bent low and slipped off her scuffed pump, revealing a foot that had no toes. Not one. A smooth stump, a block of flesh resting innocently on the faded carpet.

'See,' she said, her voice defeated as she kicked off the second shoe to reveal an identical state of affairs. 'I just . . . stuff the ends with paper, so it don't matter what size you bring.'

It was a sight, and I have not forgotten it; the Englishwoman who showed me her toeless feet. At the time, perhaps I was repulsed. We always say the young have little truck with ugliness, have not learned to mask shock. I wasn't that young, really; twenty-six. I don't know what I did in the moment, but I do recall telling Cynth, on the way home to the flat we shared off Clapham Common, and her whooping with delighted horror at the thought of those toeless feet. 'Stumpy McGee!' she shouted. 'She comin' to get yuh, Delly!' And then, with an optimistic pragmatism; 'At least she wear any shoe she want.'

Perhaps that woman was a witch coming to herald the change in my path. I don't believe so; a different woman did that. But her presence does seem a macabre end to that chapter of my life. Did she see in me a kindred vulnerability? Did she and I occupy a space where our only option was to fill the gap with paper? I don't know. There does remain the very slim possibility that all she wanted was a new pair of shoes. And yet I always think of her as something from a fairy tale, because that was the day that everything changed.

OVER THE LAST FIVE YEARS since sailing to England from Port of Spain, I'd applied for many other jobs, and heard nothing. As the train from Southampton chugged into Waterloo, Cynth had mistaken house chimneys for factories, the promise of plenty of work.

It was a promise that turned out to be harder to fulfil. I often fantasized about leaving Dolcis, once applying to a national newspaper to work as a tea-girl. Back home, with my degree and self-regard, I would never have dreamed of serving any soul tea, but Cynth had said, 'A one-eye stone-deaf limping frog could do that job, and they still won't it give to you, Odelle.'

Cynth, with whom I had gone to school, and with whom I had travelled to England, had become besotted with two things: shoes, and her fiancé, Samuel, whom she had met at our local church off Clapham High Street. (Sam turned out to be a great bonus, given the place was normally full of old tanties telling us about the good old days.) Because of finding him, Cynth did not strain at the bit as I did, and it could be a source of tension between us. I would often declare that I couldn't take it any more, that I wasn't like her, and Cynth would say, 'Oh, because I some sheep and you so *clever*?'

I had telephoned so many advertisements which stated experience was not essential, and people sounded so nice – and then I'd turn up and miracle, miracle! every single job had been taken. And yet, call it folly, call it my pursuit of a just inheritance, but I kept on applying. The latest – and the best I'd ever seen – was a typist post at the Skelton Institute of Art, a place of pillars and porticoes. I'd even visited it once, on my monthly Saturday off. I'd spent the day wandering the rooms, moving from Gainsborough to Chagall, via aquatints by William Blake. On the train home to Clapham, a little girl gazed at me as if I was a painting. Her small fingers reached out and rubbed my earlobe, and she asked her mother, 'Does it come off?' Her mother didn't chide: she looked like she damn well wanted the earlobe to give its answer.

I hadn't scrapped with the boys to gain a first-class English Literature degree from the University of the West Indies for nothing. I hadn't endured a child's pinch in a train carriage, for nothing. Back home, the British Consulate itself had awarded me the Commonwealth Students' first prize for my poem, 'Caribbean Spider-Lily'. I'm sorry, Cynth, but I was not going to put shoes on sweaty Cinderellas for the rest of my life. There were tears, of course, mainly sobbed into my sagging pillow. The pressure of desire curdled inside me. I was ashamed of it, and yet it defined me. I had bigger things I wanted to do, and I'd done five years of waiting. In the meantime, I wrote revenge poems about the English weather, and lied to my mother that London was heaven.

THE LETTER WAS ON THE mat when Cynth and I got home. I kicked off my shoes and stood stock-still in the hallway. The postmark was London W.1, the centre of the world. The Victorian tiles under my bare feet were cold; my toes flexed upon the brown and blue. I slid one finger under the flap of the envelope, lifting it like a broken leaf. It was the Skelton Institute letterhead.

'Well?' Cynth said.

I didn't reply, one fingernail pressed into the floral Braille of our landlord's Anaglypta wallpaper, as I read to the end in shock.

The Skelton Institute
Skelton Square
London, W.1

16th June, 1967
Dear Miss Bastien,
Thank you for sending your application letter and curriculum vitae.

To thrive, under whatever circumstances life presents us, is all anyone can hope for. You are clearly a young woman of great ability, amply armoured. To that degree, I am delighted to invite you to a week's trial role in the typist position.

There is much to learn, and most of it must be learned alone. If this arrangement suits you, please advise me by return of post whether the offer is to be accepted, and we will proceed from there. The starting salary is £10 p/w.

With warm wishes,
Marjorie Quick

£10 a *week*. At Dolcis, I only got six. Four pounds would make the difference of a world, but it wasn't even the money. It was that I was a step closer to what I'd been taught were Important Things – culture, history, art. The signature was in thick black ink, the 'M' and 'Q' extravagant, almost Italianate in grandeur. The letter smelled faintly of a peculiar perfume. It was a bit dog-eared, as if this Marjorie Quick had left it in her handbag for some days before finally deciding to take it to the post.

Goodbye shoe shop, goodbye drudgery. 'I got it,' I whispered to my friend. 'They want me. I blimmin' got it.'

Cynth screamed and took me in her arms. 'Yes!'

I let out a sob. 'You did it. You *did* it,' she went on, and I breathed her neck, like air after thunder in Port of Spain. She took the letter and said, 'What kind of a name is Marjorie Quick?'

I was too happy to answer. Dig your nail in that wall, Odelle Bastien; break apart that paper flower. But I wonder, given what happened, the trouble it led you to, would you do it again? Would you turn up at eight twenty-five on the morning of Monday 3 July 1967, adjusting that new hat of yours, feet wiggling in your Dolcis shoes, to work in the Skelton for £10 a week and a woman called Marjorie Quick?

Yes, I would. Because I was Odelle and Quick was Quick. And to think you have a second path is to be a fool.

2

I envisaged I would be working in a whole atrium of clattering typists, but I was alone. Many of the staff were away, I supposed, taking annual holidays in exotic places like France. Every day, I would walk up the stone steps towards the Skelton's large doors, upon whose panes was blazoned in gold lettering ARS VINCIT OMNIA. Hands on the *vincit* and the *omnia*, I pushed inside to a place that smelled of old leather and polished wood, where to my immediate right was a long reception desk and a wall of pigeonholes looming behind it, already filled with the morning's post.

The view in the room I'd been assigned was terrible – a brick wall smeared black with soot, and a long drop when you looked down. I could see an alleyway, where porters and secretaries from the neighbouring building would line up and smoke. I could never hear their conversations, only watch their body language, the ritual of a patted pocket, heads together like a kiss as the cigarette was flourished and the lighter caught, a leg bent coquettishly backwards against a wall. It was such a hidden place.

Skelton Square was tucked behind Piccadilly, on the river side. Standing there since George III was king, it had been lucky in the Blitz. Beyond the rooftops the sounds of the Circus could be heard; bus engines and honking motor cars, the keening calls of milk boys. There was a false sense of security in a place like this, in the heart of London's West End.

FOR NEARLY THE WHOLE OF the first week the only person I spoke to was a girl called Pamela Rudge. Pamela was the receptionist, and she would always be there, reading the *Express* at her counter, elbows on the wood, gum popping in her mouth before the big fellers showed and she threw it in the bin. With a hint of suffering, as if she'd been interrupted in a difficult activity, she would fold the newspaper like a piece of delicate lace and look up at me. 'Good *morning*, Adele,' she'd say. Twenty-one years old, Pam Rudge was the latest in a long line of East-Enders, an immobile beehive lacquered to her head and enough black eyeliner to feed five pharaohs.

Rudge was fashionable, overtly sexual. I wanted her mint-green minidress, her pussy-bow blouses in shades of burnt orange, but I didn't have the confidence to show my body like that. All my flair was locked inside my head. I wanted her lipstick shades, her blusher, but English powders transported me into strange, grey zones where I looked like a ghost. In the make-up department in Arding & Hobbs at the Junction, I'd only find things called 'Buttermilk Nude', 'Blonde Corn', 'Apricot Bloom', 'Willow Lily' and other such bad face poetry.

I decided that Pamela was the kind of person whose idea of a good night out was to gorge her face on a saveloy in Leicester Square. She probably spent her salary on hair spray and bad novels, but was too stupid to even read them. Perhaps I communicated some of these thoughts – because Pamela, in turn, would either maintain wide-eyed surprise at seeing me every day, as if astonished by my audacity to keep coming back, or express comatose boredom at the appearance of my face. Sometimes she would not even look up as I lifted the flap of the reception desk and let it drop with the lightest bang just at the level of her right ear.

Cynth once told me that I looked better in profile, and I said that made me sound like I was a coin. But now it makes me wonder about my two sides, the arch impression I probably gave Pamela, the spare change of myself that no one yet had pocketed. The truth was, I felt so prim before a girl like Rudge.

She knew no other *blacks*, she told me on the Thursday of that first week. When I replied that I hadn't known any either by that name till I came here, she looked completely blank.

BUT DESPITE THE CLUNKY DANCE with Pamela, I was ecstatic to be there. The Skelton was Eden, it was Mecca and Pemberley; the best of my dreams come to life. A room, a desk, a typewriter, Pall Mall in the morning as I walked from Charing Cross, a boulevard of golden light.

One of my jobs was to transcribe research notes for academic men I never saw, except for their nearly indecipherable hand-writing, scribbling about bronze sculptures or sets of linocuts. I enjoyed this, but my principal duty revolved around a tray on my desk that would be filled with letters I was to type up and leave with Pamela downstairs. Most of the time they were fairly mundane, but every now and then I'd pick up a gem, a begging letter to some old millionaire or decrepit Lady Whatnot on their last legs. *'My dear Sir Peter, it was such a pleasure to identify the Rembrandt you had in your attic back in '57. Would you consider using the Skelton to help catalogue the rest of your wonderful collection?'* and so on. Letters to financiers and film moguls, informing them that a Matisse was floating around, or would they fancy a new room of the Skelton being named after them, as long as we could fill it with their artworks?

They were mainly written by the director of the Skelton, a man called Edmund Reede. Pamela told me Reede was in his sixties and had a short fuse. In the war, he had something to do with recovering art confiscated by the Nazis, but she didn't know any more. The name 'Edmund Reede' for me conjured up a quintessential, intimidating Englishness, Savile Rowers in Whitehall clubs; eat the steak, hunt the fox. Three-piece suit, pomaded hair, great-uncle Henry's golden watch. I would see him round the corridors, and he would look surprised every time. It was as if I had walked in naked off the street. We studied men like him at school – protected gentlemen, rich gentlemen, white gentlemen, who picked up pens and wrote the world for the rest of us to read.

The Skelton was a bit like that world, the world I'd been taught that I wanted to be in – and just by typing the letters, I felt closer to it all, as if my help in the matter was invaluable, as if I'd been picked for a reason. And the best thing was; I was fast. So once I had finished their letters, I used a spare hour here or there to type my own work – starting over and over again, scrunching up pieces of paper and making sure to put them in my handbag rather than leaving them like evidence in the waste-paper bin. Sometimes, I'd go home with my handbag brimming with balls of paper.

I told Cynth how I'd forgotten the smell of the Dolcis stock cupboard. 'It's as if one week can kill five years,' I said, determined and rhapsodic about my transformation. I told her about Pamela, and joked about the rigidity of her beehive. Cynth paused, frowning, for she was frying me an egg in our tiny flat, and the hob was unreliable. 'I pleased for yuh, Delly,' she said. 'I pleased it going so well.'

ON THE FRIDAY OF THE first week, Reede's letters completed, I was struggling with a poem in a quiet half-hour. Cynth had told me that the only thing she wanted as a wedding gift was 'something written – seeing as you're the only one who ever could.' Touched but agonized, I stared at the Skelton's typewriter, thinking how happy Sam and Cynth clearly made each other. It made me think about my own lack; the foot, but no glass slipper. It also made me realize how I had been struggling with my writing for months. I hated every word that came from me, couldn't let any of it breathe.

A woman walked in just as I lit upon a possible phrase. 'Hallo, Miss Bastien,' she said, and the idea melted away. 'Getting on? Allow me to introduce myself. I'm Marjorie Quick.'

I stood, knocking the typewriter in my haste, and she laughed. 'This isn't the army, you know. Take a seat.' My eye darted to the poem on the reel, and I felt sick to my stomach that she might walk round and see it.

Marjorie Quick came towards me, hand outstretched, her gaze flicking to the typewriter. I took her hand, willing her to stay on the other side of the desk. She did, and I noticed the cigarette scent that clung to her, mingled with a musky, masculine perfume that I recognized from the letter she'd posted, and I would later learn was called Eau Sauvage.

Marjorie Quick was petite, upright, dressed in a way that eclipsed Pamela's efforts. Wide black slacks that billowed like a sailor's as she walked. A pale-pink silk blouse with a grey satin necktie loosely slung inside it. She looked like something out of Hollywood, with her short, silvering curls, her cheeks seeming carved from a fine honeyed wood. She could have been in her early fifties, I supposed, but looked unlike any fifty-year-old I'd ever met. Her jawline was sharp and her glamour hovered.

'Hello,' I said. I couldn't stop staring at her.

'Any bother?' Quick seemed to feel the same, fixing her dark liquid irises on me, waiting for my answer. I noticed she looked rather flushed, a bead of perspiration on her forehead.

'Bother?' I repeated.

'Good. What time is it?' The clock was behind her, but she didn't turn.

'Nearly twelve-thirty.'

'So let us lunch.'

3

She had her name engraved on a brass plate upon her door. I wondered how many women in London, in this year of our Lord 1967, had their own office. Working-class women had menial jobs, or nursed in the NHS, or were factory or shop girls or typists like me, and it had been like that for decades. But there was a world of difference, an almost unnavigable journey, between that and having your name engraved on the door. Perhaps Marjorie Quick was a scion of the Skelton family, here in some honorary position.

She opened the door, the nameplate glinting in the rays of sun through the window beyond, and ushered me inside. Her room was white and airy, with huge windows looking onto the square. The walls were bare of paintings, which I thought odd, being where we were. Three were covered in bookshelves and I spied mainly nineteenth- and early-twentieth century novels, the surprise combination of Hopkins perching next to Pound, and a smattering of Roman history. They were all hardbacks, so I couldn't see if the spines were bent.

From her large desk, Quick grabbed a packet of cigarettes. I watched as she extracted one, hesitated, and then placed it delicately on her lips. I would become accustomed to her habit of speeding up her actions, only to slow them again, as if checking

herself. Her name lived up to her, but whether it was her languor-
ous or hasty side that was more natural was always hard to tell.

'Would you like one?' she asked.

'No, thank you.'

'Then I'll go on alone.'

Her lighter was one of those heavy, refillable silver varieties, to
be left on a table rather than slipped in a pocket. It was the kind
of thing you might see in a country house, a cross between a hand
grenade and something up for auction at Christie's. The Skelton
had a lot of money, I reckoned, and Quick reflected it. Unspoken,
but present, it was in the cut of her pink silk blouse, her brave
trousers, her smoking paraphernalia. In her. I wondered again
what exactly her role here was.

'Gin?' she said.

I hesitated. I never drank much, and I certainly did not like the
taste of spirits. The smell reminded me too much of the men in the
Port of Spain clubhouses – the bubble of rum through the blood,
working to a roar of squalid pain or euphoria heard upon the dust
roads into town. But Quick unscrewed the cap of the gin from a
table in the corner and poured some into two tumblers. She delved
in an icebox with a pair of tongs and dropped two cubes in my
glass, splashed it with tonic to the top, added a slice of lemon, and
handed it to me.

Sinking down into her chair as if she'd been standing for twenty
days, Quick slugged back her own gin, picked up the telephone
receiver and dialled a number. She sparked the lighter and a fat
orange flame appeared. The end of her cigarette sizzled, tobacco
leaf crisping into tendrils of blue smoke.

'Hello, Harris? Yes, whatever it is today. But twice over. And
a bottle of the Sancerre. Two glasses. How long? Fine.' I listened
to the cadences of her voice; clipped and husky, it didn't sound
entirely English, even though it had hints enough inside it of a
draughty boarding school.

She placed the receiver back down, and flicked her cigarette into a giant marble ashtray. 'The restaurant next door,' she said. 'I find it impossible to sit inside it.'

I sat down opposite her, cradling my glass, thinking of the sandwich Cynth had made for me, its edges curling in the heat of my desk drawer.

'So,' she said. 'A new job.'

'Yes, madam.'

Quick placed her glass on the desk. 'First things, Miss Bastien. Never call me "madam". Nor am I "miss". I like to be known as Quick.' She smiled, looking rueful. 'Your name is French?'

'Yes, I believe so.'

'You speak French?'

'No.'

'To have and to be confuse me greatly. I thought people spoke French in Trinidad?'

I hesitated. 'Only a few of our forebears were indoors, speaking with the French,' I said.

Her eyes widened – with amusement, offence? It was impossible to tell. I dreaded that my history lesson was too much, too arch, and I was going to fail my trial period. 'Of course,' she said. 'How interesting.' She took another slug of gin. 'There's not much to do here at the moment,' she went on, 'but I expect Mr Reede is keeping you busy with his endless flow of correspondence. I'm worried you'll be bored.'

'Oh, I'm sure I won't be.' I thought of Dolcis, of how they overworked Cynth and me; the way the husbands watched our buttocks whilst their wives slipped on their heels. 'I'm just so pleased to be here.'

'There's probably more life to be seen in one day at Dolcis Shoes than a week at the Skelton. Did you enjoy it?' she asked. 'Touching all those women's feet?'

The question was vaguely shocking, rimed with a sexual sharpness that stung me, virginal as I was. But I would not be cowed. 'In all honesty,' I replied, 'with thirty pairs a day, it was appalling.'

She threw back her head and laughed. 'All the cheeses of France!'

Her laughter was infectious and I giggled too. It was a ludicrous thing to say, but it melted the tension inside me. 'Some people don't mind it,' I said, thinking of Cynth, how I was abasing her for this exchange, this strange game whose rules I didn't know. 'It takes a skill.'

'I dare say. But so many anonymous toes.' She shuddered. 'We have all these beautiful portraits at the Skelton, but we're really just gangling arms, gurgling intestines. The heat inside the liver.' She looked at me hard, and took another drag. 'I've had a lot longer than you to come to that conclusion, Miss Bastien. Toes, the crooks of elbows. Enjoy dignity in them while you can.'

'I'll try,' I said, unsettled once again. There was a restlessness to her; it felt as if she was putting on a performance for me, and I didn't know why.

There was a knock on the door. Quick told them to enter and our lunch arrived on a trolley, pushed by a very small, elderly porter who only had one arm. A basket of rolls, two flat fishes, a buoyant-looking salad, a bottle of wine in a cooler, and something else hidden under a steel dome. The porter glanced at me, startled like a rabbit. His rheumy eyes slid back to Quick.

'That'll be all, Harris. Thank you,' Quick said.

'We haven't seen you all week, miss,' he replied.

'Ah – annual leave.'

'Somewhere nice?'

'No.' Quick looked momentarily disconcerted. 'Just a home stay.'

The porter changed his attention to me. 'Bit different to the last one,' he said, cocking his head. 'Does Mr Reede know you've got a wog in?'

'That will be everything, Harris,' said Quick, in a tight voice. He cast her a disgruntled look and left the trolley, staring at me as he backed out of the door.

'Harris,' Quick said when he'd gone, as if to say his name was explanation enough. 'The arm got lost in Passchendaele. He refuses to retire and no one has the heart to do it.' The porter's word clung to the air. Quick stood up and handed me a plate off the trolley.

'Just use the desk to rest it, if you don't mind.' She carried her own plate round to her side of the desk. She had a slim little back, her shoulder blades slightly poking through the blouse like a pair of fins. The wine had been uncorked and she poured us both a glass.

'It's very good. Not like the stuff we use for the public.' The glug of it was loud and lush and transgressive, like she was pouring me elixir in full daylight. 'Cheers,' Quick said briskly, raising her glass. 'I hope you like lemon sole.'

'Yes,' I replied. I'd never eaten it before.

'So. What did your parents say when you told them you were working here?'

'My parents?'

'Were they proud?'

I wiggled my toes in the confines of their shoes. 'My father's dead.'

'Oh.'

'My mother is still in Port of Spain. I'm an only child. She might not even have got my letter yet.'

'Ah. That must be hard for you both.'

I thought of my mother – her belief in England, a place she would never see; and I thought of my father, recruited into the RAF, gone down over Germany in a ball of flame. When I was fifteen, the Prime Minister of Tobago had declared that the future of the islands' children lay in their schoolbags. My mother, desperate for me not to live a life like hers and Dad's, pushed me to better myself – but for what, when all the land post-independence was being sold to foreign companies who invested the profits back into their own countries? What were we youngsters supposed to do, when we reached the bottom of those schoolbags and found nothing there – just a seam, split from the weight of our books? We had to leave.

'Are you all right, Miss Bastien?' said Quick.

'I came here with my friend, Cynth,' I said, not wishing to dwell on Port of Spain, the death board with Dad's name on it, his empty plot in Lapeyrouse Cemetery that Mama still kept vacant, the Catholic nuns who'd taught me as I grew up in my grief. 'Cynthia's engaged,' I said. 'She's getting married.'

'Ah.' Quick picked up her knife and began to lift a small segment of the sole, and I had the strange feeling of saying too much without having said anything at all. 'When?'

'In two weeks. I'm maid of honour.'

'And then what?'

'Then what?'

'Well, you'll be alone, won't you? She'll be living with her husband.'

Quick always insisted on skirting her own truths whilst getting to the core of yours. She told me nothing about the Skelton, focusing only on finding out about me, and had soon skewered my darkest fear. The fact was, Cynth's imminent departure from our little flat had hung between me and my oldest friend like a silent question, heavy with foreboding. We both knew she would leave to live with Samuel, but I couldn't imagine rooming with anybody else, so I didn't talk about it, and neither did she. I boasted about my new job and she fretted over wedding invitations and made me sandwiches I overlooked. The salary from the Skelton would cover the second room she was going to vacate, and this was my only comfort.

'I enjoy my own company,' I said, swallowing hard. 'It'll be nice to have some space.'

Quick reached for another cigarette, but then seemed to change her mind. *If you were alone*, I thought, *you'd have already smoked three more.* Her eyes rested briefly on my face as she lifted the steel dome to reveal a lemon meringue. 'Do eat something, Miss Bastien,' she said. 'All this food.'

Whilst I ate my slice of meringue, Quick didn't touch a crumb. She seemed born to all this, to the smoking and the telephone orders, the tangential observations. I imagined her in her twenties, raffing round London with a glamorous set, a cat amongst the Blitz. I was piecing her together from Mitford and Waugh, dousing her with a coat of my newly discovered Muriel Spark. It was perhaps a vanity, instilled in me from the education I'd received, which was little different from the model used in English public schools, with its Latin and Greek and boys playing cricket – but I had yearned for eccentric, confident people to enhance my life; I thought I deserved them, the sort of people you found only in novels. Quick hardly had to do anything, I was so sprung for it, so willing. Starved of my past life, I began to concoct a present fantasy.

'Your application interested me greatly,' she said. 'You write very well. *Very* well. At your university, you seem to have been one of the brightest students. I take it you think you're too good to be a secretary.'

Fear ran through me. Did this mean she was letting me go, that I hadn't passed the trial? 'I'm very grateful to be here,' I said. 'It's a wonderful place to work.'

She made a face at these blandishments and I wondered what it was she wanted. I reached for a bread roll and rested it in my palm. It was the weight and size of a small marsupial and I had an instinct to stroke it. Feeling her eyes upon me, I plunged my thumb into the crust instead.

'And what sort of things do you like to write?'

I thought of the piece of paper on the typewriter in the other room. 'Poems, mainly. I'd like to write a novel one day. I'm still waiting for a good story.'

She smiled. 'Don't wait too long.' I was quite relieved she gave me this instruction, because usually whenever I told people I wanted to write, they would tell me how their own lives would make the perfect subject. 'I mean it,' said Quick. 'You mustn't hang around. You never know what's going to pounce on you.'

'I won't,' I said, gratified by her insistence.

She sat back in her chair. 'You do remind me of someone I used to know.'

'I do?' I found this immensely flattering and waited for Quick to go on, but her face clouded, and she broke the spine of the cigarette she'd left on the side of the ashtray.

'What do you make of London?' she asked. 'You came in '62. Do you like living here?'

I felt paralysed. She leaned forward. 'Miss Bastien. This isn't a test. I'm genuinely interested. Whatever you say, I won't tell a soul. Cross my heart, I promise.'

I'd never told anybody this out loud. It may have been the gin, it may have been her open face, and the fact she didn't laugh at my dream of writing. It may have been the confidence of youth, or that porter Harris, but it all came tumbling out. 'I've never seen so much soot,' I said.

She laughed. 'The place is filthy.'

'In Trinidad, we were brought up being told that London was a magic land.'

'So was I.'

'You're not from here?'

She shrugged. 'I've been here so long I can hardly remember anything else.'

'They make you think London is full of order, and plenty, and honesty and green fields. The distance shrinks.'

'What distance do you mean, Miss Bastien?'

'Well, the Queen rules London and she rules your island, so London is part of you.'

'I see.'

I didn't think Quick did see, really, so I carried on. 'You think they'll know you here, because they also read Dickens and Brontë and Shakespeare. But I haven't met anyone who can name three of his plays. At school, they showed us films of English life – bowler hats and buses flickering on the whitewash – while outside all we could hear were tree frogs. Why did anyone show us such things?' My voice was rising. 'I thought everyone was an Honourable—' I stopped, fearing I'd said too much.

'Go on,' she said.

'I thought London would mean prosperity and welcome. A Renaissance place. Glory and success. I thought leaving for England was the same as stepping out of my house and onto the street, just a slightly colder street where a *beti* with a brain could live next door to Elizabeth the Queen.'

Quick smiled. 'You've been thinking about this.'

'Sometimes you can't think about anything else. There's the cold, the wet, the rent, the lack. But – I do try to live.'

I felt I shouldn't say any more; I couldn't believe I'd said so much. The bread roll was in shreds upon my lap. Quick, in contrast, appeared totally relaxed. She sat back in her chair, her eyes alight. 'Odelle,' she said. 'Don't panic. It's likely you'll be fine.'

4

Cynthia married Samuel at Wandsworth Register Office, in a small room that smelled of bureaucracy and cheap perfume, with dark-green walls and steel chairs. Shirley and Helen, two girls from the shoe shop, came along in their finery. Sam's friend from the buses, Patrick Minamore, was best man, and he brought with him his girlfriend Barbara, a fledgling actress and a talkative presence.

The registrar eyed us. The men were in suits, Patrick's tie particularly loud – and everyone looked smart compared to the drab surround. Cynth was beautiful – I mean, she was beautiful anyway, even without love beaming through every inch of her, but in her white minidress, a simple white pill-box hat, and a pair of white shoes, given her by the manager, Connie, as a wedding present, she was radiant. She had a necklace of blue flowers made from ceramic, and two small pearls in her ears, so perfect and round, as if the oysters had made them especially for her.

Patrick, an aspiring photographer, was in charge of capturing us all. I still have some of those snaps. A fountain of rice caught mid-air, white rain upon Sam and Cynth's laughing faces as they stand on the registry steps, their two hands lifted together as the grains cascade.

In marriage, at least, Cynth had triumphed. It was never going to be simple for us to find our way, and Cynth should have had a shoe empire by then, she was that good. It was not easy to sell shoes in Clapham High Street in 1967 as a Trinidadian girl. It was probably easier to write a poem about Trinidad's flowers, send it to the British Consul and be rewarded with a prize. But at least she had Sam, and they had rubbed off well on each other – he serious and shy, she resourceful and determined – how her presence illuminated him as he signed his name in the register!

We went back to Sam and Patrick's flat in black cabs, and told the taxi men that our friends had just got married. The drivers rolled down their windows and played the blues on the same radio station in concert, so loud we were terrified we'd get arrested for breaking the peace. Back in the flat, we lifted tea towels euphorically from sandwiches, found bottle openers, corkscrews, put a record on, and watched as they cut the white domed cake that Cynth had laced with rum.

After a couple of hours, other people turned up – friends of friends. Barbara had summoned up a gaggle of hip-looking folk, girls with long hair and short dresses, fellers in open-necked shirts, who looked like they needed a shave. I only glanced at them; I had long told myself those people were not for me and neither me for them. My back was damp with sweat and the ceiling seemed lower than it had been an hour ago. A couple of Barbara's gang fell into a table, and a little red lamp with tassels tumbled to the floor. Though I'd never smoked it myself, I could smell the marijuana.

When the room was full, the mood was high and Cynth had drunk three Dubonnets and lemonade too many, she lifted the needle off the record player and announced, 'My friend Delly is a poet and she wrote a poem about love.' There was a cheer. 'And she goin' to read it now.'

'Cynthia Morley, *no*,' I hissed. 'Just 'cos you now a married woman, you can't boss me around.'

'Wha' happen now, Delly?' called Sam. 'Why yuh keeping yuh-self so secret?'

'Come on, Delly. For me,' said Cynth, to my horror drawing out the poem from her handbag as another, yet more unstable cheer rippled around the fuggy room. When I had finally showed it to her a week ago, like a schoolgirl walking the long route to the teacher's desk, she had read it in silence and then put her arms around me tight, whispering, *Good Lord, Delly, you truly blessed.*

'Is a very good poem, Delly,' she said now, as she thrust it in my hands. 'Come on, show these people what you have.'

So I did it. A little wobbly from my own Dubonnet, I glanced up only once at all the faces, small moons stopped for nothing else but me. I read my poem about love from the paper, although I knew it off by heart. My words made the room fall silent. And when I finished, there was more silence, and I waited for Cynth, but even she didn't seem able to speak.

I DID NOT SEE HIS face in the crowd when I read that poem. I did not feel his eyes on me, although he told me later he couldn't drag them off mine. I felt nothing change in the room, except the shock of my voice alone and the peculiar euphoria one feels in the wake of applause, feeling at once cheapened and triumphant.

He came up to me about half an hour later, where I was in the minuscule and cluttered kitchen, stacking the empty foil plates in neat towers, trying to make some order out of Sam and Patrick's bachelor chaos. 'Hello,' he said. 'So you're the poet. I'm Lawrie Scott.'

My first thought was to check whether there were bits of egg sandwich on my fingers. 'I'm not a poet, I just write poems,' I said, looking at my hands.

'There's a difference?'

'I think there is.'

He leant against the counter, his long legs straight, crossing his arms like a detective. 'Is your real name Delly then?' he said.

'It's Odelle.' I was grateful for the bottle of Fairy Liquid and the scrubbing pad I began to put to good use.

'Odelle.' He stared back through the doorless arch to where the party had turned without a rudder, sinking into a sea of cigarette butts and shrieks, ring-pulls, discarded hair accessories, and someone's suit jacket crumpled on the floor. Sam and Cynth would be leaving soon – for nowhere but our flat, which I'd promised to vacate for the evening. Tonight, I was to be staying in this pit. This Lawrie seemed lost in thought, perhaps a little stoned, and I noticed small purple smudges of tiredness under his eyes.

'How do you know the happy couple?' I asked.

'I don't. I'm friends with Barbara and she said there was a party. I didn't know it was a wedding. I feel rather rude, but you know how it goes.' I didn't, so I said nothing. 'You?' he persisted.

'I went to school with Cynthia. She is – was – my flatmate.'

'Long time, then?'

'Long time.'

'Your poem was really good,' he said.

'Thank you.'

'I can't imagine what it'd be like to be married.'

'I don't suppose it's much different,' I replied, putting on a pair of yellow rubber gloves.

He turned to me. 'Do you really think that? Is that why the poem was about love, not marriage?'

The mound of bubbles was rising in the sink because I hadn't turned off the tap. He seemed genuinely interested, and this pleased me. 'Yes,' I said. 'But don't tell Cynth.'

He laughed, and I liked the sound. 'My mother used to say that marriage got better with practice,' he said. 'But she was already on her second try.'

'Goodness me,' I said, laughing. I probably sounded so disapproving. Divorce, in those days, still contained the suggestion of debauch.

'She died two weeks ago,' he said.

I paused, scrubbing pad hovering over the sink, and looked at him to check I'd heard him right. 'My stepfather told me I should come out,' Lawrie went on, staring at the floor. 'That I was getting under his feet. And of all places I end up at a wedding.'

He laughed again, but then was quiet, hugging himself in his fashionable leather jacket. I had not had such a personal conversation with a stranger before in England. I could not counsel him, and he did not seem to wish for it. He didn't look like he was going to cry. I thought he might be hot in that coat, but he didn't seem disposed to take it off. Perhaps he wasn't planning to hang around. I registered my regret that this might be the case.

'I haven't seen my mother for five years,' I said, plunging a tray sticky with cake smears into the hot water.

'But she's not dead, though.'

'No. No, she's not dead.'

'I keep thinking I'm going to see her again. That she'll be there when I go home. But the only person there is bloody Gerry.'

'Gerry being your stepfather?'

His face darkened. 'Yes, sorry. And my mother left everything to him.'

I tried to gauge Lawrie's age. He could be thirty, I supposed, but the rapidity with which he was spilling himself open suggested someone younger. 'That's hard,' I said. 'Why would she do that?'

'Long story. She did leave me one thing, actually. Gerry always hated it, which goes to show what a moron he is.'

'That's good you got something. What is it?'

Lawrie sighed again and uncrossed his arms, letting them hang by his side. 'A painting. All it does is remind me of her.' He gave me a rueful smile, his mouth crooked up one cheek. 'Love is blind, love's a bind. I could be a poet too.' He cocked his head at the refrigerator. 'Any milk?'

'There should be. You know, I think it's best you remember your mother rather than try and forget. My father died. And I don't have anything of his at all. Just my name.'

Lawrie stopped, his hand on the refrigerator door. 'Whoa. I'm sorry. Here am I, going on—'

'It's all right. No, really.' I felt self-conscious now, and wished
he'd just get the milk out and busy himself. I never usually talked
about my parents, and yet I felt compelled to carry on. 'He died in
the war. He got shot down.'

Lawrie looked agog. 'Mine died in the war too. But not in a
plane.' He paused and I got the sense he was going to say something, then thought better of it. 'I never knew him,' he added.

I felt awkward with this synchronicity of our circumstance, as
if I'd deliberately sought it out. 'I was two,' I hurried on. 'I don't
really remember him. He was called Odell, but without the "*e*".
When he died, my mother changed my name.'

'She *what*? What were you known as before that?'

'I don't even know.'

This fact about myself sounded absurd and funny – at least,
in that moment it did – maybe it was the clouds of pot billow-
ing around – and we both started laughing. In fact, we laughed
straight for about a minute, that pain in your stomach when you
laugh and laugh – how one mother can rename you, how mad it
is another's suddenly dead, and you in a kitchen round the corner
from the British Museum wearing yellow rubber gloves.

Lawrie turned fully towards me, the milk bottle lolling in his
hand. Sobering up, I eyed it, worried that the liquid would start
dripping through the lid at such a terrible angle.

'Listen,' he said, 'Delly.'

'Odelle.'

'Do you want to get out?'

'From where?'

'From *here*, you crazy girl.'

'Who's crazy?'

'We could go to Soho. I've got a friend who can get us in to the
Flamingo. But you'll have to take off those rubber gloves. It's not
that sort of club.'

I didn't know what to make of Lawrie at this point. I could
describe him as grief-stricken, but arguably the grief hadn't truly
set in. Perhaps he was in shock – it had only been a fortnight. That

he was angry with someone, and a bit lost, both certain of himself and yet avoiding himself – these things could be said about Lawrie. He spoke well, and he talked of Gerry and the house and his divorced, dead mother with a practised world-weariness that I wasn't sure he was trying to escape or keep alive.

'I – I'm tired,' I said. 'I can't leave the party.' I pulled the plug from the sink. As the water drained noisily, I wondered how his mother had died.

'The *Flamingo*, Odelle.'

I'd never heard of it, but I wasn't going to tell him that. 'I can't leave Cynth.'

He raised an eyebrow. 'I don't think she needs you tonight.' I blushed, looking into the disappearing bubbles. 'Look,' he said, 'my car's outside. How about we drop the painting off at my friend's flat and then let's go dancing. It doesn't have to be the Flamingo. Do you like to dance?'

'You have the painting with you?' I said.

'I see.' He ran a hand through his hair. 'More of an art girl than a nightclub girl?'

'I don't think I'm either of those girls. But I do work at an art gallery,' I added. I wanted him to be impressed, to show him I wasn't just some innocent prig who chose to wash up crockery rather than fall around on the carpet.

A light came into Lawrie's eyes. 'Do you want to see it?' he said. 'It's in the boot of my car.'

Lawrie didn't try and touch me in that kitchen. He didn't let his hand drift anywhere near. The relief that he didn't, and the desire that he might – I think they are the reasons I agreed to see his painting. I followed him, leaving the dishes stranded in the sink.

I think he wanted me to be impressed by the fact he was driving an MG, but that meant nothing to me, once I'd laid eyes on the painting in the boot. It was not large, and it had no frame. As an image, it was simple and at the same time not easily decipherable – a girl, holding another girl's severed head in her hands on one side of the painting, and on the other, a lion, sitting on his haunches, not yet springing for the kill. It had the air of a fable.

Despite the slight distortion from the orange street lamp above us, the colours of the lower background reminded me of a Renaissance court portrait – that piled-up patchwork of fields all kinds of yellow and green, and what looked like a small white castle. The sky above was darker and less decorous; there was something nightmarish about its bruised indigoes. The painting gave me an immediate feeling of opposites – the girls against the lion, together in the face of its adversity. But there was a rewarding delicacy beyond its beautiful palette of colours – an elusive element that made it so alluring.

'What do you think?' asked Lawrie. His face seemed softer out of the glare of the kitchen light.

'Me? I'm just the typist,' I said.

'Oh, come on. I heard that poem. Make a poem of this.'

'It doesn't work like that—' I began, before I realized he was teasing me. I felt embarrassed, so I turned back to the painting. 'It's very unusual, I suppose. The colours, the subject matter. I wonder when it was painted? Could be last week, or last century.'

'Or even earlier,' he said eagerly.

I looked again at the old-fashioned fields in the background and then at the figures. 'I don't think so. The girl's dress and cardigan – it's more recent.'

'Do you think that's gold leaf?' Lawrie bent down and pointed to the lion's mane, the flowing strands which seemed to glint. His head was very close to mine and I could smell his skin, a trace of aftershave that gave me goosebumps.

'Odelle?' he said.

'It's not your usual painting,' I replied hastily, as if I knew what a usual painting was. I straightened up. 'Mr Scott, what are you going to do with it?'

He turned to me and smiled. The orange light caught the planes of his face and covered him in ghoulish shadow. 'I like it when you call me Mr Scott.'

'In that case, I'm going to call you Lawrie.'

He laughed, and my jaw tingled, threatening a smile. 'I don't think this was done by an amateur,' I said. 'What did your mother know about it?'

'No idea. And all *I* know is, she took it with her wherever she went. At home, it was always in her bedroom. She didn't like it in the public rooms.'

I pointed to the initials on the bottom right of the painting. 'Who's I.R.?'

Lawrie shrugged. 'Not my forte.'

I wondered what Lawrie's forte was, and whether I would ever find out, and why did I want to – and was that the reason I was feeling so odd?

In case he could read my thoughts, I bent my head down again towards the girl in the painting. She was wearing a light blue dress with a dark woollen cardigan – you could even see the cable knit. The head she was carrying had a long dark plait, which snaked unsettlingly out of her cradled arms, towards the red earth floor. The strange thing was, even though she had no body, the floating girl didn't seem dead at all. She was inviting me in, but there was a note of caution in her eyes. Neither figure was exactly beaming in welcome. They both seemed oblivious to the lion, which may or may not have been waiting for the kill.

'I have to go,' I said, pushing the painting away into his surprised hands. Lawrie, the party, the poem, the Dubonnet, Cynth's marriage, the painting; suddenly I wanted to be alone.

Lawrie took the painting from me and closed the boot. He looked down at me, his head cocked to one side again. 'Are you all right? Do you want me to walk you back in?'

'Yes,' I said. 'I mean, no. I'm fine. Thank you. Sorry. It was a pleasure to meet you. Good luck.' I turned away and made it to the entrance of the block of flats, before he called out to me.

'Hey, Odelle.' I looked back to see him jam his hands into the pockets of his leather jacket, hunching his shoulders again. 'I – you know – that really was a good poem.'

'It always takes longer than you think, Mr Scott,' I said. He laughed, and I smiled properly then, nevertheless relieved to be out of the street lamp's glow.

5

When I was growing up, my mother and I would always eat lunch with Cynth's family on Sundays. Four in the afternoon, a big pot on the hob, everyone coming in and out and dipping for themselves – and once the meal was done, we'd draw our chairs up to the radio at seven thirty and listen to the BBC's *Caribbean Voices*, the only broadcast that mattered if you dreamed of being a writer.

Here's the mad thing: poets from Barbados, Trini, Jamaica, Grenada, Antigua – any part of the British Caribbean – would send their stories all the way to Bush House on London's Aldwych, in order to hear them read back again in their homes, thousands of miles across the Atlantic Ocean. There seemed no local facility to enable these stories to be processed, a fact which impressed upon me at a very young age that in order to be a writer, I would require the motherland's seal of approval, the imperial sanction that my words were broadcastable.

The majority of the work was by men, but I would listen enraptured by the words and voices of Una Marson, Gladys Lindo, Constance Hollar – and Cynth would pipe up, 'One day *you* be read out, Delly' – and her little shining face, her bunches, she always made me feel like it was true. Seven years old, and she was the only one who ever told me to keep going. By 1960 that programme had stopped, and I came to England two years later with no idea what to do with my stories. Life at the shoe shop took over, so I only wrote in private, and Cynth, who must have seen the piles of notebooks which never left my bedroom, simply stopped her pestering.

She and Sam had found a flat to rent in Queen's Park, and she'd transferred to a north London branch of Dolcis. Up to that point, I'd never really known loneliness. I'd always had my books, and Cynth had always been there. Suddenly, my thoughts were enormous in that tiny flat, because there was nobody to hear them and make them manageable, nobody cajoling or supporting me, or holding out their arms for a hug. Cynth's absence became physical to me. Do you have a body if no one is there to touch it? I suppose you do, but sometimes it felt like I didn't. I was just a mind, floating around the rooms. How badly prepared I'd been for the echo and clunk of my key in the lock, the lack of her sizzling frying pan, my solitary toothbrush, the silence where once she hummed her favourite songs.

When you saw a person every day – a person you liked, a person who lifted you up – you thought you were your best self, without trying very hard. Now, I saw myself as barely interesting, not so clever. No one wanted to hear my poems except Cynth, no one cared or understood where I was from like she did. I didn't know how to be Odelle without Cynth to make me so. Cynth had done so much for me, but because she was gone, I still managed to resent her.

Her work commitments and mine meant we were only meeting once a fortnight, in the Lyon's on Craven Street round the corner from the Skelton. I barely credited Cynth for the fact it was she who always arranged it.

AT THE COUNTER, THE WAITRESS had slopped our cups so the liquid had spilled onto the saucer, and the bun I'd asked for was the most squashed. When I asked for a replacement saucer, the waitress ignored me, and when I paid for it, she wouldn't put the change in my hand. She placed the money on the counter and pushed it over, not looking at my face. I turned to Cynth, and saw a familiar expression. We walked to find a spare table, as far away from the counter as we could.

'How is it at the work?' she asked. 'You still trailin' after that Marjorie Quick?'

'She meh boss, Cynthia.'

'So you say.'

I hadn't realized how obvious it was, the impression that Quick had made on me over the recent weeks. I had tried to find out more about Quick from Pamela, who could only tell me that Quick had once mentioned the county of Kent as her childhood home. What she did between being a girl and a woman in her fifties was a grey sketch. Perhaps she had been destined for a genteel, Kentish life, a magistrate's wife or some such, but she chose instead to find a different kind of fortune in the rubble of post-war London. Her name was not in *Debrett's*: she was not a Skelton descendant, one of my initial lines of thought. Her impeccable sartorial choices exuded power, a care of herself that was for nobody's benefit but her own. Each perfect blouse, each pristine pair of trousers, was a pre-emptive self-narration. Quick's clothes were an armour made of silk.

I knew she was unmarried and lived in Wimbledon, just off the common. She smoked constantly, and appeared close to Reede in the sort of way that water is close to a stone that it has worn down over decades. Pamela said that Quick had been here as long as Reede had, when he'd taken the directorship of the Skelton, twenty years ago. How she had come to meet Reede, or why she decided to take employment, remained a mystery. I wondered what sort of battle it had been to get to where she was now, and whether she'd read those Roman histories to give her some lessons in war.

'She not like anyone I ever meet,' I said to Cynth. 'Friendly one minute, a sunlight beam. Then she like a hog-brush woman – she bristle so, it pain yuh to be near.'

Cynth sighed. 'We bought G Plan for the flat.'

'G-what?'

'Oh, Delly. Sam work hard hard, so Ah say, leh we buy we a nice G Plan sofa so he can put up he foot at the end of the day.'

'Hmm. And how your feet doin'?'

She sighed, stirring her lukewarm tea with a spoon. 'Oh, let me tell you a thing. So our new postman get the letters mix up, and our neighbour knock with them.' Cynth cleared her throat and put on a posh English voice. ' *"Oh, hell-air. Yes, this must be yours. We saw it had a black stamp."* Is a letter from *Lagos*, Delly. Meh name not on it, and eh know nobody from Nigeria. "Black stamp", I ask yuh.'

Her laugh died. Normally we would have discussed something like this in order to remove its barb, but after the waitress neither of us had the energy.

'Tell me about the feller you was talking to at the wedding,' she said, looking sly.

'What feller?'

She rolled her eyes. 'Lawrie Scott. The white one; handsome, skinny. He friend to Patrick's Barbara. Ah didn't drink *that* many Dubonnets – I saw you in the kitchen.'

'Oh him. He real dotish.'

'*Hmm*,' she said, her eyes taking on a secret glow, and I knew I'd given myself away. 'That strange.'

'Why?'

'Patrick told Sam he been asking about you.' I shut my mouth tighter than a clam and Cynth grinned. 'You writin'?' she asked.

'You only start asking me that, now you leave.'

'I not gone. I on the other end of the Tube map, that is all.'

'Like you worried I got nothing to do these days. Don't worry, I writin',' I said, but this was a lie. I had stopped entirely at this point, believing that the idea of myself as a good writer was laughable.

'Good. I glad you writin',' said Cynth firmly. 'You know, there a poetry night going at the ICA,' she went on. 'Sam's friend is readin', and he's a *real* dotish boy compared to you. His poem does send me to sleep—'

'Ah not readin' at some meet-up, Cynthia,' I said, wrinkling my nose. 'Make no mistake.'

She sighed. 'I not. Is just that you better, Odelle. You better and you know it, and you doing *nothin'*.'

'Eh *heh*,' I said. 'I busy. I work. You go with your G Plan and stop all this foolishness. What, because I got no husban' foot to worry me, I better go speakin' my *poetry* an' ting?'

Cynthia looked distraught. 'Delly! Why you so vex? I only trying to help.'

'Ah not vex.' I drained my cup of tea. 'Is all right for *you*,' I said. 'Don't tell me how to live.'

Cynth was quiet after that. I should have said sorry then and there, but I didn't. She left soon after, pinch-faced with tears, and I felt like a monster come out of the sea to grab her legs.

We didn't meet up the next week, or the one after that, and she didn't ring. Neither did I, and I felt so embarrassed, such a fool – *a real dotish gyal*, as Cynth no doubt described me that night to Sam. The longer she was silent, the more impossible it seemed to pick up the telephone.

All I really wanted to say was that I missed us living together. And I was someone who was supposed to be good with words.

6

*L*awrie found me on the fifteenth of August. It was seven o'clock in the morning, and I was doing the early reception shift. Shops were still shut, the buses that moved along Charing Cross Road less frequent. I walked on to the Mall, and the long thoroughfare, usually busy, was an empty road of greenish light. It had been raining for a week, and the paving stones were wet from a dawn downpour, trees springing in the breeze like fronds beneath the sea.

I'd seen much worse rain than this, so I wasn't too bothered, tucking the copy of the *Express* I'd bought for Pamela into my handbag to protect it from spatters, crossing up Carlton Gardens and over the circular centre of Skelton Square. I passed the plinth of the long-dead statesman adorning the middle point, a blank-eyed fellow whose frock coat was messed by pigeons. In the past, I would have found out who he was – but five years in London had purged my interest in old Victorian men. The statue's infinite gaze made me feel even more exhausted.

I glanced up towards the Skelton. A young man was standing by the doors, tall and slim, wearing a slightly battered leather jacket. He had a narrow face and very dark brown hair. As I approached, I knew that it was him. I could feel my throat tighten, a little hop in the gut, a thudding swipe to the breast. I approached the steps, fetching the Skelton door key out of my handbag. Lawrie was wearing glasses this time, and their lenses glinted in the subterranean light. He was carrying a parcel under his arm, wrapped in that brown paper butchers used to wrap their slabs of meat.

He grinned at me. 'Hello,' he said.

What was it like to see Lawrie smile? I can try: it was as if a healer had placed their hands upon my chest. My kneecaps porridge, jaw tingling, no hope to swallow. I wanted to throw my arms around him and say, 'It's you, you came.'

'Hello,' I said instead. 'Can I help?'

His smile faltered. 'You don't remember? We met, at the wedding. I came along with Barbara's gang. You read a poem, and you wouldn't go dancing with me.'

I frowned. 'Oh, yes. How do you do?'

'How do I *do*? Aren't you going to ask me why I'm here?'

'It's seven o'clock in the morning, Mr . . . . ?'

'Scott,' he said, the joy draining from his face. 'Lawrie Scott.'

I walked past him and put the key in the lock, fumbling as I did so. What was wrong with me? Despite all my fantasies about how this was going to play out, faced with the reality, I was being just as obstructive as I had been before. I pushed inside and he followed me. 'Are you here to see somebody?' I said.

He gave me a hard look. 'Odelle. I have visited every art gallery, every museum in this bloody city, trying to find you.'

'To *find* me?'

'Yes.'

'You couldn't find me in five weeks? You could have just asked Patrick Minamore.'

He laughed. 'So you were counting.' I blushed and looked away, busying myself with the post. He held up the brown-paper package, and said, 'I've brought the lion girls.'

I couldn't conceal the suspicion in my voice. 'Who are they?'

He grinned. 'My Mother's painting. I've taken your advice. Do you think someone will have a look at them for me?'

'I'm sure they will.'

'I looked up those initials you pointed out, I.R. Didn't find a single name. So it's probably not worth anything,'

'Are you planning on selling it?' I asked, head still fizzing, heart thumping uncomfortably as I moved around the other side of the wooden counter. I'd never been so direct with a boy before in my life.

'Maybe. See what happens.'

'But I thought it was your mother's favourite?'

'*I* was my mother's favourite,' he said, laying the parcel on the counter with a grim smile. 'Only joking. I don't *want* to sell it, but if it's worth something, it will get me started, you see. Any minute, Gerry the Bastard – excuse my French – could kick me out.'

'Don't you work?'

'*Work*?'

'Don't you have a job?'

'I've had jobs in the past.'

'The dim and distant?'

He pulled a face. 'You don't approve.'

The truth was, I *didn't* approve of people who did no work. Everyone I knew since coming to London – Cynth, the girls in the shoe shop, Sam, Patrick, Pamela – we all had jobs. The point of *being* here was to have a job. Where I was from, doing your own work was the only wake-up from the long sleep which followed the generations in the fields. It was your way out. It's hard to change the messages that circulate all your life, especially when they've been there since before your life was started.

Lawrie stared into the brown wrapping paper. 'It's a long story,' he said, sensing my disapproval. 'I dropped out of university. That was a few years ago. My mother wasn't – oh, never mind. But I'd like to start something new.'

'I see.'

He looked embarrassed, jamming his hands into his jacket pockets. 'Look, Odelle. I'm not . . . a layabout. I do want to *do* things. I want you to know that. I—'

'Would you like a cup of tea?' I asked.

He stopped, mid-breath. 'Tea. Yes. God, it's early, isn't it,' he laughed.

'Were you going to just stand out there until I turned up?'

'Yes,' he said.

'You're a mad boy.'

'Who's mad?' he said, and we grinned at each other. I looked at his pale face. 'Even without a job, my mother would still think you're perfect.'

'Why would she think that?' he asked.

I sighed. It was too early in the morning to explain.

WE HAD AN HOUR TOGETHER, sitting in the reception hall, the front door locked as I sorted the post and brewed the tea and coffee that Pamela and I had to keep renewing throughout the day. Lawrie seemed genuinely delighted by his cup of tea. It was as if he had never seen a hot beverage before.

He told me about his mother's funeral. 'It was awful. Gerry read a poem about a dying rose.' I put my hand over my mouth to hide my smile. 'No, you should laugh,' he said. 'My mother would have laughed. She would have hated it. She didn't even like roses. And Gerry has a terrible poetry voice. The worst voice I've ever heard. Like he's got a plunger up his bum. And the priest was senile. And there were no more than five of us there. It was bloody awful and I hated that she had to go through it.'

'I'm sorry,' I said.

He sighed, stretching his legs out. 'Not your fault, Odelle. Anyway. It's done. RIP, all that.' He rubbed his face as if erasing a memory. 'And you? How's life without your flatmate?'

I was touched he remembered. 'All right,' I said. 'Bit quiet.'

'I thought you liked quiet.'

'How would you know?'

'You didn't want to go to the Flamingo.'

'Different sort of quiet,' I said.

We were quiet ourselves then, me sitting behind the counter, and him on the other side, the brown-paper package between us, waiting on the wood. It was a nice silence, warm and full, and I liked him sitting there unobtrusive – yet, to my eyes, fizzing with the light I had sensed when we first met.

He was beautiful to me, and as I laid out the *Express* for Pamela, and did a spurious sorting of the desk, I hoped that she would be delayed somehow. Back home, I'd had one or two of what my mother would have called 'dalliances'; holding hands in the dark at the Roxy, hot-dogs after lectures, awkward kisses at a Princes Building concert, a late-night picnic on the Pitch Walk, watching the bluish light of the candle-flies. But I'd never done . . . the whole thing.

I generally avoided male attention, finding the courting business excruciating. 'Free love' had passed us schoolgirls by in Port of Spain. Our Catholic education was a Victorian relic, redolent with overtones of fallen women, irretrievable girls mired in pools of their own foolishness. We had been instructed that we were too *superior* for that exchange of flesh.

My attitude to sex was one of haughty fear, confused by the fact that there *were* girls who did it, girls like Lystra Wilson or Dominique Mendes, with boyfriends older than themselves and secrets in their eyes, who seemed to be having a very good time indeed. How they procured these boyfriends was always a mystery to me – but it no doubt involved disobedience, climbing out of bedroom windows and into the nightclubs off Frederick Street and Marine Square. In my memory, Lystra and Dominique, those daring ones, seemed like women from the moment they were born, mermaids come ashore to live among us, feminine and powerful. No wonder we scaredy-cats retreated into books. Sex was beneath us, because it was beyond us.

The Skelton front door was still locked. I didn't want it to end – the kettle whistling for more tea in the back room, him stretching and folding his legs, asking me what films I'd seen and how could I have not seen that and did I like blues or was I into folk and how many months had I worked here, and did I like being in Clapham. Lawrie was always very good at making you feel like you were important.

'Would you like to go to the cinema?' he said. 'We could see *You Only Live Twice*, or *The Jokers*.'

'*The Jokers*? Sounds about right for you.'

'Oliver Reed's in it – he's excellent,' said Lawrie, 'but isn't a crime caper too flip for you?'

'*Flip*? Why?'

'Because you're clever. You'd take it as an insult if I took you to watch stupid blokes scampering around for the Crown Jewels.'

I laughed, happy to discover that Lawrie also had a strain of nervousness about all this, and touched that he wasn't afraid to tell me about it. 'Or do you want to see one of those French films,' he said, 'where people just walk in and out of rooms, looking at each other?'

'Let's go and see the Bond.'

'All right. Excellent. Excellent! I loved *Goldfinger* – that bowler hat!' I laughed again and he came up to the counter, leaning over to take my hand. I froze, looking at it. 'Odelle,' he said. 'I think – I mean, you are—'

'What?'

'You're just . . .' He was still holding on to my hand. For the first time in my life, I didn't want a man to let go.

Outside, it began to rain. I turned my head, distracted by the rush of water beyond the door, cascading down onto the grey pavement. Lawrie leaned over and kissed me on the cheek. I turned back and he kissed me again, and it felt good, so we stood for some minutes, kissing in the reception of the Skelton.

I broke away. 'You'll get me sacked.'

'All right. Can't have that.'

He moved back to his chair, grinning like an idiot. The rain was thrumming heavily now, but this was English rain, not Trini rain. Back home, aerial waterfalls fell from the breaking sky, week on week of tropical downpour, forests doused so green they were almost black, the neon signs out, escarpments churned to mud, torch ginger flowers so red, like a man's blood had coloured the petals – and all of us, standing under awnings or hiding in houses till it was safe once more to walk the shining asphalt road. We used to say 'it rainin' ' as an excuse for being late, and everyone would always understand.

'What?' Lawrie said. 'Why are you smiling?'

'Nothing,' I said. 'Nothing.'

There was a rapping on the door. Quick was peering through the glass, under the brim of a wide black umbrella. 'Oh!' I cried. 'She early.'

I ran to the door and unlocked it, thanking God she hadn't seen us kissing. Quick stepped inside, and I thought her face looked thinner. She removed her coat and brushed off her umbrella. 'August,' she muttered.

She looked up and saw Lawrie. 'Who are you?' she said, wary as a cat.

'This is – Mr Scott,' I said, surprised at her bluntness. 'He'd like to speak to someone about his painting. Mr Scott, this is Miss Quick.'

'Mr Scott?' she repeated. She couldn't take her eyes off him.

'Hullo,' Lawrie said, jumping to his feet. 'Wondered if I've got an heirloom or a piece of junk.' He put out his hand and Quick, as if resisting a great magnet, lifted her own to meet it. I saw her flinch, though Lawrie noticed nothing.

She smiled faintly. 'I hope, for your sake, Mr Scott, it's the former.'

'Me too.'

'May I see it?'

Lawrie went to the counter and began unwrapping the paper. Quick stayed where she was by the door, fingers gripping the top of her umbrella. She kept staring at him. Rain had soaked her coat but she didn't take it off. Lawrie swung the painting up, holding it against his body for me and Quick to see. 'Here it is,' he said.

Quick stood for four or five seconds, eyes transfixed on the golden lion, the girls, the landscape spiralling out behind them. The umbrella slid out of her grasp and bumped to the floor. 'Quick?' I said. 'Are you all right?'

She looked at me, abruptly turned on her heel and walked out of the front door. 'It's not *that* bad,' said Lawrie, peering over the top of the painting.

Quick was hurrying away along the square, her head bowed, oblivious to the rain soaking her. As I reached for my own coat, Edmund Reede appeared and removed his dripping trilby.

He looked down at me. 'Miss – Baston, is it?'

'Bastien.'

'Where are you running off to?'

'To see Miss Quick. She's – forgotten her umbrella.'

'We were supposed to be having a meeting.' He turned to where Lawrie was now sitting again, the painting on his knees, hastily covered in the brown paper. 'And who's this?'

'Mr Scott has a painting,' I said.

'I can see that. Isn't this all rather a flurry for eight fifteen in the morning? Where's Miss Rudge?'

'I'm on the early shift, Mr Reede. Mr Scott came today because he was hoping someone would take a look at his painting. It was his mother's – her favourite . . .' I trailed off, desperate to follow Quick and see if she was all right.

Reede removed his wet overcoat with slow deliberation, as if I had placed the burden of the world on his shoulders. He was a tall, broad man and he filled the space with his fine tailoring and thatch of white hair, his woody aftershave. 'Have you made an appointment?' he asked Lawrie, his small blue eyes glinting with impatience.

'No, sir.'

'We're not a *drop-in* centre, you know. This isn't really how it's done.'

Lawrie stiffened, the brown paper rustling over his painting. 'I know that.'

'Well, perhaps you don't. Have Miss Bastien make an appointment for you some time next week. I have no time today.' He turned to look back through the door where Quick had fled. 'Why the hell did Marjorie just run off like that?' he said. I'd never seen Reede look worried before. As he turned back, Lawrie stood up, half the brown paper falling to the floor. Reede stopped in his tracks, his gaze on the revealed half of the painting, the golden lion.

'Is that yours?' he asked Lawrie.

Lawrie lowered his eyes and gathered up the paper. 'Yes,' he said defensively. 'Well – my mother's. Now it's mine.' Reede stepped towards it, but Lawrie moved away, putting his hand out. 'Hold on. You said you didn't have time. You said next week. Although by then,' he added, 'I may have taken it elsewhere.'

'Ah,' said Reede. He put his hands up. 'I just want to take a closer look. Please,' he added, which seemed to cost him a great effort.

'Why? A minute ago you couldn't give a damn.'

Reede laughed; a twitchy joviality. 'Look, old chap, I'm sorry if I was blunt. We get a damned lot of people coming in here with Auntie Edna's heirlooms or something they bought for three bob off a bloke in Brick Lane, and you get a bit sick of it. But what you've got there looks interesting. If you let me take a look, I might be able to tell you why.'

Lawrie hesitated, before placing the painting back on the counter. He unwrapped the rest of the paper. Reede stepped towards it, drinking in the image, his fingers hovering over the paint, the second girl's floating head, her snaking plait, the lion's passive stare. 'My goodness,' he breathed. 'Where did your mother get this?'

'I don't know.'

'Can you ask her?'

Lawrie glanced at me. 'She's dead.'

'Ah.' Reede hesitated. 'So – have you any idea where she might have got it from?'

'She bought most of her things from junk shops or flea markets, sometimes at auctions, but this one has been around since I was a little boy. It was always hanging on her wall, whatever house we moved to.'

'Where was it hanging last?'

'Her house in Surrey.'

'Did she ever talk about it to you?'

'Why would she do that?'

Reede gently picked up the painting and looked on the back. 'No frame, just a hook,' he murmured. 'Well,' he said, addressing Lawrie. 'If she always had it hanging up, it might have had particular meaning to her.'

'I think she just thought it was pretty,' Lawrie said.

'Pretty is not the word I would use.'

'What word *would* you use, sir?'

Reede blinked away Lawrie's tone. 'On first impressions, "brave". And provenance matters, Mr Scott, if you choose to exhibit things, or put things on the market. I assume that's why you brought it to us.'

'So it's worth something?'

There was a pause. Reede breathed deeply, his eyes pinned to the picture. 'Mr Scott, may I take you to my office so I can have a closer look at this?'

'All right.'

'Miss Bastien, bring coffee.'

Reede picked up the painting and gestured for Lawrie to follow him. I watched them walk up the spiral staircase, Lawrie looking back over his shoulder, his eyes wide with excitement, giving me a thumbs up.

OUTSIDE, THE RAIN WAS BECOMING a torrent. I scoured the square for Quick, but of course, by now, she had gone. With her rolled-up umbrella in my hand like a lance, I ran along the left side of the square and turned up towards Piccadilly, blindly hoping I would see her. I took another right, unconsciously heading towards the Tube station, and then I saw her, a block ahead. The traffic honked and screeched, and the statue of Eros loomed.

'Quick!' I yelled. 'Your umbrella!' Heads turned to look, but I didn't care. Quick hurried on, so I ran faster, reaching out to touch her arm. With lightning speed she pulled away from me and whirled round. Her expression was fixed on some distant point well beyond the bustling road, the tall and soot-encrusted

buildings, the colourful billboards, the pedestrians hopping desperately around the puddles. Then she focused on me, almost with
relief. She was drenched, and though her face was sopping wet, I
couldn't tell if it was rain or tears.

'I forgot something,' she said. 'At home – I've forgotten – I need
to go back and get it.'

'Here,' I said, 'your umbrella. Let me call you a cab.'

She looked down at her umbrella, then up at me. 'You're *soaking*, Odelle. Why on earth did you run out?'

'Because – well, because *you* did. And look at you.' I put my
hand on her wet sleeve and she stared at it momentarily. I was
surprised by how thin her arm felt to touch.

'Here.' She pulled the umbrella out of my hands and opened it
above our heads. We stared at each other under the black canopy,
the roar of rain bashing down upon its flimsy structure, people
brushing us as they ran to and fro for cover. Her curls were mat-
ted to her head; her powder had washed off her face, I could see
the true flesh of her skin – and strangely, without the make-up,
it looked more like a mask. She went as if to say something, but
seemed to stop herself. 'Jesus Christ,' she murmured, briefly closing her eyes. 'It's a bloody monsoon.'

'Shall I call you a cab?'

'I'll get the Tube. You don't have a cigarette, do you?'

'No,' I said, disconcerted, for surely she knew by now I didn't
smoke.

'That man – how did he come to the Skelton?' she asked. 'Do you
know him? You seemed to know him.'

I looked down. Huge puddles were forming around our shoes.
I thought of the coffee I was supposed to be making, how long I
could be out here before I lost my job. 'I only met him once before
– at Cynth's wedding. He found me again today.'

'*Found* you? That's fairly persistent behaviour. He's not – bothering you, is he?'

'Not at all. He's fine,' I said, a touch defensive. Why was Quick
talking about Lawrie, when she was the one acting strange?

'All right.' She seemed to calm a bit. 'Look, Odelle – I have to go. Tell him not to bother you with that painting.'

'Mr Reede has already seen it.'

'What?'

'He came in shortly after you. Said that you and he had an early meeting. He had one look at it and took it to his office.'

She looked over my shoulder, in the direction of the Skelton. 'What did Mr Reede say, when he saw it?'

'He seemed . . . excited.'

Quick lowered her eyes, her expression closed. In that moment, she looked very old. She gripped my hand and squeezed it. 'Thank you, Odelle – for my umbrella. You're a tribune, you really are. But take it, I'm going underground. Go back to the office.'

'Quick, wait—'

She thrust the umbrella into my hand, and turned down the steps of the station. Before I could even call again to her, Quick had disappeared.

JANUARY 1936

I

*S*arah was unconscious, her face turned sideways, her arti-
ficial curls crushed on the pillow, the cuts on her bare legs
covered in calamine smears. A soured scent of the night's
last glass rose from her mouth. On the bedside table was an over-
filled ashtray, a pile of detective novels, and her *Vogue* magazines,
their corners curled. Her clothes were everywhere on the dusty
floorboards, here, stockings like sloughed snakes, there, a blouse,
flattened in the effort of escape. Her rouge had melted in its pot. In
the corner of the room, a lizard flicked across the tiles like a mote
upon the eye.

Olive stood at the door, the letter from the Slade School of Fine
Art gripped in her hand. The letter was only two weeks old, but it
had a handkerchief's flutter, the creases almost oiled from so much
refolding. She walked over to her mother's bed and perched on the
end to read it again, although she knew it off by heart. *It is our pleasure to invite you to undertake the Fine Art degree course . . . The
tutors were highly impressed . . . rich imagination and novelty . . .
continuing the rigorous yet progressive tradition of the school . . . we
look forward to hearing from you within the next fortnight. Should
your circumstances change, please inform us.*

If she read it aloud, maybe Sarah would hear her through the
fug, and that would be that; Olive would have to stick to her word,

and go. Maybe a shock like this was best administered under the residual effects of a sleeping pill? When Olive had received the letter, back in London, she wanted to shout from the skyline what she'd gone and done. Her parents had had no idea – they didn't even know their daughter still painted, let alone that she'd applied to art school. But part of Olive's problem was that she had always been used to secrecy; it was where she was comfortable, the point from which she began to create. It was a pattern she was superstitious to break, and so here she was, in this village in the south of Spain.

As she gazed at her mother's sleeping form, she remembered showing her father a portrait she'd made of Sarah from art class at school. 'Oh, Liv,' he'd said as her heart hammered, the expectation inching up her spine. 'Give it as a present for your mother.'

That was all he'd said on the matter. *A present for your mother.*

Her father always said that of course women could pick up a paintbrush and paint, but the fact was, they didn't make good *artists*. Olive had never quite worked out what the difference was. Since she was a little girl, playing in the corners of his gallery, she would overhear Harold discussing the issue with his clients, both men and women – and often the women would agree with him, preferring to put their money behind young men rather than anyone of their own sex. The artist as naturally male was such a widely held presupposition that Olive had come at times to believe in it herself. As a nineteen-year-old girl, she was on the underside; the dogged, plucky mascot of amateurship. But right now in Paris, Amrita Sher-Gil, Méret Oppenheim and Gabriele Münter were all working – Olive had even seen their pieces with her own eyes. Were *they* not artists? Was the difference between being a work-aday painter and being an artist simply other people believing in you, or spending twice as much money on your work?

She found it impossible to express to her parents why she'd applied, the portfolio she'd collated, the essay she'd written on background figures in Bellini. Despite all she'd absorbed about women's shortcomings in art, she'd gone and done it anyway. This was what she couldn't understand; where the urge had come from. And yet, even though an independent life was just within her reach, still she was sitting at the foot of her mother's bed.

Turning again to Sarah, she considered fetching her pastels. Once upon a time, her mother would let Olive parade in her furs, or her strings of pearls, or take her for eclairs at the Connaught, or to hear this violinist or that clever poet perform his work at the Musikverein – always friends of Sarah, and always, Olive had gradually realized as she grew up, in love with her. These days, no one knew what Sarah Schloss might say, or do. She resisted the doctors, and often the pills seemed pointless. Olive felt like she was nothing but a dreg, jetsam in her mother's wake. So she drew her, in secret, in ways that Sarah would probably never forgive.

THE LONG WINDOWS WERE AJAR, and a breeze made the curtains dance. The dawn wind had lifted an impressive cloudscape from the mountains beyond Arazuelo, a duck-egg sky striated gold and pink. The letter still in her hand, Olive tiptoed towards the balcony and saw blank fields spanning towards rugged foothills in the distance, patched with scrub and wild daisies, where kites circled and grasshoppers sawed in the empty melon fields, oxen dragging ploughs across the earth in preparation for later seeding.

Oblivious rabbits hopped across the orchard and far off in the hills goats were being herded, the bells on their necks clanking atonally and out of rhythm, a calming sound because it lacked any conscious performance. A hunter's gun rang out, and birds rose in chaos against the baroque Andalusian morning. Sarah did not stir, but the rabbits scattered, expert hiders, deserting the surface of the waiting earth. Olive closed the windows and the curtains dropped. Her mother probably hoped her long-sought tranquillity was to be found here – but there was a wildness under the tolling convent bell, the chance of wolves in the mountains. The futile yaps of a dog in a barn would puncture every silence. And yet, since their arrival, Olive personally found the landscape and the house itself energizing, in a way that was unfamiliar and wholly unexpected. She had taken an old wood panel that she'd found in the outhouse at the end of the orchard, carrying it up to the attic as if it was contraband. She had treated it in readiness for paint; but it remained blank.

Her father strode into the room, his large foot skidding a *Vogue* under the bed. Olive jammed the letter in her pyjama pocket and spun round to face him. 'How many?' he asked, pointing at the sleeping figure of his wife.

'Don't know,' said Olive. 'But more than normal, I think.'

'*Sheiße.*' Harold only swore in German in moments of great stress or great freedom. He loomed over Sarah and lifted a stray strand of hair delicately off her face. It was a gesture from another time, and it made Olive squeamish.

'Did you get your cigarettes?' she asked him.

'Eh?'

'Your *cigarettes*.' Last night, he'd mentioned needing to get cigarettes from Malaga and visiting an artist's studio – hoping to sniff out another Picasso, he'd said, laughing, as if lightning really did strike in the same place twice. Her father always seemed to slip out of the days like this – bored quickly, yet demanding an audience whenever he turned up again. They'd barely been here two days, and already he was off.

'Oh,' he said. 'Yes. They're in the car.'

Before he left his wife's room, Harold poured his beloved a glass of water and left it by her bedside, just beyond the orbit of her reach.

Downstairs, the shutters were still half-closed and the minimal furniture was in shadow. The air had a tinge of camphor laced with old cigar smoke. The finca could not have been lived in for several years, Olive supposed. A large catacomb above the ground, each of its rooms reticent at her presence, long corridors furnished in colonial habits, dark hardwood cabinets empty of homely objects. It felt like everything was as it had been in the 1890s, and they were characters out of time, surrounded by the discarded props of a drawing-room play.

The vague moisture in the air was already evaporating. Olive threw open the shutters and sunlight bleached the room, a day of exposure but no warmth. The view was an uncultivated slope, which led down to the high wrought-iron fence and onwards, to the beginnings of the village road. She looked out; scraggy bushes and empty flower borders, three fruitless orange trees. Her father had said these mansions were always built outside the villages, near to well-irrigated and lush earth, where in summer, he declared, they would enjoy olive groves and cherry blossom, flower gardens of *dama-de-noche* and jacaranda, fountains and leisure and happiness, happiness.

Olive still had on her winter pyjamas and stockings, and an Aran jumper. The flagstones were so cool, it felt as if rain had just fallen on their large smooth squares. *Just do it*, she thought. *Tell him you've got a place, and go.* If only it was easy to act on thoughts. If only it was easier to know what was the best thing to do.

In the pantry, she discovered a tin of coffee beans and an old but functioning grinder. It was all there was for breakfast, and she and her father decided to drink it on the veranda at the back of the house. Harold went to the room where the telephone was. He had chosen this finca as it was the only one hooked up to a generator, but it was a surprise they had a telephone, and Harold was very pleased.

He was murmuring in German, probably to one of his friends in Vienna. He sounded insistent, but he was too quiet for her to make out the words. When they'd been in London, and he'd had news of what was happening in his home city – the street fights, the hijacked prayer meetings – he would plunge into dark silences. As she ground the beans, Olive thought of her childhood Vienna, the old and the new, the Jewish and the Christian, the educated and the curious, the psyche and the heart. When Harold said it was not safe for them to return, Olive could not quite take this in. In the circles they moved, the violence seemed so distant.

He'd finished his conversation and was sat on the veranda waiting for her, on a tatty green sofa someone had left out in the open air. Over his coat, he was wearing a long spindly scarf that Sarah had knitted, and he was frowning over his correspondence. He always had a knack of making sure that his post would be waiting for him, wherever they landed.

Olive lowered herself into a discarded rocking chair, hesitating for fear damp had weakened the glue, woodworm seeing to the joints. Her father lit a cigarette and placed his silver box on the flaking veranda floor. He sucked on the tobacco leaf, and Olive heard the satisfying crackle as his breath intensified the heat.

'How long do you think we'll be here?' she asked, trying to sound casual.

He looked up from his letters. A thin line of smoke rose straight from the cigarette tip, no breeze up here to shift its journey. The column of ash accumulated, curving downwards and scattering onto the peeling boards. 'Don't tell me you already want to leave.' He raised his dark brows. 'Are you –' here, he sought the particularly English word – '*pining*? Is there someone we left behind in London?'

Olive stared listlessly at the January-thin orchard, briefly wishing that there *was* some chinless Geoffrey, with a white stucco house in South Kensington and a job at the Foreign Office as an under-secretary. But there was no one, and there never had been. She closed her eyes and could almost see the dull metal wink of imaginary cufflinks. 'No. It's just – we're in the middle of nowhere.'

He laid the letter down and regarded her. 'Livvi, what was I supposed to do? I couldn't leave you on your own. Your mother—'

'I could have been left on my own. Or with a friend.'

'You always tell me you don't have any friends.'

'There's – things I want to do.'

'Like what?'

She touched her pyjama pocket. 'Nothing. Nothing important.'

'You never made much of London anyway.'

OLIVE DID NOT REPLY, FOR her eye had been caught by two people standing in the orchard, waiting at the fountain that lay beyond the immediate ribbon of grass that surrounded the house. It was a man and a woman, and they made no effort to hide themselves. The woman was wearing a satchel against her body, and she seemed at one in this garden, the canes in the parched earth the only remnant of the tomatoes, aubergines and lettuces that must have thrived here once, when someone cared.

The man had both his hands stuffed in his pockets, his shoulders hunched, chin down, but the woman stared up at the muscular satyr in the fountain, poised with his empty canton. She closed her eyes, breathing in the air. Olive breathed too, the faint wafts of charcoal fire and fields of sage, the emptiness of this place, its sense of desolation. She wondered if there was a means to get that water flowing.

The couple began to approach the house, both of them with a pace as sure as the mountain goats, avoiding rabbit holes and minor rocks in their seemingly inexorable desire to approach. It jolted Olive, this confidence. She and her father watched them come near, their progress punctuated by the light snap of bracken beneath their feet.

The woman was younger than Olive had thought. Her eyes were dark, her satchel bulky and intriguing. She had a small nose and a little mouth and her skin was burnished like a nut. Her dress was plain black, with long sleeves that buttoned at the wrist. Her hair was also dark, thick and braided into a long plait, but as she turned to look at Harold, strands within it glinted redly in the morning sun.

The man had almost black hair, and was older, probably in his mid-twenties. Olive wondered if they were married. She couldn't take her eyes off him. His face was that of a Tuscan noble, his body a sinewy featherweight boxer's. He was dressed in pressed blue trousers, and an open-necked shirt like those Olive had seen on the men in the fields, although his was pristine and theirs were threadbare. His face was fine-boned, his mouth had an agile facility. His eyes were dark brown, and they grazed Olive's body like a small electrical current. Were these two together? Olive was probably gawping, but she could not look away.

'We bring bread,' the man said in accented English, as his companion fumbled in her satchel and raised a loaf aloft.

Harold clapped his hands with delight. 'Thank God!' he said. 'I'm starving. Hand it over here.'

THE PAIR MOVED TOWARDS THE veranda. Although she was about the same height as the girl, Olive felt much bigger than both of them, and uneasy for it – her arms too long and her head too large, her limbs out of control, giving her away. Why the hell was she still in her pyjamas like a schoolkid?

The girl placed a hand on her own chest. '*Me llamo Teresa Robles,*' she said, pronouncing it in the Spanish way.

'*Me llamo Isaac Robles,*' the man said.

'*Me llamo Olive Schloss.*'

She must be his wife, Olive thought, for why else would he be with her at this time of the morning? The couple laughed, and she felt a flare of rage. Being called 'Olive' in Spain might be funny, but it was hardly the same as being called 'Anchovy', or 'Apricot'. Olive had always been teased for her name: first, as Popeye's woman; then as an adolescent, a cocktail nibble. Now, on the cusp of freedom, she was being laughed at for being the fruit upon the Spanish tree.

'Harold Schloss.' Her father shook hands with both of them, and Teresa handed him the bread. He beamed at it, as if it was a bar of gold and Teresa one of the Magi. 'I'm her father,' he added, which Olive felt unnecessary. Teresa knelt down, and with the careless precision of a magician, she produced from her satchel a strong-smelling hard sheep's cheese laced with sprigs of rosemary, a cured sausage, three small quinces and several enormous lemons. She placed each fruit with a flourish on the scarred wood, where they glowed like planets, a solar system in which she momentarily became the sun.

'Having a picnic without me?'

Sarah had appeared at the kitchen door, shivering in her silk pyjamas, wearing one of Harold's flying jackets and a pair of his thickest hunting socks. Even haggard from a bad night's sleep and the champagne they'd picked up in Paris, she looked like an off-duty movie star.

Olive saw the familiar reaction; Teresa blinked, dazzled by the bright blonde hair, the air of glamour that clung to Sarah wherever she went. Isaac knelt and plunged his fingers into the satchel. Something living appeared to be at the bottom, and it stirred, and the satchel began to move of its own accord.

'Jesus!' Olive cried.

'Don't be a coward,' said Sarah.

Teresa caught Olive's eye, and smiled, and Olive felt furious to be so publicly humiliated. Isaac pulled out a live chicken, its loose feathers floating to the floor, scaly feet dangling comically in his grip. The bird's reptilian eye swivelled; fear twitched in its toes, tensing into claws. With his left hand, Isaac kept it still on the floorboards. It was making a muffled cluck, straining for the cool of its mistress's bag. Slowly, Isaac placed his right hand on the back of the bird's head, and cooing quietly, he tightened his grip. With a determined twist, he broke the chicken's neck.

The bird slumped onto Isaac's palm like a stuffed sock, and as he took his hand away and rested the creature on the veranda, Olive made sure he saw her look down at the drying bead of its eye.

'You will eat today,' Teresa said, directly to Olive. Olive couldn't tell if this was an offering or an order.

'I've never seen anything like it so up *close*,' said Sarah. She gave the newcomers a radiant smile. 'I'm Sarah Schloss. So who are you two, then?'

'It's just a bloody chicken,' Olive snapped, her heart contracting as Isaac Robles laughed again.

II

*T*eresa watched the group move indoors as she collected her offerings from the veranda. She hadn't wanted to come; it looked so obvious to her, so needy. *There's another rich* guiri *turned up with his wife and daughter*, Isaac had said. *You should see the car, the travelling trunks. There's a gramophone roped to the roof.* 'Who is he?' she'd asked her brother, but neither he nor anyone in the village knew. All that was clear was that a week ago, the duchess's old finca had finally got some new inhabitants.

It was not that unusual for wealthy foreigners to come to this corner of southern Spain, bringing their industrial inheritances and discontentments with city life. Indeed, Teresa had worked for two sets of them before. They came down via Paris or Toulouse, Madrid or Barcelona, laden with boxes of paints and novels – and typewriters to write their own novels – and initialled trunks, which sometimes fell onto the road because of their clumsiness with the local mules. They were bohemian millionaires, or, more commonly, the bohemian children of millionaires, from Texas, Berlin, or London, wanting to dip their brush and dissolve in the sierra like one of their barely used watercolour squares. They arrived, they lived for a bit, and most of them departed.

Teresa could see out of the corner of her eye that Olive had not gone inside. The toes of her woollen socks had been inexpertly darned, which Teresa thought was a shame. People like this should dress better. Olive came towards her and knelt down. 'I'll help you,' she said – in halting Spanish, which was surprising. Under the girl's fingernails were crescent moons of vivid green paint. Her bob haircut needed a trim – untamed, it coped her head like the cap of a wide mushroom. When Olive smiled, Teresa was struck by how Sarah's features had been repeated in her daughter's face, but it was as if they had missed a beat and become a jarring echo.

'I'm still in my pyjamas,' Olive said, and Teresa did not know how to reply. That much was obvious, wasn't it? She picked up the floppy chicken and shunted it into the satchel.

'It's beautiful here,' Olive went on, weighing one of the lemons in her palm. 'My Baedeker says North Africa isn't far. *"The Catholic kings wrenched this land from the Moorish Caliphates. Crucifying heat in the summer, and skin-peeling cold in the winter, enormous night-time skies all year round"*. I memorized it.'

She seemed jumpy. Teresa had watched the girl when Sarah had called her a coward; she'd looked as if she had the words to fight back, but was keeping every single one locked inside her skull. There was an urgency in Olive's body, in the movements of her hands. She reminded Teresa of a trapped animal, restless because someone had approached the bars of her cage.

'So,' Olive said, in Spanish again. 'How long have you been married?'

Teresa stared at her. 'Married?'

Olive frowned. '*Casados* – that's right, isn't it?'

Teresa laughed. 'Isaac is my brother,' she said, now in English. She saw the blush spread over Olive's face as she pulled a loose thread of wool from her jumper.

'Oh,' said Olive. 'I thought—'

'No. We have – we had – different mothers.'

'Ah.' Olive seemed to gather herself. 'Your English is very good.'

Teresa removed the lemon gently from Olive's grip, and Olive gazed in surprise at the fruit, as if she had no recollection of taking it up.

'There was an American lady in Esquinas. I worked for her,' Teresa said. She decided not to mention the German family she had also worked for, who, before returning to Berlin merely months before, had given her a rudimentary facility in German. Life had taught her that it was wiser not to play all your cards at once. 'Her name was Miss Banetti. She did not speak my language.'

Olive seemed to awaken. 'Is that why you're here today – you want to work for us? What does your brother do?'

Teresa crossed the veranda and stared out at the skeleton trees in the orchard. 'Our father is Don Alfonso. He works for the woman who owns the land and this house.'

'Is it really owned by a duchess?'

'Yes. Her family is very old.'

'She can't have been in this finca for a long time. The dust! Oh – but I'm not saying it's your fault—'

'*La duquesa* is never here,' said Teresa. 'She lives in Barcelona and Paris and New York. There is nothing for her to do here.'

'I'm sure *that's* not true,' Olive replied.

'You are English or American?'

'Half English. My father's from Vienna. He married my mother, who's English, but thinks she was born on Sunset Boulevard. We've lived in London for the last few years.'

'Sunset Boulevard?'

'Never mind . . . so – you're from Arazuelo?'

'Will you stay long?' Teresa asked.

'That's up to my father.'

'How old are you?'

'Nineteen,' Olive replied, and when she caught Teresa's frown she went on, 'I know. It's a long story. But my mother's not well.'

'She looks well.'

'It's deceptive.'

Teresa's skin prickled at the hard edge that had crept into Olive's tone. She wondered what was wrong with the beautiful, brittle woman in the oversized jacket. 'You will need someone here, señorita,' she said. 'This is not London. You cook?'

'No.'

'Clean?'

'No.'

'You ride a horse?'

'No!'

'I will help.'

'Well, how old are *you*?'

'Eighteen,' Teresa lied, for in truth, she was sixteen years old. She had learned that foreigners often had a romantic, infantilizing attitude to age, keeping their children as children much longer. This girl was clearly a case in point. Teresa herself had never had such a luxury; sometimes she felt as old as stone. 'My brother—' she began, but stopped. She didn't feel like talking about Isaac any more than was necessary. From her pocket, she brought out three envelopes. '*Tomate, perejíl, cebolla*,' she said in Spanish.

'Tomato, parsley, onion?' Olive said.

Teresa nodded. She had not intended these seeds as a gift. She had in fact brought them to the finca in the hope that she could quietly sow them in the duchess's more fertile soil, and ultimately harvest them for herself. 'They are for you,' she said to the other girl. Teresa had never, in sixteen years, given anyone a present.

Olive looked over her shoulder into the dark of the house. From deep within could be heard Sarah's laughter, and the lower bass of the men. 'Let's plant them,' she said.

'Now?'

'Now.'

From the outhouse at the end of the orchard, Olive found two rusting garden forks and handed one to Teresa. Teresa was struck by the other girl's readiness to be here with her, turning over hard earth, weeding as she went. She didn't want to be so happy about it, but she couldn't help herself. Surely it was rare that a girl like Olive might choose to be here, rather than with those inside? When she protested that Olive should put on some boots over those socks, Olive looked down at her feet in surprise. 'Oh, I don't mind,' she said, wiggling her darned toes. 'I like the feeling of the ground.'

Teresa thought that only a rich *guiri*, with more pairs of socks than sense, would ever say such a thing. Miss Banetti, who'd also come for the rustic life, might have said it and appeared an imbecile. But there was something different about Olive, her thoughtless determination, her acceptance that was so whole-hearted, that Teresa not only forgave the girl her whim, but was delighted that she had no care for shoes.

Olive rolled up her sleeves and lugged two huge watering cans of spring water from the well at the end of the garden, and Teresa admired the sinews in her forearms, their pale endurance, the fact that nothing was lost along the way. Up and down the newly furrowed earth they walked with the cans, and as the water fell, Teresa spied a rainbow arching in the drops. If Olive felt the hard soil poking into her soles, she said nothing.

III

*H*arold invited Teresa to start by cleaning the ground-floor rooms, sweeping away the cobwebs that draped from corner to corner. Using rags ripped from a man's shirt, dipping them in a bowl of vinegar and some of her lemon juice, she scrubbed the windows where dirt had layered round the frames. From the garden, she burned rosemary and sage on the flagstones. In a cupboard in the pantry Isaac found two electric heaters and set them up in the front east room, warming up the bare chalk walls as the sunlight moved over them. He promised them firewood.

Teresa made the Schlosses lunch from the chicken, refusing to eat it with them, although Isaac accepted the offer. By the time the chicken was out of the stove, it was clear to Olive that they had a new servant. But what of Isaac – under what pretence could they keep him near?

The clock in the hall dragged its pendulum four times. 'God!' Sarah said, as they sat at the dining-room table. Her mood was excitable, a great improvement on the day before, but not without its dangers. 'Where's the day gone? It's so cold – I thought the south of Spain was supposed to be hot?' She'd changed into a long-sleeved cream house jacket covering new red woollen trousers, and a blouse in matching scarlet polka dots. At some point she'd painted her toenails, and Olive saw ten small squares of vermilion on the terracotta floor.

'It will get hotter,' Harold said.

From the kitchen, Teresa clanged the tin plates on the draining board, a noise like an armoury.

'Oh well then, I shall fetch my bathing suit,' said Sarah. 'Have you ever been to London, Mr Robles?' she asked, turning to where he sat on her left, pouring coffee into his small white cup. 'Do you smoke? Would you like an almond?'

'Yes, I do. And no – thank you.'

'Please, have one of mine. Harold snaffled some in Malaga. He'll only smoke German ones, so that's all we've got.' Sarah fiddled with the box on the table and pulled out a cigarette; her wrists were burdened with bangles, and they clinked together. Isaac removed the cigarette from her proffered fingers and lit it himself.

'I have not been to London,' he said, weighing the city's name with something like awe. London in calligraphic letters, Henry VIII, the Tower, Middle Temple. Olive's London was not like that – it was a lonely walk through St James's and along the Mall to the National Portrait Gallery to see her favourite Holbein; a penny bun at Lyon's on Craven Street after, or a stroll through Embankment Gardens. That was what she missed – certainly not the other London, the stifling cocktail chit-chat, women's over-rosied flesh, the lemon tang of Trumper's wet shaves fresh on older men; red acne rashes of boys down from Oxford, with nothing much to say.

'London's all right, I suppose,' Olive said, intending to sound jokily arch. 'The people can be ghastly.' Her mother flashed her a look.

'I have been to Barcelona many times,' Isaac said. 'And Madrid.'

Olive thought of their travelling trunks upstairs, the wooden brackets shiny from handling by so many porters, labels from Paris and Buenos Aires, Marseilles, New York; peeling like old skins the Schlosses had shed. She could barely remember any of it now, and nineteen felt like ninety.

'But you have you always lived in Arazuelo?' Harold asked him.

'Yes. I am a teacher in Malaga.'

'What do you teach?' Sarah asked.

'Lithography,' he said. 'At the San Telmo School of Art.' Olive stared hard at her plate.

'Harold's an art dealer,' Sarah went on. 'Kokoschka, Kirchner, Klimt, Klee – all his. I swear he only sells artists whose surnames start with a K.'

'I admire Kokoschka,' Isaac said, and Olive sensed her father become alert.

'Herr Kokoschka painted blue fir trees in Olive's nursery in Vienna,' Sarah said. 'Mr Robles, your English is excellent.'

'Thank you, señora. I taught myself,' he said. 'I have English acquaintances in Malaga, and I practise with Teresa.'

'Do you paint, or only print?' asked Harold.

Robles hesitated. 'I paint a little, señor.'

'You should bring me some of your work.'

Generally, Harold was allergic to people who said they painted. Whenever a hopeful artist got wind that Harold was a dealer, they always misjudged it. Sometimes, they displayed aggression, as if Harold was withholding something to which they were specifically entitled – or they offered a simpering humility that fooled no one. But here was Herr Schloss, asking this young man for his work. Olive was used to how it was when Harold's attention was caught – how he would dog, cajole, flatter, act the father, act the pal – whatever it took, hoping he would be the one to uncover next year's genius. It always hurt.

'What I paint would not interest you, señor,' said Isaac, smiling.

Harold tipped up the pitcher and poured himself a glass of water. 'Let me be the judge of that.'

Isaac looked serious. 'If I have the time, I will show you.'

'The time?' said Harold. Olive's skin tingled.

'When I am not at San Telmo, I am occupied with the workers' union in Malaga. I teach them how to read and write.'

There was a pause. 'Does your father know you're a red?' Sarah asked.

Isaac smiled again. 'I am twenty-six, señora. I do as I must. I supported the workers' strikes. I travelled to Asturias to help the miners. But I am not a red.'

'Shame. That would have been exciting.'

Olive sat on her hands, staring at her mother. Sarah's entire life was predicated on the docility of the workers who propped up her family's famous condiment business. She saw herself as a free spirit, but it was the work of her great-grandfather – starting with his barrel of oranges in Covent Garden and ending up an industrialist with a seat in the Lords – that paid for their travel, the flat in Curzon Street, the cottage in Sussex, the house off the Ringstrasse, the Schiaparelli dresses. Harold's business was certainly successful, but Sarah's inheritance underwrote the lot.

'You are who you are because of the very people you would never deign to consort with,' Harold had once shouted at Sarah, after an evening when she hadn't come home and he'd had to call the police. Sarah, who had in fact passed out on her host's chaise longue and couldn't be roused till the morning, had shouted back that he didn't have a leg to stand on, because he too benefited directly from the family's Finest Cut Marmalade, so he could shut his mouth, unless he fancied finding himself a proper job and a flat in Camden.

'My father and I do not often agree,' Isaac was saying. 'He works for the duchess. All this land is hers. She is eighty-five years old and she won't die.'

'I'm going to be like that,' said Sarah, and they all laughed.

'The people who work her land – how do you say in English? – *tienen un gran hambre—*'

'They're starving,' said Olive.

Isaac looked at her in surprise, and again Olive felt the current that ran through her, the thrill of his attention. 'Yes,' he said. 'Thousands. Across the region.'

'How terrible,' said Sarah.

Olive willed Isaac to look at her again, but he leaned forward and spoke to her mother. '*La duquesa*'s men will give you a job, if you promise to vote for her family and keep her powerful. The poor beg to work her land, for almost nothing, because that is all the work. But she does not remember them if their wife dies, or if their mother is sick. If *they* are sick. She only shows her face during the time of election.'

Teresa appeared at the door of the dining room, and stood with her arms crossed. Her hair had frizzed from the kitchen's steam, her apron covered in bloodied smears. Isaac looked up, seeming to hesitate. Olive noticed Teresa almost imperceptibly shake her head, as Isaac blinked away her warning and barrelled on.

'My father finds her men to work her land,' he said, 'but he only picks the young men, the strong men, not the older ones with families. So more people are starving. And there is no rule on the price for your work here, so *la duquesa* pays you nearly nothing. We tried to change that in the last election, but it has been changed again. And if you complain about how little you get of the harvest – or how bad condition is your house – *la duquesa* and her people will hear. You will not work.'

'But the church must help them,' said Harold.

'Shall I tell you a secret? They say that our Padre Lorenzo has a lover in the village of Esquinas.'

Sarah laughed. 'It's always the priest what done it.'

Isaac shrugged. 'They say Padre Lorenzo wants to make private the fields between the church and the house of his lover, so no one can see him when he makes the journey.'

'Is that a joke?' asked Sarah.

'Who knows, señora? Padre Lorenzo is the cousin of the duchess. He has more interest in territory maps than prayer books.' He sighed, tapping the ash of his cigarette into the ashtray. 'We had a vision. Land, church, army, education, labour – all to change. But we are – how do you say it? *Cogidos*?'

'Caught,' said Olive, and Isaac looked at her again. She blushed. 'You're caught.' She turned away, unable any longer to meet his eye.

'Mr Robles isn't *caught*,' Sarah said. 'He speaks English. He's been to Madrid.'

Isaac inhaled sharply on his cigarette. 'Action may be the only answer, señora. We need the tyranny gone.'

'Tyranny?' said Sarah. 'What tyranny?'

'Most people here are just trying to plant their cabbages and eat them in peace,' said Isaac. 'But many of the children in Arazuelo do not even go to school because they are working in the fields. They need to know who's pulling the sheep over their eyes.'

'Wool,' said Harold. He'd barely spoken, and they all looked at him as he reached into his pocket for his lighter and dipped his head to ignite his cigarette. 'The word you mean is *wool*.' Being Viennese, he pronounced it *voohl*.

'Are you planning a revolution, Mr Robles?' asked Sarah. 'Perhaps we should call you Lenin.'

He held up his hands in surrender, laughing as he glanced at Olive once again. She could barely cope; he was looking at her this time because he wanted to, and she felt as if her head might be on fire. He was the most beautiful man she had ever seen. 'You will see, señores,' Isaac said. 'You are new here, but you will see.'

'*Are* you a communist?' Harold asked.

'No. I am a member of the Republican Union party. And the poverty in our region is visible, it is not in my imagination. Mud huts, ten or eleven children inside them, men asleep on the fields.'

'Isaac—' said Teresa, but he interrupted her.

'It is not just the poor – small farmers, they live on the land, they improve it for the owners – and then they are charged a high rent because they have made the land so productive, that they can no longer afford it. Their labour counts for nothing—'

'You should be careful when you talk about "tyranny", Mr Robles,' Harold said. 'If you insist on being a revolutionary, you will make the people with means to support you fly to the arms of a fascist.'

Isaac lowered his eyes. 'But the people with the means to support us will never support us. I believe there is a way to universal happiness.'

'The coercive redistribution of wealth,' said Harold, looking grim.

'Yes, that will do it. The people—'

'Nothing destroys a country's sense of balance more than the word *coercive*, Mr Robles. But look,' he beamed, 'we are destroying your sister's lunch.'

Teresa stared at her brother. Olive thought of the thin wraiths they'd seen in the fields on their way here, stopping their work to stare at the car like it was a vehicle from a land of fantasy. 'Mr Robles is right,' she said. 'I saw it.'

'Oh, not you too, Liv,' said Harold. 'Not after all those bloody school fees.'

Olive looked to Isaac, and he smiled.

Late that night, after Isaac and Teresa had left, with promises to return in a couple of days with firewood, Olive went up to her bedroom in the attic and locked the door. *Union*, *onion*; this brother and sister had come with their words and their seeds and Olive had never seen their like. Had she and her parents let them in, or had they simply entered, sensing a weakness in the fortifications? No one was like this in Mayfair, or Vienna; you left calling cards, not chicken carcasses. You spoke of the poor with pity, not anger. You did not plough your own land.

Blood alive, head singing from the way Isaac had looked at her, Olive grasped her easel, pulling open its three legs and fastening them tight. She found the wooden panel she had taken from the outhouse, and placed it on the easel. She opened her window to let in the moon, lit the oil lanterns and switched on the electric light beside her bed. She knelt before her travelling trunk like a pilgrim at an altar, and ran her fingers over the paint tubes hidden under the cottons. As she pulled them out, Olive felt a familiar connection, as if her heart was slotting into place, a moment to breathe. Not one of her colours had burst in transit, all her powders intact, the sticks of pastels not cracked in half. They had always been loyal to her, when everything else was falling out of place.

Moths hurled themselves at the bulbs as she worked, but she paid no mind. For the first time in a long time, all else was eclipsed by a purer sense of purpose and the image that was emerging on the old wooden board. It was a view from the bottom of the orchard, in exaggerated colours, the finca behind it, its peeled red paintwork on every window. It had its feet in the earth, but the sky above was enormous and swirling, with a hint of angelic, silver-grey. The scale of the house made it look smaller in the painting, the trees in the foreground laden with such fruit that in reality was not there.

You could just about call it figurative, but it was not realistic. It had a new form of surreality Olive had never executed before. For all its grounded colours on the fields – ochres and grasshopper-greens, the folkloric tenderness of russet furrows and mustard browns – there was something other-worldly about the scene. The sky was a boon of promise. The fields were a cornucopia of cereal crops and apples, olives and oranges. The orchard was so lush you might call it a jungle, and the empty fountain had turned into a living spring, the satyr's canton now gushing full of water. The finca rose up like a welcoming palace, her father's house with many mansions, its windows huge and open to her gaze. The brush strokes were loose, and colour dominated technical accuracy.

Olive fell asleep beside it at four in the morning. The next day, she stood before the painting as the sun cracked low along the sky beyond her window. She never knew she was capable of such work. She had made, for the first time, a picture of such movement and excess and fecundity that she felt almost shocked. It was a stubborn ideal; a paradise on earth, and the irony was it had only come from this place, this lonely part of Spain to which her parents had dragged her.

Stiffly, Olive moved to the trunk where the letter from the art school was hidden. She pulled it out, read it, smoothed it, folded it neatly, and kissed it, placing it back at the bottom of the trunk, buried deep and out of sight.

IV

*L*ast year,' Isaac said, in English, 'I meet a man waiting for my train at Barcelona station. A journalist. We talk. He tells me, "It is coming. It has happened before and it is going to happen again."'

'What's happened before?' Olive asked. She was standing with Isaac in the orchard, helping gather the chopped wood as he sliced it in half with his axe. She turned briefly towards the house, and saw a shadow move behind the lace curtains of her mother's room. To hell with her; this was Olive's time with him. Sarah always wanted to be the centre of attention, and was very good at it, but Olive loved these stolen moments in Isaac's company.

Out of the corner of her eye she watched his shirt lift, and saw the flash of dark brown flesh, a trail of hair leading away. She felt such pleasure when he handed her the split pieces of wood, as if he were offering her a bouquet. From a decade of devouring novels, Olive knew that charming men were deadly. Their story had been played down the centuries, unharmed through the pages, whilst girls were blamed and girls were lost, or girls were garlanded, mute as statues. Be Vigilant and Prize Your Virginity was a subtitle many of these stories could have taken, most of them written by men. Olive knew all this and she didn't care. She didn't give a damn.

He had been coming to the house with less regularity than Teresa, partly because of his job in Malaga, and partly because he did not have as much of an excuse. It pleased Olive so much to see that their piles of firewood were probably the highest for several miles. If he wanted to tell her about the state of his country, she was more than happy to listen.

He had not noticed her new hairstyle, the gobs of her mother's pomade she had applied, to try and make it smooth and slick. These were not the sort of things a serious-minded man might notice, of course, Olive supposed. Not when his country was in a state of unrest. Not when he was thinking of the people. She decided that to make the most of her time with him, it would pay to be more politically aware.

'What happened before? Chapel tombs smashed open, the corpses of nuns on the ground,' said Isaac. 'Houses like this one, robbed.' They both turned back to look at the finca, and the figure at the curtains dipped rapidly away. 'They say a priest was taken from his sacristy and left hanging on a tree, found next morning with his balls in his mouth.'

'Isaac!' Olive cringed. The word *balls* made her nervous, and she felt childish.

'The newspapers make it seem worse than it is – but they never ask the question as to why the looting happens in the first place. So, this journalist.'

'Yes?'

'He starts talking to me about a polar bear.'

'A *polar bear*?'

'Yes. He tells me he interviewed a duke in his house,' Isaac said, laying the wood blocks on her open hands. Olive saw how the tips of her fingers were stained red. She hadn't stopped painting since meeting him. She was working on smaller canvases, filling notebooks with sketches; it was as if she had plugged herself in – to what, exactly, she wasn't entirely sure – and although she was terrified that this long seam of inspiration was going to end, she felt that as long as Isaac was close, and that she was ready for it, for him, her output might continue.

She knew that by staying down here, she had avoided a confrontation about her true self – no art-school confession with her father was required. And yet, she was happier than she'd been in a long time.

'He told me the duke had a polar bear in his drawing room,' Isaac went on. '*Lo había cazado?*'

'He'd hunted it down.'

'Yes. With a gun.'

Olive curled her fingers up, hoping he might comment on their dyed appearance, so she could say, *Oh, I paint a bit too. Would you like to see?* He would come and see the painting and reply, *This is extraordinary, you are extraordinary. How did I not see?* And then they would kiss, him taking her face in his hands, bending down to brush his lips on hers, full of astonishment at how good she was. She so desperately wanted him to see how good she was.

But Isaac did not notice her fingers, and so Olive turned instead to the anomalous polar bear in her mind's eye, a piece of the Arctic, a grotesquery in the Spanish heat, the barbarity and expense of it, the chill in the heart of the home. 'Why did you tell me about that priest?' she asked, trying to assert herself. 'Were you trying to frighten me?'

'No. I want you to see what's happening here. So when you go home, you will tell other people.'

'I'm not going home, Isaac.'

She waited for him to express his pleasure, but he did not. 'Isaac, you do know I'm not like my parents, don't you?' she said.

'What do you mean?'

'They're frightened of things. I'm not.'

She only wanted to communicate that whatever he thought *they* were, she was the opposite. She didn't see things in black and white, like they did. She was nothing like them at all. It felt very important that he should know this.

'There's a gypsy camp, out in the hills,' he said, as if he hadn't heard her. 'They lost one of their boys. Not *lost*,' he corrected himself. 'They didn't lose him. He was beaten by a gang of men. He was twelve. He died.'

'How awful.'

Isaac put down the axe and walked towards a slope at the end of the orchard. '*Ven aquí*,' he said. *Come here*. Together, they surveyed the land before them. A couple of far-off buzzards wheeled in the sky in search of prey along the ground. The skies were so large, the mountains beyond so solid; it seemed the only violence possible here was the violence of the natural world.

'It'll be all right,' Olive whispered. She imagined slipping her hand into his, the two of them, standing here for ever.

His face was hard. 'The people hold this soil in their blood. That is why the landlords fear them.' He paused. 'I worry for my sister.'

Olive was surprised by this. 'Teresa? She'll be fine.'

At the beginning, Teresa had come every other day to clean and cook. Now she was coming daily. The house still had its dark corners, and its sense of absent occupancy, but it had benefited from her quiet and watchful presence. She never said much, just going about her business through the rooms, taking the weekly envelope of pesetas from Harold with a nod.

'Teresa is not married,' said Isaac. 'She is not rich. She is nothing that fits.'

'What do you mean?'

'She's the daughter of a gypsy—'

'A *gypsy*? How romantic.'

He raised his eyebrow. 'And the sister of a socialist. I do not know which is worse for her.'

'Why?'

'The police, the mayor, the *caciques*. My own father. They do not like me. I've been in fights. And she is too close—'

'Isaac, don't worry,' Olive said, attempting a tone of mature assurance. 'We'll look after her.'

Isaac laughed. 'Until you leave.'

'I *told* you. I'm never going to leave.'

'What do you want from this life, señorita?'

'I – I don't know exactly. I know I'd like to stay here.'

Isaac looked as if he was going to say something, and her whole body willed him to say how glad he was to hear this – but he was interrupted by the sound of crunching leaves. Teresa appeared at the bottom of the slope, her satchel strapped across her body, a flat expression in her eyes. '*La señora te necesita*,' she said to Isaac.

'Why?' said Olive. 'Why does my mother want him?'

Teresa and her brother stared at each other, until eventually Isaac capitulated, sighing as he moved back down the slope, not saying another word.

AS ISAAC MOVED THROUGH THE trees, Teresa imagined for a moment that she and Olive were hunters together, watching their prey before deciding to let it go, preferring instead to stand side by side in the cold air. It was not the thrill of the kill they wanted, but simply the companionship that came from sharing a mutual target.

Isaac was fond of saying that Teresa was the kind of girl who'd sell her grandmother if she had to, not that she'd ever had a grandmother to sell. The worst thing was, Teresa sometimes *did* feel a sort of icy indifference to those around her, who'd never helped her, making it clear that she wasn't worth the bother. She looked over at the furrows she and Olive had made with the gardening forks. The seeds were still deep in the soil, and would not show green shoots for months. Teresa was relieved that she had wanted to hand Olive those seeds. Olive somehow reminded her that she was still capable of feeling something akin to happiness.

'Let's go and smoke on the veranda,' said Olive. 'I stole three of my father's cigarettes.'

ONLY OLIVE SMOKED. FROM ABOVE them inside the house, came the sound of a slamming door. 'Do sit,' she said to Teresa, but only after Harold's motor car had revved down to the rusting gates at the bottom of the slope did Teresa obey. 'That's Daddy out again,' Olive said.

'Will your mother see us? I must work.'

'You don't have to work every minute of the day, Tere. They won't get rid of you for sitting down for five minutes. And besides.' Olive lit the cigarette and took an inexpert drag. 'She's talking to your brother.'

Teresa had seen the empty pill bottles in Sarah's room, the indecipherable stretch of words around the small brown vials. She'd heard Sarah sobbing once, trying to bury the sound in her pillow, and had seen a flash of silvery white scars running down in crisscross lines at the top of her legs. Surmising from the stolen cigarettes that Olive was in a more reckless mood than the last time she'd brought this up, Teresa asked, 'Is your mother very sick?'

'She's a depressive.' Olive sat back in the rocking chair, blowing out a funnel of blue smoke.

'A *depressive*?'

'Smiles in ballrooms, weeps in bedrooms. Ill, in her head.' Olive tapped her temple. 'And here.' She touched her heart. 'She gets worse, gets better. Gets worse again.'

'That is hard,' Teresa said, surprised by the other girl's frankness.

Olive turned to look at her. 'Do you mean that, or are you just saying it?'

'No, señorita. I mean it.' And Teresa did mean it; but really her wish was for Olive to confide in her about everything, and she would say what she had to, in order to make it so. Olive looked out at the orchard. To Teresa, she seemed more at ease in her skin. Her clothes, unusual and boyish, suited her; even her untameable crown of hair seemed intrinsically to fit. Being here in Arazuelo seemed to have brought her out of herself.

'It is hard,' said Olive. 'Daddy calls them her "storm clouds", but that's just a nice way of saying that she drags us around. The doctor says her mind's like honeycomb, chamber upon chamber, broken, rebuilt again. She sees her pain in colours, you know. Steel Blue, Yellowed Bruise, German Measles Red.' Olive gave a grim laugh, and

Teresa tried to process the language. 'It's an illness we've always had in her side of the family. I've got a great-grandmother buried in an unconsecrated grave, an aunt – whom no one speaks of – locked in an asylum. Then there's a cousin, Johnny; he hated boarding school, and tried to drown himself in the Ouse. It's wretched really, and I'm so selfish, I just worry I'm next.'

Teresa could hear the snag of Olive's breath in her throat, before she inhaled deeply again on her father's cigarette. 'I can feel it sometimes, in my bones – just how easy it might be to catch it off her.' Olive turned to her. 'Do you think you can catch it, Tere?'

Worry flickered over Olive's face, the spray of freckles over her nose, her dark brown eyes, her mouth ajar. 'I do not think you will be mad,' she said, and Olive laughed and nudged her, and the touch of her shoulder on Teresa was shocking.

'Well, that's that, then. If you don't think I'll be mad, I won't be. Just my mother.' Olive paused. 'Do you think she's beautiful?'

'Yes.'

'Of course. I think she's a sex maniac.' Olive laughed, but the sound died quickly, because the description had the vague air of medical viability and seemed less funny than she might have wanted. The girls sat in silence for a while, watching the kites circle in the distance. Teresa wanted only that time might cease, that this view, and this strange, confiding peace, be all that existed. To have a friend like this would be to own the world.

'I should be engaged to be married by now,' Olive said.

'There is a man?'

'Oh, no. No. It's just – most of the girls I know in London – I wouldn't call them *friends* – are "taken" now. I'm not. But whenever I see their engagement rings, I feel sad. They're so eager to run away, change their names. It's all so *uniform*. Maybe they all like being the same as each other.'

Olive seemed to be talking to herself now, and Teresa was failing to manage the unstoppered bottle that was Olive's English, pouring out words and words that seemed to have been waiting inside a long time.

'And the fiancés!' Olive said. She hooted ferociously. 'They're so peripheral. Do you know what "peripheral" means?'

'No.'

'On the outside. Not important. They've got interchangeable names, like Philip and Ernest and David. Just one floating face, of a man with no discernible chin. When I said I wouldn't get married, one of these girls said to me, "You wouldn't *understand*, Olive. You've been to Paris – I haven't made it past Portsmouth." Imagine being so idiotic! Imagine thinking being a married woman is the same as travel!'

'Perhaps it is?'

Olive glanced at her. 'Well, there are plenty of miserable wives in Paris. Some of them are my parents' friends. One of them's my own mother.'

'Yes?'

'Marriage is a game of survival,' Olive said, and it sounded as if she had heard this somewhere else, before repeating it herself.

'How did your parents meet?'

'A party. Paris. Mother was seventeen. "An English nettle" – her words. Daddy was twenty-two. It was a bit shocking, her becoming engaged to a Viennese Jew. Her family took a while to accept it, but then they loved him.'

Teresa nodded, thinking this a simplification. Harold was not easily loveable, she thought. He reminded her of a beetle, deep within the wood and plaster of the finca's walls. He needed his hard wings to be kept shiny, his antlers polished with a soft cloth, his body buffed and fed so he didn't bite.

'He was interned during the war,' Olive said. 'They let him out and he worked for the British government. He never talks about that. He represented everything Mummy's life didn't, I suppose. She gets bored so easily, and likes to cause a stir. Condiment Heiress, Cocaine Flapper, Rebel with Hun Groom. It's all so garish,' she added, and although Teresa did not understand the adjective, she could taste its jealousy.

'It's astonishing,' Olive continued, 'how easily she can hoodwink other people that she's whole, when inside she's spiralling, as broken as a shattered pot. I sometimes wonder whether we could have had a stable life – Daddy, walking daily to the Foreign Office – bowler hat, club on St James's, mother at home doing embroidery. I doubt it. Don't you doubt it?'

Teresa didn't know what to say to this fizzing girl, with her plaintive, open face. The Schlosses were so short-handed with each other, that it usually neutralized any depth of reference to their past lives. They were actors in costume, in the moment, performing through the house as if it were a theatre stage and Teresa their sole audience. She desperately wanted to see what happened when they took off their robes and walked into the wings, the darker corners where memories shifted. Olive had now lifted the curtain a little, and shown her the shapes and patterns beyond. Teresa worried that to say something wrong would make that curtain drop again, and break the spell of their solicitude.

'Do you think you'll marry?' Olive said, in the face of the other girl's silence.

'No,' Teresa said, and she felt that this was true.

'If I do, it will be for love, and not just to annoy my parents, like my mother did. Do you think Isaac will marry?'

'I do not know.'

Olive grinned. 'If he does, you'll be alone in your cottage. You'll have to come and live with me and my husband. I wouldn't want you to be lonely.'

'Your husband?'

'Let's call him . . . Boris. Boris Mon-Amour.' Olive laughed and kicked her heels. 'Oh, Boris,' she shouted, opening her arms to the sky. 'Come to me, take me!' Breathless, she turned to Teresa and beamed. 'I haven't felt like this in ages.'

'What do you feel?' said Teresa.

'Happy.'

Teresa drank in the image of this girl, in her Aran jumper and old brown shoes, who didn't want her to be lonely, who had a foolish imaginary lover called Boris, and who had come to the ends of

Spain to discover she was happy. And then she noticed the dried
blood, crusted under Olive's fingernails, and she remembered
the axe, and Olive out here with her brother, and panic rose. She
grabbed Olive's hand.

'What is it?' Olive looked shocked by the contact, and stopped
her rocking.

'Your fingers.'

Olive stared down at her rust-coloured nails trapped in Teresa's
little paw. 'I'm fine.'

'It's blood. Did he—'

'Did he what? It's not blood, Teresa.' Olive hesitated. 'It's paint.'

'You are in pain?'

'Not pain, *paint*. I didn't clean up properly.'

'I do not understand.'

Olive considered. 'Teresa, if I told you something, would you
promise to keep it to yourself?'

It was a risky question, riddled with unknowns, but the alter-
native was being shut away from Olive, and that was something
Teresa could not countenance. 'Of course,' she said.

Olive held up her little finger. 'Put your finger round mine. Do
you swear?'

Teresa linked her own with Olive's, feeling the intensity of
Olive's gaze. '*Lo juro*,' she whispered. 'I swear.'

Olive reached out and crossed her fingers over Teresa's heart,
and Teresa, as if under a spell, lifted her hand and marked Olive
with the same gesture, the heat of the other girl's skin coming
through her woollen jumper.

'Good,' Olive said, standing up and pulling Teresa to her feet.
From inside the house, they heard Sarah's laughter. 'Come on, follow me.'

V

As he sat with Sarah in the front east room, Isaac's gaze flicked up to the ceiling. The room above their heads was the place, eleven years ago, where he'd lost his virginity. His father had just taken the job of estate manager for the duchess, and the finca had been unoccupied. Isaac had stolen the keys from his father's office and crept in with a couple of his schoolfriends. More young people from the surrounding villages turned up around midnight, and he'd got drunk properly for the first time in his life, two bottles of his father's Tempranillo to himself.

In the morning, he'd woken sprawled on one of the covered beds with a woman – Laetitia was her name – fast asleep beside him. When she woke, they started kissing, and in the drugged, dry-headed haze of his first hangover, Laetitia and he had sex. Laetitia, Isaac recalled now, had been twenty-seven years old. He had been fifteen. A vase had been smashed downstairs, and when his father appeared at their bedside with the pieces in his hands, he chased Laetitia out of the room and came back to beat his son. Not for the sex – just the vase. *I thought you were a poof*, his father had said. *Thank God.*

Isaac wondered where Laetitia was now. She'd be thirty-eight, about the age of Sarah, who was pouring out their glasses of lemonade. He looked out of the window, down the slope towards the village path. He had never been able to hold Arazuelo in proportion. It never stayed the same, and yet it always seemed the same. It was a self-reflecting place, insular and welcoming by turns. He was continually trying to leave it, although he could never exactly say why. Arazuelo was part of his body. Madrid was the moon, Bilbao was outer space, Paris a place of biblical fantasy – but Arazuelo could overtake a man like no place else.

'Mr Robles?' Sarah Schloss was talking to him, and he smiled. He could hear his sister and Olive making their way up the creaking stairs to the first floor, and then up again to the attic. If Sarah heard them too, she made no comment. She was smoking again, always smoking, and her legs were tucked up underneath her as she sat on the green sofa. 'So, do you think it's a good idea?' she said.

Well, did he? He knew there was something wrong about it, that he should say no. But he couldn't put his finger on it. 'You must be terribly busy,' she went on, in the face of his silence. 'But I haven't had one for years, and it will be such a surprise for my husband.'

'Does he like surprises, señora?'

'Well,' she said. 'He's always surprising me.'

Isaac thought about her offer. That he was a good painter, he knew. He might even be a great painter one day. As he and Tere had grown up in the shadows, as Alfonso's illegitimate children, his father had often bunged them money, on the understanding that Isaac would grow up and leave all this left-wing, artist stuff behind. Alfonso, on hearing that his son was now 'consorting' with union leaders, Anarchists and divorced women, had confronted him. Isaac had no intention of leaving his work at the San Telmo school, so Alfonso had stopped his cash flow. He hadn't told Teresa.

He had very little income from the school, as cuts to government initiatives had affected its ability to run classes and pay the staff. In a few months, Isaac knew he was going to be very poor. But he could never ally with his father, whom he considered the biggest hypocrite this side of Seville.

'I pay very well,' Sarah said. 'Whatever you need.'

Although he bristled at the ease with which she thought she

could buy him, he considered what a pleasure it would be to paint a face like Sarah Schloss's. 'Thank you, señora. I accept. But allow me to make this a gift.'

Her eyes closed in a brief pause of pleasure, as if she had always known he would assent. As much as Isaac disliked witnessing this, he admired her self-belief. He felt that he did not want to give her any assurance about her beauty. She clearly knew she had it in abundance.

Sarah smiled. 'Oh, that won't do. This has to be a transaction. How many sittings will you need me for?'

'I think six to eight, señora.'

'And should we do it here, or at your house?'

'Whatever is easiest for you.'

Sarah leaned over the tray as she lifted a glass of lemonade and handed it to him. 'This is your sister's recipe,' she said. 'It's better than any I've had elsewhere. What do you think her secret is?'

'I leave my sister's secrets to her, señora.'

Sarah smiled. 'Sensible. I think it should always be like that – everyone's happier that way. I'll come to you. Harold is in and out all the time, and I don't want him getting suspicious.'

'When is his birthday, señora?'

'His birthday?'

'This is not a present for his birthday?'

'Oh, no,' she said. 'It's just a surprise.' She lifted her glass. 'Cheers. Here's to my painting.'

OUTSIDE HER BEDROOM, OLIVE STOPPED her hand on the old wrought-iron handle and faced Teresa. 'Remember,' she said. 'Keep this to yourself.'

Teresa nodded. She could hear her brother and Sarah talking below. Olive pushed down the handle and let her in.

They were in an unexpected atrium of thick gold light, a huge space that ran along at least half the span of the house, with exposed beams, splintered with age and cracking plaster. Teresa blinked, adjusting her sight, the dust in the shafts of honeyed daylight swirling in Olive's wake. Isaac had been in this house before, running round it like a mad boy, but Teresa had been too young, and so she hadn't known such a room existed.

She stood rigid at the door, looking furtively around for whatever it was that Olive had been hiding up here. She could not smell an animal, nor hear any muffled cries; she could see only travelling trunks, a messy bed, clothes on a chair, books piled up in towers. It was the type of room she dreamed of for herself.

'Shut the door, nincompoop,' Olive said.

'*Nincompoop?*'

Olive laughed. 'I didn't mean it. I just – I don't want them to hear us.'

Teresa was uneasy. Olive was supposed to be the fish out of water, walking round in her socks. But now, standing by the window on the other side of the room, she looked so different. She had walked into the sunlight straight-backed, certain of herself, her arm resting gracefully on the sill, lost in thoughts that Teresa didn't have the ability to reach.

'Teresa,' Olive said. 'Close the door. Come over here. I want to show you something.'

Teresa obeyed, as Olive knelt down under the bed and pulled out a very large, flat piece of wood. When she lifted it up and turned it round, Teresa's breath caught in her throat. '*Madre mía*,' she said, and laughed.

'Why are you laughing?'

'You did this?'

Olive hesitated. 'I did. It's called *The Orchard.* What – do you think?'

It was one of the most extraordinary things Teresa had ever seen. Some of Isaac's paintings were pretty decent, but this one, *this* one, stood before her like a . . . person. It was not a case of thinking, it was a matter of feeling. The painting in its power overwhelmed her.

Her eyes darted all over it. She felt saturated. Who painted like this, a nineteen-year-old in her school pyjamas? Who knew such colours, who could take the land she had only just arrived in, and turn it into something better, and higher, brighter than the sun that flooded the room? For surely, this was the finca and its orchard, reimagined in a riot of colour and dancing shapes, identifiable to Teresa but so essentially changed.

Isaac had talked on occasion about art, about famous painters and what made someone stand out from the rest. *Novelty*, he always said, *makes the difference.* It was the fact that they were unlike the rest. *You can be a brilliant draughtsman*, he said, *but that means nothing if you're not seeing the world differently.* Teresa felt almost a wave of pain run through her. This wasn't just a case of novelty. This was something else, beyond words, an elusive power that was too much for her to comprehend. She didn't know if she believed in God, but she knew this girl was blessed.

'You don't like it,' said Olive, her mouth thinning to a line. 'I knew I should have worked more on those fruit trees. And perhaps there should be figures in it—'

'I like it,' said Teresa. They stood in silence before it. 'Is – this what you do, señorita?'

Olive considered the question, laying the painting on the bed as delicately as one might a lover. 'I got into art school,' she said. 'I sent my pictures and I got a place.'

Teresa's eyes widened. 'But you are here?'

'Yes. I'm here.'

'But you have *un gran talento.*'

'I don't know about that.'

'If I had the money I would buy your painting.'

'Would you?'

'I would be proud to have your painting on my wall. Why are you not at the school?'

Olive looked away. 'I don't know. But it's funny. Just before we left for Spain, I purchased this green, a vivid grasshopper green – and a shade of scarlet, an oil called Night Indigo, a plum and a silvery grey – all colours I'd never used before. I just picked them up and put them on the counter. And it was as if I'd *known* that only here would those paints come into their own, and help me. That they would flesh out my fears and dreams.'

Teresa could not hide her confusion. 'Look, Teresa, it's not easy to explain. My parents, the girls in London . . . Something's clicked down here. It was as if this painting had been stalking my mind and now it's in the light. I've never felt so connected to the *doing* of the thing.'

'I see.'

'But now that it's done and . . . and out of me, I can't help wondering that the paints didn't do it on their own. As if my involvement was nothing at all.'

'No, no. You have done it. If *I* touch the paints, nothing good will happen. But with you, it is different.'

Olive smiled. 'Thank you for being so nice about it.'

'Do you have more paintings?'

'Not here, but I do have these.' Olive went over to one of her trunks and pulled out a large sketchbook, handing it to Teresa.

Teresa opened the pages and saw inside small sketches of hands and feet, eyes and bottles, cats, trees, flowers – completely unlike the painting in their realist, engraved style. Over the next page, she saw a portrait of Sarah, called *Mother, London*, and one of Sarah and Harold together, a still-life sketch in pastel of the lemons Teresa had brought that first day.

She pointed at the lemons. 'I asked you where they went. You said you didn't know.'

Olive blushed. 'Sorry.'

'You stole them?'

'If you want to put it like that.'

'Why is this a secret?'

'It's not a *secret*. I just – don't tell anyone. Except you.'

Teresa glowed, hiding her pleasure in the pages of the sketchbook. The images were extraordinary, as if they might leap off the page. She kept turning, and was arrested by a double page of her brother; *Isaac Chopping Wood, Isaac with Coffee Cup.*

Teresa felt a surge of pain and Olive yanked the book from her grip. 'Just sketches,' she said. Downstairs, Sarah's laugh rang out, a little bell.

'What will you do with this painting?' Teresa asked.

'So practical,' said Olive. 'Not everything has to have a purpose, you know, an end point.'

Teresa flushed, because this was exactly how she thought; pragmatically, like a jackal hunting for a rib. Still, she had detected a defensiveness in Olive's responses which mystified her. If she had half of Olive's skill, she'd be in Barcelona by now, far from Arazuelo. 'You are going to hide it under your bed for ever, where no one will see it?' she said.

'Of course I'm not.'

'So why do you not show it now? You could put it on the wall.'

Olive went rigid, sitting down on the bed next to *The Orchard*. The old mattress gave way beneath her, and Teresa thought suddenly how squalid the bed looked, and how stupid Olive was to put up with such a state of being when she could clearly afford something better. They could even go into Calle Larios in Malaga to buy a new one – she could offer to take Olive, letting her try mattress after mattress until they found the perfect one. But Teresa kept silent, the deft pencil edges of her brother's face reworking themselves in her mind's eye.

'I don't want it on my wall,' said Olive.

Teresa frowned. It seemed a flat protest. She came up to the edge of the bed, her hands on her hips. 'You could sell this in Malaga, señorita,' she said. 'You could make money.'

Olive flicked her eyes up. 'Money? We've got money coming out of our ears.'

Teresa flushed. 'You could go away.'

'But I like it here.'

'Paris. London. New York—'

'Tere. I don't *want* people to know. Do you understand?'

'If that was mine, I would show the world.'

Olive looked over at the painting. 'Say you do show the world. But the world might not like it. Think of that. All those hours, all those days and months – years, even—'

'But *I* would like it, so it would not be important.'

'So why bother trying to please the world in the first place? And, I can assure you, you will never truly like it, if you do it yourself.'

'Then why are you doing it?'

Olive got up, lit a cigarette and stared out of the window. 'I don't *know*. I've never known. I just do it.' She looked over at Teresa. 'All right, I know that's vague. It's just – it feels as if there's a place, a shining citadel of perfection I have in my mind. And with each canvas and sketchbook, I'm inching closer and closer to it, to the place where my paintings will be a better reflection of the person I am, a *different* reflection. And I will fly.'

She rubbed her forehead and came back to lie on the bed. 'Why are we so trapped by the hours, the minutes of every day? Why can't we live the life that's always out of reach?'

Her voice broke, and Teresa reached out a hand to Olive's arm. 'I'm sorry, Tere,' Olive said. 'I'm probably mad. But it's how it's always been. I just wanted to show someone. I'm glad you liked it.'

'I love it. *Me ha encantado.*'

'Here.' Olive was brisk again, leaping off the mattress with her cigarette still in her hand. 'Take these. You might like to look at them.' She reached down for a book on Renaissance painters, and an old *Vogue*, and handed them over. 'The magazine is my mother's, but she won't mind.'

Teresa flicked through the Renaissance book, colour plates of men and women in their finery, their skin taut as boiled eggs, bulging eyes, delicate ringed fingers and swathes of damask on their shoulders. Strangely elongated Virgin Marys, darted with a yellow beam of the Annunciation; nightmarish scenes of mythical beasts; men with five legs; women turning into pomegranates. She read the names silently: *Bellini, Bosch, Cranach*. It was another language to learn and assimilate, to wield like a weapon.

The *Vogue* was well out of date, but Teresa didn't care. It was hers. She was glad it was already a year old. Sarah barely glanced at her magazines before dumping them on the floor of her bedroom, their colours and allure a siren that Teresa was astonished her mistress couldn't hear. But she didn't want Olive getting into trouble.

'Are you certain your mother will not mind?' she said.

'She won't even notice. Isaac is still here I think,' Olive said, putting away the sketchbooks and *The Orchard* under the bed. 'We should go and see what my mother wants with him.'

Teresa pushed down the cloud that rose in her chest at the mention of Isaac, closed the Renaissance book and followed Olive out.

Isaac picked up the second glass of lemonade and clinked it against Sarah's. He was used to women being like this around him; feline, flirtatious, sometimes giddy. He never encouraged, but this only seemed to make their behaviour more pronounced. It was almost clownish – and yet he had learned not to assume immediately what women wanted from him. It might look like one thing, but it was quite often another.

He thought of how essentially different Olive was from her mother, so innocent, reaching out to him like a drowning girl, more obviously than she probably imagined. And yet she intrigued him in a way that Señora Schloss did not. Sarah dazzled immediately, but there was something supple and interesting about Olive, beneath her awkwardness. She was a survivor of her parents' marriage. He wondered whether if Olive stayed with them indefinitely it might work out badly for her.

He heard footsteps, and Olive appeared at the door, switching her attention between him and her mother, as if she was trying to work out a difficult sum. Teresa was peering from behind Olive, with a strange look of triumph on her face that made Isaac wary.

'Liv,' said Sarah. 'Guess what?'

'Do I have to?'

'Mr Robles is going to paint my picture.'

'What?'

'As a surprise for Daddy,' Sarah went on. 'I've given Mr Robles a commission.'

'But he hates surprises.'

'Well, so do I, Olive. But Daddy is getting this painting, whether he likes it or not.'

Olive came forward, seating herself on the moth-eaten arm-chair, left at a careless angle to the sofa. 'Have you got time to paint this, Mr Robles?' she asked. 'With all the work you have?'

'It will be an honour,' he said. Olive looked towards the unlit fireplace, filled with logs that Isaac had piled up for their conve-nience. Teresa remained in the doorway. She was sneering slightly at him, and he felt irritated with her. She lived in a bubble, she had no idea how many times over the years he'd protected her.

'I should be in the painting,' Olive announced.

'Livvi,' said her mother after a pause, realigning the crease of her trouser leg. 'It's my surprise.'

'I think Daddy would like us both to be in the painting. We sat for one years ago. We should do it again.'

'We did?'

'You've forgotten. Yes, we did. Mr Robles, don't you think that would be a good idea?'

Isaac felt the pressure of the women's attention like a physical weight. 'You must decide,' he said. 'He is your father, your hus-band.'

Sarah picked at a bobble. 'Mr Robles, if I agreed to sit with my daughter, would you need to paint us together?'

'Not always, señora.'

'Well then,' she sighed. 'We shall work it out between us, won't we, Olive?'

Olive tipped her chin in Sarah's direction. 'Yes, Mother,' she said. 'We will.'

VI

*O*live and Sarah were to have three initial joint sessions, arranged when Isaac was not teaching in Malaga. Teresa was to guard the secret. 'Tell Harold that we're at the market in Esquinas,' Sarah had instructed her. 'Or seeing the local doctor. You can think of something, Teresa. You're so clever.'

By the second session, as Isaac painted Olive and her mother in the dimming light of his cottage kitchen, Olive knew something was wrong. Sarah, in a semi-sheer lavender blouse and a brown silk skirt, kept her spine continuously at a slight arch, one arm draped behind Isaac's kitchen chair. She was concentrating on being her best self for the artist, but Olive could see how bleak and drawn Isaac looked.

She thought he should be happy; his party had just won the national election. It had been on the wireless, on the front pages of the newspapers her father brought back from Malaga. A left-wing coalition was in power, something that surely must make him feel triumphant.

'What's wrong?' she asked, when Sarah excused herself for a moment.

He looked up from where he was painting, with a surprised expression. 'Another boy was killed,' he said. 'I knew him a little.'

'Killed?'

'Last night. A local boy called Adrián, a member of the Anar-chist party. He worked in a factory in Malaga. Started by tying red ribbons on donkeys and bicycles, and ended up burning his boss's property records. He had a loud mouth, but he was only a kid. Some bastards shot him and tied him to the back of a truck.'

'Oh, Isaac. That's awful.'

'They are calling it a crime of passion, which is a joke. He didn't have time for love.'

'Have they arrested anyone?'

Isaac's expression darkened. 'No witnesses. He tied himself to the truck, of course. He didn't have any feet left by the time they'd finished.'

'Good God. Who would do such a thing?'

'Everyone, no one. The Civil Guard are saying it was a Commu-nist gang, mistaking him for some rich kid. Others are blaming it on the gypsies. Anarchist, Communist, Falangist or Socialist, *oligarco*, *gitano* or what? Maybe his father did it?' Isaac spat.

Olive wanted to comfort him, but she knew her mother would be back any moment. She tried to be steady. This was a one-off, she told herself, a hideous thing, but still unique. The boy was a symbol of nothing, just an unlucky human put out too soon. But she remembered what Isaac had told her – the polar bear, the priest swinging from a tree, the soil of the land coursing through the people's veins. She thought of *The Orchard*, waiting in her attic, her perfect, multi-coloured paradise, and felt ashamed of her igno-rance, her foreign and insistent make-believe.

The next evening, Teresa sat at the kitchen table in the cottage, whilst Isaac skinned rabbits he'd shot for a stew. She had before her the *Vogue* which Olive had given her, and she handled it as delicately as if it was a first edition of a precious book. The woman on the cover stared delicately back. She was blonde, wearing a long cream cape, one black-and-white-striped beach shoe peeping out. She was leaning on the side of an open-top car, shading her eyes against the sun but looking upwards nevertheless, at some invisible point. The sky behind her was deep blue. HOLIDAY – TRAVEL – RESORT FASHIONS ran along the bottom of the picture in a clean, attractive font.

'You've been quiet,' Isaac said. 'Are you worried about what I'll do?' When she remained silent he said, 'Jesus, Teresa. You should be worried *for* me.'

'Just be calm about all this, Isaac. Nothing you do will bring back that boy Adrián. Stealing honey from the duchess's beehives is one thing, but putting yourself in danger is another—'

'I could say the same to you.' He pointed at the magazine with his knife. 'You should behave, too.'

'But I'm not in danger.'

'Are you sure? Remember last time, Tere. I won't bail you out twice.'

'I haven't taken a thing. Olive gave me this.'

Teresa remembered how it had been with Miss Banetti. The loneliness, the drudgery. The woman had had so many belongings that she didn't even notice when they began to disappear. It had been so tempting, so easy. Small things first, a ring, a silver matchbox. Then on to empty scent bottles, and finally a necklace of emeralds. Teresa had seen these items, always overlooked by the rich foreigners in her care, as fair payment for a grey life. She buried the trinkets in a tin out by the well, and she would visit them sometimes, never actually putting them on her own body, only holding the emeralds to the sun, watching them wink in green complicity. She loved them so much that she felt no guilt.

It was the German family who had caught and dismissed her. Isaac had gone to talk to them, explaining that she had mental problems – which was a lie, but was better than letting the Frau report her to the Civil Guard. He'd returned everything to them, but she kept quiet about the Banetti box, the emerald necklace hidden in their garden. It was her little private escape.

'Tere,' Isaac said more softly, bringing her back into the room, the sound of the rabbit innards slick on the blade. 'Olive can't be your friend, you know.'

'You should take your own advice.'

'I know it must be lonely for you when I'm in Malaga. But she's some rich kid drifting around after her parents and before you know it, she'll be gone again. I don't want you to—'

'I'm not lonely. And I'm not a child. You don't need to be so patronizing. I don't want to be her friend.'

'Good.' He began to dismantle the rabbit's leg. 'Come and help.' She slunk from the table and stood next to him. 'You can't tell me what to do, either, Tere,' he said.

'I can try.'

He laughed, and she did too. 'Haven't I always looked after you?' he asked.

'Yes, Isa. But I never needed you to.'

Harold had not seemed to notice his wife and daughter's absence particularly. He seemed distracted, sitting at his desk in the middle of his study, marooned on the Moroccan tapestries he'd bought from a rug trader in Malaga, elbows digging into the fraying leather top, barely acknowledging Teresa as she dusted round him, or left him a glass of fino at his side. He looked like the captain of a drowning vessel who had found a piece of driftwood and was clinging on for dear life.

On the day the women were having their last painting session, and Teresa was in the finca preparing a stew, the telephone rang. She waited, but Harold was nowhere to be seen. 'Señor?' she called. The house was silent, except for the telephone ringing and ringing. She tiptoed along the corridor towards the study, listening through the door before she went in, making her way across the rugs. As she hefted the Bakelite handle to her ear, she knew she'd made a mistake.

'*Harold, bist du es?*' It was a woman's voice. Teresa remained silent, listening to the caught pocket of air as the woman inhaled sharply and the line went dead. She looked up; Harold was standing at the door, in his coat, holding his hunting rifle.

'What are you doing?' he said. 'Teresa, what the hell are you doing?'

Teresa looked dumbly at the receiver, wishing in that moment that she'd never come to this finca, that she'd found work elsewhere. It had not been enough for her to move only between the tissue layers of the Schlosses' lives – she had wanted to be closer, to the scars and the spots and the hot red mass of their hearts. But now she remembered the danger of knowing other people's secrets.

Harold came towards her as she slammed the receiver down. He put his hand on top of hers, and she was surprised by how warm it was. 'Teresa,' he said, smiling, his hand exerting the minimum of pressure. 'Who could you possibly be wanting to call?'

She looked at him in confusion, and then she understood, rearranging her face into humility, still hearing the echo of the woman's hopeful voice, her panicked breath when she realized Harold wasn't on the other end.

'I am sorry, señor,' she said. 'I wanted to speak to my aunt in Madrid.'

They fixed their eyes upon each other and Harold released her hand. He walked round and sat in his chair, opening the breech of the rifle. 'All you had to do was ask, Teresa.'

'I am sorry, señor,' she repeated. 'It will not happen again.'

'Good. All right. Off you go.'

She was at the door when he spoke again. 'Where is my wife?' he asked her, and Teresa turned back to face him, fear bursting in her stomach.

'She is at the market, señor.'

'At six in the evening?' Harold locked the rifle and pushed back his chair.

'Yes. But she wanted to visit the church after.'

'The church?'

'Yes. *La iglesia de Santa Rufina.*'

He laughed. 'You know Mrs Schloss is not well, Teresa. If she keeps wandering off like this, you must tell me. Keep an eye out for her.'

'*An eye out?*'

'Keep watch for her. Wait here until she comes back. And when she does, tell her I've got work in Malaga. She'll understand.'

'*Sí, señor.*'

'Is Olive with her, at the church?'

'Yes.'

'I'm glad they're spending time together.' He laid the rifle on his desk. 'Teresa, I want your opinion.'

'Yes, señor?'

'Do you think the villagers would like us to hold a party?'

Teresa imagined that a party held by the Schlosses would be the most glamorous thing any of the villagers had ever seen – and she would be in the centre, organizing it. They wouldn't mock her after that – no more gypsy slurs or bastard comments. The power of Harold and Sarah Schloss would reflect in glorious technicolour – on her. 'I think it would be wonderful, señor,' she said.

She hurried back to the kitchen to see to the stew, and heard Harold pacing in his bedroom, the stop-start of his feet as he moved back and forth from his closet to try on several outfits. He reappeared in a beautiful wheat-coloured suit, with a blue shirt underneath, which set against his dark hair and made him look incredibly refined.

His motor car revved and when he was gone, Teresa felt heavy again, burdened by *Harold, bist du es?*, by the secret they both knew he had entrusted her to keep. He had left a trail of cologne. An ambery echo of dark leather chairs and darker corners.

When she returned to the cottage, Isaac was packing away his paint materials in his bedroom. In the kitchen, a sheet was over the painting, as he would not allow anyone to see it before it was completed. Sarah had left, but Olive lingered at the table. She looked tired, and Teresa watched out of the corner of her eye how her hands moved constantly. Teresa could not marry this urchinous twitcher with the stately, confident artist up in her attic. She wondered if Olive had painted anything new, and whether she'd be permitted to see it.

'Your father asked where you were,' Teresa said. 'I told him you had gone to the church of Santa Rufina with your mother.'

'Where's that?'

'In the village square.'

'My mother doesn't know about this.' Olive rose to her feet. 'I'll have to get to her before Daddy does.'

'He's gone out,' Teresa said.

Olive's face fell. 'Of course he has.' She sat back down.

'Are you enjoying being painted?' Teresa asked.

'I don't think I make a very good subject. My mother loves it, of course.'

'Your father will be very happy to see it.'

'Maybe. If it's any good. Isaac won't let me look.'

'Your father – he tells me he is going to have a party.'

Olive groaned. 'Is that what he said?'

'Do you not want a party, señorita?'

'You haven't been to one of my parents' parties. I think I'd rather visit the church.'

She was in an irritable mood, and Teresa wondered quite how badly the portrait session had gone between Olive and her mother. All Teresa could conclude was that whilst Sarah was born to be watched, Olive was more of a watcher.

She walked to the counter, fetched an onion and a knife, and began to chop. 'Do you know the story of Santa Rufina?' she asked, hoping to distract Olive from her gloom.

Olive gazed towards the darkness of the corridor, where Isaac was moving around in his room. 'No.'

'It is a story about two sisters. They were Christians. They lived in Seville, in . . . *la época romana*?'

'Roman times,' said Olive.

'Yes. They made pots and bowls. The Romans wanted them to make pots for a party. A pagan party. But the sisters said, "*No, no we won't. Our pots are our own.*" And they broke the mask of the goddess Venus.'

'Goodness me.'

'They were arrested. They threw Justa down a well. And Rufina – they made her fight a lion.'

Teresa noted with pleasure how Olive had stilled, listening to her story, as the shadows threw black dancers up the walls and the onion sweated in the pan.

'A big lion,' she went on. 'A hungry lion. *En el anfiteatro*. All the people watching. But the lion did not want to fight. He sat, he did not move. He would not touch her.'

'What then?' whispered Olive.

'They cut off her head.'

'*No.*'

'And they threw it down the well to meet her sister.'

Olive shivered. 'That's awful.'

Teresa shrugged. 'I like the lion.' Her eye was caught by Isaac standing at the door. 'He knows the value of peace. He keeps his place.'

'Maybe he didn't like the taste of bony girl,' Isaac said. Olive turned to him. He folded his arms and fixed Teresa with a look. 'Telling stories again, Tere?'

'She's a good storyteller,' said Olive. 'Imagine waiting down in the darkness whilst your sister faced a lion. Imagine holding her head in your hands; the rest of her, disappeared. What happened to Justa?'

'She died of the shock,' said Teresa.

'So would I,' said Olive.

'You don't know that, señorita,' said Isaac. 'You might be strong.'

'Oh, no. I'd definitely faint.' Olive looked thoughtful. 'Do you know, I might visit that church.'

'Señorita?'

'Why not?' said Olive. 'At least then we could say that one of our lies was actually a truth.'

PART II

Belonging

AUGUST 1967

7

*L*awrie and I made it to the cinema for our first date. In the end, we went for *You Only Live Twice*. There was so much bare flesh and sadism in it, I was embarrassed for making the suggestion. No romance, just gadgets and Sean Connery's chest that looked borrowed from an ape. I think, on reflection, I would have preferred to watch Catherine Deneuve, but I was happy simply to sit with Lawrie, to catch his lovely scent, the dense warmth of his body, this person who in turn had chosen me.

Over the next two weeks, we saw each other nearly every single day. It was a fabulous sickness. We went to the Wallace Collection and the National Gallery, to see if we could spot any more paintings with the initials I.R. (no success). We went to the theatre, and I still have the ticket stub. It was called *Play* by Samuel Beckett, and I had never seen anything like it. I remember my delighted shock as the curtain went up, the three actors revealed – one man and two women, playing his mistress and his wife – stoppered to the neck in giant grey funeral urns, unable to move, gabbling incoherently before they began interspersing their stories to the audience, remaining oblivious of one another.

We went to Soho restaurants and bars – All Nighters, the Flamingo – and discovered that we danced together very well. I didn't like having to shout to be heard over the noise and it got very smoky past eleven. We saw gangsters and their girls there: slick hair, gold rings, a shimmer of malevolence. But the important thing was the live music. It was wonderful – ska, calypso, jazz and blues.

I didn't know it, but a bond had been sealed, and who'd suggested what, who'd wanted what – that strange dance of allusion and manners that distinguishes the first time for anything – had faded. We were dependent on each other without really knowing each other, in that way the young can be when they have never been burned or hurt or discarded, when they share everything, making the mistake that the other person is the answer to their confusing sum. He was lonely and I was lost – or was it the other way round? We hadn't slept together; it hadn't got to that yet. It was very innocent, in its way.

Since our exchange in the rain on Piccadilly Circus, I'd hardly seen Quick. Only Pamela and I – and a couple of the academics, who normally kept to the basement with the archives – seemed to come in dutifully every day. Quick seemed to be absent more than you would consider acceptable, often only coming in for a couple of hours. We were attached to the research part of the building, not the gallery round the front on Jermyn Street, so it was always quiet. I missed Quick's attention.

In her absence, Pamela invited me to eat my sandwiches with her in the courtyard, leaving the reception desk unattended. I'd hesitated, firstly because I was still finishing my Muriel Spark book, a collection of short stories and radio plays she'd had published six years before. The second reason was that I did not really want to hear more about 'people like you' – a phrase that Pamela occasionally slipped into our conversations – but my lack of contact with Cynthia, and the absence of Quick, was making me miss female company. And thirdly: I really thought someone should be manning reception.

Pamela's lunchtime questions about life in Trinidad were a lesson to me in how little her school days, and all the days after, had taught her of the Empire's reaches. But she also had a genuine curiosity – the weather and what humidity and heat did to books, to clothes, and how they shaped the food your mother once made you, the music you listened to, the people you knew – Pamela's questions made me realize how far away from it I really was. It conjured Cynth, our long journey together, and then it reminded me of our stupid stand-off, and I thought I might cry, so instead I pushed Pamela to talk. She told me about her mother the seamstress, and how her father portered meat at Smithfield. She had five brothers – and a sister, she said, who'd died when Pamela was eight.

'I've got to ask, Odelle – you got a feller?' she said. 'You been looking sort of dopey these last few weeks.'

I hesitated. I so wanted to talk about Lawrie, about love – what it might feel like, and whether I was in it. 'No,' I said, instead. 'I haven't.'

Pamela narrowed her eyes. 'All right. You keep your secrets. *I've* got a boyfriend. Billy. He works behind the scenes at All Nighters, but I wouldn't expect you'd go there.'

'Why?' I said.

She laughed. ' 'Cos you're too sensible to waste your youth dancing in clubs.'

I laughed back, intuiting true flattery in her comment, that for the first time, she was imbuing me with some sort of sophistication and status. But I could still picture how Lawrie and I had danced in that very club, the sweat running down our backs. It did feel like a different me.

Pamela wore Billy like a medal, but thinking of the men I'd seen there, I wondered if he was more of a bronze than a gold. As the days wore on, and our sandwich lunches continued, my book of Spark stories still unfinished, I found myself surprised to feel sorry for Pamela, whose company I was coming to enjoy. 'Billy's got big dreams,' she'd say, but never elaborated about what exactly, and I had the feeling they didn't really include her.

REEDE HAD TELEPHONED LAWRIE, SAYING he'd had an 'inordinate piece of luck' with the Prado gallery in Madrid, and could Lawrie come as soon as possible. On the morning he was due at the Skelton, he was already waiting for me on a bench in the middle of the square.

'Hel-lo,' I said, sitting down next to him. 'Excited for news of the lion girls?'

He smiled. 'A bit.' As he leaned over to kiss me, a man walking past tutted loudly. I couldn't be sure, but I thought I heard the word *'disgusting'*. We ignored him; I was never going to say anything, however much I might have liked to, but I did wonder if Lawrie might speak up.

'Come on,' I said, when it was clear that either Lawrie hadn't noticed, never assuming such a comment might be directed at him – or that he didn't consider it worthy of attention. 'You'll miss your appointment with Mr Big Shot. But you go in first, I'll follow.'

'Why?'

'I don't want Pamela to know about us.'

'Are you embarrassed about me?' he said.

I laughed. 'Of course I'm not. It's just – well, if she finds out about you, I'll never hear the end.'

Sitting at my desk, having safely outwitted Pamela, I couldn't stop thinking about what was going on in Reede's office above me. I was very curious about Lawrie's painting. And although my mother always said that if you listen at doors you deserve every burned ear you get, I knew Reede wasn't going to tell me a thing. Quick was away that day, and Lawrie couldn't be trusted to relay every particular.

I took the back stairs to the next floor and hesitated before putting my eye to the keyhole. I could feel my pulse beating hard, fearful that one of them inside would turn, and hear me. Lawrie's painting was propped up on the easel by the desk. It was a perfect rectangle, filled with vibrant colours; vermilion, lavender, indigo, terracotta, livid greens. And to my complete surprise, sitting in one of Reede's low-slung leather armchairs, was Quick. Once upon a time, the Skelton had been a domestic house – most of the panelling was original – and I imagined Georgian ladies sitting where Quick was now, playing with a spree of little dogs and wondering what syllabub to feed their guests.

What was Quick doing here? She was staring into the empty grate, her arms wrapped around her body. She looked nauseous, as if she was waiting for an explosion. She reached down into her handbag and brought out her cigarettes, busying herself with lighting one.

'So. Isaac Robles,' Reede was saying, pulling out a photograph from a buff folder on his desk. 'Ever heard of him?'

'No,' said Lawrie.

'The Prado in Madrid sent me this. They think it's him, in Malaga, around 1935 or -6. We don't know who the woman is, but the photo was most likely taken in his studio, and she's probably a model he used. It matches up to other images of him in Madrid earlier in the thirties. He was just beginning to enjoy a bit of fame when this photograph was taken. But of course, what has excited me most is that the painting in progress on Robles's easel looks *exactly* like it could be yours.'

There was a silence. Lawrie had his back to me, so I couldn't see his expression through the keyhole, but he was very still, as if he'd been stunned.

'What?' Lawrie said, quietly. 'Is that possible?'

Reede smiled. 'Thought you'd like that. He's only started on the lion by the looks of it in the photograph, but it's fairly emblematic, wouldn't you say?'

Lawrie took the photograph from Reede's outstretched hand. His shoulders were hunched, head bent in concentration. Quick remained seated, watching him, dragging deeply on her cigarette.

'Where did the Prado get this?' Lawrie asked.

'They don't know for sure. Their records from the thirties are not complete, for obvious reasons. Robles might have left it with someone to keep it safe when war broke out. They might not have known what to do with it, so gave it to the Prado. Isaac Robles wasn't very popular with the authorities, and his work wasn't

really to their taste. You didn't want to be caught with evidence
that you were friends or acquaintances with undesirables.'

' *"Undesirables"*?'

'From what we know, Robles moved in quite left-wing circles.
That meant he could have been a political agitator. They probably
accepted this photograph and slipped it in their files. Robles didn't
survive to match Miró or Picasso in output and trajectory. But what
he *did* make is superlative. One theory for his small output, other
than an early death, is that he destroyed a lot of his work. That sort
of practice always makes a painter more special – it's his rarity. Now,
to the point. I believe this painting of yours is what we call a sleeper.'

'A sleeper?'

'Yes, it's been lying in wait for us, overlooked for years. We're looking at 1936, perhaps,' Reede continued. 'The fact there is no frame
is unfortunate. You can learn a lot from a frame's quality. I assume
Robles wouldn't have had access to many, if he was back and working in the south of Spain. But if this *is* by Robles, and I think it is,
then it was painted as he reached the cusp of his powers before war
came. Look at the colours, the surreal narrative, the playfulness. It's
highly unusual. I see why he was so prized at the time.'

'What happened to him?' Lawrie asked.

'War happened, Mr Scott. There are several theories. One is
that he went north to join forces with other Republicans as Fran-
co's troops inched up from the south. They never found a grave,
but at that time, it wasn't uncommon. He was from the south,
Andalusia, and he lived and worked in Malaga for a time, fairly
unsuccessfully. He travelled to Madrid and Barcelona – there are
a couple of his lithographs there, fairly minor.'

'I see.'

'But at the time *this* photograph was taken, Robles wouldn't have
been so worried about war. He was working well. He'd abandoned
his idealistic, figurative aesthetic once he was back home, and it
appears that he started to paint quite differently. A few months
before Spain cracked apart, he painted a work that caused a real
stir. It's called *Women in the Wheatfield*. Have you heard of it?'

'No.'

Reede turned towards the door, and I swore he looked at the keyhole. I froze.

'It's not particularly famous, but it's a special painting,' said Quick, and Reede turned back to her. Gradually, I edged my heart back down my throat.

'Why is it so special?' asked Lawrie.

'I've done a little investigating,' Reede went on before Quick could say anything more. 'We know that Robles sold *Women in the Wheatfield* in Paris, around the time this photo was taken. A man called Harold Schloss sold it.'

'I see,' said Lawrie. Even through the keyhole, I could see that he was uncomfortable.

'It went to New York for a while, and now hangs in Peggy Guggenheim's house in Venice. I've seen *Women in the Wheatfield* myself,' Reede went on, 'and it has similar qualities to yours. Extraordinary in the flesh.' He touched the edge of Lawrie's painting. 'Sometimes, I think he would have been a genius, had he carried on.'

'Why?'

'That's not always easy to define. But you see, with most artists, you have one thing or the other – the visionary with sub-standard technical skills, or a short time frame of astonishing output that diminishes in quality, for one reason or another. These fellows have no training in composition, and most of them can't therefore subvert it. Or, you have the excellent trained draftsman with no imagination, who will never paint the world anew. It's actually quite hard to find someone who has it all. Picasso has it – you should see his early works. It's subjective, of course, but I think Robles had it too. And I think your painting demonstrates his skills to a higher level than *Women in the Wheatfield*. Some say his scant works are political; others find them to be escapist *tours de force*. That is the quality they have – perpetually interpreted, yet always standing up to every iteration. Robles has lasted. You don't get bored. You see new things. Moreover, on a basic aesthetic level, they wash gorgeously over the eye whilst never being twee.'

'But you can't prove this is a Robles,' Quick said.

Reede narrowed his eyes at her. 'Right at the moment, I can't, Marjorie. But there are avenues. He painted other pictures. It's a case of tracking them down and lining this up with them. Your mother is – recently deceased, I understand, Mr Scott?'

'That's right.'

'I wonder – do you think she kept receipts?'

'Receipts?'

'Yes, of things she bought. Paintings, for example.'

'She wasn't the sort of woman who kept receipts, Mr Reede.'

'Pity.' Reede looked thoughtfully at the painting. 'Anything you have regarding the purchase would be very useful. I ask about the provenance, not just in the instance of your wishing to sell the picture, or us perhaps to exhibit—'

'Exhibit?' Quick said.

Reede blinked at her. 'That's right. I ask, Mr Scott, because this painting may be a legal matter.'

'What do you mean?' said Lawrie, the panic palpable in his voice.

Quick stubbed out her cigarette. 'Perhaps there's no need to get into that now, Mr Reede. It's not really the Skelton's approach, an exhibition for a single painting—'

'You're probably aware of what happened in the thirties in Europe to valued works of art, Mr Scott,' Reede interrupted. 'A lot of them disappeared. The Nazis took them off gallery walls, removed them from private homes—'

'This painting wasn't stolen,' Lawrie said.

'You sound so sure.'

'I am. My mother wouldn't have stolen anything.'

'I'm not suggesting she did. But she could easily have purchased a stolen item. Robles was Spanish, working solely in Spain, as far as we know, although his paintings sold in Paris. Did your mother have any connection to Spain?'

'Not that I know of.'

'Well. Here's one theory. Artworks moved around Europe quite freely in those days. Harold Schloss was a well-known Viennese art dealer specializing in early twentieth-century modern art. If he sold *Women in the Wheatfield*, he might have sold more of Robles's work. Schloss had a Paris gallery, so it's possible your painting was there around the same time.'

'This painting went from Spain to Paris?'

'Possibly. By this point Robles was back in Malaga, so maybe Harold Schloss visited him down there. Dealers will go anywhere to sniff out talent.'

'This is all just conjecture, Mr Scott,' Quick murmured. 'Just an avenue—'

'Many of the gallerists in Paris were Jewish,' Reede went on. 'I don't know about Schloss's history, we'd have to find that out – but in '42, when the Nazis had occupied Paris for a year, they closed a lot of the businesses down and sent the owners to be interned before they went onwards to – well, to the camps. Many paintings were never recovered. Others were hidden away, only to turn up in the strangest of places. Junk shops, for example. Suitcases. Old train tunnels. Flea markets.'

There was a silence. On the other side of the door, I was barely breathing.

'Jesus Christ,' said Lawrie.

'After the war, the Nazis who were captured claimed they'd burned the lot. Poppycock, of course. They stole too many to have destroyed them all. And they knew what they were doing. They knew that what they were taking was valuable, even as they claimed it didn't fit the new aesthetic of the Reich.'

'What do you think happened to Harold Schloss?' Lawrie said.

Reede looked annoyed. 'I'll be investigating that, as I said.'

'This painting wasn't stolen,' Lawrie repeated.

'There's no way to be certain – at least at the moment. The first half of this century was a mess for the art market, and we're still picking up the pieces. Art has always been used for purposes other than pleasure, be it for political leverage or a loaf of bread.'

'All right.' Lawrie ran his fingers through his hair.

'I'm speaking to a representative at the Guggenheim foundation, who is being a great help in investigating what – if anything – they have on Isaac Robles, which may shed more light on this painting here.'

Lawrie exhaled slowly. 'Thank you – I think,' he said. He went to take the painting off the easel, but Reede stretched out his arm.

'Don't you think, Mr Scott – all things considered – that it might continue to be safer here? We have a night watch and an alarm system. I fear that in Surrey—'

'The crime capital of the world?'

Quick intervened. 'Your mother's death – was it announced in the papers?'

'It was.'

This surprised me – what sort of people had their deaths announced in the papers?

'That is the kind of thing that attracts art thieves,' said Reede. 'People who get death notices in papers usually have things worth nicking,' he went on. Reede's use of the word *nicking* pinged out to me; it was the sort of word Pamela would use. 'I know it sounds preposterous, Mr Scott, but even so. Allow us to look after it for you. It will be safer.'

Reede was a slick act; polite, pressurizing, authoritative, conciliatory all at once. 'All right,' said Lawrie. 'A little longer.'

'Thank you. Sincerely. I'll be in touch as soon as I have news. This is very exciting, Mr Scott. I can only thank you for choosing the Skelton as your base of investigation—'

'Can I keep this photo?' Lawrie said, holding up the battered square.

Reede looked puzzled. 'Keep it?'

'Until we meet again. Just to have a closer look.'

'Marjorie will get Rudge or Bastien to make a Xerox copy for you.'

I tingled at the sound of my name, terrified Reede would discover me hiding here, but I was unable to drag myself away. 'I'm convinced that photo's an original, Mr Scott,' Reede said, 'and I can't let it go. Marjorie – are you all right?'

Quick jumped. 'What?'

'I *said*, will you get one of the girls to make Mr Scott a Xerox copy of this photograph.'

Quick gathered herself and took the photograph from Lawrie. She carried it by the tips of her fingers, not even looking at it. I backed away from the keyhole and moved as fast as I could down the corridor.

I wasn't fast enough.

'Odelle?' Quick's voice was low and quiet. I stopped and turned, relieved to see she had closed the door behind her. 'Come here,' she said.

I walked towards her, shamefaced. 'You were listening,' she said. Given the faint glint of amusement in her eyes, I saw no point in lying; I'd been caught creeping down an otherwise empty corridor.

'I'm sorry,' I said. 'Please, don't—'

'Apparently, we're not supposed to look through keyholes.'

'I know.'

She looked down at the photograph in her hands and went still. 'Think he's got a talent?' she said.

'I do. Do you believe that's a genuine Isaac Robles in there?'

She pushed the photograph into my hands. 'If Reede says so. He's the one that knows. And it looks like it matches the one in this image. But what do *you* make of it?'

'I'm not an expert.'

'I don't want a bloody expert, Odelle. I just want to know if you like it. It's not a test.' She looked exhausted, and I noticed her hands were trembling slightly.

'It unnerves me.'

She leaned against the wall. 'Me too.'

'But it's very beautiful.'

'The subject matter is insidious.'

'What do you mean?'

'It's as if there's an extra layer to the painting we're not privy to. You can't get at it, but it's there.'

I looked closely at the photograph. It was bent, splodged, with a liquid stain in the bottom left corner. It was in black and white, and looked as if it had been through the wars. And yet the image was clear enough – a man and a woman, standing in front of a large, half-finished canvas. They were in a workshop of some sort. The man alleged to be Robles was without a jacket, his sleeves rolled up, a cigarette dangling from his mouth. He was unsmiling, staring straight at the photographer. He had thick, slightly wavy hair, and dark brows, a slender face, nice cheekbones, compact body – and even in this locked-away moment in time, his eyes were attractive, his glance determined. He was holding a large palette covered in many paints, and his body was turned all the way to the camera. He seemed defiant.

The woman on his right looked happy. She had an open face – she couldn't have been much more than a teenager really, but in those old photos, girls always look like women before their time. She was really laughing; her eyes were almost invisible, they were so creased. She had that cheery unselfconsciousness that always makes a person beautiful, however unremarkable their face. Her hairstyle was half-crimped, close to her head in the thirties style, but flyaway, as if she didn't care. She was pointing to the painting, and in her hand she held a brush.

'Who's the woman?' I said.

Quick closed her eyes. 'His muse, probably. Or just a model.'

'He's an Italian Paul Newman,' I said, and Quick laughed.

The photo jarred something in me. It was so potent, so full of a story. I flipped it over, and amidst the marks of time, at the bottom left, I read the handwritten caption, *O and I.*

'Did you see this, Quick – who are O and I?' I asked. 'Is it *I* for Isaac?'

But Quick was no longer in the mood for speculation. 'Don't stand there gawping, Miss Bastien,' she said. 'We haven't much time. Go and copy that for Mr Scott, will you? Off you go.'

8

*T*hree days later, Quick invited me to her house. I had mentioned in passing that my birthday was coming up, and I found a small card, left on my desk, asking me to lunch on the Saturday. I was thrilled. It was not normal for employers and employees to mix like this, but my curiosity overrode any reservations I might have had. I told no one I was going.

My shoes clipped the pavement and my sense of adventure rose. It was the very last of summer; London was a motor-car fume, a cigarette stub on the paving, a cirrus sky. By now, I was a fully-fledged observer of the uneven spurts and scars of London housing. The postcodes, the brick, the rose bush absent or present, the foot scraper, the height of your front steps or the lack thereof was a language I had learned to speak. You couldn't live here and not notice the difference where roads reigned in peace or chaos, a mangy dog lolling by the gutter, ragged kids, a neat box hedge, the flicking net curtain. In London, there were many different ways to live, but few to change the life you had.

The bombings of the war had left odd patterns in so many streets, and Quick's long road was a familiar mongrel, starting with a handful of stately Victorian survivors, a slew of Edwardian terraces, a sudden and squat apartment block that had been erected in the fifties, with wide white balconies, concrete walls

and a midget ivy that someone had planted in an attempt at green-
ery, but which barely reached the first-floor window. Then, further
along, was where she lived, on the edge of Wimbledon Common.

I stood before Quick's house. It was a low-slung, pale-blue-
coloured Georgian cottage. You but half closed your eyes, and a
woman with a muslin dress and bonnet could so easily just have
slipped within. *Why the woman working if she have a place like
this?* I wondered. I thought Cynth would love to see this cottage,
and how unlikely it was she ever would. I used the knocker, an
old copper handle specked with verdigris, and waited. There was
no reply. Honeysuckle spilled everywhere around me, framing the
door. From within I could hear the strains of a classical piece, the
simple steps of a piano, complicating itself as the stanzas went on.

I wondered if the burn on my back was indeed eyes watching
me, or just my worried imagination. I hadn't been into a white
person's house, not even Lawrie's. This was, shall we say, a very
white street. The bolt slammed back, the door pulled open and in
a rectangle of gloom, Quick was before me. That silvery short hair,
those liquid pupils shrinking in the sunlight. She looked smaller
than at work. 'You came,' she said. I had never entertained the
thought that I might not. The piano was much louder now, playing
through the house like a theatrical opener to our pas de deux.

She gestured for me to step inside. It was a deep house, set back,
and the floor stretched down a corridor, on towards a glimpse of
garden, where leaves moved in a light breeze and the silhouette
of a solitary cat was shaped like a waiting vase. 'Garden?' Quick
asked, but it was not a question really, for she was already walking
towards it. She was taking delicate steps as if she didn't quite trust
her own feet. I swivelled my eyes to the left where the front room
opened out, and saw a brief glance of polished floorboards, wide
rugs, pot plants and an upright piano. Wherever I looked, the front
room, the corridor – the whitewashed walls were bare of pictures.

It looked decidedly un-English, no heavy Victorian tiles under-
foot, no raised flock wallpaper, no cornicing, no heavy wood.
There were bookshelves though, and I longed to pry. To the right,

a flight of stairs began; I doubted I would ever see where they led. Another room opened off to the left as we carried on down the corridor, towards the square of light. It had a desk in it, and wind-up gramophone from where the dying notes of the classical recording was emanating. I thought it was quite old fashioned of her to have a gramophone.

When we reached the kitchen and the open garden door, Quick stopped. The cat skittered out into the undergrowth, where it settled, a pair of pale yellow eyes regarding me between the leaves. 'Lunch,' Quick announced. A large tray waited on the table. On it were bread rolls in a basket, a brash yellow cheese, some cold chicken legs, a pork pie and small red tomatoes, jewels of condensation running plumply off their sides. It all looked good, and I said as much.

'It's very simple,' Quick said. I offered to carry the tray into the garden. 'Not at all,' she said, batting me away, before conceding, 'but perhaps you can take those.' She indicated a large earthenware jug of water and two glasses, and I took them outside, following her stiff gait. 'Something stronger?' she asked over her shoulder, and this time it was a question. I declined.

Her garden was not large, but it was full of trees and bushes, and pink hollyhocks, more honeysuckle, the drone of accompanying bees, a little wilderness at the end. A church bell rang in the distance, a sombre line of twelve dongs to hold the time before it slipped away once more.

The garden moved in the breeze. Quick put the tray down on a stone table and a car revved in the road. 'Pull up a pew,' she said, gesturing to one of the three sun chairs. Two were old and saggy and had clearly seen much use. I obeyed, compelled by her authority. Lowering herself down gingerly into one of the older chairs, she slowly extended one leg after the other upon the grass. Kicking off velvet slippers, she revealed petite bare feet, browned by exposure. Looking at Quick's ten toes, I felt trussed in my winkle-pickers, my wedged pill-box hat, my plain green dress. She pushed a pair of sunglasses down onto her face and I lost sight of her expression.

'There are days like this,' she said, 'that I wish could go on for ever.' She poured us each a glass of water, struggling a little with the weight of the unwieldy jug. She glugged her glass and smacked her lips. 'Please eat,' she said. In her own habitat, she seemed much more relaxed. Gone was the haunted expression in Reede's office, even the debonair diffidence she sometimes employed for me and Pamela. I took up a quarter of the pork pie and began to eat it with a piece of bread roll. It was a good pie; the pastry melting away, the cool of the jelly, the rich shock of pig.

'I hope we're not giving you too much to do at the office?' she asked.

'Oh, no,' I said. 'It's all manageable.'

'Good.'

'How's your married friend?'

I looked at Quick, worried she was a mind-reader. 'Fine, thank you. She and her husband have moved to Queen's Park.'

'You're not lonely?'

'No.'

'Writing anything?'

'A little.'

'Can I read it?'

'*Read* it?'

'Well, that's what people usually do with writing, isn't it?' She looked amused.

'I don't—'

'I'd be honoured if you showed me.'

'It's not very good,' I said.

She pulled a face. 'Does it matter whether you think it's any good?'

'Of course.'

'Why?'

'Well – because – because I have to be critical of it, to make it better.'

'Well, that's a given. But isn't writing something as natural to you as breathing?'

'In some ways. But I have to work at what I write,' I said, my voice rising. 'Every writer does.'

'But you pick up a pen and write without much preamble.'

'I suppose.'

'And are you proud of breathing? Do you *revere* your ability to breathe?'

'It's who I am. So if it's not any good, then neither am I.'

She stared at me. 'Do you mean as a person?'

'Yes.'

'Oh, no. Don't be *moral* about this, Odelle. You're not walking around with a golden halo beaming out of you depending on the power of your paragraph. *You* don't come into it, once someone else is reading. It stands apart from you. Don't let your ability drag you down, don't hang it round your neck like an albatross.' She lit another cigarette. 'When something is considered "*good*", it draws people in, often resulting with the eventual destruction of the creator. I've seen it happen. So whether you think it's "*good*" or not should be entirely irrelevant, if you want to carry on. It's tough, but there it is. And of course, whether *I* think it's good should also be neither here nor there. Even more so, in fact. I think you're worrying too much.'

I was silent. I felt like I'd been shot.

'Do you want to publish your work, Odelle?' she went on, as if we were talking about nothing so substantial as a train timetable.

I dug my shoes into the grass and studied the tips intently. 'Yes.'

Surprisingly, my honesty created a companionable silence, a moment of reprieve. To publish my work was what I wanted; it was the only goal I'd really ever had.

'And do you hope to marry one day?' she asked. 'Have children?'

This was a swerve, but I had grown used to her staccato, jumping thoughts. Often with Quick you got the sense there was a whole other conversation going on underneath her words, one that only she could hear. The idea of being a wife was vaguely odd to me; the thought of being a mother, completely alien. Even so, the mind is elastic, so I thought of Lawrie and leapfrogged prematurely into the future. 'Maybe one day,' I said.

'The only problem is, children grow up. Or maybe that's a good thing, in your case. They can look after themselves, you can look after the words.'

'Can't I look after both?'

'I couldn't tell you. I've never tried.' I considered the house behind us; Quick had no sign of a family, children or otherwise. I tried to imagine Quick as a child, and I couldn't do it. She was too sophisticated and strange to ever have been such a rudimentary being.

Quick placed her cigarette in the ashtray. She readjusted her glasses, and forked a tomato with such expert precision that not a seed escaped. She plunged it into her mouth, and swallowed it. 'Mr Scott brought his painting to the Skelton because of you,' she said. 'Didn't he?'

My stomach flipped. 'I – what? – I—'

'Don't worry, Odelle. You haven't done anything wrong.'

'He didn't – it wasn't me, it was the Skelton's reputation – he—'

'Odelle,' she said firmly. 'I saw you kissing in the reception.'

'I'm sorry. We shouldn't have – I don't want—'

'Oh, don't worry about that. Are you happy?'

I thought about this. 'Yes.'

'Just be careful of him.'

I sat back in my chair, overwhelmed. 'Do you – know him?'

Quick lit another cigarette, her fist gripped so tightly round the lighter that her knuckles had turned white. She breathed out the bluish smoke. 'No, I don't know him. I'm only looking after you. That's my job. I recruited you, and I value you, and I want you to be all right. Men are not always – well – just make sure you don't do anything you don't want to do.'

I realized then, that Quick was not a person to make herself vulnerable. That in fact, she would do anything to avoid such a predicament. 'I won't,' I said. It felt like Quick was admonishing me; this flash of a harsh demeanour had curdled the garden's lovely atmosphere, where even the bees seemed to fall silent. 'He's not like that.'

She sighed. My bones felt like lead. But I could have got up, I could have thanked her for the pork-pie quarter and the bit of bread which was all I'd managed to eat, and walked through the cool bare corridor, back out to life and Lawrie and Cynth and the future, and never have talked to Quick personally again. Things might have been easier if I had.

'Has he told you anything about the painting?' she went on.

'Only that he's pleased it might be an Isaac Robles,' I said, dully.

'But he'd never heard of Isaac Robles before this?'

'No.'

She looked thoughtful. 'Why do you think he wanted a copy of that photograph?'

'I don't know,' I said, trying my best to hide my irritation. 'To look at it more closely, I suppose. To put the pieces together.'

'Odelle, does Mr Scott understand that Mr Reede would like to make this painting a big splash – not just for the Skelton, but for himself? He spoke of the possibility of an exhibition. Is that what Mr Scott wants?'

'I don't know what he wants. But surely an exhibition can only be a good thing.'

'Men like Edmund Reede are circus masters. They will spin a reputation from thin air. They will wrap it up and increase its wonder, just so what they possess increases in value. What I mean is, Odelle – be careful to remind Mr Scott what he's actually *looking* at. Don't let Reede take what he has away from him.'

'But I thought you agreed with Mr Reede that the Skelton should keep his painting safe.'

'Only until Mr Scott has made his decision.' She took a long drag on her cigarette and stared into the hollyhocks. 'If I was Mr Scott, I would keep it. I would keep it and enjoy it. His mother clearly did, and so should he.'

'But if it is an important painting, he could sell it, he could use the money. He's stuck, you see.'

She turned to me. 'So he *does* want to sell it. He's worried about money.'

'I don't know the ins and outs. But the painting could be useful. If there was an exhibition of it – a long-lost painting come to light, that sort of thing – I'm sure that would be popular. Lawrie could be involved. He could help with organizing. He's very clever. Enthusiastic. People like him.'

'You're not his mother.'

'And you're not mine.'

The words came out before I could stop them. Quick winced; I was horrified. 'I'm sorry,' I said. 'I'm very sorry—'

'No – you're right,' she said. 'You're quite right. You must think I'm interfering.'

'I didn't mean – I'm only trying to help him.'

'Mr Scott isn't stuck,' Quick said. 'I'm sure he could do many things. His existence doesn't hinge on that painting. He should just take it home and enjoy it for what it is. A very good painting – an *excellent* painting, designed for private pleasure.'

'But isn't it better that more than one person can see it?' I asked. 'Isn't that the ethos of a place like the Skelton – shouldn't it be shared?'

'That's fair. But like Reede said, we don't know enough about the painting yet. We need to go slowly. You don't just *happen* upon a painting like that, Odelle. People always have something to hide. Listen to the words Mr Scott isn't saying.'

'Lawrie is an honest person,' I said, my voice rising again.

'Of course,' Quick said, her own words tightening with emotion. 'Of course he is. But you can still be honest at the same time as having something to hide. And if there is something to hide, then the Skelton could look very foolish indeed.'

She levered herself out of the chair and walked slowly into the cottage. I sat, stupefied, unable to think properly. What was going on here? The bees appeared to drone again, looping from flower to flower. Above, the sky was now cloudless. Suddenly everything seemed so very alive, vibrating, the green leaves turning slightly gold, moving in a psychedelic pattern as the sunshine rippled.

For a mad moment I imagined Quick might be fetching a revolver, that she was going to point it at me and demand answers that I couldn't give. Something had switched rapidly over the brief course of our picnic, a change of energy like the light through the leaves, impossible to catch. But when Quick came back, she was holding a beautiful octavo leather notebook. 'I bought this for you,' she said, holding it out.

I could almost laugh, thinking about this scene now – no, it was not a firearm, but Quick knew full well it was still a weapon.

'For me?' I said.

'Just a small present, to say thank you for doing such a wonderful job. I'm very glad we found you, Odelle. Or you found us, more to the point. Happy Birthday.'

I took the notebook from her. It was handmade, thick calfskin leather with a matte green finish. The pages were the colour of cream. It was a Stradivarius of notebooks, compared to the flimsy numbers I bought in Woolworth's. 'Thank you,' I said. 'It's so kind.'

From somewhere over the fences, a lawn mower ground itself up to a mechanical whine, and a child shrieked. 'Well,' said Quick peaceably. 'Don't they always say? You never know when inspiration is going to strike.'

9

On Sunday, I sat on my bed with my new notebook from Quick, and thought about what she'd said in the garden. Like most artists, everything I produced was connected to who I was – and so I suffered according to how my work was received. The idea that anyone might be able to detach their personal value from their public output was revolutionary. I didn't know if it was possible, even desirable. Surely it would affect the quality of the work?

Still, I knew I'd gone too far in the opposite direction, and something had to change. Ever since I could pick up a pen, other people's pleasure was how I'd garnered attention and defined success. When I began receiving public acknowledgement for a private act, something was essentially lost. My writing became the axis upon which all my identity and happiness hinged. It was now outward-looking, a self-conscious performance. I was asked to repeat the pleasure for people, again and again, until the facsimile of my act became the act itself.

Cynth's wedding poem was to me a perfect example of how I felt my writing to be bound up with obligation. I'd been writing for so long for the particular purpose of being approved that I'd forgotten the genesis of my impulse; unbothered, pure creation, existing outside the parameters of success and failure. And somewhere along the line, this being 'good' had come to paralyse my belief that I could write at all.

So admitting to Quick that I wanted to be published was no small step. It communicated, to a certain degree, that I believed I should be taken seriously. And here she was, telling me, *Well, maybe you're not that special, maybe you are – but that doesn't actually mean anything, and it certainly doesn't have any bearing on whether you can write. So stop worrying, and do it.*

She had told me that the approval of other people should never be my goal; she had released me in a way I hadn't been able to myself. She trusted me. Quick had encouraged me to lay myself bare, and it had not been that difficult at all.

I ran my fingers over the leather of the notebook and remembered. I first started writing as a little girl because I liked imagining parallel possibilities. That was all it was. That Sunday, I picked up my pen for the first time in a long time, and began to write.

At the end of the day on Monday – my actual birthday – I left a short story typed up on Quick's desk. I wasn't completely bullish – the top-grade schoolgirl dies hard – I did not creep into her office without a feeling of trepidation. I put no note on the top; she'd know who it was from.

I appreciated the irony that just like at school, at university, I was delivering a story for someone else to approve, but I had been too long inculcated with the act of writing for an audience. This time, however, I wasn't going to hinge everything on my audience's response. If Quick didn't like it, maybe that was a good thing. It was now out of my control.

Pamela stopped me as I was leaving. 'You can't hide it any longer, you know,' she said.

'Sorry?'

'Oh come on. You're going round like Cupid smacked you in the chops. You forgot to put stamps on these envelopes. That ain't like you.'

I winced; Pamela was more observant than perhaps I'd given her credit for. 'I don't know what you mean,' I said.

'Odelle, I'm only gonna keep askin'. Gonna be your Scotland Yard. It's you and that feller, isn't it? There was barely five minutes between you when he turned up.'

I weighed up my options. Don't tell Pamela, and suffer her interminable hypotheses, which, knowing her, would become more outlandish and indefatigable – or just tell her, and be done. 'Maybe,' I said.

'Lawrie Scott, eh. Bit posh, ain't he?'

'How do you know his first name?'

She looked pleased with herself. 'It's *right* here, in the appointment book. Written by your own fair hand. Shall I draw a heart round it for you?'

'Shut up.'

'Does Quick know?'

'Quick knows.'

'How?'

'Saw us kissing in the reception.'

'Hoo-ee!' Pamela whooped with laughter and I couldn't help a smile; it was a thrilling admission. 'Bloody *hell*, Odelle, I didn't know you had it in you. She must like you, 'cos most girls woulda been out on their ear.'

'Pamela, shut *up*.'

'Ahh, you *like* him.'

'Don't be an idiot.'

'All right, all right.' Pamela put up her hands, and her ringed fingers glinted in the light. 'I was like that when I first met Billy,' she said. I suspected no two men were more different than Lawrie and Billy, but I let it pass. 'It's like you can't *breathe*,' she said.

'I can breathe perfectly well.'

She laughed. 'Miss High and Mighty. Honestly, Odelle, are you sure you ain't a secret African queen?'

'I'm from Trinidad.'

'Keep your knickers on. Or maybe *not*.'

'*Pamela.*'

'Come on,' she whispered. 'Have you done it yet?'

'Mind your own business.'

She smirked. 'That'll be a no then. Get on with it, Odelle. You don't know what you're missing.' She fished under the reception counter and placed a brown-paper bag before me. 'Happy birthday,' she beamed, mischief dancing in her black-kohled eyes.

I eyed it suspiciously. 'What's inside?'

'Take a look, Miss Bastien.'

I lifted the edge of the paper. Inside were two strips of pills. 'Are *these*—'

'Yep. Got some spare. I thought you might want them.' Pamela looked at the expression on my face, and her confidence faltered. 'You don't have to take them—'

'No, thank you. I'll take them.'

Pamela grinned. It was funny to me, the different gifts people gave to show their friendship – with Quick it was a notebook, with Pamela, the contraceptive Pill. I'd spent weeks pressing novels onto Pamela, which in many ways says all you need to know about me. Pamela's offering was a reflection of her utilitarian sensuality; a pragmatic approach to the pursuit of pleasure. It was no small thing for an unmarried girl to get hold of the Pill in those days; no doctor would prescribe it.

'How did you get these?' I asked.

She winked. 'Rubbed a lamp, didn't I.'

'Come on, how?'

'Brook Advisory,' she relented. 'Gold dust.'

I shoved them into my handbag. 'Thank you, *Rudge*,' I said, skipping down the Skelton steps before Pamela could ruin the moment with a salacious addendum. Still – she was a woman of the new world, giving me a slice of freedom. I should have been more grateful.

FOR MY BIRTHDAY, LAWRIE WAS taking me to the house in Surrey. Gerry was away, he said, and he wanted to show me the place. In the near six years I'd been in England, I'd not seen that bucolic heaven peddled to us in Trinidad. I was ready for hedgerows, crumbling Eleanor crosses covered in yellow lichen, the dip of autumn trees overburdened by their fruit, village shops selling eggs in boxes by the step. In fact, when I saw Lawrie's house, this wasn't actually far off, which made me think that perhaps the only truth my colonial educators had told me was the one about the English countryside.

Lawrie's family lived near a place called Baldock's Ridge, in a detached red-brick Victorian farmhouse. In a childlike simplicity, it was called The Red House. It had a mature orchard of apple trees in the front, and peeling paintwork on its windows. It was enchanting. Inside, however, there wasn't much evidence of feminine life, despite how recently his mother had died. I wanted ball gowns hanging up in dignified tatters, tobacco-infused dining chairs, chocolate-box paintings on the wall, the smell of dog hair on old picnic rugs. But there was nothing like that. Either she'd lived as a spartan, or Bastard Gerry had cleared his dead wife out.

I sat in the kitchen, and closed my eyes as Lawrie made the tea. *Just be careful of him. You don't just* happen *upon a painting like that, Odelle.* I pushed Quick's words away with a flash of anger. Did she want to ruin this for me?

'Here we are,' said Lawrie, handing me a chipped blue cup. 'It's still lovely and warm out. Shall we sit in the garden?'

I followed him, my hands wrapped round the cup, padding along the rugless hallway.

THE BACK GARDEN WAS A bit of a mess in a Hodgson Burnett way; overgrown bushes and gnarled plum trees, broken terracotta pots sprouting mint, wild pansies faring perfectly. There was a greenhouse at the end of the long lawn, its windows streaked with dried mud and rain so it was impossible to see inside. Who had tended this place? Perhaps Lawrie had, once upon a time, up and down the furrows.

'How long have you lived here?' I asked.

'On and off all my life. We had a flat in London, too, but my mother stopped liking the city. She preferred it here.'

'I can see why. It's beautiful.'

He sighed. 'It has its moments.'

We sat in silence for a while, listening to the blackbirds in the dusk. 'Are you excited for what Reede might discover next?' I asked.

He stared out at the orchard. 'What if it *was* stolen?'

'It wouldn't be your fault – or your mother's.'

'Well – no. No, I suppose not. Imagine if it's worth a fortune. God, the look on Gerry's face. The only thing she left me and it's worth a bomb.'

'If you sold it, you wouldn't have anything of your mother left.'

He turned to me, a shrewd expression in his eyes. 'Don't you go soft. My mother was the least sentimental person I knew.'

'I think it is quite sentimental, leaving you a single painting in her will.'

'You didn't know her,' he said. 'It's more likely a loaded gun.'

'What do you mean?'

Lawrie cast his eye over the wilderness before us, sipping on his tea. 'She always attracted trouble. I think she would have liked you very much.'

'Why? I never attract trouble.'

'And she could be a pain in the arse as well.'

'*Hey.*'

He said he had made a shepherd's pie; I was impressed that he could cook. I wondered when Lawrie had learned, and had the suspicion he had spent quite a lot of his life looking after himself. He said he'd lay the table, I was the birthday girl – so whilst he was doing all that, heating up the oven and looking for forks, I took the opportunity to go upstairs.

I WENT INTO ONE OF the large back rooms, evening sunbeams slanting through its windows, a shade of deep whisky, dust motes swirling in the shafts. Again, no rugs or carpets on the floor, no paintings on the wall, just the bed frame and a wardrobe, empty save for a percussive clutch of wire hangers when I opened its door. Upturned bluebottles were scattered against the skirting.

There were piles of documents and boxes of paper everywhere, curled and faded with time.

I tried to imagine Lawrie's mother in this house; what she looked like, her marriage to Gerry, what she'd done in her life after her husband died in the war. There were no photos of her anywhere, but there was the faintest trace of perfume in the air; sophisticated, woody, alluring. I sat gently on the edge of the metal bed frame, wondering whether another family would fill this place again with life, with second chances, hopes and failures. I felt a pang of anxiety that Cynth would never speak to me again. *You must telephone*, I thought. *It's gone on too long. Or write, at least.*

I rose from the bed and approached the window to view the rolling Surrey hills in this extraordinary light. I rested my elbows on yet another pile of old papers, and Quick's caution over Lawrie entered my thoughts again. What was it that bothered her so much? It was none of her business, but I couldn't budge her comments from my mind.

Absently, I sifted through a pile of papers on the windowsill. They were receipts mainly, one for a butcher's delivery back in 1958, a Guildford shopping centre parking ticket, electricity bills, an order of service for the Baldock's Ridge Carol Concert, 1949. Here was someone who didn't throw things away, yet Lawrie had said his mother was not the type who kept receipts.

Underneath the carol service sheet was a tissue-thin pamphlet for an exhibition of young British artists, from 1955. I opened it. It had been held in the London Gallery on Cork Street, and whoever had attended had put a line through the names of the artists and their works one by one with a pencil. *No Sign*, they had written at the bottom. No sign of what? I wondered. The frustration of whoever had written this was evident in the pressure of lead upon the paper.

I folded the pamphlet in two, slid it in my pocket and went downstairs, telling myself that in that mess of papers up there, no one would miss it.

LAWRIE HAD LIT CANDLES, WEDGING them into empty wine bottles and a burnished, sinuous candelabra that had more than a hint of murder weapon about it. We sat in the kitchen, the day now faded, eating his shepherd's pie, drinking cider that the neighbour had made from the orchard. 'Happy birthday, Odelle,' he said, and raised his glass.

'Thank you. I feel like we're hiding from the world out here.'

'Sounds good to me.'

'It doesn't seem obvious that Gerry lives here. Upstairs is a bit of a mess.'

'That was my mother, more than him. I expect Gerry will sell the house.'

'How long were they married?'

Lawrie poured more cider into our glasses. 'Let's see. I was fourteen – so that's sixteen years.'

'How did she die?'

Lawrie visibly prickled. I saw his closed expression, sensed his self-protection. I regretted the question immediately, feeling like a blunderer.

He placed the bottle down gently. 'It's hard to explain.'

'You don't have to. I shouldn't have asked. I'm sorry.' Now I was interfering, just like Quick.

'My mother killed herself,' Lawrie said, and the words weighed down the air between us, the kitchen's atmosphere thickening to a soup. Looking at Lawrie, I saw how a ghost could suck the air from your throat.

'I'm sorry,' I said. 'I'm so sorry—'

'It's all right. No, really, it's all right. I would have told you eventually. Don't apologize. I mean, don't feel bad about it. In all honesty, it wasn't that much of a surprise.'

I tried desperately to think of something to fill the silence, but the admission seemed to open something in him: 'We tried to help. We were always trying. And now I can't even look at bloody Gerry, because every time we look at each other I know he's thinking,

What if you'd done more?, and I'm thinking exactly the same. But it's not his fault. It's just a horrible game of blame.'

'I can't imagine it.'

'Well, neither can I, and I was her son.'

He was very still, his voice very quiet, and I wanted to get up and give him a hug. But in the soupy air I felt unable to move, and I wasn't sure he wanted one anyway. I thought of the kitchen at Cynth's wedding, how Lawrie must have been reeling from his past two weeks – and me, mocking my own mother, rude when he tried to be nice about my poem—

'Anyway, that's that,' he said. 'But she *was* spirited, and she did a lot of things, and enjoyed herself a great deal, and that's really why she reminds me of you. And now there's her painting.'

'Yes.'

'So.' He exhaled brusquely. 'I've told you *that*. Jesus. I promise you that's the worst. Now you tell me something.'

'I don't have anything.'

'Everyone has at least one thing, Delly.'

I stayed quiet. He leaned back in his chair, fishing around in the dresser drawer behind him. 'A-ha. Gerry always leaves a few lying around.' He brandished a box of slim cigars. 'Care to join?'

WE WENT TO THE BACK room and Lawrie pushed open the French windows. The night was still fragrant with the smell of damp grass and wood smoke, bats dipping in and out of the garden.

'It's like paradise,' I said, even enjoying the smothering scent of Lawrie's cigar. I sat on the sofa and watched him, propping himself against the window frame.

'I don't know about that,' Lawrie replied. 'But one thing is – you can't hear the road. When I was little, my favourite book was *Peter Pan*. I used to pretend this garden was Neverland.'

'And was Gerry Captain Hook?'

'Ha, no, this was before Gerry. It was just me and Mum at that point.'

'I was just with my mother too.'

He turned to me. 'What happened to your dad in the war?'

Given what Lawrie had told me about his mother's suicide, I felt I had to dredge it up, although I really didn't want to. 'Well,' I said. 'My dad sold his bicycle and trumpet to pay for his passage to England in '41. He walked to the Air Ministry, passed the medical, and got himself twelve weeks' basic training. He served as an air gunner in the RAF. Then three years later, my mother found his name chalked on the death board in Port of Spain.'

He came over, and put his hand on my shoulder; it was warm, and I focused on it with particular concentration. 'I'm sorry, Odelle,' he said.

'Thank you. I don't remember him, but I know what it was like not to have him. My mother took it bad.'

He sat beside me. 'What was it like, on the island, in the war?'

'People were terrified what would happen if Hitler won. We've got one of the largest oil refineries in Trinidad. U-boats were already torpedoing British ships off our coastline.'

'I didn't know that.'

'We knew what Hitler wanted; the plan for a master race. We were always going to want to fight. My dad was no exception.' I sipped on my cider. 'England wasn't too keen on the colonies helping out at first, but as things turned bad they wanted the help.'

'Do you think you'll go back?'

I hesitated. Most English people I'd met would ask me questions about the island with the expectation that I should fit the complexity of Trinidad into my single body for their benefit. None of them had ever been there, so to them we were specimens of curiosity, realities risen from a tropical petri dish that until very recently sat under a British flag. Most of the time, as with Pamela, the Englishers' interest was not malicious (except when it was) – but their questioning always served to make me feel *different*, when I'd been brought up to feel perfectly understanding of British ways, because I was a child of empire too.

In the time I'd known him, Lawrie hadn't asked me a thing about Trinidad. I didn't know whether he was being polite, or whether he was genuinely uninterested – but either way, I was mainly glad of his failure to highlight our differences in life experience. I'd learned Latin and read Dickens, but I'd also seen the lighter-skinned girls get more of the boys' attention, in a way the boys probably didn't even understand themselves. Most of our 'differences' had been created by the white skin of the English. And yet, by the shores of the Thames, the complexity of our island life was reduced to one phenotype: *black.*

Practically every Englishman, even the enlightened ones, believed we would have more in common with a Sudanese than with them. But what did I know of the Sahara, of a camel or a Bedouin? My ideal of beauty and glamour for my entire childhood was Princess Margaret. With Lawrie, I'd talked about James Bond films, or my strange boss, or the painting, or Gerry the Bastard, dead parents. Stuff that bound us together as a duo, that didn't make me a representative of a whole island that I hadn't seen for five years. When Lawrie didn't ask me about Trinidad, I felt more of an individual again.

'Odelle?'

'Let me tell you about London,' I said.

'OK.'

'When I first got here,' I went on, 'I could not believe the cold.' Lawrie laughed. 'I'm serious, Lawrie. It was like the Arctic. Cynth and I arrived in *January.*'

'Of all the months.'

'I know. When I was a little girl, I was Autumn in a school play about the seasons. I didn't even know what autumn *was,* let alone winter.'

I was quiet for a minute, remembering my smaller self, in her little boater and English pinafore, telling her mother she needed 'russet leaves' pinned to a leotard – and my mother, who had no idea either what frost on the tips of grass might look like, what a conker was, how it felt to inhale London's November air and feel a sliver of ice in your lung – doing her darnedest to make this English costume in the humid Caribbean.

'I remember,' I went on, warming to this reminiscence, feeling that I could do this with Lawrie, that I was safe – 'an early day I was here – a feller saying to me in the shoe shop, "Your English is very good." My *English*! I told him, "English is a West Indian language, sir." '

'And what did he say?' Lawrie asked, laughing. I realized that never in Lawrie's life would anyone say to him what that man had said to me.

'He thought I was simple. I nearly lost my job. Cynth was furious. It's true though – I'd be quite at home with Queen Elizabeth and that tall Greek husband of hers, drinking a cup of tea and petting those funny midget dogs she loves so much. Quite at home. "Your English is not as good as mine," I should have said. "It does not have the length and the breadth, the meat and the smoke. Come at me with my Creole, with its Congo and its Spanish and its Hindi, French and Ibo, English and Bhojpuri, Yoruba and Manding." '

Lawrie laughed again. 'Oh, to see his face,' I carried on, draining my cider glass. 'With his Anglesaxon—'

'Angle what?'

'Two-up, two-down, a window with a view people never truly look at, because they think they know every shrub and flower, the bark of every tree and the mood of every cloud. But we made room for their patois too—'

'Odelle,' Lawrie said. 'I would be happy with you for the rest of my life.'

'Eh?'

'You have this light, and when it switches on I don't think you even realize what it does.'

'What light? I was talking about—'

'I love you, Odelle.' His face was hopeful. 'You inspire me.'

We sat in silence. 'You tell it to all the girls,' I said desperately, unsure what to say.

'What?'

'You're not serious.'

He stared at me. 'I *am* serious. I feel like time's tricked me, as if I've known you from before. Like we passed each other in our prams. Like it's been a waiting game to meet with you again. I love you.'

I said nothing, unable to respond. He looked down at the carpet.

No one had ever told me they loved me before. Why did he have to ruin our evening with talk of love and . . . *prams*? I felt panicked. Quick's warnings flashed again through my mind – and I cursed her inside. Why should I be careful – and yet why could I not bear to hear Lawrie's words?

I got off the sofa and walked to the windows. 'You probably want me to go,' I said.

He sat, motionless, looking at me with incredulity. 'Why would I want you to go, after what I've just said?'

'I don't know! I – look, I'm not—'

'It's fine,' he said. 'I'm sorry. It's fine. I shouldn't have—'

'No – it's just, I was – and then you—'

'Forget I said anything. I – please, forget it. If that's what you want, then I'll drive you home.'

SO LAWRIE DROVE US BACK in silence up the deserted A3. I clasped my handbag tight to my body, feeling utterly miserable, my fingers clenched around the pamphlet I had stolen, and the pills Pamela had handed me only hours before. How could I explain to Lawrie that this was terrifying for me, and that I couldn't exactly say why? We'd only just started, he barely knew me. I felt like he'd hoisted me onto a pedestal and left me with my legs dangling, and of course I'd managed to turn it into a trauma for the pair of us. Being alone was always so much easier.

I glanced only once at him, his profile coming in and out of the orange light as the car moved under the street lamps. His eyes were on the road, his jaw set. I didn't know which of us felt more humiliated.

When we reached my flat, he pulled in. 'I left your present in Surrey,' he said, the engine still running.

'Oh – I—'

'Anyway. I'd better go.' I got out, he revved the car and was off. I stood in the road, until the noise of his engine was replaced in my head by the sound of a silent scream.

I LAY IN BED AWAKE, my bedside light still on past three. In my chest, my stomach, in my aching head, I felt pain for us both. That Lawrie loved me, I could not easily believe. Though he had never made me feel like an outsider, I couldn't help worrying that he only liked me because I looked different to all the other girls in that gang he'd turned up with at Cynth's wedding.

Lawrie had rushed in with his declaration of love – but did he really *see* me? I couldn't imagine being someone who dived in for another like that; the sense that one's molecules were being recalibrated; the sheer, multi-layered joy of being seen and adored, and adoring in return, the cycle of shyness to confidence as each new step was taken. To seek your beloved in a crowd, to lock your eyes and feel you have no truer place – it seemed impossible to me. I was – both by circumstance and nature – a migrant in this world, and my lived experience had long become a state of mind.

I didn't know if I loved him, and that was also frightening – not to know, to be sure. *Just be careful of him. You don't just* happen *upon a painting like that, Odelle.* I had tried so hard to shut Quick's voice away. I wondered if she was the reason I could not drop my anchor with him as confidently as he'd declared his love. I leaned over, switching off the light, hoping in the dark for sleep. As I lay there, I couldn't tell which fears were mine, now Quick had slipped her own inside my head.

FEBRUARY 1936

VII

The painting Olive had finished was propped against the wall. She was more proud of it than even *The Orchard*, and felt that she was creeping ever closer to that shining citadel. The new piece was a surreal composition, colourful, disjointed to the gaze. It was a diptych; Santa Justa before her arrest and after, set against a dark indigo sky and a shining field. Olive had decided to call it *Santa Justa in the Well*.

The left half of the painting was lush and glowing. Olive had used ordinary oils, but had also experimented with gold leaf, which glinted in the light as she held the painting up. She'd always thought of gold leaf as an alchemist's dream, a contained ray of sun. It was the colour of queens, of wise men, of shimmering land in high summer. It reminded her of the Russian Orthodox icons she had always wanted to touch as a little girl, when her father took her to the Kunsthistorisches Museum.

In the middle of the healthy land on this left-hand side stood a woman, her hair the colour of the crop. She was carrying a heavy pot with deer and rabbits painted on it, and in its centre was the face of the goddess Venus. Both the faces of the woman and Venus looked proud, staring out at the viewer.

On the right half of the painting, the crop was deadened and limp. The woman appeared again, except this time she was curled inside a circle, hovering over the crop. This circle was filled with an internal perspective to make it look as if it had depth, as if the woman was lying at the bottom of a well. Her hair was now severed and dull, her pot had smashed around her, a puzzle impossible for anyone to piece together. Around the rim of the well, full-sized deer and rabbits peered down, as if set free from the broken crockery. Venus had vanished.

Olive could hear soft knocking at the attic door, and she sat up. 'Who is it?' she asked, her voice half-strangled with hope that it might be him.

'It is Teresa.'

'Oh.'

'The party is in a few hours, señorita. Can I come in?'

Olive leapt up and hid the painting under the bed. 'Yes,' she said.

Recently, Teresa had begun to help Olive keep her room in order. It was an unspoken agreement. Olive had not invited it, but she liked it; the attention, the paint brushes laid out for another day's work. Her clothes were always neatly folded on her chair or hanging in her cupboard, her unfinished canvases were turned to face the wall, the way she liked it when it was time for bed. Olive would turn them back in the morning, and work up there unbothered.

Teresa stood at the doorway, her satchel across her chest. 'Is there anything I can do?'

Olive lay back on the bed. 'I want to look like Garbo,' she said languorously, stretching herself out, running her fingers through her hair. 'Tere, how good are you at making waves?'

The girls set up a chair in front of the oval mirror, which Teresa had found in a spare room and nailed to the wall. The glass was foxed and misty round the edges, but the centre was clear enough. They were using a series of illustrations from one of Sarah's *Vogues* in an attempt to recreate Greta Garbo's look. Teresa lit candles around the room as the light outside faded.

'I've never been able to have finger waves anyway,' Olive said. 'My hair's too thick. But we should be able to do these curls.'

They remained in companionable silence for a good five minutes, Olive enjoying Teresa's calming administrations through her hair; a repetitive, smoothing motion that made her sleepy. 'I suppose it's good news about the election, but I keep thinking about that poor boy Isaac knew,' she said finally.

Teresa kept her eyes down, working at the nape of Olive's neck. 'One day, left, next day, right. The government changes the street names more than I change my bed. And at the end of it, señorita, I never see the difference.'

'Well, thank goodness there are men like your brother who *do* care.'

Teresa was silent.

'Do you like your father, Tere?' Olive said.

Teresa frowned at the back of Olive's head. 'I do not like the stories.'

Olive opened her eyes. 'What stories?'

Teresa wrapped small portions of Olive's sizeable mass of hair round and round her finger, before securing it tightly with the pins sequestered out of Sarah's bedroom. 'They say that once he cut a man's thing off and nailed it to a door.'

Olive swivelled her head round, and the hair sprang from its curl, the pin skittering across the floorboards. 'What? To a *door*?'

'He was his enemy.'

They looked at each other, then burst out laughing, high on the night to come and the violence they believed was safely avoided, because it had gone before their time, because neither of them had a *thing*, and because they were safe up here.

'Teresa, that's disgusting! Why would he *do* that?'

'It's just a rumour,' Teresa said, picking up the pin.

'But no man would drop his trousers to prove it.'

'And yet Don Alfonso never denies it.'

'Jesus, Teresa. And I thought I had problems with my father.'

Teresa looked up. 'What problems?'

Olive sighed. 'Oh, nothing really. I just . . . I feel a bit invisible, that's all. He never takes me seriously. I never know how to *make* him take me seriously. The only things he thinks about are his business and whether my mother has taken her pills. And she's never really taken the time to understand me either. When I have children, I am never going to be like her. I wish I was free of my parents. I suppose I *could* be free of them, if I put my mind to it.'

'If you had gone to the art school, you would be free.'

'You can't be sure. And painting here makes me feel freer.' Olive looked serious. 'Although I'm learning something else out here.'

'What is that?'

'That if you really want to see your work to completion, you have to desire it more than you'd believe. You have to fight it, fight yourself. It's not easy.'

Teresa smiled, working through the mass of Olive's hair with a level of attention that Olive wanted to bask in for ever. She had never had a friend like this, in her private room, combing her hair, listening to her, talking about silly nonsense and the uselessness of one's parents; how the future was perfect, because they hadn't lived it yet.

'I always find that the time *before* a party is happiest,' Olive said. 'Nothing's had the chance to go wrong.' Teresa lifted her hands away from Olive's head. 'Why have you stopped?' she asked, as Teresa walked over to her satchel.

Teresa removed a small, square package wrapped in tissue paper. She held it out, nervously. 'For you,' she said.

Olive took it. 'For *me*? My goodness. Shall I open it now?'

Teresa nodded, and Olive gasped when she saw the green flash through the paper, emerald strung on emerald, emerging like a stone snake, a necklace of such beauty and intensity she had never seen before. 'My God. Where did you get this?'

'It was my mother's,' Teresa said. 'Now for you.'

Olive sat frozen on the chair, the necklace swinging from her fist. No one had ever in her life given her such a present. This was everything Teresa possibly had of her mother; to take it would be a selfish act. 'No,' she said. 'I couldn't—'

'It's for you.'

'Teresa, this is too much—'

In the end, it was Teresa who made the decision for her, scooping the necklace out of Olive's grasp, laying it round her neck and fixing the clasp. 'It is for *you*,' Teresa said. 'For my friend.'

Olive turned to the mirror. The emeralds looked like green leaves, shining upon her pale skin, enlarging in size towards her clavicle. Stones from Brazil, green as the ocean, green as the forest her father had promised they would find in the south of Spain. These were not jewels, they were eyes, winking at her in the candlelight, watching the girls who watched themselves.

VIII

By the evening, Harold had returned from Malaga with supplies for the party. He was loping around the house, a cigar clamped between his teeth, calling for more gramophone records. Isaac was helping carry extra chairs and tables loaned by the villagers.

'Olive,' he said to her. 'The painting is finished.'

'Oh,' she said.

'You are not pleased? I did not think you liked being painted.'

She didn't know what to say; Isaac's finished painting just meant less opportunity to see him.

Sarah emerged, dressed in a long plum-coloured gown. In London, when they had parties, she would often come in fancy dress – the Little Mermaid, or Snow White – and one memorable year as Rapunzel, when her entire false plait went up in flames and they'd put her out with champagne. But tonight was a Schiaparelli number, *truly sophis*, as the girls at school might have said – with two women's faces embroidered on the back in sequins, their red lips glittering from the hundreds of candles Harold had brought back from the city, and which Teresa had been instructed to light. The dress was one of Olive's favourites; she had always been mesmerized by the Janus-like embroidery.

Sarah's eyes were drawn to the emeralds around her daughter's neck. 'Who gave you those?' she demanded, as Harold popped a bottle of Veuve Clicquot.

Olive realized that she had heard the sound of glasses clinking over trauma all her life. Annoyed that her mother had not even noticed her new hair, she tipped her chin and stroked the green stones. 'Isaac,' she replied.

IT WAS A RECKLESS EVENING. The guests began to arrive up the finca path at around eight o'clock, and Olive and her parents stood at the door to greet them. One of the first to appear was a man in an expensive-looking cream suit with a large cravat, as if it was cocktail hour on an ocean liner. His large black moustache had been oiled at the tips. Behind him, two younger men followed in neat suits. Olive wondered who they were – his children, perhaps? They seemed more like his hired guards than anything else.

The man proffered his hand. 'Señor Schloss,' he said. 'Don Alfonso Robles Hernández. I have been away on business for the duchess.'

'Don Alfonso,' said Harold, putting out his own hand. 'We meet at last.'

He spoke good English, and Olive saw echoes of Isaac in the man's face – but there was something inherently theatrical about the Don that his son did not share. Despite his flashiness, there was an intelligence in Alfonso's small eyes; calculation and black humour. She thought of the story Teresa had told about him, and tried to quell her anxiety.

'Gregorio, give Señora Schloss our offerings.' One of the boys hopped forward. 'Almond cake and a bottle of good port,' said Alfonso.

Sarah took the presents. 'Thank you,' she said.

'Are you settled in well?'

'Very well.'

Alfonso peered past Harold into the darkness of the hallway. '*Díos mio*, the kitten has grown into a cat,' he said, knocking one heel to the other in a cod-military gesture. The clipping heels of his boots and the creak of patent raised the hairs on Olive's skin. She looked back to see Teresa scowling in the dark.

'Still so scared of me, Tere?' Alfonso said, in Spanish. 'I don't know why. I've heard about your claws.' The younger men laughed. 'She's not giving you trouble, I hope?'

Harold glanced at Teresa, who stared at him with round black eyes. 'None at all,' he said.

'Well, let me know if she is.' Alfonso looked up at the finca's many windows, every one illuminated with tiny, flickering flames. 'Señor Schloss, I hope we are not going to be burned alive. I thought this house was blessed with electricity?'

'We wanted a little atmosphere tonight, Don Alfonso. Please come in.'

'I brought Gregorio and Jorge – you don't mind if they come too?'

'Not at all. Everyone is welcome.'

The three men moved past Olive and her mother, Jorge's gaze lingering a little too long on Sarah.

'Is that brother of yours here?' Jorge asked Teresa.

'Maybe. But he won't be talking to you,' she said.

IN TOTAL, SIXTY-SEVEN RESIDENTS OF Arazuelo came to the party. The presence of this small family from London and Vienna imbued the locals with a carnival, topsy-turvy feeling. There was a permissiveness in the air, as if a taboo had broken apart, and its scent was going to drown them all. Don Alfonso stayed in a corner of one room – a few people came up to him, but generally he was left alone.

The guests wrote their names in a book that Harold produced. Some inscribed their signatures eagerly, happy to be included in this cosmopolitan event, with its dancing lights and jazz music, and the smell of oleanders in every room. They jotted short messages of approval or goodwill – *buen vino* or *Dios bendiga*. Others were more cautious, looking worried about being permanently embedded in this foreign book, as if it might be a politically controversial gesture. Olive remembered Adrián, the murdered boy from Malaga, Isaac's concerns about what was going to happen to the country, and wondered if they had a point. Nevertheless, she wrote down her own name, directly underneath those of Teresa and Isaac.

Having drunk three glasses of champagne, Olive sensed the ghost of the boy moving through the rooms. She sat back in her wicker chair, and saw his bloodied body drag itself between the guests. She imagined there was a determination to their drinking, their dancing, their shouts and claps, as if they were pushing him back to the land of the dead, to reclaim this house for the living.

A woman wore a long satin dress the colour of a dawn mushroom. The candle flames sparked a glint in a brass cufflink, lifted with a crystal glass of moonshine. Teresa scurried hither and thither, always with a tray of drinks, or some meats and cheeses, or slices of cake. She was studiedly avoiding her father. The room was full of voices, the music pulsed from the gramophone in the corner – and there was Sarah, in her double-faced purple dress, flitting between the groups. She laid her hand on Isaac's arm, and made him laugh. People turned to her as they might to a beacon of light.

Olive watched Isaac wherever he went, feeling her attraction sing up to the wooden beams above her head, down to the slosh of champagne in her glass. Her curls had begun to droop and she tugged them nervously, worried she was walking around with a half-hairstyle. Now he was deep in conversation with the local doctor, looking sombre at something the man had said. He too had not spoken to his father. He was wearing that perfect pair of dark-blue trousers, cut close to the line of his body; a dark linen jacket, a blue shirt. She imagined what colour his skin was underneath. When was he going to turn round and notice her? She touched the emeralds around her neck and downed a fourth champagne. The fumbling child she'd been all her life was soon to be a spectre; one more glass would flush that kid away.

Two of the guests had brought guitars, and from their fingers cascaded a confident duet, note after perfect note, up and down the fretboards. People cheered when they heard it, and someone lifted the needle off the gramophone, scratching the record. There was a moment's worried hush, but Harold, very drunk by now, roared with approval and shouted, 'Let them play! I want to hear this magic! *¡Quiero oír el duende!'*

At this, the party seemed to surge as one. The father and son who'd brought the guitars knew flamenco songs as well as the popular *canciones*, and they played a couple, a wide ring of people around them, before a woman in her sixties stepped forward, and began to sing, opening her mouth to let forth a soaring sound of pain and freedom. For a second time that night Olive felt the hairs on her neck rise up. The woman had the room under complete control. She sang, clapping her hands in a fast, percussive rhythm, and there were shouts around the room of '*¡Vamos!*', people stamping their feet and crying out in admiration.

Gregorio whirled two little girls around the room, and they screamed with delight as the guitars and the singing grew ever more fevered. The woman's voice was like an ancient sound come to life, and Olive stood up, drinking down a fifth glass of fizz – except no, this wasn't champagne, this was a spirit of some sort, a firewater that set her insides burning. The woman's voice was rough and plaintive and perfect, and outside the night deepened, and moths flickered to die amongst the lanterns. In this room of strangers, Olive had never felt more at home.

HER FATHER WAS CALLING THAT it was time for the fireworks. '*Fuegos artificiales!*' he bellowed in a terrible accent, and Olive's eyes roved the room for Isaac. She spied him slipping through the door. The crowd began to move into the back of the house, out onto the veranda to watch the fireworks exploding over the orchard. Olive stopped, dazed by the flow of people in the corridor. Then she saw him going in the other direction, crossing the hallway and out of the front door. She was mystified – why was he running away from the centre of the world?

She began to follow him, stumbling onwards, away from the light of the house and into the pitch dark of the February night.

Above her, the sky was soaked with stars. The moon was high but she lost sight of him, and her blood was quickly cooling, but on she went, out of the rusted main gates onto the dirt path towards the village, stumbling on stones, cursing that she had been idiotic enough to come out in heels.

A hand clamped on her mouth. An arm locked round her neck and dragged her to the side of the path. She wriggled and kicked, but whoever had her pinned had a strong grip. Olive brought up her hands and began tugging; she opened her mouth to bite hard on the fingers that wouldn't let her breathe.

'*Mierda!*' said a voice, and Olive was released.

'Isaac?'

They stood, panting, both bent over in disbelief.

'Señorita – I thought someone was following me.'

'Well, they were. *Me*. Jesus bloody Christ!'

'Are you hurt?'

'I'm fine. How about you?'

'Please, do not tell your father—'

Olive rubbed her neck. 'Why would I tell him? Do you make a habit of jumping out at people like that?'

'Go back to the party. Please.'

Olive could tell he was agitated. 'Where are you going?' she asked.

'Nowhere.'

'That's a lie.'

'Go *back*. It's dangerous for you.'

'I'm not scared, Isaac. I want to help. Where are you going?'

She couldn't make out his expression in the dark, but she sensed his hesitation, and her heart began to pound harder.

'I am going to church,' he said.

She laughed. 'To confess your sins?'

'Something like that.'

She put out her hand and reached in the darkness for his. 'Lead the way,' she said.

LATER, WHEN OLIVE WAS LYING awake and going over everything back in her bedroom, she supposed it was the alcohol that did it. When Isaac was painting her, she couldn't stand it. She didn't feel enough of a satisfying subject, and she couldn't match her mother. But here, she and Isaac were equals, not watcher and watched. In the dark she could be her real self, a woman who took men by the hand and forced them onwards, down the path.

'YOU MUST BE COLD,' HE said, and she could hear that he was quite drunk too. When he took off his jacket and put it round her shoulders, Olive's skin sang, her whole body almost dipped in pleasure at his solicitousness and concern.

In ten minutes, they reached the church of Santa Rufina, which abutted the main square of Arazuelo. The place was deserted, as most of the village were up on the hillside, revelling in the music and the manzanilla they had rolled up in barrels as a gift to their host. Olive and Isaac turned back to see the fireworks which had begun to explode in the sky; red and green and orange, gigantic sea urchins, falling fountains. Isaac forced the door of the church and slunk in, and Olive followed – frightened now, choked by the smell of stale incense. The moonlight came through the window, touching the beeswaxed pews, the baleful saints, set into the wall. She felt Isaac's hand slip from hers, and heard his footsteps padding away up the nave.

'Isaac—'

The gunshot rang out beyond the pews from where she stood, and then another, then another. Olive was too terrified to scream. Beyond the walls of the church, the fireworks continued. She was rooted to the spot, cowering in terror. Suddenly, Isaac was next to her, his hand on her arm.

'*Now*,' he said. 'We have to go.'

He took her hand and they fled. 'What have you done?' she hissed. 'Was the priest – Isaac, what the hell have you done?'

They ran all the way back to the finca. Olive had to kick off her shoes and go bare-footed, the skin on her feet tearing on the occasional stone. At the gates, they stopped, breathless. The fireworks were still exploding, and she could smell the sulphuric tang of gunpowder.

She collapsed against the gate. 'Am I an accessory to murder?' she whispered. 'Jesus, I'm not even joking.'

Isaac put his hand on her face. 'For Adrián,' he said.

'What do you mean?'

He began to kiss her, cupping her face with his hands, scooping her by the waist. Olive felt the pride he had in her in the way he was clasping her hair, running his lips along the side of her neck, down on to her chest, under the emeralds which had heated with her skin. She'd proved herself to him, at last.

Isaac ran his fingers over the stones. 'Where did you get these?'

'A friend.' She kissed him on the mouth to stop him asking more. She'd never known her body could feel this way, or that she could inspire a man to do such things to her.

He kissed her again, and Olive parted her lips and put her hands through his hair, the rusted railings hard against her back. They pushed into each other, kissing, kissing, kissing, as the old woman in the finca resumed her plaintive music, and a figure watched them, silhouetted at the door.

IX

*O*live tried to sit up, but a lightning bolt of agony split her brain. Her mouth was a desert, her neck was lead. Lying in the mussed sheets, guts addled, scalp stinking of a thousand cigarettes, her hands flew to her body. She wasn't wearing any clothes. Jesus, where were her clothes? She winced to her left. Someone had folded her dress neatly over a chair; her stockings laddered and bloodstained on the soles, her fox stole swinging off the arm. It looked like a hunter's trophy, skinned and broached overnight, a dead glass eye in the head, those awful glued teeth. She touched her neck. The emerald necklace was still there, a snake upon her collarbone.

She heard the gunshot again – the church, the darkness, the fireworks, a rusting gate – had it been a dream? So much, all in one day. Far off, she could hear the telephone ringing. What if the civil guard were waiting outside, ready to take her away?

Isaac. The kiss – how was it possible she had endured life until now without that kiss – how had she lived? He'd dragged her through the darkness to let a pistol off inside a church, and then he'd kissed her. She wanted another kiss from Isaac more than she wanted to breathe.

SHE FELT AUGMENTED, AS IF a door, long hidden inside her, had been opened, revealing a sinuous corridor, and she herself was running through it. Since the moment she met him, this man had clung to her imagination. He had made her feelings enormous, the depths of her horizons doubling. For once in her life, Olive had been made to feel monumental. The nervousness of what might come next went hand in hand with a desire for him so extreme that she wondered whether even being possessed by Isaac would assuage it.

SHE HADN'T NOTICED TERESA, AT the end of the bed, scanning the peaks and hollows of the sheets. 'I have made you a bath,' Teresa said, looking quickly away in the face of Olive's nakedness.

'Who was that on the telephone?'

'No one.'

'No one?'

Olive saw Teresa hesitate. 'I do not know.'

'Are the police here?'

'No, señorita.'

'I'm never drinking again.'

'There is a glass of milk by your head.'

'I can't.'

'There is a bucket by your side.'

Olive leaned over and looked into the bucket. Bits of soil from the garden were scattered in the bottom. She retched into it, wanting to expel the sick feeling, her eyeballs hard as rocks.

'Señorita,' Teresa said, 'my brother is going to show his painting today.'

'What?' Olive groaned, collapsing back onto the bed. 'Tere – was there – has there – been any news today, from the village?'

'Someone broke into the church last night. They shot the statue of the Virgin Mary.'

'What?'

'Padre Lorenzo is crazy,' Teresa went on. 'He has taken her into the centre of the main square and he's shouting.'

Olive tried to speed up her thoughts. 'Taken who?'

'*La Virgen*,' Teresa repeated, in Spanish. 'She was very old wood, very expensive. She was shot three times. They took her to the office of Doctor Morales. As if he could bring her back to life,' Teresa added, with a slight sneer. 'Do you know what the men are asking, señorita? They are asking, who is the kind of man who puts a bullet through the tit of the Madonna?'

Olive said nothing, and closed her eyes. 'My brother looks more sick than you today,' Teresa said.

'Well, it was a good party.'

'I know. I have been cleaning for four hours. Come, get into the bathroom before the water is cold.' Teresa stood at the side of the bed and opened out a huge bath sheet. Olive obeyed; Teresa wrapped her up and shuffled her from the room.

Outside, Teresa's seeds were growing well; tiny leaves emerging from the fertilized furrows, where back in January she and Olive had marched up and down. The cork oaks and sweet chestnuts had turned a deeper green, and the sun was a few degrees warmer. Although the flowers were not in bloom, and the air was still thin, Teresa could smell the departure of winter, the inexplicable awareness the body has of the change to the most hopeful of seasons.

Sitting on the tatty green sofa in the front east room, she could hear Olive upstairs, draining her bath. She thought of Adrián, how it was inconceivable someone so young should be dead. She thought of the Schlosses' mad party, of Isaac's anger, their surly father, the shot Madonna. Everything was so uncertain. And yet, with regards to today's unveiling, Teresa had never felt so sure. She'd asked her brother whether he would miss painting Sarah and Olive, but he'd ignored her, trudging off down the hill to fetch the table and chairs that Doctor Morales said they could borrow for the party.

This morning in the cottage, Teresa put her head round Isaac's door and told him that if he wanted she would take the portrait over and prepare it for a grand unveiling. 'I'll put it on an easel in the front east room,' she said.

Isaac, flannel on face, lying in the dark of his bedroom, lifted it once, peered at her and said, 'Fine. I'm glad it's done. But wait until I get there before you show them.'

TERESA HAD CHILLED ONE OF the remaining bottles of Clicquot, leaving it out on the veranda overnight. All the windows had been thrown open to let fresh air into the corners where cigarette smoke clung. Stubborn patches of spilled sherry attracted columns of ants. Teresa crushed them with her foot, arranged the sofa and the other chairs in a semicircle around the easel, and draped a white sheet over the artwork. She put the champagne in a metal cooler and went to the kitchen. She had never felt so clear-headed, nor had she ever felt a greater sense of purpose than today. The excitement for it almost made her feel sick.

THIRTY MINUTES LATER, EVERYONE WAS gathered. Harold, the best recovered of the family, was in an impeccable suit. Sarah looked frail, a tremor in her fingers as she passed a champagne flute to her daughter, who looked green at the sight of it. Isaac was perched on the edge of the sofa, dragging deep on a cigarette, his foot jigging. This was his moment to shine – here, in the presence of the great dealer, Harold Schloss. Teresa saw his eyes meet Olive's, and the girl's smile was an open beam of pleasure. Harold was looking in puzzlement at his wife, as to what this was all about.

Teresa wondered whether he had answered the telephone this morning, for she had vowed never to pick it up again.

Sarah rose to her feet. 'Darling Harold,' she said. 'Well done from all of us, for *such* a wonderful party. It seems, even down here at the end of civilization, you haven't lost your touch.'

Everyone laughed, and Harold raised his glass. 'Now, as you know, things have been a little up and down of late,' Sarah said.

'But we like it here, don't we, darling? And we're doing well. And I – well, *we* – wanted to give you a little present to say thank you. It's Liv and me, darling,' she said, pulling the sheet off the painting. 'Mr Robles painted us – for you.'

Teresa swallowed the champagne she'd been offered, and a sick, irresistible tide of fear flushed through her, the bubbles filling her mouth, the metallic fizz agitating her blood. Isaac ran his fingers through his hair. As the sheet cascaded to the tiles, Olive's knuckles turned white on the arms of her chair. There was a small collective gasp.

OLIVE WAS IN DEEP DISLOCATION. She couldn't understand what she was seeing. The painting was two-thirds drenched in indigo blue, there was a glint of golden wheat, and two women, one holding her pot aloft in a shining field, and the other, curled in semi-defeat, surrounded by her broken shards.

It was her painting. It was *Santa Justa in the Well*. She turned to Isaac; he, too, was staring in confusion. What was it doing down here – why wasn't it upstairs, hidden in her room? Olive looked at Teresa; the grim triumph on her face.

There was a sound of clapping. Her father was looking at her painting. Her father was *applauding*. 'Bravo, Isaac,' he was saying. 'Bravo. What you've *done*!'

Sarah frowned, hands on hips. 'Well, it isn't quite – what I was expecting. But I like it. Which of us is which, Mr Robles? Do you like it, Harold?'

'I've not seen something like this in a very long time. Liv, you look like you've seen a ghost,' her father said. 'You're not upset that Mr Robles hasn't done you a society turn?'

Olive couldn't speak. All she could do was look at her own painting, her father pacing around it. 'This is *wonderful*,' he went on. 'I *knew* you had something in you, Robles. Lithography, my eye.'

Harold's voice was intense and warm; it was like this whenever a new painting was speaking to him. It was a silent conversation; the painting slowly heating him up, running round his mind – and Harold was working on it like a child might a boiled sweet, sampling its flavours, softening its corners, edging inexorably towards its core.

Olive felt as if she too was being honed away, soon to snap and disappear. 'This is real. Oh, this is good,' her father was saying, and it felt like she was hearing him from the bottom of a well. 'Look at the pot – and the deer. Oh, this is *good*! This is excellent.'

Isaac was staring at the painting. His eyes began to dart around it, as if the colours, the composition, the line might speak to him too. Was he angry? Olive couldn't tell. Like her, he wasn't saying a thing. She wondered where Isaac's painting was, whether he was going to speak up. She turned to see Teresa staring at her, her look of triumph now replaced with one of urgency.

'Mr Robles, you're a star,' said Sarah, placing her hand on his arm. 'Well *done*.'

Teresa nodded at Olive, her eyes wide – and in that moment, Olive understood. She knew, then, what Teresa wanted her to say – *That's mine. I did that. There's been a mistake* – although she could not understand Teresa's desire. She felt her mouth open, the words almost there, but then her father spoke.

'We should take this to Paris,' Harold said. 'I think this might be something a few collectors over there would be interested in. I'd like to act for you, Isaac. I'll get you a better fee.'

'*Paris?*' said Olive, and then she closed her mouth.

'What's it called?' Harold asked.

'It has no title,' said Isaac.

Harold stared at the painting. 'I think we should avoid any mention of Liv and Sarah in it, given that I might be selling it. How about *Girls in the Wheatfield*?'

'Harold,' said Sarah. 'This was a present for you. You can't just sell it.'

But Harold wasn't listening. 'Perhaps *Women in the Wheatfield* is better.'

'Poor Liv, painted curled in a ball like that,' said Sarah, draining her glass of champagne, and pouring herself another. 'Mr Robles, you really are terrible.'

Isaac stared at Olive and Teresa. 'Yes,' he said. 'I am.'

He got to his feet. The painting had caused an almost alchemical transformation in him. The new Isaac was solidifying, like smoke into gold, before their very eyes. He was a real artist, something about him they could all sense but not quite touch – however much they wished to.

'Teresa,' Isaac said, and Olive could hear the shake in his voice as he uncharacteristically stumbled over his English. 'Come and help me in the kitchen. I brought the turnip you wanted for that soup.'

X

'What the *fuck* have you done?' Isaac hissed. He pushed his
sister inside the kitchen, jabbing his hand between her
shoulder blades.

'I haven't done anything,' Teresa hissed back. 'I can't believe
you said that thing about a turnip—'

'Shut up. I had to think of something.' He closed the door.
'Whose painting is that?'

Teresa stuck her chin in the air. 'It's Olive's,' she said. 'It's
Olive's, and it's better than yours.'

'*Olive's?*'

'She paints every day. She got a place at art school and stayed
here instead. You didn't ask her that, did you, when you had your
tongue rammed down her throat.'

Isaac slumped at the kitchen table and put his head in his
hands. 'Oh, Jesus. She put her own painting up there.'

Teresa flushed. 'No, she didn't. I did.'

'*You* did? Why?'

'You're going to break her heart.'

'Oh, Jesus. This is about me kissing her?'

'You sneaked in here—'

'And what else did you do but creep through the orchard with
your chicken as an offering, like a bloody Indian to Columbus—'

'I help them, every day. They'd be lost without me.'

'You could be anyone, Teresa. You're just the maid.'

'And you just cause trouble.'

'Sarah Schloss *asked* me to paint her, so I did. And you might as well know. Alfonso has stopped my money.'

'What?'

'You heard – he doesn't like the "taste of my politics". And so the money from Sarah Schloss was supposed to keep us going. I wanted to keep this professional, Teresa—'

'And you expect me to believe that?'

'I've got more important things to worry about than some rich *guiri* with a taste for big parties—'

'What, like shooting your pistol in the church and lifting Olive's dress?'

'You're just a spy. A stirrer.' He stood up, his voice low and vicious. 'You came to these people, Tere, because you knew how your life was going. You've been doing it since you were little. With a dad like ours and your gypsy mother – don't pretend to me you're some saint. Don't think I don't know where Olive's necklace came from. I know all about your little box in the garden. And now what? What are we supposed to do?'

'You're going to admit it isn't your painting,' Teresa said, pinch-faced and shaken, 'and give Olive the credit she's due.'

'No, he isn't,' said a voice from the doorway. 'He isn't going to do that at all.'

OLIVE HAD OPENED THE KITCHEN door quietly, and had been listening at the threshold. Her expression was not easy to read. She looked incandescent – but with rage, or sorrow, or excitement, neither Isaac nor Teresa could easily tell. They froze, waiting for her to speak again. Olive moved inside the kitchen and shut the door.

'Why did you do it?' she asked Teresa.

Tears sprang into Teresa's eyes. 'I wanted to—'

'She wanted to punish me. She saw us at the gate last night,' said Isaac. 'This little trick is Teresa's revenge.'

'No! It is not revenge, señorita,' Teresa pleaded. 'Your father should see how brilliant you are, how—'

'That's not your responsibility,' said Olive. 'Tere, I trusted you. I thought we were friends.'

'You can trust me.'

'How?'

'I am sorry, I did not—'

'It's too late,' Olive sighed. 'We can't all just stand here like some mothers' meeting. They'll be wondering what's going on.'

'I will tell them it isn't mine, señorita,' said Isaac. 'It is not fair Teresa should trick your parents. They have been good to her. And my own painting is ready. Teresa brought it over this morning.'

Olive looked thoughtful. 'Where is Isaac's painting, Teresa? Fetch it.'

Teresa went into the pantry. They heard her dragging barrels across the tiles, and she came tottering out with the large canvas, propping it up against the wall before she pulled away the protective cloth.

Olive stared in silence. She and her mother were recognizable, but their eyes had been made gauzy, their lips had a generic redness. Behind their heads were strange nimbuses of light, and beyond that, a plain green background. There was no humour, no spirit or power, no exciting use of colour or line, no originality, no intangible magic. No hint of secrets, no play, no story. It wasn't terrible. It was two women on the front of a Christmas card.

Olive glanced at Isaac. He was looking at his own work, arms folded, a frown of concentration as he assessed his effort. What was he thinking? Was he pleased – did he think this was *good*? There was nothing wrong with the kind of art that Isaac had replicated – after all, why should everything be an intellectual gauntlet? It was easy on the eye, but it was juvenile. Her father would hate it.

She realized, in that moment, that despite her discomfort of sitting for a portrait, part of her had wanted Isaac to be really good. It would have been easier than him having no gift at all. Perhaps she was more her parents' daughter than she thought. It was always easier to admire someone with a talent, and pity was the path to indifference. Olive closed her eyes, resisting the potential damage to her heart that this painting, or Isaac's lack, might cause. She told herself that Isaac didn't deserve to face her father's disdain. When she opened her eyes, Isaac was looking at her, and she gave him a bright smile.

'Isaac, you heard what my father said. He wants to take the painting to Paris. He wants to sell it.'

'You see, señorita,' said Teresa. 'I know you said you did not care for the recognition of the world – but look at what has happened. I am glad I took the risk for you—'

Olive turned to her. 'I didn't want you to.'

Teresa set her jaw. 'Are you sure about that?'

'Tere, enough,' said Isaac.

'But – we must tell him, now,' said Teresa.

'My father thinks Isaac painted *Santa Justa in the Well*, or *Women in the Wheatfield*. He wants to take Isaac's painting to Paris, not mine.'

'But all you need to do is tell him that you painted it.'

'But would it be the same painting?' Olive asked.

Teresa frowned. 'I do not understand.'

The exclamations and murmurs from the front room could be heard through the kitchen door. 'I don't think my father would have quite the same enthusiasm if he knew I'd painted it,' said Olive.

'No,' said Isaac. 'That is not true.'

'How can you be so sure?' she said. 'I want my father to go to Paris, you see. I want him to take it. It might be fun. I simply want to see.'

'This is not right,' Teresa pleaded. 'Your father, when you tell him – he will be surprised, yes – but then he will see your other paintings—'

'No.'

Olive held up her hand for silence, but Teresa ignored her. 'You do not see your father. He will—'

'Oh, I see my father, thank you very much.' Olive's voice was hard. 'And my mother too. They believe it's Isaac's painting, and that's all that matters, isn't it? What people believe. It doesn't matter what's the truth; what people believe becomes the truth. Isaac could have painted it – why couldn't he have painted it?'

'He could never have painted it,' said Teresa, and she stamped her foot.

Olive made a sound of frustration. 'You're to blame for this. So you'd better be quiet.'

'But I did not want for you to—'

'This is madness,' Isaac said. 'This is *una locura*. My painting is here.'

'Isaac, it's just a bit of fun.'

'This is not a game,' said Isaac. I have my painting here—'

'Please, Isaac. Look, he might not sell *Women in the Wheatfield*. So it stays in the family after all. This will be forgotten. Then you can give him your one.'

'But what if he sells yours? What if he sells an Isaac Robles that has not been painted by Isaac Robles?'

'If it sells – well, I don't want the money, and you *need* the money. I heard what you said about your father. If *my* father sells the painting, you could spend the money any way you wanted. New schoolbooks, trips out, food, equipment for your students, the workers.' Olive paused. ' "*What do you want in this life?*" Isn't that what you asked me, Isa? Well, I want to be useful.'

'Art is not useful.'

'I don't agree. It can make a difference. It can help your cause.'

'I cannot do this.'

'Isaac. Claim the painting in the other room. It means nothing to me.'

'I don't believe that, Olive.'

'Let me do something useful. Let me be needed. I've never done anything useful in my life.'

'But—'

'I'm not going to admit that the painting in the front room is mine, Isaac. Not to my father, at least – and in this case, he is the only person who matters.'

'But he has *praised* it. Teresa is right. I do not understand—'

Olive drew herself up, her face pale. 'Listen. I cannot tell you how rarely my father has this reaction. Let's not risk damaging that. Be the Isaac Robles that's out there now. Just one painting.'

Isaac said nothing for a minute. He had a look of misery, his mouth downcast. Next to him, Teresa was pulling nervously at her cardigan. 'But it is not *his*,' she whispered.

'It is, if I give it to him,' said Olive.

'You will be invisible, señorita. You are giving yourself away—'

'I'm doing the absolute opposite of giving myself away. As far as I'm concerned, I'll be completely visible. If the painting sells, I'll be in Paris, hanging on a wall. If anything, I'm being selfish. It's perfect; all the freedom of creation, with none of the fuss.'

Isaac looked between his own painting and the kitchen door – beyond which, down the corridor, *Women in the Wheatfield* was waiting on the easel, and Harold's exclamations could still be heard. The bottle of champagne Teresa had prepared popped, and Sarah laughed. Back and forth Isaac's eyes went, between two possible selves.

'Do not do this, Isaac,' Teresa whispered. 'Señorita, go in there and tell them that it is yours.'

'Isaac, this could be our chance to do something extraordinary.'

Isaac pushed through the door and lumbered along the corridor. When he'd disappeared, Olive turned to Teresa, her eyes alight.

'Take this upstairs for me. And don't sulk. It's all going to be fine. Hide it under the bed.' She studied Isaac's poorly rendered version of her face. 'Is that what he thinks of me?'

'I do not know,' said Teresa. 'It is just a painting.'

'I know you don't really think that,' Olive said, with a smile.

If the smile was supposed to be a gesture of forgiveness for what Teresa had done, it did not lift her spirits. She watched as Olive skipped down the corridor, following Isaac's path. The door of the front room opened again. Alone in the kitchen, Teresa heard laughter, and the repetitive clinking of glass.

XI

Isaac walked back to the cottage in a daze. He was so tired, so hungover. Harold had got some woman on the telephone about the painting; she'd expressed interest, and he was off to Paris in the morning. The Schlosses had implored Isaac to stay for a celebratory dinner, but he couldn't bear it. He felt like half a man. He almost hoped the thing wouldn't sell, that Olive's vendetta against her parents was a delayed adolescent whim soon to be forgotten, something she would look back on in years to come and laugh. The *people*. She wanted to help *the people*. She wanted to help herself, and Isaac knew he had made it possible.

He patted his pockets for his cigarettes, lit one, inhaled deeply and breathed out the smoke on a sigh. What was he doing? As he began the ascent to the cottage, the kites circled above him. He pushed open the door and thought again about the party, that kiss against the finca gate. It seemed half a year had passed since then. Olive's insistence on coming to the church had showed a spontaneity and rebelliousness that he'd admired. He just didn't realize quite how deep that spirit went.

He should simply have kept away from the finca from the very beginning. He should have said no to the commission, he should have told Teresa to find work elsewhere, he shouldn't have stopped

Olive in the dark, in her evening gown, hair flying everywhere. He should have marched into the front east room, bearing his own painting. He wasn't up to pretending, and he didn't want it.

The sound of feet on the gravel made him turn. It was Olive, running up the hill after him. She stopped to catch her breath, and he waited, immediately wary.

'I just wanted to say, don't worry. It's going to be all right, I promise. If he sells it, the money's yours. That's it. The end.'

'It's done now.'

'I promise you, Isaac. Just the one painting.'

'Fine.' He began to turn away.

'And was it just the one kiss?' she asked. He turned back to her, and she came closer, stopping just beyond his reach. They surveyed one another.

Isaac was done with her words, and tired of himself. He took her by the waist and pulled her towards him, kissing her hard on the mouth. Beneath him, Olive sprang to life, and he felt the power of her body responding as she kissed him back. He forced himself to pull away.

'I've wanted this,' Olive said. 'Since the day we met.'

He gave a harsh laugh. 'Wanted what?'

She stepped back. 'You've allowed me this chance, Isaac. And I wondered why – and I thought – well, I thought—'

'I did not allow you this chance. You took it.'

'I think both of us can see this pretty clearly.'

'Are you sure? What we have just done is exactly what a child would do. The three of us, whispering like children in the kitchen. It is make-believe. Only my sister tried to inject a bit of honesty into it.'

'I wasn't talking about the painting, Isaac.' He was silent. A look of fear flickered over her face. 'You don't want me, then,' she said.

Isaac felt something collapse inside himself. He turned towards the cottage and could hear Olive following him. 'I just – I want it to be you,' she said. He carried on walking, and could hear her steps.

He closed the door, and they stood facing each other. The light was dim, but he watched as Olive reached up and undid the top button of her blouse. She carried on, methodical as a sergeant major, button after button, letting the blouse fall off her shoulders, no brassiere beneath.

She stood before him, and her torso was perfect, her skirt a fabric stillness over the shape of her thighs. She must have thought Isaac was thinking of her, but he was not. He was thinking of that long-lost woman, Laetitia, twenty-seven years old and him, fifteen – and how grateful he was for her generosity to him that morning, how she'd never laughed, how she'd treated him like the man he'd been so desperate to become.

Isaac stepped forward and wrapped his hands around Olive's waist. She gasped as he lifted her onto the table, her feet just touching the floor. She sat rigid as he drew a single finger all the way from her neck, between her breasts, down to the top of her skirt. She shivered and arched her back, lifting her hips and Isaac thought then, *Why not, why not*, and he brought his mouth to her breasts, kissing and kissing her, hearing her sharp inhalation as his finger stroked up the side of her leg and slid inside her knickers. Her legs tensed. 'More?' he murmured.

There was a pause. 'More,' she said.

He ruched Olive's skirt up around her waist, dropped to his knees and prised apart her thighs. When he ran his tongue down the fabric of her knickers, Olive gasped again. He stopped.

'More?' he asked. 'Yes,' she said, so he pushed the fabric aside and dipped in his tongue, dipping and lapping, opening his mouth onto her.

'Is this a real thing?' Olive whispered, and then her words were lost.

He carried on, and soon Olive was pushing her hips hard into him, her moans turning upwards into a huge sigh. She shuddered onto the table, her arms thrown back on the wide, gnarled wood. Isaac stood up and surveyed her, his hands holding the sides of

Olive's legs, how her arched spine now lay flat, how her face was turned away, closed to everything except her smile, her undeniable triumph and bliss.

'More?' Isaac asked.

Olive opened her eyes, widened her legs, and looked at him. '*More*,' came her reply.

PART III

The Lion Girls

OCTOBER 1967

10

The first story I ever published in England appears on pages seventy-four to seventy-seven of the *London Review* of October 1967. It was called 'The Toeless Woman', and they even paid someone to draw an accompanying illustration. They missed the *e* off the end of my first name, so it looks like my father wrote it. I still have two copies of that particular edition – the one that I'd purchased myself, and the other I'd posted to my mother in Port of Spain, and which was returned to me years later, after her death.

My mother had annotated her copy with the words *'My girl!'* and to my amusement, added the missing *e* in biro. Years later, at her funeral, my second cousin Louisa told me that Mrs Bastien had passed that *Review* round all her friends like a one-woman lending library, strictly insisting that they could only have an evening with it each. I think more people in Port of Spain read that story than in the literate sections of London town. What they made of it, I'll never know.

It was Quick, of course, who was to blame – or thank – for the story finding its way to the editor. I think she relished the symmetry of it – how, after my leaving the raw thing on her desk, she was able to leave a copy of the magazine containing it on mine. I thought it was odd, how she had sat in her garden and exhorted me to disregard the opinions of others, only to go and submit my work for mass approval.

'Find page seventy-four,' she commanded, scratching aggressively at the base of her neck. I obeyed her, sitting in that viewless room in the Skelton, wishing she would go away, so that I could be in private to study this vision of my almost-name on the page. But Quick did not leave, and I had to hold in the tsunami of sound I wanted to unleash across the square, a cry of satisfaction so loud it would have travelled over the rooftops to the coast of Kent. My father's name, *Odell Bastien*, his daughter's writing underneath. Next time, I swore there would be no missing *e*. But for now, it would do. The words, at least, were mine.

Quick smiled, and the effect on her gaunt face was transformative: gleeful, youthful, briefly illuminated with pleasure. She was dressed that day in a dark green pair of trousers, slightly flared, and a pussy-bow silk blouse with a seasonal repeating pattern of brown leaves. I noticed the slight sag of the material on her thighs; she was definitely thinner. 'It was an excellent story,' she said, 'so I sent it in. I even got you a fee. Thirty pounds.'

'Thirty *pounds*?'

'I hope that was all right. You don't mind I went ahead?'

'I don't know how to thank you. Thank you.'

She laughed, sitting down opposite me, fumbling in her trouser pocket, lighting a cigarette and taking a deep drag. 'Don't thank me,' she said. 'It was a fantastic read. Did you base it on something that happened at Dolcis?'

'Sort of.'

She gazed at me. 'How does it feel, to be a published writer?'

I looked back down at the page; the ink that couldn't be rubbed away, the deceptive permanence of the paper. I felt exalted, my mind a cathedral, with an actual congregation who wished to visit my altar. 'Incredible,' I said.

'You'd better write some more,' she replied. 'Keep going at it. It seems to work.'

'I will. Thank you, thank you again.'

She went to the window, cigarette in hand, and looked down at the alley where the smokers gathered. I couldn't imagine her mixing with them, a bird of paradise amongst the canaries. 'Would you have let me look at it,' she asked, 'if you'd known what I might do?'

'I don't know,' I said. It was a good question.

'I wondered. Anyway, you've got a terrible view here. Did Pamela choose this room? We can get you a nicer one.'

'I'm fine, thank you. A nice view would probably distract me from my work.'

She raised an eyebrow. 'How puritanical.'

Quick could tease me as much as she wanted; I didn't care. I was published. She remained at the window, her back to me again. 'How about Reede's news on Mr Scott's painting, eh? He's looking very pleased with himself. Looks like we are going to have an exhibition. He wants to call it "The Swallowed Century". But we cannot exhibit only one painting.' I could hear the disdain in her voice. Her body was slightly curled over, as if she was shielding a ball of pain.

'I didn't know,' I said.

She turned. 'No? Is everything all right between you and Mr Scott?'

'Yes. No. Just a misunderstanding.'

'I see.' She straightened up, leaning against the wall. 'Want to talk about it?'

'There's nothing much to say.' Quick fixed her gaze on me, so reluctantly, I went on. 'I went to his mother's house, in Surrey.'

'Nice?'

'Nice. We had dinner. And then afterwards, he told me he loved me. And I didn't say it back. And it all went wrong from there. I haven't spoken to him for three weeks.'

Quick inhaled thoughtfully on her cigarette. 'No harm done. I saw the way he looked at you. You've got him in the palm of your hand.'

'I don't think so. I wasn't very polite.'

'Odelle, you don't have to say, or do, anything you don't want to. I don't suppose he loves you for your politeness.'

'But he hasn't called. I haven't seen him.'

'Does that bother you?'

I was astonished at the tears pricking my eyes. 'Yes.'

'Then it'll work itself out. Don't go flailing back in. Never helps, in my experience. Did you stay long in the house?'

'A few hours.'

'Big place?'

'Fairly. I didn't see much.'

I considered telling Quick about the pamphlet I'd smuggled out in my handbag, but something stopped me. Maybe it was my reluctance to look like a thief, but there was also something about the way Quick constantly hovered over the issue of Lawrie and the painting that made me wary. Given her attitude towards Lawrie, she might jump on anything to use against him – although what a long-forgotten pamphlet might mean in all this was anyone's guess. Lawrie and I may not have been quite on speaking terms, but I didn't want Quick to make him even more defenceless in the face of any attack.

'Come and have dinner with me tonight,' she said. 'Let's have champagne.'

'Champagne?'

'I'm feeling victorious. I've got a couple of lamb chops that need eating. And someone needs to give you a pat on the back.'

I hesitated. Being alone with Marjorie Quick was always a very intense experience, and after the last time in her garden, I didn't know if I was up to it. But then I thought about another night in the empty flat, with only the crackle of the radio and my overly read books for company, and suddenly I didn't want to be alone. 'Thank you,' I said. 'Shall we ask Pamela?'

'She wouldn't want to come. Besides, I've only got two chops.'

I felt I couldn't insist, because it wasn't my house, my dinner, my champagne. But I do remember thinking it would be no problem at all to pop to a butcher and buy Pamela an extra chop. Quick seemed keen to have me there alone.

'Good,' she said, taking my silence for assent. 'That's settled. See you later, Odelle. We can take a taxi home together. And well done again. I'm very proud.'

11

When I went to find Quick in her office at the end of the day, her door was closed. Voices were coming through the wood – hers, and that of Edmund Reede, more angry than I'd ever heard.

'We should use these discrepancies as opportunities,' he was saying. 'Why are you undermining me, Marjorie?'

'Edmund—' she began, but he interrupted.

'I've tolerated a great deal from you in the past, but your doggedness over this is ridiculous.' There was a silence. Reede sighed. 'You've seen the accounts, Marjorie. You've seen what's happening to us. I just cannot fathom your reluctance. It's a stunning painting. It has a story. It has a handsome young man on the end of it. Two, in fact, if you put owner and painter together. We'll have a crowd; we might even have a sale. The Guggenheim are going to send me what they have, but there's already so much here. The mystery of Robles – how did he die? Who ordered his death, and why?'

'That's got nothing to do with the painting, Edmund,' Quick said.

'I disagree. His personal tale reflects the international stage. It prefigures by less than a decade the vanishing of hundreds of artworks under Nazi rule, and, in many cases, their creators and families.'

'But the art first, eh, Edmund?'

He ignored this reproof. 'Robles is universal. When we tell the tale of this artist, we tell the tale of war.'

I heard the flick of Quick's lighter. 'I'm surprised you of all people want to tell the tale of war,' she said. 'I don't see this painting as political at all.'

'Look here, Marjorie, what's the problem? We've always been frank with each other.'

'Have we?'

'Oh, come on. As frank as it was possible to be.'

Quick was silent for what seemed a long time. 'There is no problem,' she said. 'It just isn't political in the way you think it is. It's not about war in the way you see it, Edmund. It's not about the artist as a man. It's about the canvas. Two girls facing down a lion.'

I was astonished at the way they were talking to each other, so fluid and intimate. Pamela said they had known each other for years, and it showed. It was almost fraternal, and he was talking to her much as he might talk to one of his friends at the club.

'We'll agree to disagree, Marjorie,' Reede said. 'As we have done for longer than I care to remember.'

I could hear Reede moving towards the door, so I ran back along the corridor to my own desk, waiting instead for Quick to come and find me. It seemed that Quick had capitulated – to what exactly, I was not sure. She was resistant to the idea of an exhibition – but the true focus of her reluctance, this wavering derision and fear, was still not clear to me. It seemed that she was placing herself in opposition to whatever Reede thought philosophically about the painting, more than she was against the idea of actually exhibiting it.

QUICK INDEED TURNED UP AT my desk shortly after, looking drawn and upset. 'Ready?' she said. 'There's a taxi downstairs.'

We walked past the reception desk together. I glanced at Pamela, and saw the confusion in her face. I was surprised to feel that I was betraying her, going off with Quick like this, when Pamela worked just as hard as me and had been here longer. But I couldn't turn back. I was too drawn to Quick's enigma, too determined to find out what was really going on.

After our dinner, Quick invited me into the sitting room at the front of the house. She lowered herself into a sleek grey armchair, its wooden arms carved like the strings of a harp. Everything she owned, apart from the gramophone, seemed stylish and modern. 'Keeping an old woman company,' she said. 'I feel guilty.'

'Hardly old,' I replied. 'I was very happy to come.'

We hadn't talked of much over dinner; a little about Pamela, Reede and the donors he had to court, how he hated flirting with old marchionesses holed up in damp castles, where God knows what treasures were rotting in the lofts. 'You've known Reede a long time?' I asked.

'A long time. He's a good man,' she added, as if I'd said otherwise.

We were drinking brandies, a quiet piano concerto floating through from the gramophone in the other room. Quick closed her eyes, and she was so still, neither of us speaking, that I thought she'd dropped to sleep, the glow from the electric table-light beside her turning her face orange. She didn't strike me as the kind of person to invite a guest over and then fall asleep in the middle of a conversation. She was in her fifties, not her nineties, but it was peaceful to watch her in repose and I didn't wish to disturb. I wondered why she was so interested in me – placing my story in the magazine, the invitations to lunch, the solicitous questions over Lawrie and my future.

The electric fire was switched on, although it was a mild October. Quick even had on a shawl. I felt the brandy overheating my body and thought maybe I should leave, and I was on the point of rising from my chair when Quick said, her eyes still closed – 'Did you ever talk to Lawrie Scott about his mother?'

I sat back down. 'His mother?'

Her eyes snapped open and I saw their leonine intent. 'Yes. His mother.'

I thought about the suicide, and realized that it might have taken place in one of the very rooms I'd wandered through. I suddenly missed Lawrie. I wanted us to start again – a trip to the cinema, a walk in the park – but I had no idea how on earth to make it possible. I couldn't let him float adrift as well as Cynth.

'He didn't talk about her at all,' I lied.

'Then he must be thinking about her an awful lot. I'd lay money on it, if I were a betting man. Grief's a pressure cooker if you don't deal with it. One day, you simply explode.'

'Do you?'

She drained her brandy glass. 'Things crumble. Bit by bit. They shift, you don't notice. Then you notice. Jesus Christ, my legs are broken but I never moved my feet. And all the time, it's been coming towards you, Odelle – orchestrated in the hearts of strangers, or a God you'll never meet. Then one day, a stone is hurled – and by accident or design, that stone hits the car window of a powerful idiot who wants revenge, or who wants to impress his mistress, and – whoosh – the foot soldiers move in. The next day, your village is burning down, and because of stupidity, because of sex, there's a coffin for your bed.'

I couldn't think how to reply to this. Sex, death, coffins – how many brandies had she had? I didn't see what this had to do with Lawrie at all. I stared into the electric bars.

Quick leaned forward, and the arms of her chair creaked. 'Odelle, do you trust me?'

'Trust you with what?'

She leaned back again, visibly frustrated. 'You don't, then. If you did, you would have just said yes.'

'I'm a cautious person. That's all.'

'I trust *you*, you know. I know you're someone I can trust.'

I think I was supposed to be grateful, but instead I felt a simmering unease. The bars of the fire were making me hotter and hotter, and I was tired, and she was in a strange mood.

Quick sighed. 'It's my fault. For all my conversations with you, I'm probably even more guarded than you are.'

I couldn't disagree with this, so I didn't try and persuade her otherwise.

'I'm not well,' she said. 'I'm not very well at all.'

IT WAS CANCER, SHE SAID. Late stage, pancreatic cancer with an inevitable outcome. My own body ached at these words, which was selfish, but entirely predictable. I assumed that the outrageous fact of her cancer had made Quick want someone at home with her – a desire which had possibly surprised her and made her even more brusque. Quick, who had been alone with her secrets for so many years, no longer wished to be alone. Perhaps submitting my story, and therefore making me obliged to her, was a baroque plan to satisfy her simple need for company? When life is running out, such decisions may not seem so invasive or dramatic, and you willingly commit. This was why she spoke to Edmund Reede with no fear of reprisal; she knew she was soon to be reprised entirely.

I do think, looking back, that Quick perhaps regarded me as the child she never had, as someone who would perpetuate her essence after death. She told me at our first meeting that I reminded her of someone she once knew. I suspect that person was the closest companion she ever had. I'll never be sure of this, and she never mentioned a name, but her expression when she said those words makes me think that it was so. She looked at me tenderly, mingled with terror, as if to come too close would lose whatever she'd lost all over again.

Sitting in that overheated front room, I realized quite how thin she was, how tired. And although I probably thought it unfair that someone should suffer something like that alone, I don't imagine I cried in front of her. Quick was not someone you would sob in front of unless you absolutely had to, and when it was a question of her own pain and loss, you might feel a monstrous booby to cry when she herself was dry-eyed, dragging on the cigarettes that were helping to kill her. She was a curio, out of her time, not given to standard emotion – and in her presence, you did what Quick did.

'Well, say something,' she said.

'Does Mr Reede know?' I asked.

Quick snorted. 'God, no. And he's not to.'

'Does anyone else know?'

'No one else, but don't worry, I haven't told you because I want you to be my nursemaid.'

'Why have you told me?'

Quick reached for the brandy bottle and refilled her glass. 'Do you know, I got my diagnosis the day you started at the Skelton?'

'Goodness me,' I said. I remembered Quick coming up to my desk that first day; her flushed face, the way she batted away the porter's questions over her absence from work.

'Indeed,' she said. 'A day of ups and downs. Death imminent, followed by Odelle Bastien.'

'I can't imagine I was much of a tonic.'

She lit a cigarette, the last of the packet. 'You have no idea.'

I couldn't help wondering how long she had left, but I didn't want to ask if she knew, nor enquire about medications, or anything practical. It seemed too brutal, as if I was asking about her expiration date. She was still here, still vital, still mercurial.

IN THE SILENCE BETWEEN US, I reached into my handbag and handed over the art gallery pamphlet. I still wonder why I did it, even though it felt like a betrayal of Lawrie. I think it was the pride I felt, from knowing that Quick had confided in me. It was my consolation offering in return, even though I didn't know if it was something she'd find useful.

She took it, almost as if she was expecting it. 'This was in Lawrie's house,' she said.

'How on earth did you know?'

'You've been looking like you wanted to tell me something since the moment I mentioned your visit there.'

'I didn't know I was so obvious,' I said.

She smiled. 'You're not that obvious. I've had lots of practice.' She opened the pamphlet and placed it gently on her knees, her finger tracing the pencilled message, *No Sign*. 'Was there anything else with it?' she asked.

'No. Just odds and ends on a window sill. Butcher's bills, church service sheets.'

'Church service sheets?' she repeated, her eyebrow raised.

'A carol concert, actually.'

'I see.'

'What do you think it means – where someone's written *No Sign*? The name of a painting?'

'I imagine it's simpler than that. Someone was looking for something, and they didn't find it.'

'You know what they were looking for, don't you, Quick?'

She looked up at me, the electric fire turning her irises hazel. 'I do?'

'Well,' I said. 'It's just – you're very interested in Lawrie's mother. And Lawrie's painting.'

' "Interested" is not the word I would use.'

Obsessed? Frightened? I thought. *As if I would say those words to you.* 'Well,' I faltered, sensing her stiffen, 'you seem averse to the idea of exhibiting it.'

'I'm not averse to the exhibition of that painting. I think everybody should see it.'

'All right,' I said. 'But that's not what you said last time. You said Lawrie should take it home.'

She took in a deep breath. 'Well. I'm not entirely happy with how Reede is planning to use it. Until we get more information from the Guggenheim institution, my doubts remain.'

'What doubts are those?'

Quick's face took on a haunted expression. I'd seen it before, through the keyhole at the Skelton, when Lawrie had returned to continue his discussions with Reede. Her eyes darted back and forth on the rug between us. She kept breathing in as if to speak, and not speaking. It was frustrating, but I knew that to speak myself might ruin the slim chance she would finally say something.

'Isaac Robles didn't paint that picture, Odelle,' Quick said, her fingers tightening on the pamphlet.

My heart began to thump harder. 'But he's standing in front of it, in that photograph.'

'So? I could go and stand in front of any number of artworks and be photographed. It doesn't mean I made them.'

'It was taken in his studio—'

'Odelle, it's not that I don't believe he painted it. I know he didn't.'

Her last four words sang through the air between us, and hit me in the stomach. Something shivered over me, and my skin turned to gooseflesh, the way it does when someone tells you the truth and you hear it with your body.

I must have looked dumb. 'He didn't paint it, Odelle,' she repeated. Her shoulders sagged. 'It wasn't him.'

'Then – who was it?'

My question ruined everything. Quick looked stricken, aged, weird. Looking at her, I felt a bit sick and scared myself, because she seemed terrified. 'Are you all right?' I said. 'Should I call a doctor?'

'No. It's late. I'm fine.' But I could hear that she was out of breath. 'You should call a taxi. I have a number, out in the hallway. Don't worry, I'll pay.'

I rose, stumbling over the threshold of the front room into the cool darkness of the hall, where I switched on the light standing on the telephone table. There was no number to be seen. The house behind me was silent. I sensed a presence in the shadows, and my back prickled. I turned around and something was on the stairs, moving towards me. I gripped the edge of the table, as Quick's cat emerged into the pool of yellow light, and sat very still before me, turning his green eyes. We regarded one another, only the faintest movement from his ribs dissuading me that he was stuffed.

'Look in the drawer,' Quick called in a ragged voice, and I jumped. 'There's an address book in the drawer. *T* for Taxi.' I turned back to the lamplight, feeling foolish, praying that nothing else was waiting for me in the shadows beyond the cat.

I STILL DON'T KNOW WHETHER what happened next was another of Quick's plans – her, leading me deeper into the wood – or whether in her illness, under strong medication, she just hadn't realized what I'd find.

I pulled her address book out of the drawer, where it lay amongst old maps and balls of string and unopened mousetraps. I flipped to find *T* for Taxi, and saw two things. The first; under *S*, in Quick's flowing black nib, were written the words:

> Scott – The Red House
> Baldock's Ridge
> Surrey HAS-6735

And secondly, a small white letter, folded in two, and pressed between these pages.

'Everything all right out there?' Quick called.

'Fine!' My voice quivered. 'Just getting it now.'

I looked at the Scott address in confusion. This entry might be a recent addition, of course – Quick undertaking some investigating of her own into Lawrie and the painting – and God knows it would not have surprised me. It was unbelievable that Quick might actually know the Scott family. And Lawrie didn't seem to have recognized her, did he? He was far too convincingly bemused by Quick to be hiding the fact that he actually *knew* her. And yet, here was his family's address. None of it made sense.

I opened the letter quickly, knowing I didn't have much time. A thin slip of paper fell out from the fold and fluttered to the floor. I knelt to pick it up and read it, hunched in the semi-darkness, Quick's cat still watching. It was a telegram, and my eyes bulged on the words. "DARLING SCHLOSS STOP," it read: "VERY EXCITING PHOTOGRAPH STOP WE MUST BRING R TO PARIS-LONDON-NYC STOP LOVE PEG." It was dated: "PARIS – MALAGA 2nd JULY 1936."

I can see myself even now, kneeling like a sinner in Quick's hallway, skin tingling with the twitch of connecting threads, a knowledge just beyond my reach. Schloss. *Harold* Schloss? It was the dealer Reede had mentioned. What the hell was this telegram doing here, in Wimbledon, in Quick's telephone book? Quick was in her living room, steps away from me, but there could have been a thousand miles between us.

I sat back on my heels, hoping time would stand still in order for me to think. *Peg* could be Peggy Guggenheim, *R* could be Robles; the date fitted, and it was sent to Malaga, where Reede said Robles resided. If this was real – and it looked real – then this was a piece of correspondence Reede might kill for. And here it was, out of Quick's drawer and in my hands.

'Odelle?' she called, and I heard the note of panic in her voice. 'Are you summoning that taxi in Morse code?'

'The line's engaged. I'm just waiting,' I called back. I placed the telegram on the table and picked up the letter. The date was 27 December 1935. I inhaled the scent of the old, thin paper. There was something familiar about it; but I couldn't place it. It was addressed to a person called Miss Olive Schloss, at a flat in Curzon Street. It ran:

Further to your application to the Slade School of Fine Art, it is our pleasure to invite you to undertake the Fine Art degree course, commencing 14th September, next year.

The tutors were highly impressed by the rich imagination and novelty on display in your paintings and studies. We should be happy to have a pupil such as you, continuing the rigorous yet progressive tradition of the school –

'Odelle.' Quick was calling very sharply now.

'Coming,' I said. 'There's no answer.'

I began to refold the letter in haste, placing the telegram back inside it. I was on the point of reaching for the discarded telephone book, open on the Scott entry, when Quick came into the hall. I froze, the letter still in my hand. My face must have been a vision of guilt. The living-room light shone through the fabric of her blouse. She seemed so small, the outline of her ribcage far too narrow.

She looked at me – stared, actually – deep into my eyes. She reached out, took the letter and the telegram from my mesmerized grip, placed them in the telephone book and closed it. And then my realization came, and I saw in Quick's face a younger woman smiling, a woman in a photograph, a moment of happiness as she clutched a brush. *O and I. O*, a full circle. *O*, for Olive Schloss.

'You knew him,' I whispered. She closed her eyes. 'You knew Isaac Robles.'

The cat brushed against my legs. 'I'd murder a cigarette,' Quick said.

I pointed at the telephone book. 'Who's Olive Schloss?'

'Odelle, would you go and fetch me some cigarettes?'

'You were there, weren't you?'

'I've run out, Odelle, would you mind?' She fumbled inelegantly in her pocket, and thrust out a pound note.

'Quick—'

'Go,' she said. 'There's a shop just round the corner. *Go.*'

SO I LEFT, TO FETCH her cigarettes. Numb, I floated into Wimbledon Village to buy her a packet, and I floated back. And when I returned, the house was in complete darkness, the curtains drawn. The pamphlet I'd taken from the Scott house was on the step, weighted down with a stone. I put it back in my handbag and knocked and knocked, and called her name quietly through the letterbox.

'Quick. Quick, let me in,' I said. 'You said you trusted me. What's happened? Quick, who is Olive Schloss?'

There was only silence.

Eventually, I had to push the cigarettes through the door, and they landed lightly onto the mat on the other side. I pushed through her change also, as if I was throwing money down a wishing well that would never grant me any wish. Still there was no movement. I sat on the other side of that door for a good half an hour, my limbs going stiff. I waited for the sound of her footsteps, sure that Quick would give in to the craving of her nicotine and come for the cigarettes.

What was true, and what was I already beginning to concoct? It mattered greatly to me as to whether Quick had intended for me to find the clues in her telephone book, or whether it was a mistake. It seemed as if she had been deliberate about it – why else invite me here, and grill me about Lawrie, and the painting? Why else tell me to look up *T* for Taxi? Or perhaps it had been a genuine mistake, and I had stumbled across her secrets – and now my punishment was this silent, locked door.

Outside, I could hear car doors closing arrhythmically, and see the street lamps flickering to life. I didn't want a policeman to catch me sitting there, so I got up, and walked away to the village high street to wait for a bus.

Whatever the truth was, Quick was now fragmented to me. The illusion of her perfect wholeness and easy glamour had been shattered by tonight. Despite her confession about her ill health, I realized I knew so little about her. I wanted to put her back together, to return her to the pedestal on which I'd placed her, but our encounter tonight would make that impossible. Now, when I thought about Quick, I couldn't stop thinking about Olive Schloss.

My imagination was extravagant, and I believed that Olive Schloss was a ghost I might control. But had I turned back that night, and looked up at Quick's window, I would have seen a silhouette, orchestrating my retreat.

APRIL 1936

XII

omen in the Wheatfield did sell, and it was a woman who bought it. Harold had sent a telegram to the post office in Arazuelo three days after his departure to Paris, and Olive went to fetch it. The buyer was called Peggy Guggenheim, and according to Harold, she was a rich friend of Marcel Duchamp and was thinking of dabbling in the art market.

'So not a real collector,' said Isaac.

'Well, she's got the money,' Olive retorted.

Guggenheim purchased Isaac Robles's painting at a fairly high rate for an unknown; four hundred French francs. To Olive, the sale of the painting was glorious, hilarious: it made no sense, and yet it did. It was as if *Women in the Wheatfield* was a completely separate painting from *Santa Justa in the Well*, whilst remaining exactly the same thing. The image was identical, it just had a different title and had been made by a different artist. She was free of identity, yet what came from her was valued. She could create purely, and also bear witness to the muddier yet heady side; the selling of her art.

Having had her father unwittingly sell one of her paintings, Olive could admit to herself that part of her plan to attend the Slade had been solely to spite Harold, to show him what he had overlooked.

But the Guggenheim purchase had eclipsed this desire; it was both a grander personal validation, and a much more wonderful joke.

Soon after Harold's telegram arrived with the news, Teresa began to have a dream that was strange for someone who had always lived in such a dry part of the land. It was dusk, and she was on the veranda, and the body of the murdered boy, Adrián, was lying out in the orchard. She couldn't see much beyond the small lamps she'd laid out along the ground, only the eerie glow of his body. In his tatters of flesh, he began to rise up and move towards her – and yet Teresa couldn't, or wouldn't, flee, despite knowing that to stay would be her end.

Beyond the boy's body she sensed an ocean, wide and black and churning, and she noticed what he did not – that a huge wave was coming, a looming wall of water, ready to lay waste to his life for a second time, and to wash hers away with a biblical magnitude. She could almost taste the salt in the air. Olive was screaming somewhere, and Teresa called out to her, '*Tienes miedo?*' *Are you scared?* And Olive's voice came floating back over the trees: 'I'm not scared. I just don't like rats.'

Teresa would wake at this point, just as the wave took Adrián's body away. She'd had the dream three times, and it disturbed her not only because of the content, but because she never normally remembered her dreams, and this one was so easy to recall. Once, she would have told Isaac about it, in order to laugh with him at her imagination, but she didn't much feel like sharing with him these days.

Throughout the end of February and into March, Harold remained in Paris on business, and so the women were alone in the house. Teresa began to long for Harold to come back, if only to fill the place with noise, his heavy English, even his whispered German. Too much was happening elsewhere, out of Teresa's control. It felt as if she and Olive were orbiting each other, like opposing moons. Olive would go upstairs, claiming a migraine, or women's pains. Teresa hoped she would be painting, but often Olive was nowhere to be found, at hours that normally coincided with Isaac's return from his job in Malaga.

If Sarah wondered about her daughter's sudden ill-health, these domestic absences, she wasn't saying anything. But Teresa could sense a change in the other girl; how she had become more sure of herself since the sale of the painting. Olive was crackling with energy, and the effect was remarkable. The idea that she was suffering headaches was idiotic. Teresa would watch Olive, leaning up to inhale the burgeoning jacaranda, the honeysuckle, the roses come in an early spring, her finger gripping the stems so hard that Teresa worried they were going to snap. Olive, for her part, looked through Teresa as if she was a ghost.

As far as Teresa saw it, Olive was pouring herself away into Isaac. She wondered if Olive believed that she was drawing power from pretending to be him. Teresa wanted to shake her and say, *'Wake up, what are you doing?'* But it was Teresa, not Olive, who suffered the bad dreams and painful days. She began to regret ever swapping the painting. She'd made a gamble and failed, sacrificing the only friendship she'd ever had.

Teresa had never missed a person before. It revealed a dependency within herself which outraged her. Olive's diverted attention was a pulsing wound, a peculiar type of torture; the loneliness hard to quantify when the source of it was before her, walking up and down the staircase, or round the orchard, out of the front door and away. Teresa never knew when the next pang of it was going to hit. And when it did, it was as if the floor had fallen away and her heart sprang into her mouth, stoppering her breath – and there was no one to catch her as she stumbled to a hidden corner of the finca to cry. What had happened to her?

Alone in the cottage at night, Teresa would sit up in bed and move through the pages of the old *Vogue* like a child with a storybook, savouring each image and paragraph, underlining with her nail the words she didn't understand. She ran her finger down the side of the model's face, before lifting her pillow and slipping the magazine under, a perpetual love note to no one but herself.

SINCE THE SALE OF THE painting, Sarah was gloomy, too. She would lie on her bed, not speaking, watching the blue smoke of her husband's cigarettes disappear towards the ceiling. The telephone would ring and ring, and she would never answer it, and she wouldn't let Teresa pick it up either. Teresa thought it odd that Sarah would not lift the receiver, to see if it was her husband. She wondered then if Sarah knew full well it would be a different voice entirely; a woman's voice, whispering in timid German.

Teresa could now see Sarah's faultlines – the telephone left ringing, the champagne bottles empty by three in the afternoon, the uncracked spines of discarded books, the dark roots growing from her blonde head. She stopped dismissing them as a rich women's problems, and to her surprise, in her own pitiful state, began to feel pity. Life was a series of opportunities to survive, and in order to survive you had to lie, constantly – to each other, and to yourself. Harold had the motor car, the business, the contacts, the cities and spaces he inhabited, manifold and varied. Sarah, despite her obvious wealth, had just this one bedroom and her beauty, a rigid mask that was setting her into an existential rot.

'I WAS THE ONE WHO discovered him,' Sarah said to Teresa. It was a late night, and Olive was upstairs. They could hear her, pacing back and forth. Despite everything, Teresa longed to go up there, to knock and be admitted, to see what Olive was painting. Forcing herself to stay put, she picked another camisole from off the floor.

'*I* was the one who suggested Isaac painted for us in the first place,' Sarah went on. 'And I get no thanks. Harold as usual takes the reins, riding off into the sunset. I don't even get to keep the painting, because of course he has to go and sell it. He said,

"Why would we keep it here, where only the chickens will see it?"
Because it was a painting of *me*, for *him*, for Christ's sake.'

Outside, the cicadas had started to rasp in concert, so aggressively that it sounded as if the grass was vibrating. Teresa marvelled that Sarah had managed to see herself in the images of
Santa Justa in the Well. Couldn't they all see that Olive's painting
was of the same woman, repeated twice, once in her glory and
again in her despair? Perhaps, Teresa supposed, if you were determined to see yourself in a certain way, you would – however much
the evidence presented otherwise.

'It should have stayed with us,' Sarah said. 'It's wonderful for
your brother, of course, but it's the principle of the thing. It was
something he did for us. And Harold just hands it over to the highest bidder.'

'Did Isaac accept your money, señora?'

'No,' said Sarah. 'I did try. I hope he's happy with Peggy Guggenheim's, that's all I can say.'

Teresa knew that Isaac had travelled to Malaga to pick up
the money wired from Paris, and gone straight to the Workers'
General Union headquarters, donating two-thirds of it to pay for
agitating pamphlets, clothes, an emergency fund for those laid
off, and food. In some ways, you had to admire the efficacy of
Olive's plan, turning her painting into a political cause with her
father the unwitting middleman. Isaac had kept the last third of
the money, a fact which incensed Teresa. She'd told her brother to
give it back to Olive, but he'd said that Olive wanted him to have
it. 'I have to eat,' he'd said. '*We* have to eat. Or do you fancy eating
rats this year?'

Rats. Was that why she'd been dreaming about rats?

'Teresa, are you listening to me?'

'Yes, señora,' Teresa said, folding up the last of Sarah's cami-
soles and placing them in the wardrobe drawer.

'I was his inspiration.'

'I am sure he is very grateful.'

'Do you think so? Oh, Teresa. I wish something would *happen*. I'm really beginning to miss London.'

Teresa plunged her hands into Sarah's drawer of satins and gripped her fists out of her mistress's sight. *Then go, and take me with you*, she screamed silently, even though she knew this was an impossibility. For all the pity she showed Sarah Schloss, the woman would never do such a thing in return.

XIII

*H*er father's absence made it easier for Olive to see Isaac, and they met several times a week, usually in the cottage when Teresa was in the finca working and Sarah was taking her afternoon rest. For days afterwards, Olive could almost physically summon the memory of their meetings, how it felt when Isaac entered her – the indescribable sensation of making space for him as he pushed deeper, and what she believed was his utter bliss, mirrored by that of hers.

And yet, she never felt sated. Her appetite was unstoppable, a revelation; and she felt so happy that here was something she could summon whenever she wanted, but which never ran out. She felt that he improved her, he made her the woman she was meant to be. And afterwards, at night, she would lock herself in her attic, and paint. She was growing ever more confident, and saw Isaac as her key. This was not something Teresa would ever be able to understand – Isaac as essential to her development as an artist. Olive couldn't bear to look at Teresa's mournful face, her little scowl. It was an energy the opposite of him.

The olive trees, lined in serried swoops on the hillsides, were greening. Along the road, oranges were coming into fruit, and Olive scratched her nails on the hard skin, and made a scar on the early citrus. It was fresh, it was perfect, the world was fresh and perfect.

What next to paint? What next to do? Everything was possible. She was now the Olive Schloss she was always supposed to be.

When she reached the cottage, Isaac was reading a letter by the wood burner in the kitchen. She walked towards him to give him a kiss, but Isaac held the letter out and stopped her path.

'What is it? What's wrong?'

'This is from Miss Peggy Guggenheim. Read it for yourself.'

Disconcerted, Olive took the letter, sat at the table, and read.

> Dear Mr Robles,
>
>   Harold Schloss gave me your address. Forgive my forwardness, but I do believe that in these matters, honesty of expression is invaluable. I hope that you, as an artist relatively new to these transactions, would agree. For I have no wish to be a faceless 'purchaser' – your work has enlivened my wall, and I am enthralled.

Olive looked up at Isaac, her mind racing. 'Oh, Isaac. How wonderful—'

'Read on,' he said.

> When Schloss said he had something special to show me, I was dubious. Art dealers say this a lot to me, and I am quickly learning to develop a "sang froid" when it comes to such declarations. But Schloss was adamant; even coming to Paris specifically to show it to me. He said you were from the land of the Moors and the endless starlit skies, of Arabic palaces and Catholic forts, where blood is in the soil and the sun beats the sierra. Your dealer may sound a theatrical Viennese, Mr Robles, but I have come to entirely trust his opinion.
>
>   I am so delighted I agreed to meet. The enriching effects of your painting change by the day for me. My friends, who know better than me, call it a chimaera, a chameleon, an aesthetic pleasure and a metaphysical

joy. I would rather say that *Women in the Wheatfield*
is not an easy painting to categorize, and that this
is a good thing. Whilst I admire your figurative
stubbornness in a time of abstract shapes, this is not
to say I think you are part of a reactionary, regressive
force – far from it. You are up to something new.

The colors – where to start with your colors? I joked
to Herr Schloss, "perhaps if we cut Mr Robles open,
we will find a rainbow hiding inside?" But guard your
hands, Mr Robles – I know we will only find out this
rainbow through the process of more paintings.

The overall spirit of *Wheatfield* to me feels mythical
and unbridled. Yet there is something fastidious in
your animals, as if their lines have been rendered by
a Renaissance master with a realist's touch – and the
fact you have painted oil onto wood compounds this
sense of tradition. It is both dream and nightmare,
irreligious yet striving for some faith. Yet the colors of
the women – their expressions, the sweep of the sky –
they seem derived from a somewhat more modern
soul.

This is just what I take from it, of course. You must
do as other great artists do, and ignore all "opinion".
Anyway, Mr Robles: I love it; take or discard that as
you will.

Schloss probably told you that I am planning to
establish a gallery in London next year, and I have
your painting intended for the opening exhibition. I
do not know if I shall be able to part with it for public
consumption – I do not want to share it and for now, it
hangs on my bedroom wall. There is a call to intimacy
within it, a personal struggle and defiance that seems
so essentially human – dare I say, so essentially *female*
– which has come to beat inside me like an extra heart.

But I want to be a good collector, you see – and good

collectors always share. I would love for you to see it on
the public wall.

I will never make an artist explain himself to me,
unless he himself chooses to do so – so I ask here no
questions of impulses, process, your wishes for what
may come. But here is my one request. Schloss has
assured me that there will be opportunities to see more
work, and all I ask is that you consider me a supporter.
To wit: when it comes to showing you to the wider
world, I would love to be your first port of call. The first
of anything is so often the most indefatigable.

Yours, in admiration,

Peggy Guggenheim

Olive started to laugh, giddy laughter – the laughter of someone whose lottery ticket has just come through; her winner's mind
already racing over the transformations of her life to come. 'Oh,
Isaac,' she said. 'You've made a new friend. She *loves* it.'

'She is not my friend.'

'Come on, Isa. There's nothing to worry about.'

He went very still. 'Is it true that your father has told her I have
more paintings?'

Olive placed the letter slowly on the table. 'I don't know. That's
the honest truth. But it's inevitable he would – he's a dealer. It's
half his job. He got Guggenheim – hook, line and sinker – and he
wasn't going to let her go again without a little bait.'

He ran a hand over his face. 'Did you know this would happen,
Olive?'

'No.'

'Did you *suppose* it would happen?'

'I didn't think about it.'

'You didn't think about it.'

'I – just knew I couldn't tell my father that it was mine.'

'But why not?' He pressed his finger on the letter and she

watched the skin turn white. 'Would it not be easier than all this?'

'Teresa put me on the spot. She interfered—'

'Mr Robles does not have any more paintings,' Isaac said, folding his arms. 'That was the one painting he had. And now it's sold. And now there are no more.'

'Yes, but—'

'So I am going to tell your father, the *dealer*, that I do not have time to paint. My work in Malaga does not give me the time for it.'

'Peggy Guggenheim bought you, Isaac. Her uncle—'

He made a sound of disgust. 'Listen to yourself. Peggy bought *you*.'

'Peggy bought *us*. Don't you see? We're together in this. Your name, your face: my work.'

'Olive. This is very serious. There is no balance.'

'Just one more painting. One more.'

'I have not enjoyed this. I said yes, like a fool. I was tired, I was stupid. And now you are like a drunk, searching for the hidden bottle.'

'Blame your sister, not me. I never wanted this situation, but here it is.'

'You could have stopped it. You didn't want to.'

'Did you give the money to the workers?'

'I did.'

'And didn't that feel like you were doing something? Aren't we all supposed to make sacrifices – isn't that half your credo that you've been telling me since the day we met?'

'And what sacrifice are you making, Olive? As far as I can see, for you this is a big joke.'

'It's not a joke,' Olive snapped, pushing her chair back and facing him square-on.

'You have been behaving as if it is.'

'Why do you and your sister think I'm so stupid? Do you know how many artists my father sells? Twenty-six, last time I counted. Do you know how many of them are women, Isaac? None. Not one. Women can't *do* it, you see. They haven't got the *vision*, although last time I checked they had eyes, and hands, and hearts and souls. I'd have lost before I'd even had a chance.'

'But you *made* that painting—'

'So what? My father would never have got on a plane to Paris with a painting he thought was mine. I've lived with that realization for years, Isaac. Years and years, before you and I met. When I came down here, I didn't know what I was going to do with my life; I was lost. And then I met you. And then your sister – your interfering little sister, who perhaps did me the greatest favour anyone's ever done, even though the truth of it is killing her – came along and changed everything. And I like it, Isaac, and I don't want it to stop. One day I might tell him – just to see the look on his face. Maybe that will be a joke. But not now. It's too late.'

'Too late – for what? And please do not say it is because you want to carry on helping the Spanish working man. I do not think I can tolerate it.'

'You were happy enough to take my money.'

'Peggy Guggenheim's money—'

'Which was probably double your annual salary. Do you think I truly don't care about what's happening down here?'

'You may care. But it is superficial. You do not understand it at the heart.'

'But *I'm* the one who can actually pump proper money into it, not you. And who says you're the expert?' She threw up her hands. 'All right, Isaac, I'll tell you why I want to carry on – it *is* for me. But I can help some people along the way, at least. I want my paintings to be so valuable and so important that no one can pull them off the market and hide them away because – heaven forfend – they were painted by a *woman*. And it's not just that. I've seen what success does to people, Isaac – how it separates them from their creative impulse, how it paralyses them. They can't make anything that isn't a horrible replica of what came before, because everybody has opinions on who they are and how they should be.'

'I am glad you are being honest. But it would still have been the same painting if your name was on it,' Isaac said. 'You could have changed things.'

'Oh, God, I could wring your neck. You're so naive – it wouldn't have worked out the same way at all. There'd be no flirty letter from Peggy Guggenheim, no exhibition in her new gallery on the basis of one painting, nothing like it. And it would take all my energy "changing things" as you put it, with none left over to paint – which is the whole bloody point of everything. The energy a man might use on – oh, I don't know, making good work – you want me to use on "changing things". You don't understand, because you've lived your life as an individual, Isaac. And yet everything you do as a man is universal. So enjoy the glory, enjoy the money, and do it for me, because I certainly wouldn't have been allowed.'

'A cheque from Peggy Guggenheim isn't going to change the political situation round here,' he said. 'You are the naive one.'

'Well I'd rather be naive than boring. What's wrong with the pair of you? I've given you this! You and Teresa are as bad as each other.'

'My sister is angry with me,' he said. 'She's right.'

'Well she's angry with me too. We're hardly friends. It's a mess. But let's face it, when is Teresa not angry?'

This was a brief moment of unity, of levity, as they thought of Teresa and her scowling, her defiance, her sense of what was right, and her unorthodox ways of going about it. 'I don't think she considered any of this when she put my painting on the easel,' Olive said. 'She doesn't know me at all.'

Isaac leant back in his chair and exhaled the moment of truce. 'No. It did not go according to her plan. But she still idolizes you. And I think she knows you better than you know yourself.'

'What's that supposed to mean?'

'That maybe, Olive, you didn't want your painting to be so secret after all.'

She stared at him. *What?*

'You let her into your bedroom. You showed her your paintings.

Did you never wonder that my sister might skip ahead of you a few steps?'

'I showed her my paintings as a *friend*.'

'Teresa did not do this to you maliciously. Stop pretending that she has done you a harm.'

Olive slumped onto the table. 'If you're so worried about your sister's feelings you should never have touched me in the first place. That's what's really bothering her. I don't know why.'

'Olive, you came to me – you wanted . . . All right. How about we stop this, now?'

Olive lifted her head. 'What do you want to stop?'

'This . . . *lie*. I feel I am deceiving your father—'

'It doesn't matter about him. He's happy. He's delighted. He's sold a piece of art and he's cultivating the reputation of a very promising artist—'

'Who doesn't exist.'

'But the Isaac Robles we created – *he* exists.'

'We are going round in circles.'

'Just one more painting. *One* more.'

'You are so bossy, Olive. So careless with other people's feelings.'

'Am I? What about you? You didn't even want to kiss me when I turned up.' They faced each other in silence. 'Please, Isa. I know it's a lot. But I've got a painting called *The Orchard*. We could give Peggy Guggenheim that.'

'The more we play, the more dangerous this gets.'

'Nothing bad is going to happen.' Olive knelt down by Isaac's side, her fists locked together in supplication, resting on his knee. 'No one will ever know. Please, Isa. *Please*.'

He ran his hands nervously over his head. 'What if Peggy Guggenheim wants to meet me?'

'She's not going to want to come down here.'

'What if she invites me to Paris? She has already mentioned London.'

'Then say no. Play the elusive artist.'

Isaac narrowed his eyes. 'Now is not the time for English irony.'

'No, I mean it. Isaac, *please.*'

'What will you do for me?'

'Anything you want.'

Isaac closed his eyes and drew his hand down his face, as if he was washing away his thoughts. He lifted her from the floor and rose from the table, leading her across the kitchen towards his bedroom door. 'One painting, Olive,' he said. 'And then – no more.'

XIV

saac demanded to see *The Orchard* before it was shipped to Harold's office in Paris, 'so at least I know what I am putting my name to.' Teresa suggested that perhaps Sarah should view it too, because it would be useful for her to see Isaac with *The Orchard*. This would reinforce the general belief that the painting was his, should Sarah ever mention seeing it to her husband.

Olive was surprised at Teresa's suggestion. 'I suppose it's a good idea,' she said to her. 'But I thought you didn't want anything to do with this?'

Teresa merely shrugged.

'OH, IT'S WONDERFUL,' SAID SARAH, standing in front of the painting that afternoon in the front east room. Olive scuttled away from it – rather like a crab, it seemed to Teresa – running from a great wave, unable to put her head out of her shell. Her confident attitude had evaporated, and she sat herself in her father's armchair to watch her mother. Teresa took in the vision of Sarah's red woollen trousers, the deep blood shade against her creamy skin; Sarah had clearly rallied herself. 'It's so like *our* orchard,' she said. 'But . . . different.'

'Thank you, señora,' said Isaac, in visible discomfort.

'Isn't it good, Liv?'

'Yes,' said Olive, unable to meet Isaac's eye.

Sarah insisted that Teresa fetch Isaac tea and *polvorones*. 'We're so glad to have Teresa,' she said. 'It would all be such a palaver without her. And I'm so proud of finding you, Mr Robles,' she said to him, leaning against the back of the sofa where he was sitting. She was warm, conciliatory. 'How does it feel, to be the toast of Paris?' she asked.

'What is *toast*?'

'It means you're everyone's new favourite. He'll be champing at the bit when he sees this.' She waved her hand in the direction of *The Orchard*. 'Honestly, Mr Robles, I'm so glad I commissioned you in the first place, although it's hard to share you. It's just a shame my painting is hanging on another woman's wall.'

'Yes,' he said.

'Well,' she sighed, and it sounded like twenty words in one. 'My husband will be home soon.' The marital noun made it sound as if Isaac would have no idea who Harold was.

'It will be good to see him,' said Isaac.

Sarah smiled and left the room, and Teresa felt as if the wattage of the day had dimmed as they listened to her moving back up the main staircase. Olive stepped quickly to the door and shut it. 'Well, Isa?' she asked, whirling round. 'Do you like it?'

They all stared at the painting, the undulating patchwork of fields, the surreal intensity of colour, the white house which once was his to roam and now the home of someone else. 'Does it matter whether I like it?' he asked.

Olive looked uncomfortable. 'You don't like it.'

'I can see its merit, but it is not what I myself would paint,' he said.

'He does not like it,' said Teresa.

'It is not that simple,' Isaac snapped.

Olive stood before the painting. 'I think it is that simple, really. What don't you like about it?'

'My God!' he cried. 'Why do I have to *like* it? Is it not bad enough I am pretending I have made it?'

'Do keep your voice down,' she said.

'You have even painted my initials.'

'A necessary touch.'

He stood up. 'I hate it,' he said. 'I hope your father does too.'

'Isaac—'

'Good day, señoritas.'

Olive looked as if he had slapped her in the face. When he left the room, Olive ran to the window, watching his figure disappearing down the slope to the rusting gates. He pushed them open roughly, not looking back once.

'Do not be upset,' said Teresa, stepping forward. 'What does it matter if he doesn't like it?'

Olive made a sound of frustration. 'He can hate what I create, but I can't *create* if he's angry with me. I just can't.'

'But why not? You painted before you knew him.'

Olive gestured at *The Orchard.* 'Not like this, not like this!' She pressed her forehead against the peeling wooden shutter. 'And if he doesn't like it, how can we be sure he'll ship it to my father? It has to go soon. We'll lose momentum with the Guggenheim woman.'

'I am sure she will wait for genius.'

Olive wrinkled her nose. 'That's a word that gets bandied about too much. I'm not a genius. I just work hard.'

'Well, she will wait. And if my brother will not do it, I can take it to the port myself.'

'You?'

'You can trust me.'

Olive kept her face hidden, still leaning her forehead on the shutter. 'You broke my trust when you put that painting on the easel. I never know if you're my friend or not.'

Teresa was silent for a moment. She couldn't hide her pain. Sometimes Olive was as coquettish as her mother, for all her determination to be different. 'You cannot see? You can trust me with your life.'

Olive lifted her head. 'Never mind about my life, Tere. Do you mean it about the painting? You'll take it to the port?'

'Yes.'

Olive peered down the slope towards the gate, through which Isaac had long disappeared. 'I've never had a true friend.'

'Neither have I.'

'Have you ever been in love? Have you ever been with a man?'

'I have not.'

'Been with a man – or been in love?'

'Been with a man.'

Olive turned to her. 'But you've been in love.'

Teresa felt her cheeks flame. 'No. I do not think so. I do not know.'

THAT NIGHT, TERESA DID NOT go back to the cottage. She was permitted to install herself in the corner of Olive's attic, sorting the artist's brushes and her clothes, a heady bliss that followed truce. Olive revealed that she had been painting a portrait of Isaac. It had been a long time coming, Teresa thought – given the speed with which the girl could usually work, the sketchbooks overflowing with the pencilled planes of his face.

Glancing over at Olive by the easel, Isaac's features developing on the wood before her, Teresa could see it was an astonishing beginning. He had greenish skin, and a consumptive, claustrophobic look in his eye. But his head seemed on fire, sweeps of dandelion and canary yellows up to the top of the painting, where red flecks were being spattered like the wake of murderous thoughts. It was a livid rendering, and Olive looked to be as if in a trance. Teresa knew that the balance between her brother and this girl wasn't right, but she doubted Olive was aware of these layers of infatuation and fear, manifesting by her very own hand.

OLIVE FINISHED HER FIRST GO at Isaac in the small hours. At three in the morning, exhausted, she lay back on her mattress, staring at the roof beams and flaking ceiling plaster, its rough, raised corners illuminated by the weak glow from her bedside candle. A wolf howled, distant in the mountains.

'Come and sleep here,' she said to Teresa. Teresa, who'd been reading one of Olive's books in the corner, put it down and obeyed, climbing onto the old mattress, lying rigidly next to Olive under the dusky pink coverlet, unable to move for fear that to do so might expel her from this magic kingdom.

They lay side by side, staring at the ceiling together as the atmosphere lightened in the room, the energy of Olive's work and concentration dissipating into the air, until all that was left was the glowing green face of Isaac on the easel. Beyond the window, into the land, no rooster or dog or human cry broke their silence as they fell asleep, fully clothed.

Two days later, Olive decided to go with Teresa to Malaga, 'to make a day of it,' she said, 'and why not?'

'But how long are you going to be?' asked Sarah. Teresa supposed she was agitated, because for the first time in months she was going to be alone.

'We're going to the shipping office for Mr Robles, and then I thought we'd have a lemonade in Calle Larios,' said Olive.

'Well, make sure you get that farmer fellow to bring you back before nightfall.'

'I promise.'

'He isn't a red, is he?'

'*Mother.*'

The Orchard was a large painting, and it took both girls to carry it down the finca path, as if it was a stretcher missing a body. Teresa looked back up at the house and saw Sarah watching, staying at the window right until they were down in the valley and she disappeared from their sight. The mule man was waiting for them in the town square. Teresa tried to ignore the uneasy feeling in her gut when she imagined Sarah on her own. She couldn't pinpoint the worry, so she focused instead on the pleasure of a day trip. She was in her best blue dress; she'd washed her hair and doused herself with the distilled orange blossom Rosa Morales, the doctor's daughter, sold out of her kitchen. It could almost be *feria* time, for the sense of holiday Teresa felt.

As she sat with the wrapped parcel of *The Orchard* propped beside her, on the back of a mule cart thirty kilometres along the Malaga road, Teresa was surprised at how bulky the package was under the string and paper. She did not question it, simply because she was now deliciously in Olive's good books again. She would do as she was bid. Olive's hair was flying in the wind, and her white-framed sunglasses made her as glamorous as her mother. Why would you want to ruin such a blue-sky day?

The mule pulled along the white-dust road, and Olive pointed out more red ribbons that had been tied around the girths of the cork oaks. The vision was vaguely unsettling, like shining lines of blood fluttering in the breeze. 'What are they?' she asked in Spanish.

The mule driver turned over his shoulder and said, 'They're trouble.'

Teresa saw them as an omen for what violence might come to this land, as it had so many times in centuries before. No one ever saw who tied these ribbons – Adrián had been one of them, apparently – but the fact that there were people determined to adorn the trees suggested an undercurrent of defiance, a desire to turn things on their head. Teresa didn't want anything turned on its head. She had only just managed to achieve this day.

Full of self-importance and happiness, they reached the shipping office and arranged with the mule man when and where he should come back to fetch them. They made the post office just before it closed for siesta, sending off the parcel for today's shipment to France. *The Orchard* was off to the Galerie Schloss on Paris's Rue de la Paix.

Afterwards, they walked the wide boulevards, admiring the wrought-iron lamp-posts adorned with hanging baskets, trailing petunias and geraniums in hot pinks and scarlets. They looked through shop windows, pointing out to each other the best-dressed of Malaga's high society. They went inwards to the narrower, cobbled streets, all shutters closed against the midday heat. It was metropolitan, so different to their rural hideaway on the slopes of Arazuelo. Teresa was pleased to see how impressed Olive was with her native city. It might not be London, but it was by turns stately and timeless, as the sun beat down on the stone, or reflected off the polished vitrines and ornate wooden frames of department stores and pharmacists.

They walked down to the harbour and sat to enjoy a lemonade, wondering which of the enormous ships that pulled in and out with such constant frequency would be taking away their duplicitous cargo.

'Isaac knew the painting would go,' Olive said. 'He just didn't want to be the one who sent it. Do you think I'm being fair to him?'

'What you mean to ask is – will my brother carry on doing this for ever.'

Olive looked at her in surprise. 'Yes, I suppose I do.'

Teresa gazed out to sea. 'The money will never be a good reason for him.'

She was telling the truth; it had never been enough for either of them. Even though he had kept some aside from the sale of *Women in the Wheatfield*, they had both always wanted things that money couldn't buy; legitimacy, love. Teresa did think that Olive was being thoughtless, that her use of Isaac's name as a front for her own work was not something he would continue to tolerate. As for herself, as long as Olive wanted it, she was happy to oblige.

Olive frowned. 'That sounded like a threat.'

'No, no,' said Teresa. 'But – he is a man, you know.'

'What do you mean?'

Teresa couldn't answer with the precision she wanted in English. And although she worried that Olive's actions were bringing her closer to some undefined, simmering danger that was coming, which Teresa couldn't name but could almost taste – she was so happy to be here, by the sea, the lemonade, that she didn't want Olive's thoughtlessness to stop.

'My brother can speak for himself,' she said obliquely, and Olive, not wishing to go any deeper into the sourer elements of this plot of theirs, turned away to look at the gigantic liners moving out to sea.

THEY RETURNED TO THE FINCA at dusk, tired and happy. 'Teresa,' Olive said, as they reached the front door.

'Yes?'

'I won't let anything happen to you. You can trust me, I promise.'

Teresa smiled, amazed to hear her own words being spoken back to her, the second half of the same spell. When they went inside, Sarah was nowhere to be seen.

'Where is she?' said Olive, and the panic in her voice was so childlike, so easily accessed.

'She has probably gone out for a walk,' Teresa said.

'My mother doesn't go for walks.' Olive ran out into the orchard, and on the pretext of searching for Sarah in the upper rooms, Teresa took the opportunity to slip into the attic and confirm her suspicions. It was as she thought. The green-faced portrait of Isaac was nowhere to be seen. By now, it was deep in the bowels of a liner, on its way to Peggy Guggenheim.

XV

Sarah began frequent walks out of the finca estate, an unprecedented gesture for someone usually more inclined to smoke on a sofa. She began to pull the ready vegetation from the rented land, piling it up in a wide wicker basket, the earth-encrusted roots still attached. She would announce her trip to the village to buy artichokes, and soon there was a molehill of them in the kitchen. The vases of wildflowers had multiplied so considerably that Teresa was running out of receptacles.

Ten days after their trip to Malaga, a telegram from Harold arrived. Teresa went down to pick it up, and ran all the way back to the finca, handing it to Olive, who was shelling peas with her mother at the kitchen table.

'GREEN FACE GENIUS GOES TO GUG STOP ALSO BOUGHT MAGNIFICENT ORCHARD STOP BACK END OF WEEK STOP,' Olive read aloud. 'Peggy Guggenheim bought them both,' she breathed. 'Isaac will be pleased.'

'I wasn't aware there were two,' said Sarah, one fingernail flashing down an open seed-pod. The lacquer, Teresa noted, had chipped, and her mistress had done nothing to remedy it.

'There was *The Orchard*, but Isaac had another painting. A self-portrait.'

'You saw it?' asked Sarah.

'Briefly. It looks like Daddy's coming back.'

'Just when that telephone finally stopped ringing,' Sarah sighed.

Teresa went to the sink to busy herself with the washing up. Sarah laid down her empty pea pod. 'Darling,' she said. 'Do you like it here?'

'I've got used to it. I like it very much now. Don't you?'

Sarah looked through the kitchen window. The garden and the orchard beyond it were now abundant with fruit and flowers, honeysuckle, *dama-de-noche* and all the oranges and olives Harold had promised his wife and daughter back in January, when, cold, bedraggled and shaking off the after-effects of one of Sarah's storm clouds, they had arrived here, knowing no one.

'I don't know if *like* is the word I'd use. I feel I've lived here about ten years. It sort of . . . saturates you, a place like this. As if it's the living embodiment of Isaac's painted fields.' She turned to her daughter. 'It's extraordinary – how he captured it, isn't it?'

'Yes.'

'How do you think he does it?'

'How would I know?'

'He's a genius.'

Olive sighed. 'Nobody's a genius, Mother. That's lazy thinking. It's practice.'

'Ah, practice. I could practise for ever and not produce anything as good as that.'

'You seem better, Mummy,' said Olive.

'I do feel a lot stronger. Daddy got me that last round of pills from Malaga and I haven't touched them.'

'Really? Is that a good idea? You gave me and Tere a real fright when we got back from Malaga and you weren't here. I was worried you'd—'

'I wouldn't do that, Livvi. It's not like it was.'

They continued shelling peas in silence. Her mother had caught the sun, and she seemed peaceful; self-contained. It was once again painful to Olive how attractive her mother was, and how Sarah barely registered this fact – her hair a bit of a mess, her sundress crumpled as if she'd just pulled it out of a trunk. Her roots had now grown out considerably, and she didn't seem to care. Her natural dark blonde was a stark, yet oddly pleasurable visual contrast to the peroxide ends. Olive had the itch to paint her, to capture this ease, in the hope that she too could have some of it for herself.

'Summer's nearly here,' Sarah said, breaking Olive's thoughts. 'It's going to be so hot.'

'You were complaining when it was cold.'

Sarah laughed at herself. This too, was rare. 'It wasn't a terrible idea of your father's to come here. Not a terrible idea at all.' She reached over and squeezed her daughter's hand. 'I do love you, you know, Liv. Very much.'

'Goodness. What's wrong with you?'

'Nothing. Nothing. I just think you should know.'

SARAH WENT OUT ONTO THE veranda with her packet of cigarettes and the latest Christie shipped over from a friend in London, and Teresa began to mop the flagstones in the hall. Olive followed her, standing on the dry patch Teresa hadn't yet reached.

'Teresa, will you sit for my next painting?' she asked, her voice quiet. 'I'd love to use you as a model.'

Teresa's spine stiffened, her fists tightening round the mop handle. 'You didn't tell me about the second painting we took to Malaga,' she said.

'I didn't want to get you into any more trouble.'

'Trouble?'

'Look, I know you think this whole undertaking demeans me as an artist.'

'*Demeans*?'

'Makes less of me. You think Isaac gets more importance round here than he deserves. But it's what I want. I want the freedom. You're my friend, Tere. Let me give this to you.'

Teresa straightened, meditatively plunging the head of the mop into her bucket of filthy water. She knew, in a way, that she had wanted this moment ever since she saw Isaac in the sketchbook. And the decision to help Olive in her deceptions – taking the paintings into Malaga, making sure Sarah still believed they were by Isaac, keeping the attic clean – had all been leading to this less than noble truth; that Teresa wanted to be painted. She wanted Olive to want her as a painting.

As Teresa walked behind Olive upwards to the attic, she knew she had departed from her place in the script. She turned back once to view the floor, half-agleam, the mop resting, accusatory. She was no longer the servant who rid the house of stains; she was going to make a mark so permanent no one would ever forget it.

IT WAS TO BE A painting of Rufina, Olive told her, locking the attic door. 'I've done Justa in the Well, and you'll be my Rufina. It was you who told me the story, after all. I've been wondering what part of it to tell.'

Teresa nodded, not daring to speak. What would Isaac say, when he found out Olive had painted his face green and sent it as a self-portrait to Peggy Guggenheim? When would he realize that painting after painting would come out of this girl? Olive believed Isaac was the source of her inspiration, but Teresa thought that nothing he could do now – no tantrum, no withholding of affection – would stop the flow.

'Rufina with her pots, Rufina with the lion, or Rufina, beheaded, with her sister?' said Olive, mainly to herself. 'The last one's grim, but it is the apogee, even though she's down a well.'

Teresa heard the unusual word, and thought Olive had said *apology*. 'There is nothing to be sorry for,' she said.

Olive smiled. 'I'm glad you think so, Tere.'

She had decided to abandon the diptych format that she'd used for *Women in the Wheatfield*, and paint just one scene. In the end, she wanted all the stages of the story involved. So Rufina would be there in her full body, but she would also be carrying her own head.

'You could put your face in it, too,' said Teresa, then immediately wished she hadn't, for she was probably overstepping herself.

Olive bit her lip, considering the idea. 'Well, let's paint yours first,' she said. 'I'll decide later whether to add mine. It is supposed to be one person, after all. But I'm definitely going to lay gold leaf on the lion's mane. He'll be tame as a pussycat.'

Olive placed her on the chair she usually sat in when Teresa brushed her hair. There was a surety to Olive's touch, she was operating in her space of confidence and possibility. 'Such solemn eyes,' Olive told her, as she put her paintbrush to the treated panel. 'So dark and watchful above your little snub nose. You and Isaac have become as engraved in my mind as a woodcut.'

Her expression grew distracted as she began to draw away from the outer elements of the room and closer to her artistic vision. Teresa was locked out of it, and yet she felt the source of it. She willingly sank into this phantom role, where she could disappear and be anything Olive wanted. She had never felt so invisible, and yet so seen.

XVI

In the end, Harold returned the first week of June, driving himself back from Malaga airfield. 'Where is he?' he called, as soon as he'd parked up the Packard. 'Where's my prodigy?'

The women stood on the front step, shielding their eyes from the sun. Harold's wave was breezy. *He's been with her*, Teresa thought, surveying him as he neared the front door. He looked sated, well fed, and yet his grin was a little fixed. He seemed to have the air of a man rolling away from vice and back into the straits of virtue. *Maybe he sent her a ticket to Paris.* The anonymous woman's timid German, which had grown fainter in Teresa's memory, now returned. *Harold, bist du es?*

Teresa glanced over to Sarah. She had a self-contained look, as if she was conserving her energies, girding herself. *Does she know?* Teresa thought. *She knows.*

'Hallo, darling,' Sarah said. 'Isaac doesn't live here, you know.'

Harold stalked forward, depositing two kisses either side of his wife's face. 'It's Isaac now, is it?' He turned to Olive. 'You look well, Liv. In fact, you look glorious.'

Olive smiled. 'Thank you, Papi. So do you.'

Teresa cast down her eyes, hoping Harold wouldn't see her thoughts. '*Buenos días*, Teresa,' he said. She looked; the journey had left him with a day's stubble. She discerned the smell of travel, the possibility of someone else's perfume mingled on his skin.

'*Buenos días, señor.*'

'Fetch my suitcase, will you.'

She descended the step, feeling folded inside the Schlosses' life with such cloying intensity that she could hardly breathe.

THAT NIGHT, TERESA WAITED FOR Isaac outside their cottage, as the shadows lengthened and the cicadas began to build their rasping wall of sound. He appeared at the base of the hill at about seven o'clock, and she was struck by how tired he looked, burdened down by an invisible weight as he moved towards her.

'He's back,' she said, by way of greeting.

Isaac dropped his knapsack on the grass, where it clunked.

'What's in there?' she asked.

'You'll see.' He sank to the earth and lay on his back, his hands enlaced beneath his head.

'There's something you should know,' she said, irritated by this evasion. 'Olive didn't tell you, but she sent an extra painting to Paris. Don't be angry. He's sold it. I wanted to tell you before Harold did.' Isaac remained prostrate, and he nodded, patting his jacket pocket, pulling out a box of battered cigarettes. 'Are you angry, Isa?'

'No.'

'I thought you would be. Why aren't you?'

'Do you want me to be angry? What's the point? She's done it. And it doesn't surprise me.'

'More money for the cause, I suppose.'

'Always that.'

'Isa. I know what's going on.'

He looked up at her, sharply. 'What do you mean?'

'I know what you two do. Apart from the painting stuff. That she's in love with you.'

A look of relief passed across his face as he lit a cigarette. 'Olive,' he said.

'Are you in love with her?'

Isaac sat up and dragged on his cigarette, hunching his knees as he looked down over the sierra. It was dusk by now, and the bats had started to appear out of the copses at the foot of the valley. The air was warm, the earth still giving off its heat. 'They'll leave,' he said. 'They won't last here. They belong in the city. In the salon.'

'Sarah, yes. Harold, maybe. Not Olive.'

'She's turned you into a romantic.'

'The opposite. I understand her, that's all. She won't leave you. She'll follow wherever you go.'

'What makes you so sure of that?'

'She says she can't paint without you.'

He laughed. 'True in one way, perhaps. Well, if she does love me, that doesn't make any of this all right.'

'I don't think she needs you at all.'

'And that doesn't surprise me either, Teresa.'

PARIS HAD BEEN A TRIUMPH, Harold said; Isaac Robles was now the pole star in the firmament of Galerie Schloss Paris. The next afternoon, Harold, legs stretched out in the front east room, drinking a glass of fino, told them in no uncertain terms that thanks to *Women in the Wheatfield*, *The Orchard*, and *Self-Portrait in Green*, he and his partners were enjoying a renaissance.

'People heard through Duchamp that Peggy wants to buy art,' he said. 'But I got there first. She's incredibly excited about the next one, your companion piece to *Women in the Wheatfield*. She wants a photograph of it in progress, though, if that's possible. Is it possible, Isaac?'

Olive slugged back another fingerful of sherry. 'The "companion piece"?' said Isaac.

'Am I rushing you?' said Harold. 'Tell me if so. We don't have to send her a photograph if you don't want that. It's what's best for you. You have a great gift, Isa. Truly. I cannot wait to see your future.'

'It will not be what any of us expects,' Isaac replied. 'Mr Schloss, I have brought something for you.'

Olive put the sherry glass down and began to rise from her chair, but Isaac reached into his knapsack and withdrew a pistol, the barrel made of shining steel. No one spoke as he weighed it in the flat of his hand.

'Is that real?' Sarah asked.

'Real, señora.'

'Why on earth have you brought us a gun?' said Harold, laughing. 'Bring me a painting, for Christ's sake.'

Olive sat back, the relief visible on her face. 'Do you shoot, señor?' Isaac said.

'I can. I have.'

'Can the women shoot?'

'Of course we can't,' said Sarah. 'Why do you ask? This is terribly dramatic.'

ISAAC HUNG AN OLD FLOUR sack, packed with earth, upon a protruding branch of a cork oak at the end of the garden. One word covered the rough sacking, H A R I N A, and they agreed that the makeshift bullseye was the space between the 'R' and the 'I'. They all trooped past the empty stone fountain and lined up to have a go, and there was almost a carnival atmosphere to their endeavour; the silly swinging sack, the birds scattering out of the oak at the crack of Isaac's pistol.

Harold hit the last *A*. Sarah shot into the bark and handed the pistol back to Isaac, saying she would never touch it again. She went to lie on her back in the grass, staring at the sky, her hands resting on her stomach. Isaac shot the middle of the *N*, and looked sheepish. He handed the pistol to Olive, and Teresa watched the intertwining of their hands.

Olive lumbered over to the shooting spot and raised the pistol. She squinted, and pulled on the trigger, releasing the bullet with a gasped shock as the pistol recoiled in her hand.

'Liv,' cried her father.

'I'm fine.'

'No, you nearly shot the centre.'

Olive looked in surprise towards the sack. 'Did I?'

Teresa thought it natural that Olive should have such a good eye, a steady hand. 'Do that again,' Harold said.

'No. It was a fluke.'

Sarah lifted her head up to look at the bullet-riddled sack. 'Liv, you've got a hidden talent. Maybe we should enter you in competitions.'

Teresa hurried over to take the pistol from Olive, and Isaac came to check she was reloading it correctly. Teresa brushed him off, setting the pistol perfectly on her own. 'You bought this with her money, didn't you?' she whispered to him.

'It won't be the last. It's a Soviet T33,' he replied, with a note of admiration.

'Are you giving this gun to them?'

'They might need it.'

'Why? Are you trying to protect them, or put them in danger?'

'Keep your eye on the target, Tere. And your voice down.'

Teresa wondered where Isaac was finding the means to source Soviet weapons, but part of her didn't want to know. She concentrated on raising the pistol, her legs apart, her other hand supporting her wrist. Her body was taut, every muscle tensed on her spare frame, the set of her jaw fixed as hard as the stone satyr in the fountain. She inhaled deeply and pulled the trigger. *You're not the only one who shoots rabbits*, she thought. The pistol went off and the bullet sailed through the air, hitting precisely through the knot attaching the sack to the branch. To Isaac's cry of frustration, the entire thing tumbled to the grass. The packed earth spilled everywhere, and the game was ruined.

Late that afternoon, Harold said he was driving to Malaga. He wanted to visit a bodega, pick up some new supplies of sherry. Sarah announced that she would accompany him. 'I need a chemist,' she said. 'Then I'd like a coffee on Calle Larios and a walk along the sea.'

Teresa saw Harold's hesitation, but he said, 'That's a good idea, get some air into your lungs. Isaac, would you join us? A man with local knowledge might help when it comes to the sherry.' But Isaac, who Teresa knew would once have craved a drive in such a powerful car, who had to content himself with a bicycle, did not wish to join them at all. He demurred, politely. 'Of course,' said Harold. 'You've got work you want to do.'

Outside the finca, Olive and Isaac waved her parents off. 'We could take the photograph for Peggy Guggenheim now,' she said, as their car disappeared. 'Daddy has a camera in his study.' Isaac was silent, staring at the swinging gate, gaping open on the path towards the village. 'What is it?' she asked.

'I was foolish,' he said.

'You're weren't.'

'I thought your confidence, your happiness, was out of love for me.'

'It was. It is.'

'I do not think so. I think this has always been inside you, waiting to come out. I just happened to be there, at that particular time, in order for you to use me as your canvas.'

'I love you, Isaac,' she said. The words landed short between them.

'Your love is not with me. It is for the walls of the Guggenheim house. How is this going to end, Olive?' he said. 'Because it is going to end.'

Olive turned to him, placing a hand on his arm, but he brushed it off. 'I've made you angry,' she said. 'But I do love you—'

'You say one more painting. But then there is one another. A green face, one more, one more, one more.'

'I'm sorry. I'm so sorry. This will be the last. I promise, I swear. I swear on my life.'

He turned to face her squarely. 'Did you and my sister plan all this from the very beginning?'

'Of course not.'

'She seems very comfortable with the situation now. She sounds like you. Always, she has a plan.'

'No, there was never a plan, Isaac. This just happened.'

'Teresa is a survivor. She was the one who put you on the easel, but don't think she will always put you first.'

'What are you talking about?'

He laughed, without humour. 'I am famous in Paris, a city I have never even seen. I paint portraits of my own face I have never even seen. You are stealing me, Olive. I feel like I am becoming invisible, the more visible I become.' The breath had got stuck in his throat, and he looked embarrassed, his words breaking up. 'And after all this, you expect me to believe you love me.'

'I don't expect anything, Isaac. I never wanted you to feel like this. I do love you. I never expected you to love *me*. I've got carried away, I know that. But I – we've – been so successful, I never thought it could be so easy—'

'It is not easy, Olive. It has never been easy. I cannot, I will not do this any more. And if you send that Guggenheim woman one more picture, then I cannot promise my actions.'

'What does that mean? Isaac, you're frightening me.'

'The painting you are working on – you must destroy it.'

She looked horrified. 'But I can't.'

'Why not?'

'Because it's the best thing I've ever done. Because they're waiting for it in Paris.'

'Then you cannot expect me to have anything to do with it.'

'Isaac, please. *Please—*'

'You promised me, Olive. You went behind my back.'

'And you haven't touched me for four weeks. Is that the price you're forcing me to pay, for once in my life doing something brilliant?'

'And what about the price you are forcing me to pay? No man would put up with a woman who asks so much. A man needs a woman who understands him, who supports him—'

'Who puts him first?'

'My absence from you is an exchange you seem more than willing to make, as long as Miss Guggenheim continues to sing your praises.'

'That's not true. I miss you.'

'You do not miss me, Olive. You miss the next chance to send a painting over.'

'I do miss you. Just come upstairs and see it,' she pleaded. 'And then tell me if you still feel the same.'

THE PAINTING WAS THE SAME size as *Women in the Wheatfield*, and yet it felt bigger. Up in the attic, Isaac stood before it, staggered by its sensuality and power. Even though it was still unfinished, the lion already looked possessed by the sight of the double-headed Rufina. This piece was breathtaking, sinister, revolutionary.

'Is that you?' he asked. He pointed at the disembodied head. 'And is that Tere?'

'Yes, and yes,' said Olive. 'But it's supposed to be the same person. It's called *Rufina and the Lion*. That's Rufina, before and after the authorities got hold of her.'

Isaac stared at the painting, the riot of colours and gold leaf, the curiously level gazes of Rufina carrying her head; the lion, waiting to take action.

'Do you like it?' she asked.

'It's wonderful.'

She smiled. 'It happens sometimes. My hand guides my head without much pause to worry or think.'

In that moment, all she wanted was for Isaac to see her as talented and confident – and to love her for it. 'We've done a wonderful thing, Isa,' she said. 'The paintings are going to be famous.' But Isaac kept his focus on *Rufina and the Lion*. 'Let's use the camera,' she said with a bright voice. 'Peggy wanted snaps.'

'*Snaps?*'

'Photographs. Of the painting. Isa,' she said gently, 'do you really want me to destroy it?'

He looked at the floor, and Olive knew in that moment that she had won this battle, if not the war. 'You could fight a lion too, Isaac – if you had to. I know it.'

'And a lion would run away from you. Do you know how to use the camera?' he asked.

'Of course,' she replied, unnerved, unable to pinpoint what was happening between them. 'But – I was hoping Teresa would take a photograph of the two of us, together.'

Isaac closed his eyes, as if in pain. 'Let's get it done,' he said. 'Call her.'

'I'M A LION,' TERESA ROARED, putting her free hand up, a pantomime paw as she hovered her finger over the camera button. She'd been taking rather formal pictures for the last half-hour – of the painting, of Isaac next to it, but in this moment, Olive threw back her head in laughter, eyes slightly closed, whilst next to her, Isaac, impervious to his sister's humour, gazed straight down the lens with a look of such possession on his face that Teresa forgot she was the king of the jungle at all.

Teresa knew then, as she pressed that button and captured them in these poses, that something had broken in this room. And she understood, for the first time, that they could never go back.

WHEN ISAAC WENT TO PICK up the developed film in Malaga a week later, he discovered that in some of the pictures, Teresa had put Olive in the centre of the image, and the painting itself was half-obscured. He thought he looked funereal in every single one. Olive, because she had been moving so much – jumpy in the face of his acute reluctance that afternoon – was slightly blurred, her mouth ajar, her lips making a silent *O* of pleasure. The sight of her – her expression of freedom and joy – made his conscience flicker briefly before dying away.

When Harold was shown a photograph of the painting on its own, cropped closely so you couldn't tell its location, he asked Isaac, 'Why is the girl carrying a head?'

'In my mind, it stands for duplicity,' Isaac replied. 'Because we are surrounded by lies.'

XVII

*O*live continued to paint *Rufina and the Lion* throughout the
rest of June and into July. Harold's telephone began to ring
again in his study, every two or three days, and he would
close the door on them in order to answer it, his voice hushed
and incomprehensible. When he'd been in Paris, he said, the news
from Vienna had not been good. Businesses were closing, crimes
going unpunished; but not even smashed shop windows were as
frightening as the political rhetoric being hurled from one side to
the other. Jews were coming in from Germany for shelter, but he
wondered how long their luck would last.

He told his family that he would focus on the Paris gallery, trying
to work out the logistics of getting his artworks out of Vienna before
the business suffered. Peggy Guggenheim was going to open her
gallery in London, and he was hoping he might be able to trans-
fer some of his stock to her there. In Vienna, he told them, Jewish
friends were selling their art for knock-down prices to raise capital
to pay for train fares, lodgings, food, new lives beyond the borders
of Austria. People who had prided themselves on varied, intelligent
and abundant collections of old masters and new were forced to
accept prices they would have baulked at twelve months earlier.

Harold was unsurprisingly gloomy, only perking up when there
was talk of the next work by Isaac Robles. Isaac Robles had become

his raison d'être, two fingers to the nationalistic narrowness peddled in every paper; his colourful child, his man with a vision, his
delight and defiance. 'Paint, Isa,' he said one night, drunk. 'God
knows we need you to paint.'

It was odd to think such tempests were happening all around
Europe, for Arazuelo seemed relatively peaceful. Sarah continued
with her walks out; by now there was a mountain of artichokes in
the kitchen. They would never be able to consume them against
the pace that Sarah was coming home with them, and Teresa
regarded them with a sense of foreboding. She noticed how freckles had appeared over the bridge of Sarah's nose, from the punishing July sunshine; she had lost some of her brittle elegance, and
seemed somewhat more grounded in her surroundings. At night,
Teresa could hear the Packard's engine as Harold trundled it down
the slope and through the gates towards Malaga. Sarah seemed
serene about Harold's leave-taking. She slept in, and complained
of headaches, rising late enough for her husband to have made his
way back home in the dawn, as if he'd never left.

Olive no longer commented on her father's disappearing acts.
Teresa wondered whether she was using it as a spur, duping her
father as he was duping her. Perhaps Olive's pursuit was not one of
success, but of an enemy's humiliation? Teresa wasn't exactly sure.
Olive simply seemed most herself when painting, day and night, to
finish *Rufina and the Lion*.

JULY WAS A GOOD MONTH in Arazuelo. The smell of sage fields
and rosemary, lizards making their way like small secrets out of
the walls, jerky and neurotic in motion, ever wary of predators in
the sky. But when they stilled themselves to bask, how poised they
were, such pragmatists of nature, soaking up the heat of the sun.

It was a time of long evening shadows, the raw rasp of crick-
ets filling the hot night. The fields were now shades of parsley,
lime and apple. Wildflowers; spattered reds and royal purples,
canary-yellow petals moving in the breeze. And when the wind
got up, salt tasted on the air. No sound of the sea – but listen,

and you could hear the articulated joints of a beetle, trundling through the corn root.

From the hills came the dull music of bells as the goats overtook these smaller sounds descending the scree through the gauze of heat. Bees, drowsing on the fat flower heads, farmers' voices calling, birdsong arpeggios spritzing from trees. A summer's day will make so many sounds, when you yourself remain completely silent.

They didn't see it coming. Of course they didn't. Who wants to look for trouble, every single day? You turn away, as long as you can. Even the government didn't see it coming. Perhaps later, when the locals recalled how no one had ever been brought to justice over Adrián the factory boy, or when they considered those red ribbons tied to the trees, or the shot statue of the Madonna, they would turn to each other, and say, *Ah yes; the writing was on the wall.*

The Schlosses were too wrapped up in their own internal battles to realize what was going on north in Madrid, what was going to surge up towards them from Morocco. They were not paying attention when on the twelfth of July in Madrid four Falangists shot dead the socialist lieutenant of the Republican Assault Guard. In retaliation, his friends assassinated the country's monarchist deputy, a prominent right-winger. Life in Spain, and life in the finca, was on the cusp of being broken apart, letting in a flood of recriminations, ambitions and long-buried resentments. But at the same time, in those early days, it didn't seem that war was on its way at all.

Sarah and Olive heard it on the radio first. On the eighteenth of July, four generals, out of the eighteen that ran the national army, rebelled against their left-wing government and took over their garrisons. The Prime Minister, frightened of revolution and mass unrest, ordered all civil governors not to distribute arms to the workers' organizations, who would inevitably want to resist potential armed rule. He then resigned that night.

Isaac came racing up to the finca. Harold was out – in Malaga, of course. 'Get the pistol,' he was calling, and on hearing him, the women had spilled out of the house.

Later, Teresa would think about the Schloss women's conflicting expressions. Olive looked relieved. Perhaps she still believed that Issac still cared about her – so much so that he had run all the way because some soldiers were throwing their weight around. Teresa remembered Sarah's smile of pleasure, her steady hand as she poured him a glass of water.

Seville was the nearest city to Arazuelo to fall to the army rebels. Its conquering general was a man called Queipo de Llano, who used the radio at ten o'clock that night to broadcast his intentions. Isaac and the three women sat listening in Harold's study, the fear they felt mirrored in each other's faces as Queipo de Llano's haranguing crackled through the speaker:

'People of Seville: to arms!' he bellowed. *'The Fatherland is in danger and in order to save it a few men of courage, a few generals, have assumed the responsibility of placing ourselves at the forefront of a Movement of National Salvation that is triumphing everywhere. The Army of Africa hastens to cross to Spain to join in the task of crushing that unworthy Government that had taken upon itself to destroy Spain in order to convert it into a colony of Moscow.'*

'A colony of Moscow?' said Sarah. 'What the hell is he talking about?'

'Shut up!' hissed Olive.

'All the troops of Andalusia, with whom I have communicated by telephone, obey my orders and are now in the streets . . . all the authorities of Seville, and all who sympathize with them and with the so-called Government in Madrid, are under arrest and at my disposal.'

'Isaac,' Olive whispered. 'He's talking about you. Isaac, you have to run.'

He looked up at her, and she saw the hollows under his eyes. 'Run? I am not going to run,' he said. 'You think I am going to hide from a man like him? You think because Queipo de Llano has telephoned some people, they will do as he says? We have already mobilized. We will fight back. They did not succeed in Madrid or Barcelona, and they will not succeed here.'

'*People of Seville!*' the general bawled on. '*The die is cast and decided in our favour, and it is useless for the rabble to resist and produce that racket of shouts and gunshots you hear everywhere. Troops of Legionnaires and Moroccans are now en route to Seville, and as soon as they arrive, those troublemakers will be hunted down like vermin. Long live Spain!*'

'Isaac,' Olive said, her voice rising in panic. 'They've got troops. Weapons. Trained soldiers. What would men like that do to you?'

They could hear the sound of Harold's motor, fast and loud, crashing up the hill. The car door slammed. 'Are you there, are you there? Have you heard?' he shouted through the hallway.

Teresa veered away from the desk, stumbling along the unlit corridor, bashing into the walls as she fought her way through the kitchen and onto the veranda, as far away as possible from everybody else. She ran down into the darkness of the orchard and felt the bile come, her body retching the words she could not find to spell out the terror inside – that this was it, the wave was here, the land ripped, her brother taken, and Olive – Olive would leave. She kept shaking her head, willing herself to get a grip, that she'd got this far – but in her heart she could hear the soldiers. Stomping jackboots along dark routes, *thump thump thump*, butt of a gun, split head; no place to hide.

'Tere? Tere!' It was Olive, calling for her. 'Tere, don't be scared. Where are you?'

But this was how she would end, Teresa knew. Here, on her knees, in the dark, in the company of those Spanish wolves.

PART IV

The Swallowed Century

NOVEMBER 1967

12

When the telephone rang in the hallway two days after I was locked out of Quick's house, I ran downstairs, still in my dressing gown, to pick it up. When I heard the person on the line say, 'Wha' happen now, Delly?' I was so glad, I nearly cried. It wasn't Quick I wanted, nor Lawrie. Her voice was permission to live.

'Cynth!'

'You still alive, girl?'

'Just about.'

'Ah – Ah free today. You want to meet up?'

IT HAD BEEN JUST OVER two months. I saw her before she saw me. Cynthia was immaculate as ever, leaning on one of the lions in Trafalgar Square, wearing a thick sheepskin coat which I'd never seen before, and a new pair of denim flared trousers. She looked . . . cool. She'd let her hair out of its French plait, and it was cut in a new shape; the beginning of a rounded Afro. I felt frumpy in comparison, in my thick tights and sensible heels, my woollen scarf and hat clamped round my ears like something out of a Blyton book. But still. A cold November morning in London; you do not mess.

My heart surged at how wonderful Cynth was. The realization of how far I'd travelled alone swamped me, as I saw her face, my friend, my oldest friend. Cynth caught my eye as I moved towards her, her arms wide open like a flightless bird trying to flap her wings.

'Ah sorry, Cynth,' I said. 'So sorry. Ah was dotish, Ah was mess up—'

'Hey, Delly,' she said. 'Ah marry and lef' you. Ah sorry too. What I was thinking?' But there was a twinkle in her eye. 'Ah miss you real bad, girl.'

'Me too. Me too. Me too.'

Her face broke open in a smile, and we turned shy. My emotion left me embarrassed – how I, a grown woman, could be so child-ish, so effervescent. My heart thumped in my ribs to be near her; I was giddy with her, my giddiness exacerbated by the fact she seemed to feel the same. We walked down under Admiralty Arch and into St James's Park, finding a bench to sit. 'Sherbets,' Cynth said, opening her handbag, proffering me a paper sack of sweets. 'You thin, Delly. What goin' on?'

'Ah pining for you,' I said, mocking myself, trying to show I still had grit. When she laughed aloud, the sound almost hurt. How good it always was to make her laugh.

'Nah, come now,' she said.

SO I TOLD CYNTH EVERYTHING – about meeting Lawrie after the wedding, and our dates after that – the mother he lost and the painting she left – and how Quick's attraction to the artwork seemed mingled with repulsion. I told her how the name 'Isaac Robles' came up, Edmund Reede convinced that this was a long-lost artwork by a forgotten genius, and how Quick was more doubtful about this, until her declaration last night that actually, the painting was nothing to do with Isaac Robles at all.

Cynth was much more interested in Lawrie, how it was going, and was it serious – but I tried to keep the focus on the conundrum of Quick, rather than of my own heart. 'The worse of it, Cynth,' I said, 'is that she dyin'.'

'Dyin'?'

'Cancer. She tell me is in a late stage. They didn't catch it early. Pancreatic.'

'Poor woman,' said Cynth. 'She sound scared about it, invitin' you round. Why she worrying about paintings when she goin' to dead?'

'This is what bothering me. Because listen to this; she running out of time on something, I sure of it.'

'What you sayin'?'

'Reede find out that the person who first sell Lawrie's painting in 1936 is an art dealer called Harold Schloss,' I said. 'The thing is, I find a letter in Quick's house addressed to *Olive* Schloss, inviting her to study at the Slade School of Art.'

'Delly, you snoopin' round a dyin' woman house?'

I tutted. 'No! It there in her telephone book she *tell* me to fetch. But listen – Quick also have telegram address to Harold Schloss, date of July of 1936.'

'What, just lyin' there in her telephone book, thirty year later?'

'I know. I know. But – is like Quick want me to find it. Is like she lef' it out, because she dyin' and don't want the truth to die with her.'

'Delly . . .'

'Quick too interested in where Lawrie get the painting from. And then she tell me last night is not Isaac Robles who paint it. Olive Schloss is key to this, Ah sure.'

'But who is this Olive Schloss?'

I exhaled, and my breath made condensation in the air. 'That is the question, Cynthia. That is *it*. Clearly a body who could paint, otherwise they wouldn't have been offered the Slade. Someone probably relate to Harold Schloss.'

'His wife?'

'Maybe. But if you going to art school, you usually younger, a student.'

'His daughter, then?'

'That's what I think. Olive Schloss was Harold Schloss's daughter. And at the Skelton, it have an old photograph of a man and

woman standing by Lawrie's painting. On the back someone write
"*O and I.*" That stands for Olive and Isaac. Quick say that Isaac
Robles didn't paint the pictures. Then who did it, and how she
know? I don't think Quick who she say she is.'

'Delly . . .'

'It always bother me, how she never have any painting on her
wall. Why's that? And the thing is, Quick went funny when I ask
her about Olive Schloss. She shut the door on me, lock me out. Is
like she *want* me to know, to get closer to the truth of it, and at the
same time – she cyan bear it.'

Cynthia appeared to be thinking, staring at the ducks gliding
across the pond before us. Beyond the trees, the spindly brown
turrets of Westminster poked up into the air. 'I always thought
Marjorie Quick was a funny name,' she said.

We sat in silence for a moment. I loved my friend for believing, for not saying I was mad, for accompanying me as I moved
to and fro over my narrative. It gave me permission to enter-
tain seriously the possibility that Quick might once have gone
by another name, lived another life, a life she was desperately
trying to remember – and to tell me – before it was too late. I
couldn't imagine the pain of seeing someone else take credit
for your work, whilst you languished unnoticed, uncelebrated,
knowing death was so near.

'The English mad yes,' said Cynth. 'So you goin' to ask her about
all this commesse?'

'But what Ah goin' to say?' One couldn't exactly confront Quick,
and I wasn't sure if I wanted the woman I knew to vanish further under scrutiny. I felt that if I could show her my support, this
might coax her out of the corner, but I wasn't sure of the best way
to go about it. 'Ah think she keeping secrets for a reason,' I added.

'Shoe shop was never like this,' Cynth sighed. 'You put a shoe on
woman foot and that is it.'

We laughed. 'No, that is true,' I said. 'But you know what else?
Quick help me publish a short story, so I in her debt.'

Cynth only heard the bit she wanted to hear, and her eyes lit up. 'Oh now, published! Oh, that is *good*. What it called?'

' "The Toeless Woman". Remember that woman who come in and have those blocks of feet?'

'Oh, my God. Yes. I have to read this.'

Tingling with pleasure at her excitement, I told her it was in October's *London Review*, but that if she liked I could send her a copy, I could send her ten. I told her how it had all unfolded, Quick sending the story personally to the magazine.

'I think she like me,' I said. 'I think she trust me. I just don't know exactly what she trustin' me with.'

Cynth nudged me. 'It take some white lady to get you to do it, eh, not me?' I started to protest that I'd had no idea what Quick was planning, but Cynth put her hands up. 'I jokin', I jokin',' she said. 'I just glad. Is about time.'

'How's Sam?' I asked, wanting to change the subject away from me, suddenly nervous that Cynth was going to read the dramatization of our joint life in that story about the toeless woman.

'He good. He very good.' She looked shy. 'It have somethin' I want to tell you, Dell. I want to tell you first. Ah havin' a baby.'

She looked very nervous about telling me this, which was a shame. But then again – consider how well I'd handled her getting married and leaving me alone in the flat. But this time, I was not going to get it wrong. I was genuinely excited for her. How could you not be, when you saw her pleasure and fear and wonder – that right now, there was this little thing in there, such a good thing, such a good mother to meet it when it finally showed its face.

'Oh, Cynthia. Cynthia,' I said, and to my shock tears filled my eyes. 'I sitting here talking about mysterious women and you the greatest mystery of all.'

'Delly, you sound like a poet even when you chokin' up.'

'Come here. I proud of you.'

We embraced, I held her tight and she held me, breathing out relief and crying a bit, because my happy reaction just made her happier still.

She was due at the beginning of April. She was terrified but excited, and worried they were not going to have enough money for it. 'You'll manage,' I said, thinking how much Cynth's life was going to transform, whilst mine was going to stay exactly the same. 'Sam have a good job. An you too.'

'So, Lawrie,' she said, dabbing her eyes with tissue. 'Don't wriggle. You had a fight.'

I was unable to hide my surprise. 'How you know?'

'Because I know you, Delly. I also know that if things were harmony, you would da be seein' him today, but you at some long loose end and see your boring ol' friend instead. Let me guess. He tell you he love you and you run a mile.'

'Is not like that.'

She laughed. 'He is miserable, Delly. Mis-er-ab-le. He the one who pining.'

'What? Come on, how you really know?'

'I hear it from Patrick, who hear it from Barbara, who see the feller mopin' around like someone chop off his arm. He lost. And he's a good one, Dell. Don't be dotish. He say he love you and you push him off a cliff.' Even though it was an admonishment, Cynth wheezed with laughter.

'But what if Ah don't love him? Why I have to love him?'

'You don't have to do anything, Delly. You don't have to rush. But you could give the feller explanation. If only to give his friends a break.'

'Lawrie the type of man to push a rhino down a rabbit hole. It won't work.'

'You a rhino though, Delly, so it would be amusing at least.'

We laughed, me from relief at being able to talk about it, and Cynth because it refreshed her to tease me, to be her younger self, to pull on the old ties and discover they were still intact. I still didn't know what I wanted, but it was sad to know Lawrie was going around feeling like someone had severed a limb.

After another hour or so, we embraced outside the Tube station, Cynth descending north on the Bakerloo to her new life in Queen's Park. We promised to see each other before Christmas, and I thought how bittersweet it was, how once upon a time, we'd have made sure we were catching up within the week.

I watched Cynth move down the steps carefully, thinking that surely she had no need to be so ginger. She stopped and turned back. 'One thing, Dell. If you do speak to Lawrie again, maybe keep this Olive Schloss story to yourself.'

'Why? If it true—'

'Well, yes. But you don't know it true for a fact, do you?'

'Not yet, but—'

'And he want to sell that painting, if I hear it right through Barbara. His stepfather selling the house and that painting is all he have. You goin' around sayin' that what he have is not an Isaac Robles – it goin' to knock his ship right out of the water. Don't make trouble where it don't have any, Delly. Think of your heart for once, not that clever head.'

I watched her go, knowing that there was sense in what she said, but also aware that Quick's behaviour wasn't something I was going to let lie.

I called Lawrie that night, but Gerry the Bastard answered. It was a shock to have him pick up.

'Who's this, calling on a Sunday?' he said.

Immediately, I put on my BBC tones. You couldn't help it – you heard an Englishman like Gerry, you just tried to make your voice sound the same as his. 'This is Odelle Bastien,' I said. 'Is Lawrie there, please?'

'Lawrence!' he yelled. Gerry must have put down the receiver because I could hear him move away.

'Who is it?' said Lawrie.

'Couldn't catch the name. But it sounds like the calypso's here.'

There was a wait, and then finally Lawrie put his mouth to the receiver. 'Odelle? Is that you?'

The sound of relief, mingled with wariness in his voice, was painful to hear. 'It's me,' I said. 'How are you, Lawrie?'

'Fine, thanks. You?'

'Fine,' I lied. 'I got a story published.'

'You called to tell me that?'

'No – I – it's just. It's what's happened, that's all. Was that Gerry I spoke to?'

'Yes. Sorry about that. Well done on the story.'

We were silent for a moment. Ironically, I didn't know how to shape these particular words, how to tell him that I missed him, that strange things were happening with Quick, that my best friend was having a baby and I felt like a teenager out of my depth.

'I'm coming to the gallery tomorrow, as it happens,' he said, his voice more hushed. 'Is that why you've called?'

'No. I didn't know.'

'Reede's had more information from a fellow who works at Peggy Guggenheim's palazzo in Venice. A couple of interesting things, apparently.'

'I see.'

'So why did you call? I thought you didn't want anything to do with me.'

'No – that's not – I do. I do. I spoke to Cynthia. She said you've been miserable.'

There was quiet on the line. 'I was miserable.'

'You're not miserable any more?'

He was silent again. 'I shouldn't have rushed in like that,' he said.

'No, it's fine – I mean—'

'I won't ever say what I said to you again.'

'I see.'

'Not if you don't want me to.'

'I don't really know what I want you to say, or not say,' I admitted. 'I just know that when I heard you were miserable, that made me sad. And I realized I'd been miserable too. And I was wondering whether it might be a bit easier – if we were miserable together.'

Quiet on the line again. 'Are you – asking me on a date, Odelle?'

I didn't – couldn't – say anything. 'Well, there's a first time for everything,' Lawrie went on. 'Thank you. Let me just check my diary – oh, no need. I'm free.'

A pleasurable warmth spread through my stomach and I couldn't hide the smile in my voice. 'Convenient,' I said.

'Isn't it?' he replied. 'Now, where would you like to meet?'

13

We met early the next morning, as early as we could, in the middle of Skelton Square, before I started work and Lawrie went in to see Reede. He was clutching a bottle of champagne. 'For your first published story,' he said, handing it over. 'That's vintage, you know. Sorry about the dust. Nicked it from the house.'

'Gosh, thank you.'

'Actually . . . I knew about the *London Review*.'

'What?'

'We do take modern periodicals in Surrey, you know. I read it.' He looked down at his shoes. 'It was just brilliant.'

'Shut up.' I took the bottle, my head about to explode with pleasure. I read the label: *Veuve Clicquot*. 'Lawrie, can we start again?' I said.

He sighed. 'I don't know if that's possible.'

I sat down on the bench, trying to bat away my despondence. I was so sure he'd say yes. He was here, wasn't he? 'I suppose not,' I said, looking up at him.

'You could hit me over the head with that champagne bottle,' he suggested.

'What?'

'Knock the memories out of me. But then I'd lose the first time

I saw you, reading that poem. Or the first time I spoke to you; those yellow rubber gloves. Or the way you pretended to like the Bond film, your nose all wrinkled up. Or when you out-danced me at the Flamingo and the manager offered you a job, or when you told me about that idiot in the shoe shop. Or when we had that shepherd's pie, and I messed everything up. It's all part of it, Odelle. It's not going to be perfect. Personally, I don't want it to be. I'd go through that horrible drive up the A3 again, just for the sweetness of hearing your voice after so long. I wouldn't change any of it. I don't want to start again, because that would make me lose memories of you.'

I couldn't say anything for a moment. Lawrie sat down next to me and I felt the warm solidity of his body. I took a deep breath. 'I – get scared,' I said. 'I don't know how else to explain it. I get feelings that I'm lost, that I'm no good, that if someone likes me there must be something wrong with them.'

'But why?'

'Well, if I knew that, Lawrie . . . and when I met you, I told you things I'd never told anyone. Then you swept in with your declaration that you loved me, and – well – it felt that like you were filling out a form, obeying some pattern.'

'A pattern?'

'Of what people do, what they think they're supposed to say.'

'No one tells me what to say.'

'But I also realized I didn't want you *not* to say it. I just wanted you to say it – when I wanted to hear it.'

He laughed. 'You really are a writer, aren't you? All right. How about, whenever I feel that I might be about to say I've fallen in love with you, or that I love you, or that you're wonderful, we agree on a sign that such a declaration is coming – and you recognize the sign, and give me the go ahead or not as to whether I can say it.'

'You make me sound mad.'

'I'm joking. I'm sorry. Whatever you need. I just want to see you, Odelle. Is that OK?'

'Yes,' I said. I hesitated. 'More than OK.'

'Good. Right,' he said. 'Let's go and hear what the venerable Mr Reede has to say.'

'Good morning, Odelle,' Quick said, stopping smoothly at my door. Lawrie had been with Reede for about thirty minutes. Quick looked tired, a little apprehensive. Her appearance was a world away from my first week, when she had breezed up to my type-writer and suggested a light lunch – in order to pick my brains – for what exactly, I still wasn't sure.

'Good morning, Quick.'

She froze, her eyes on the champagne bottle standing on the desk. 'Where did you get that?' she asked.

I swallowed, intimidated by the look on her face. 'Lawrie gave it to me.'

She turned her gaze to me. 'Friends again?'

'Yes. He's here. He's talking to Reede,' I said. 'I think they're discussing the exhibition.'

'I know they are. I scheduled the meeting.' Quick came in, clos-ing the door. To my surprise, she walked over and sat down oppo-site me, taking the bottle in her lap. 'Lawrie gave this to you?'

'To say well done for getting "The Toeless Woman" published. Is there something wrong with it?'

She ran her thumb across the neck, leaving a clean smear through the dust. 'It's vintage,' she said.

'I know that. Quick—'

'Odelle, what happened on Friday night—'

I sat up straighter. 'Yes?'

'It shouldn't have happened. I broke a professional barrier when I told you about my illness. I've compromised you. I've compro-mised myself. I don't want the attention.'

'You've done rather a good job of getting mine, though.'

She looked at me, sharply, but I refused to shrink away. 'I want you to know – that whatever happens – your job is completely safe.'

'Safe?'

Quick seemed to suffer a spasm of pain, and the bottle sagged heavily in her lap. 'They've got me on rather strong painkillers,' she said. 'No choice but to take them now. I'm hallucinating. I can't sleep.'

'What are you hallucinating?' I said. 'What is it that you see?'

I waited, barely able to breathe, my fingers drawing away from the typewriter and resting in my lap.

She didn't answer, and we sat in silence for a few moments, the clock on the wall syncopating my heartbeat. I took the risk. 'On Friday night, you said that Isaac Robles didn't paint the picture. Do you remember that, Quick?'

Quick sat, staring at her hands. She was swallowing hard, her throat constricted.

'Did he paint *any* of the pictures, Quick – the ones in the Guggenheim?'

Still, Quick remained silent.

'If he didn't paint those pictures, who did—'

'All I wanted,' she said, abruptly, in clear distress. 'I just wanted to see.'

'What, what was it that you wanted to see?'

I watched in horror as Quick fanned her fingers open on the neck of the bottle, and the entire thing slid between her legs and cracked against the floor. The base smashed clean off and the champagne gushed between us, fizzing and pooling everywhere. She jumped up crookedly, staggering from the mess before us. 'I'm sorry,' she mumbled. 'I'm so sorry.'

'It was an accident,' I said. I stared at Lawrie's ruined bottle, lying on the floorboards in a puddle of champagne. The green glass was so dark it was almost black, winking as the overhead lights caught its jagged edges. I'd never even got a taste. I swallowed hard and looked at Quick.

She was drained of colour. I knew the conversation was over, that I would get no further now. Would she really go so far as to sabotage my present from Lawrie? I ushered her to her own office, and she leaned on me, snaking her arm through mine. I could feel her bones so easily through the skin. Now I knew about the cancer, I could see how ill Quick was. But it wasn't just the cancer in her body. I was also witnessing her psychological recalibration.

I wouldn't say Quick's mind was diminishing, despite her protests of hallucinations and insomnia. It was almost the opposite to her body; an augmentation, her imagination inhabiting more than just the present. Somewhere inside her memory, a drawbridge had been lowered, and the foot soldiers of her past were pushing through. She wanted to talk; but couldn't. She didn't have the words.

'Please lock the door,' she said, beginning to rally a little. 'Odelle, I'm so sorry about your bottle.'

'It's all right.'

'I'll make it up to you in my will.'

Her black eyes glimmered with gallows humour. 'Got a cellar in Wimbledon, have you?' I said in kind, trying to chivvy her spirits.

'Something like that. Fetch my handbag, would you? I need the pills.' She moved slowly to the drinks table. 'Gin?'

'No thanks.'

I watched her pour one, breathing deeply, corralling herself as the clear liquid glugged into the tumbler. 'Those are bloody strong,' she said as I handed her the pills. 'I fucking hate them.'

The expletive, the bitterness in her voice, shocked me. I forced myself to sit, reminding myself I was a junior employee, and must be mute and mild. Pushing Quick to tell me things I wanted to know was clearly not going to work. I'd suspected that it wouldn't, after the night with the telephone book, and now I had one smashed champagne bottle as confirmation. As frustrating as I found it, I had to be her blank canvas. Patience was never my strong suit, but as long as it kept her talking, it was better than silence.

'There's a fellow called Barozzi in Venice,' she said, lowering herself into her leather chair and reaching for her cigarettes. 'Works for Guggenheim. Around the time Mr Scott's painting was being made, Peggy Guggenheim was attempting to open a gallery in London.' Quick stilled herself for a minute, before finding the strength to continue. 'She succeeded. The place was on Cork Street, before the war turned it on its head and it closed.'

'I see.'

'You don't. The point is, she – or others at her gallery – are good with keeping paperwork. Barozzi found some rather interesting correspondence in her archives, sent it to Reede, and he's beside himself.'

Cork Street. I knew the name – it was the street that the pamphlet came from. My skin began to tingle.

'He now has evidence that Mr Scott's painting was a commission for Peggy Guggenheim, as a twin to *Women in the Wheatfield*.'

'A twin?'

'He's found a telegram addressed to Isaac Robles, which for some reason was never sent. It was destined for Malaga in Spain, dated September '36, enquiring how much longer she will need to wait for the "companion piece" to *Wheatfield*, which Robles had called *Rufina and the Lion*. Barozzi has acknowledged that no deposit was actually given Robles for the Rufina piece, otherwise Mr Scott could have found himself in a lot of trouble, given that he's apparently got no proof of purchase. The Guggenheim could have tried to claim it as theirs.'

I marvelled that Quick could talk about another discovered telegram, as if the one hidden in her own house wasn't inextricably tied up with all this too. Not only was she acting as if the smashed champagne bottle was not deliberate sabotage, she was now pretending that our evening with the telephone book had never happened.

'*Rufina and the Lion*,' I repeated. 'That's what Lawrie's painting is called?'

'That's what Reede believes. Ever heard of Saint Rufina?'

'No.'

Quick sipped her gin. 'The image of Mr Scott's painting fits the story perfectly. Rufina lived in Seville in the second century. She was a Christian potter, who wouldn't kow-tow to the authorities' rules when they told her to make pagan icons, so they chucked her in an arena with a lion. The lion wouldn't touch her, so they cut off her head. And with this mention of a "companion piece", Reede believes he's found a connection between Mr Scott's painting and the more famous *Women in the Wheatfield*, which might change the way we look at Robles entirely.'

I gazed at her, feeling determined, ready to enter into a battle of wills. 'But you told me that Isaac Robles didn't paint it.'

Quick slugged back another painkiller. 'And yet, we have a certified telegram from a world-class art collector, stating that it was intended as a companion piece to one of the most important paintings to come out of Spain this century, currently in the Guggenheim collection in Venice.'

'Yes, but there was someone else in that photograph too. A young woman.'

I waited for Quick to speak, but she did not, so I carried on. 'I think she was called Olive Schloss. In that letter at your house, it appears she won a place at the Slade School of Art around the time that Isaac Robles was painting. I think she painted *Women in the Wheatfield*.'

'I see.' Quick's face was impassive, and my frustration grew.

'Did you think she made it, Quick?'

'Made what?' Her expression turned hard.

'Do you think Olive ever made it to the Slade?'

Quick closed her eyes. Her shoulders sagged, and I waited for her to reveal herself, to release the truth that had been broiling in her ever since seeing Lawrie's painting in the hallway of the Skelton. Here it came, the moment of confession – why she was in possession of the telegram from Peggy Guggenheim and the letter from the Slade – how it was her own father who had bought Isaac Robles's painting, a piece of art she had created herself.

Quick was so still in her chair, I thought that she'd expired. She flicked her eyes open. 'I'm going to hear what Mr Reede is saying,' she said. 'I think you should come too.'

I followed her down the corridor, disappointed. But I was getting nearer, I was sure.

WE KNOCKED ON REEDE'S DOOR and were told to come in. Lawrie and he were sitting facing each other in the armchairs. 'Can I help you?' Reede said.

'Miss Bastien and I will be the ones on the front line once this exhibition gets underway,' said Quick. I saw how tightly she was gripping the door frame. She was torturing herself. 'It might be wise if we were to sit and take notes, to understand what you're proposing.'

'Very well,' said Reede. 'You can sit over there, ladies.'

We looked to where he was gesturing; two hard wooden chairs in the corner. Either Quick was being punished, or Reede was blind to how frail she was. Lawrie caught my eye as I sat down; he looked excited, alive with the possibilities of his painting. *Rufina and the Lion* was propped up on the mantelpiece, and I was no less overwhelmed by its power than the first time I saw it, by how much that girl and the severed head she held in her hands had already changed my life. If Lawrie hadn't used it to try and take me on a date, would any of us even be sitting here today – would Quick be unravelling like this, despite her insistence on blaming the cancer and its painkillers?

Directly above Reede's head sat the lion, imperial and implacable as so many painted lions are. Yet today, it looked so curiously tamed. I gazed at the white house in the distant hills; its painted red windows, how tiny it was compared to the vast, multicoloured patchwork of fields which surrounded it. Rufina and her second head stood looking back at me, at all of us. Thirty years ago, Isaac Robles and a girl I was sure was Olive Schloss stood before this very picture, for a photograph. What had Isaac and Olive been to one another?

Inevitably, I looked to Quick. She seemed to have gathered herself from her earlier distress; sitting straight now, notebook on her lap, eyes on the painting. Whatever the truth was, it seemed to me that she was going to let this exhibition go ahead with no sabotage on her part, and I felt confounded by her capitulation.

'As I was saying, Mr Scott,' Reede went on, 'three years ago, Peggy Guggenheim's entire Venetian collection came to the Tate on temporary loan. Whilst *Women in the Wheatfield* was here on the Tate's public walls, your own Robles painting was hiding in the shadows. It's extraordinary to think we could have matched them then, had we known. There was so much to-ing and fro-ing over that exhibition, between the British government and the Italian authorities,' he said. 'Tax issues, mainly. But that was for a hundred and eighty-odd pieces, and I've only asked for three. So the good news is, they're letting us borrow their Isaac Robles pieces.'

'That is good news,' said Lawrie.

'It's wonderful. It'll really bolster the exhibition. I hope the news pages will give us coverage as well as the arts sections. We're getting *Women in the Wheatfield*, a landscape called *The Orchard*, and rather brilliantly, something I wasn't aware of – his *Self-Portrait in Green*. And what will be exciting about the reunion of *Women in the Wheatfield* with *Rufina and the Lion* is that it could change the way we view Isaac Robles generally.'

'Why?'

'Rufina was one of a pair of sisters,' Reede said. 'Justa was the name of the other.'

'Justa?'

'The story goes that Justa was thrown down a well to starve. I believe that *Women in the Wheatfield* is actually the story of Saint Justa – and that there's only one girl in it, not two. We see Justa before and after her punishment, once in happiness, and then in torment. The smashed pots around her back up this idea. It's the mask of the goddess Venus, broken in half, and that appears in the myth.'

'I see,' said Lawrie.

'There have been different interpretations of the circle that the woman lies in over the wheatfield. Some art historians say it is one of Dante's circles, others says it's the moon – and some identify it as the rotundity of planet earth, particularly with those woodland animals around it. But I believe she's actually lying at the bottom of a well, as per the myth. Here,' he said, handing Lawrie four pieces of paper, which had copies of paintings on them. 'Robles wasn't the only Spaniard to paint Rufina and Justa. Velázquez, Zurburán, Murillo and Goya, all four great Spanish painters, painted those sisters. I'm trying to get a loan of at least one of these paintings to complement the exhibition.'

'Do you think you'll get them?' asked Lawrie.

Reede rose to his feet, and rubbed his hands together. 'Maybe. Maybe. I really do hope for it.' He smiled. 'It would be something extraordinary. The chances are Robles was well aware of these other works. I've told the galleries who have these pieces that I want to examine the particular Hispanic pathology around the myth of Justa and Rufina.'

'The Spaniards have always been incredibly subversive artists,' said Quick.

'Yes,' said Reede, looking at her more warmly, one arm propped up on the mantelpiece. 'Creative rebellion against the status quo. Just look at the Goya. He would be the one to put in a lion, kissing her toe. And can you imagine what Dalí would do with it?'

'But why is the Guggenheim Robles called *Women in the Wheat-field*, with no reference to Saint Justa, if mine's called *Rufina and the Lion*?' Lawrie asked.

'Harold Schloss might have called it *Women in the Wheatfield*, not Isaac Robles,' said Reede. 'Robles might have easily called it *Saint Justa*, for example. We'll never know. He may not have given it a name at all.'

At the mention of Harold Schloss, I glanced over again at Quick. Her head was bowed, and she was massaging her temple. I wondered if she needed another painkiller. She seemed determined to get as close to Reede's plans as possible, despite the visible trauma it was causing.

'The salesman in Schloss,' Reede went on, beginning to pace around us, 'probably wanted to make the painting more attractive for Guggenheim's purchasing sallies. She hadn't bought much before this; he didn't want to scare her off. It's the same sort of thing as Picasso wanting *Les Demoiselles d'Avignon* to be called *The Brothel of Avignon*, and his exhibitors changing the name, apparently to make it more appealing. And Schloss may not have known that a companion piece to Justa and her well was on its way. Somewhere along the line, I believe that what Isaac Robles wished to communicate in these paintings was lost.'

'And what did he want to communicate?' said Lawrie.

I looked at Quick again; she was gazing up now at Reede, with a blank expression on her face.

'I think Robles was very interested in this myth,' Reede said. 'And discovering this connection between the Guggenheim Robles and the Surrey Robles allows us a new window on to his artistic process, to reinterpret his preoccupations – to reinvent him, if you like. This exhibition may be "The Swallowed Century", but we are still trying to digest it, so to speak.'

'Reinvent him?'

'Succeeding generations do it all the time, Mr Scott. Don't be alarmed. We can never bear to think we haven't thought of something new. And tastes change; we have to be ahead of them. We are resurrecting an artist at the same time as enacting his retrospective. My approach will allow us to describe Robles's awareness of a glorious national historical tradition – Velázquez and the rest – whilst being something of a contemporary international star, cut down in his prime.'

'You've really got it all planned, haven't you.'

'That's my job, Mr Scott. I can't tell you yet what exactly he was trying to communicate, but I want to take a political slant with your painting in particular. Rufina, the defiant worker saint, facing down the lion of fascism. Have a look at this,' he said, handing over yet another document for Lawrie to read. 'I was sent that from Barozzi at the Guggenheim foundation. Harold Schloss wrote it to Peggy Guggenheim when he was in Paris again, and she had returned to New York.'

'Mr Scott,' said Quick, and the men jumped. 'Could you read it out loud? Neither Miss Bastien nor I are furnished with a copy.'

Lawrie obliged.

'Dear Peggy,

Forgive me for not making my presence known to you in time before you left Paris. Everything, since my departure from Spain to my arrival back in this city, has been very difficult. I tried to bring Rufina with me, but have failed. I know how much you were looking forward to it, and I am deeply sorry.

I have a couple of early Klees you may like to look at instead – I myself will not travel to Vienna, but am organizing them to be sent to London – or perhaps, if you're staying in New York for some time tying up matters, and are interested, I may send them straight there?

My best to you, as ever,

Harold Schloss.'

Lawrie looked up at Reede. 'He doesn't mention Robles at all.'

'I think we can do something with that. I'd like to blow this letter up large, and have it on one side of the gallery wall. We could speculate on what happened to Robles.'

'What do you mean?'

'I don't think he made it through the war. We would surely have heard about him if he had. There was a lot of bombing in the south of Spain in those days. Say the rest of Robles' paintings went up in flames. We could consider how the immolation of Robles' body of work reflects the disappearance of the artist himself.'

Reede began to pace again, his hands behind his back, lost to us as he expounded his vision. 'We could extend the metaphor, into the conflagration of the Iberian corpus, and the world war to come. The man is a symbol, as much as an individual. He was a vision of Spain's future, which was annihilated.'

Lawrie crossed his legs, his voice hard. 'But you don't know his works went up in flames. You can't build an exhibition on a rumour. They'll laugh at me.'

'They won't laugh. People love a rumour, Mr Scott. You can do more with rumour than you can with fact. And the fact is, we have a limited supply of paintings. Another fact: Harold Schloss did not have *Rufina and the Lion* when he went back to Paris. Where was it? That's where you come in.'

'Me?' said Lawrie. Something in his tone of voice made me turn. I looked to Quick; she had clearly thought the same as Reede, for her eyes were on Lawrie, concentrating hard.

Reede came to sit opposite Lawrie, and spoke more gently. 'I think that Harold Schloss realized it was untenable to remain in Spain, and in fleeing, the painting fell out of his possession, either through theft or carelessness. It is unusual for a dealer to confess so openly a loss, as he does in that letter. Normally they're glib, smooth talkers. I think Harold Schloss came back to Paris with his feathers ruffled.'

'And you think the painting was left behind in Spain?' said Lawrie.

'Well, Schloss doesn't seem to have it. He's got no reason to lie to his best collector. But I don't know, Mr Scott. The next person to be attached to it was your mother. And apparently, we have no idea how she got hold of it.'

Lawrie gazed up at the painting, and down again, into the empty grate. 'It's always been on her walls,' he said quietly. 'I don't remember a time it wasn't there.'

'So you say,' Reede sighed. 'Well, we can play with the question mark. I don't think we have a choice. The survival of an artwork through the Spanish Civil War and a world war to a house in Surrey is not without its romantic possibilities.'

'What do you think happened to Isaac Robles, in the end?' asked Lawrie.

'Mr Reede,' said Quick, her voice hard and clear across the room. 'What is the timescale for this? When are you planning to open this exhibition?'

Reede turned to her. 'A delegation from the Guggenheim is coming in two weeks with the paintings. And two weeks after that, I believe we can open.'

Quick looked down at her diary. 'Four weeks from now? That's ridiculous. That's no time at all.'

'I know, Marjorie. But it's what I want.'

I watched as Quick marked the day of November 28th in her diary, a slight tremor in her hand, the pen drawing across the page in a thick black cross.

14

That evening, Lawrie and I took the commuter train to Surrey. He told me that he'd already sold the MG. 'I just didn't use it much,' he said, but he sounded wistful. I considered that perhaps there was more pressure than I initially imagined to sell his mother's painting.

As we pulled out of Waterloo, me with the Xeroxes from Reede on my lap, I looked at the four paintings of Rufina and Justa by the older Spanish artists. I loved the passive lion in the Goya, but my favourite overall was the Velázquez; a young girl with dark hair and an inscrutable gaze, holding two little bowls and a plate in one upturned palm, and a huge plume in the other. Velázquez, like Robles, had painted Rufina on her own too. I moved on to the copy of Harold Schloss's letter. Schloss had written by hand, and had started it neatly enough, but in places it became barely legible. His rounded arcs and sweeping curves descended into crossings-out and ink blots everywhere. I did not think it was the letter of a happy man.

'We're here,' said Lawrie.

We were not normal passengers getting off at Baldock's Ridge; the normal passengers were men in their late forties, paunch incoming, signet ring, *Telegraph* under their arm, an embossed briefcase. Women, country-tweeded, middle-aged with distant faces, thoughts buried deep within their handbags, coming back from a day in town.

'After you left the meeting, Reede said he could try and sell the painting for me,' Lawrie said as he opened the door and helped me down. 'For a commission.'

'How much does he think it will fetch?'

'It's hard to say. *"Art doesn't always behave itself like other things you might put up for sale, Mr Scott"*,' Lawrie said, parroting the pomposity Reede could stray into when on home turf. 'He said it isn't like a late Van Gogh coming onto the market.'

'What does that mean?'

'Well, apparently everyone would want one of those. But *Rufina and the Lion* is unique in a different way. Reede said he doesn't want to underplay it, but neither does he want to over-egg the pudding. He said selling always has its risks.'

'But he's so enthusiastic about it.'

'As a historian, maybe. As a personal preference, yes. But perhaps as an auctioneer he wants to manage my expectations. Not everyone's going to like Isaac Robles.'

'You could always donate it to a public institution.'

Lawrie laughed. 'Odelle, I haven't got any money.'

QUICK AND I HAD NOT had a chance to talk for the rest of the day. She had gone home shortly after the meeting with Lawrie and Reede was finished. She claimed a headache, but I knew of course it was more. I felt torn; I wanted to be with Lawrie, to revel in the rush and headiness of making up, of realizing how much a person means to you, the thrill of having nearly lost them only to be reunited. But at the same time, I was the only person who knew something was very wrong with Quick, that her pain seemed to be worsening, and yet I had no idea how to help her manage it.

'Are you all right?' said Lawrie.

'Just thinking about Quick,' I said. 'She's – not very well.'

'She didn't *look* very well.'

Lawrie leaned in to kiss my cheek as we walked down the

station path. There was an intake of breath behind us. I turned;
one of the tweed women, trying to look as if she hadn't made the
noise at all.

'Come on,' said Lawrie quietly. 'Let me take you out of the eighteenth century.'

Except it wasn't the eighteenth century, was it, Lawrie? It was
late October, in 1967, in Baldock's Ridge in Surrey, and you weren't
allowed to kiss me without comment. Or perhaps, more accurately,
I was not allowed to be kissed.

WHEN WE GOT TO THE house, the lights were on. 'Oh, Jesus,' he
said. I turned; Lawrie looked genuinely frightened.

'What is it?' I asked.

'I thought Gerry wouldn't be here. We should go.'

'I don't want to go,' I said.

'Odelle, Gerry isn't – I don't think he— I just want to warn you.'

'Let me guess. I'm one of the natives.'

'Oh, God, this is going to be a disaster. He's – very old-fashioned.'

'We should get along perfectly, then.'

'You won't. You shouldn't have to—'

'*Lawrie*. I don't want you to protect me. Let me be the judge of
Gerry. Just as no doubt he'll be the judge of me.'

How to describe Gerry? Gerry the Bastard, Gerry the Merry. As
soon as he clapped eyes on me, his face lit up. 'I thought Lawrence
was a queer!' The tone with which he said it made me think that
Gerry was possibly inclined that way himself. I have never met a
man like him since; that particular strain of upper-class English – so
camp and Wodehousian, a madness at which no one bats an eye.
Anything that was inappropriate to say, Gerry would say it. He was
overweight, and handsome, but he looked like a man closing down
on himself. I could smell the grief; six months down the line, you'd
find him a puddle of skin on the floor.

'I understand you work at an art gallery, Miss Baschin?' he said, pouring yet another whisky.

Lawrie winced at Gerry's mispronouncing my name, and I could see he was about to correct his step-father. 'That's right,' I said quickly. 'As a typist.'

'Set up home here, then?'

'Yes, sir. Nearly six years now.'

'Odelle's father was in the RAF,' said Lawrie. I could hear the desperation in his voice, and it annoyed me. I knew what Lawrie was trying to do, of course – repackaging me in a context the man might understand. But I did not feel I needed my father's military record as any introduction; I felt, in a strange way, that Gerry was accepting me regardless. By some weird alchemy – perhaps because I was inside his house – Gerry seemed to exempt me from the unconscious hierarchy of colour he also inadvertently revealed now and then. Perhaps he was whitewashing my skin? Perhaps he rather liked the thrill, his colonial days coming back to him? Or perhaps he just liked me. Whatever it was, I felt invited in.

WE ATE A JUMPY DINNER – well, Lawrie was the jumpy one; Gerry and I fumbled our way through. At least he didn't mention calypsos again – or bongos, or the miracle of my excellent English.

'We went to the Caribbean once,' Gerry said, as Lawrie cleared the plates. He drained his tumbler of whisky, and stared at it.

'Did you like it?' I asked.

Gerry didn't appear to hear me. 'Worked in India after I left Oxford.' I looked at Lawrie's expression: thunderbolts at the tablecloth. 'Was there for years. I think the travel bug was in my blood from then on – probably got bitten by something. Beautiful place, India. Difficult though. Incredibly hot.'

'Which islands did you go to, in the Caribbean?' I asked.

'Feels like a lifetime ago now. I suppose it is.'

'Odelle asked you a question,' said Lawrie.

'It's all right,' I said.

'Jamaica,' the man replied, with a sharp look at his step-son. 'I'm not senile, Lawrence. I heard her.'

'I've not been to Jamaica,' I said.

Gerry laughed. 'How extraordinary. I thought you all just hopped between the islands?'

'No, sir. I have been to Tobago, and Grenada, and Barbados. I do not know the other islands. I know London better than I know Jamaica.'

Gerry reached for the whisky. 'It wasn't my choice to go there,' he said. 'But Sarah said everyone went to Jamaica. She loved heat, needed it. So off we went. I'm glad we did. The sand was so soft.'

Lawrie snatched the whisky bottle. 'Let's go and listen to that record we bought,' he said.

'Who's Sarah?' I asked.

Gerry looked at me through bloodshot eyes. 'Lawrence didn't even tell you her name?'

'Whose name?'

'His mother,' Gerry said, sighing when Lawrie turned away. 'My beautiful wife.'

15

*L*awrie lunged up the stairs, three at a time.

'What's wrong with you?' I said. 'He just misses her. He wants to talk about her.'

Lawrie stopped on the landing and whirled round at me. 'Don't think he's some sort of saint,' he said.

'I don't, Lawrie.'

Lawrie seemed to be battling with a particular thought. He looked half fearful, half furious. 'When my dad died,' I went on, trying to sound soothing, 'my mum used to hear his voice in the radio. Saw his face in every man she met. You've got to be patient.'

'She was my mother.'

'Of course.'

'I was the one who found her. In that room down there.'

'Oh, Lawrie.'

I turned to the darkness where he was pointing, and felt a preternatural repulsion, an overwhelming desire to walk in the opposite direction. But I didn't move; I didn't want him to see me scared. 'Gerry's held together with whisky and sticking plasters,' I said. 'You should be kind to him.'

'And what about me?'

'I'll be kind to you,' I replied, taking his hand.

WE LAY SIDE BY SIDE on Lawrie's eiderdown, hearing Gerry shuffling beneath us, until a door closed and the house fell silent. 'You shouldn't live here,' I said.

'I know.' He turned on his side to face me, propping himself on his elbow. 'But it's all I have. This place, Gerry and a painting.'

'And me,' I said. 'You've got me.'

Gently, he ran his hand down the side of my face. The window was still open, and I heard a blackbird, so musical and effortless, singing in a tree like it was dawn. 'Come on, Writer. What's your favourite word?' he asked.

I could see he wanted to change the subject, so I obliged. 'You're asking me to pick? All right. *Lodgings*.'

He laughed. 'You had it ready – I knew you would. That's so stodgy, Odelle.'

'Is not. It's cosy. *"My lodgings were clean and comfortable."* You?'

'*Cloud.*'

'Such a cliché,' I said, inching towards him and giving him a squeeze.

We talked on – for now, mothers and step-fathers and paintings forgotten, or pushed away at least, banishing them to the outer edges of our memories as much as we could. We talked about how beautiful the English language could be, in the right hands – how varied and nuanced and illogical. *Hamper* and *hamper*, and words like *turn*, that seemed boring at first but were deceptive in their depths. We discussed our favourite onomatopoeia: *frizz* and *sludge* and *glide* and *bumblebee*. I'd never been so happy alone with another person.

Because of the blackbird singing in the tree, we ended up drifting into a game of bird-tennis, our intertwined hands the raised-up net, and a kiss for each bird that we exchanged. *Plover* to *lapwing*, *honey-creep*, *lark*. *Coquette* and *falcon*, *manakin*, *hawk*. His hands upon my skin, *curlew*, *oriole*, and mine upon his. *Jacamar*, *wren*. Then the birds flew away, their names turned to kisses, a silence to spell a new world.

The next morning, I woke very early. Lawrie was in a deep sleep, his expression peaceful. I considered the astonishing moment he'd pushed inside me, how that was never going to happen for the first time again. I put on my knickers, his shirt and woolly jumper, slid out of the bed and tiptoed along the corridor to the bathroom. Had Gerry known I'd stayed? How mortifying it would be to cross him now.

I went to the toilet and felt between my legs; a little dried blood, but the more obvious symptom was the stomach pain I could feel, slight, low-seated, a dull ache, a sense of having been opened up and bruised. I had never even been naked with a man, had never been touched like that before; it was strange that one might feel pain over something that had been so pleasurable.

We had broken through a frontier, and I had told him, very quietly, that I loved him, and Lawrie had pressed his ear to my mouth, saying, *You might have to repeat that one, Odelle, because I'm getting on and these days I don't hear so well.* And so I said it again, slightly louder, and he kissed me in return.

I LOOKED AT MY WRISTWATCH; five-thirty. Below me, I could hear Gerry's snores. What a place to be, I thought; urinating in a clapped-out Victorian toilet in deepest Surrey over a man called Gerry's head. I would not have predicted it; and I was glad of the lack of forewarning. Had I known such things were going to be promised me, I would have been too intimidated by their weirdness and they probably wouldn't have happened.

I finished, washed my hands and face and used a little soap on my upper thighs. I felt the sudden desire to tell Pamela that this had happened, to give her the gift of my gossip, to make her birthday present worth it after all.

I came out of the bathroom and was about to head back to Lawrie's room, when I hesitated. I turned to my right, looking down the long corridor. There would be no other time, I knew; with Lawrie awake it was unlikely he would lead an expedition down here. And for me, the curiosity was too great.

The door was slightly ajar. It was her bedroom, Sarah's bedroom; you could tell. There were still lipsticks on the dressing table, a silver powder compact in the shape of a shell; paperback novels and old magazines. Along the sill were china and glass ornaments, vases of flowers, now dried out. The curtains were open, but the sun was not yet up. The silhouettes of naked trees were crooked against a lavender sky.

I looked at the bed. Had it happened here? There was no sense of the scene, for which I was grateful. I felt deeply sorry for both these men, clearly lost without her – or confused, at least. Gerry was right – Lawrie had been so evasive about his mother. Gerry, far from being a heartless bastard, appeared to want to discuss her. It was Lawrie who wouldn't. Only now, being in the house with him and his step-father together, could I see how deeply Lawrie had been affected by Sarah, by this second marriage, by the manner of her death.

In the corner of the room was a large wardrobe. I opened it, and a cloud of camphor hit the back of my throat. Hanging inside was a solitary pair of delicate red trousers, and I pulled them out and held them against my body. If these were Sarah's, and I assumed they were, she had been tiny. They barely cut the middle of my shins. They were made of scarlet wool, which in many places had been attacked by moth, most unfortunately at the groin. Yet you could tell that these trousers had been particularly stylish. They made me think of Quick. She'd have liked these, holey groin or not.

'They won't fit, you know,' said a voice. 'But I couldn't bear to throw them away.'

I jumped. At the door was Gerry; scant, sandy hair on end, large body wrapped in a deep blue dressing gown, his hairy legs and bare feet sticking out at the bottom. Embarrassed, I stammered something incomprehensible as I moved to put the trousers back. I felt terrible for thinking that Gerry had just cleared away his wife without a second thought. This place was like his little shrine. He probably visited it every morning, and I was an intruder. I was beyond mortified. I'd stayed over; I was just wearing a man's shirt and jumper. I'd had sex under his roof. Thank God Lawrie was much taller than me, in terms of my modesty, but I might as well have had the word SEX emblazoned on my forehead, I felt it was so obvious.

But Gerry seemed uninterested in the morals of his step-son and girlfriend. Perhaps he was more modern than I gave him credit for. That, or he was too mired or hungover in his grief to care. He waved his hand as he padded in. 'Don't worry,' he said, sitting heavily on the end of the bed. I was still holding the trousers. 'You can have a look around. She was a mystery to me too, in many ways.'

With his glum expression and rotund stomach, Gerry reminded me of the morose Humpty Dumpty from Lewis Carroll's *Looking-Glass*. And I felt like Alice – being riddled and challenged in every direction I turned.

'I'm sorry,' I said. 'I shouldn't be in here.'

'Don't be. Lawrie really doesn't talk about her, does he?'

'Not much. Mr Scott, can I ask—'

'I'm not Scott,' said Gerry. 'That was Sarah's maiden name.'

'Oh.'

'Lawrence chose to keep her name rather than mine,' Gerry said, shaking his head. 'Still, he was sixteen by then, and you can't tell a sixteen-year-old what to do. Never really understood him.'

'He didn't take his father's name?'

Gerry looked at me shrewdly. 'Not a very good idea to call yourself Schloss in the school playground in the forties.'

I stood, frozen to the spot, the red trousers hanging limply in my grasp. 'Schloss?' I repeated. 'Lawrie's father was Schloss?'

Gerry looked up at me, interested by the energy in my voice. 'Well, strictly speaking, yes. Sarah gave him the surname Scott from the moment he was born, but in terms of his father, it's Schloss. Her first husband was an Austrian of all things, just before the Great War.'

'Austrian?'

Gerry looked amused. 'You seem a little perturbed by all this. Is everything all right?'

'Oh, I'm fine,' I said, trying to look as casual as I could, in Lawrie's oversized woollen jumper, clutching his dead mother's trousers, as if this news about Lawrie's father meant nothing to me at all.

'When she came back to England and had Lawrie, she thought it prudent to give him her own name. Nobody trusted a German name in those days.'

'What was her husband's first name?'

'Harold. Poor bastard. God, when I think what happened. Sarah never talked about it, but I think perhaps she should have, now I look at Lawrence. The man is so pathological when it comes to his parents.'

I tried to recall how Lawrie had behaved, on the occasions that Reede had mentioned the name Harold Schloss. I didn't remember any particular show of emotion, or moment of recognition. But he had asked if Reede knew what had happened to him – I did remember that.

'What happened to his father?' I asked.

Gerry bared his teeth in a grim smile, revealing long incisors. 'He doesn't tell you much, does he? Well, it's a sensitive subject.'

'Clearly.'

'Perhaps you two don't have time spare for talking. I was the same, once.'

I tried to turn my blush into a weak smile, half wanting to flee, half wanting to find out from this man more than Lawrie would ever tell me. 'He has a point, not talking about it,' Gerry said. 'It's useless for a man to rake over things he can't even remember. Lawrie never even met the fellow.' He ran his hand over his head and fixed me with a look. 'Hitler happened to Harold Schloss, that's what. Like he happened to us all.'

I went to speak, but Gerry rose to his feet, yellow-nailed against the dark wood floorboards. 'It's very early to be talking about all this,' he said. 'I'm going for a walk to clear my head. I suggest that you go back to bed.'

16

I returned to Lawrie's room. He stirred and opened his eyes with a smile, throwing his arms up to let me into the warm, crumpled sheets. I stood at the side of the bed. 'What is it?' he said, the smile fading. 'What's wrong?'

'You're Lawrie Schloss,' I said. 'Your father sold *Rufina and the Lion*. That's how you have the painting.'

I admit, there might have been a better way to approach the situation – *your father* this and *your father* that – talking of a dead man Lawrie had never met, at six fifteen in the morning. I think it was because I had always thought of Lawrie as fundamentally honest; had even defended him to Quick when she was raising her doubts. And I realized now, that time and again, Lawrie had evaded the question not just of his mother, but of how she might have come into possessing such an artwork.

Lawrie lowered his arms and surveyed me. 'I'm Lawrie *Scott*,' he said. He closed his eyes. 'You've been talking to Gerry.'

'You lied,' I said.

He opened his eyes again, and propped himself on an elbow. 'I didn't bloody lie. I just never told you the whole truth.'

'But why? What does it matter who your father was?' He said nothing. 'Lawrie, have you really sold your car?'

He rubbed his eyes, frowning as if trying to slot his thoughts into place. 'Yes, I have really sold my car. Gerry's definitely planning to sell this house. And then what will I do?'

'He'll never sell it. There's a room along this corridor devoted to your mother. It's even got her clothes and make-up still inside.'

There was confusion in his eyes. 'How d'you know about that?'

I sat down slowly on the side of the bed. 'It's where I just bumped into Gerry.'

'You were snooping?'

I looked away, embarrassed. 'He told me about your mother giving you her maiden name when the war was on. When Reede mentioned Harold Schloss – why didn't you just say something?'

He fell back against his pillow. 'It would have made things too complicated.'

'It would have simplified them. That's how you have the painting in your possession. Provenance and all that.'

'It might simplify things for Reede, but not for me.' He clasped his hands together into one fist. 'Look, we never, ever talked about him, Odelle. My family doesn't *talk* about things. And if you've spent your whole life never talking about something, do you think you're suddenly going to be able to discuss it – just like that – to some stranger who's after your painting?'

'But why—'

'I don't have the words for it, Odelle. I don't have the words for something that happened when I wasn't even alive.'

'But surely your mother talked about him? He was your *father*.'

'I knew his name, that's it. I knew my mother changed hers when she came back to England. It was her and me for sixteen years, and then Gerry came along. I wasn't going to claim a dead man just to satisfy Edmund Reede's little genealogy.'

'All right. I'm sorry.'

'There's nothing to be sorry for.'

'I just . . .' I thought of Quick. 'I'm just trying to make sense of the painting, that's all.'

He sat up. 'My mother never told me how she got that painting,

Odelle. I wasn't lying. My only guess is, my father never managed to get it to this Peggy Guggenheim – and then in the chaos that followed leaving Spain, my mother took it with her and brought it to England.'

'What happened to their marriage, if he was in Paris and she was in England?'

Lawrie sighed. 'I don't know. She came to London; he stayed there. And then the Germans occupied Paris. My mother never even wore a wedding ring before Gerry.'

'And you never asked her about it?'

'I asked,' he said, his voice tight. 'She didn't like it, but she told me he died in the war being brave, and that now it was just the two of us. I heard that line at three years old, at ten, at thirteen – and you hear something like that over and over again, it just becomes the way things are.'

'Perhaps she wanted to spare you the grief of it,' I said.

Lawrie looked grim. 'I don't think my mother ever really thought about sparing me anything. My guess is, either he walked out and chose not to have contact with her, or she was the one who severed ties. It was a nice idea, her and me, against the world, but it got a little claustrophobic. She was very over-protective. Said I was her second chance.'

'And that's all she said?'

'You don't know what she was like. It just wasn't something you talked about to her. And lots of people had missing dads, you know. It was after the war, lots of widows. You don't pick at someone else's grief.'

'Of course.' I knew it was time for me to stop. I wanted to ask if Sarah had ever talked to him about Olive; how she might fit into all this. As I'd discussed with Cynth, a young woman with that surname could easily be Harold Schloss's daughter – but Lawrie had never mentioned a sister, however much older than him she would have been. And if Lawrie knew as little about Harold as he was claiming to, this hardly came as a surprise. I looked at him, trying to see echoes in his face of Quick's. I couldn't imagine how I'd broach the subject that he and Marjorie Quick were possibly related.

Lawrie sighed. 'I should have told you about it. But things were up and down between you and me, and it wasn't on my mind. I'm sorry you had to bump into Gerry. I hope he was wearing his dressing gown, at least.'

'Yes.'

'Small mercies.'

'Can I get in?'

He lifted up the blankets and I snuggled under. We lay in silence for a while, and I wondered if Lawrie would ever have told me about his father, if I hadn't pushed it. When it came to our blossoming relationship, I had to consider whether it mattered, either way. Lawrie was still Lawrie to me, surely, regardless of who his father was. But it did sting a little, the amount I didn't know about him, what he'd chosen to hold back. I suppose I was holding things back, too. 'We sat looking at Harold's writing on the train,' I murmured into his shoulder.

'I know.'

'Did you feel anything, looking at it?'

'Not in the way you probably want me to. I was a little sad, I suppose. The way life works out.'

'Yes,' I said, and thought again of Marjorie Quick. 'You never quite know how it's going to end.'

17

*Q*uick telephoned in sick on Monday, and was still not back by Wednesday, and I was too tied up working with Pamela to get everything ready for the opening night of the exhibition to go and see her. Reede was amassing an impressively eclectic list of attendees for 'The Swallowed Century', and had placed Pamela and me in charge of organizing the invitations. Reede wanted coverage, relevance, attention – for the Skelton Institute to be cool and viable, a place where money flowed – and *Rufina and the Lion* was going to help him. Mixing high culture with pop, there was even a rumour that a Cabinet minister might turn up. And it had to be said, *Rufina and the Lion*, as both an intellectual challenge and an aesthetic offering, more than stood up to it. Reede had commissioned a frame for the painting, the first it had probably ever had. He had good taste; it was a dark mahogany, and it radiated Rufina's colours even more.

Julie Christie had confirmed she was coming, as had Robert Fraser, the art dealer. Quentin Crisp, Roald Dahl and Mick Jagger had all been invited. I thought the Jagger invitation an unusual choice, but Pamela pointed out that earlier in the year, when the Rolling Stone had been put in custody on a drug charge, the papers reported that he'd taken with him forty cigarettes, a bar of chocolate, a jigsaw puzzle, and two books. Pamela knew everything about the Stones. Mick's first book was about Tibet, she told me. The second was on art.

The newspapers picked up the story of the exhibition, as Reede had hoped they would. The *Daily Telegraph* ran a headline on page 5: *The Spanish Saint and the English Lion: How One Art Expert Rescued an Iberian Gem.* According to the journalist, *An extraordinary, long-lost painting by the disappeared Spanish artist Isaac Robles has been discovered in an English house, and will be brought to public recognition by Edmund Reede, art historian and Director of the Skelton Institute.* I wondered what Lawrie might make of this last sentence – or indeed, Quick – for both of them, in very different ways, were helping Reede achieve his aims. It annoyed me, but it did not surprise me.

In *The Times*, the art correspondent, Gregory Herbert, wrote a long essay focusing on rediscovered artists like Isaac Robles – and how paintings such as *Rufina and the Lion* both reflected and extended our understanding of the turbulence of the first half of the twentieth century. Herbert was invited for a private view, and he told us, as he stood before the painting, that he'd fought in the International Brigades in 1937, before the Spanish government had sent the volunteers home.

In Auschwitz and at Hiroshima, Herbert wrote, *the toll has been written in ledgers and carved on sepulchres. In Spain, the Republican dead can be tallied only in the heart. There are few marked graves for those who lost that war. In the name of survival, the damage was internalized, a psychic scar on toxic land. Murderers still live near their victims' families, and between neighbour and neighbour twenty ghosts trudge the village road. Sorrow has seeped into the soil, and the trauma of survivors is revealed only by their acts of concealment.*

Even today, Pablo Picasso still stays away from the Andalusian city of Malaga, despite being its most famous son. When Spain broke apart, many artists escaped the cracks, fleeing to France or America rather than endure isolation, imprisonment and possible death. Life in its variety was cauterized, and so was art. For the poet Federico García Lorca, it was too late to escape. One can only surmise that his fellow Andalusian, the painter Isaac Robles, may have met a similar fate.

Spain's past is a cut of meat turning green on the butcher's slab. When the war ended, people were forbidden to look back and see the circling flies. Soon they found themselves unable to turn their heads, discovering that there was no language permitted for their pain. But the paintings, at least, remain: Guernica, *the works of Dalí and Miró –* and now Rufina and the Lion, *an allegory of Spain, a testament to a beautiful country at war with itself, carrying its own head in its arms, doomed for ever to be hunted by lions.*

By the end of Herbert's essay, you would imagine that Isaac Robles was well on his way to becoming highly collectible, enjoying a second renaissance of prices the likes of which the humble painter himself would never have dreamed. Herbert sounded so sure that he knew what the painting was about, that Isaac Robles had intended a political commentary on the state of his country. But I thought the painting, combined with the images of Justa in *Women in the Wheatfield*, seemed more personal – sexual, even.

By Thursday, when Barozzi and the other Guggenheim people from Venice arrived with their paintings – an ambassadorial art entourage, with better presents and suits – Quick was still not back, and Reede was furious.

'She's not well,' I said. Quick wasn't answering her telephone. The nearer the exhibition had drawn to opening night, the further she had shrunk away from it. Even though I feared the pressure of the impending opening was crushing her, I almost hoped it would crack her open whatever the consequence, so the secret she was hiding from me would be forced into the light.

'I don't care if she's on her death-bed,' Reede raged, and I shuddered at his macabre accuracy. 'This is the most important visit to happen to the Skelton in all my twenty years and she can't even be bothered to show up?'

He was in an extremely bad temper, for he had failed in his bid to get the Prado museum in Madrid to loan him the Goya. 'Then who's the person I can speak to in the convent with the Murillo?' I had heard him saying through his open door one afternoon.

In Quick's absence, Reede had directed the hanging of the paintings himself, ordering Pamela and me to oversee the tea-making and the clearing up of boxes, packing crates and twine. The Venetians were very friendly, I recall, and slightly disturbed by the freezing London winter. 'Have you ever been to Venice?' one of them asked me.

'No,' I said.

'Go. It is like the theatre has been turned onto the street.'

The photograph of Isaac Robles and the unnamed woman had been blown up to cover four enormous boards. Two archivists were trying to affix it to the end of the gallery wall. No one dared point out that the camera was clearly centred on the slightly blurred face of the smiling young woman, holding the brush. 'It's the only photograph we have of him,' Reede said, 'so it's going in.'

The Venetians pulled their own Isaac Robles out of a crate and a gasp went up from Pamela.

'Oh, Dell,' she said. 'Look.'

The Orchard was indeed worth gasping at. It was stunning, far larger than I was expecting, at least five foot long and four high. The colours had lasted well over the past thirty years – it was so vibrant and modern in its sensibility, it could have been painted yesterday. There were echoes in the patchwork fields of *Rufina and the Lion*, but the detailing was almost hyper-real, diligent on the ground, giving way to a symphony of brushstrokes in the sky.

'It is my favourite,' admitted one of the Venetians.

'It's beautiful.'

'Where does Signor Reede want it?'

I looked at the plan. Reede wanted *Rufina and the Lion* to share a wall only with *Women in the Wheatfield*, which was still in its crate. *The Orchard*, because of its size, was unlikely to share wall space. 'Put it here for now,' I said, indicating that the Venetians could park it safely in a corner of the gallery.

Although it was very exciting to be in that space that day –
opening the wooden crates, like Christmas on a grand scale; saw-
dust and nails everywhere, and a magical sense of occasion – I
had a deep feeling of unease. Yes, there was the momentousness
of this being Isaac Robles' first ever London exhibition – but the
one snag was that Quick didn't think Isaac Robles painted these
paintings at all.

I wandered down the gallery to take another look at the photograph, and stood before the woman I was so sure was Olive Schloss,
Rufina and the Lion half-finished behind her. It felt imperative that
I understand this photograph, that it was the key to unlocking the
truth about that painting, and what was happening to Quick. I
sought in that girl's slightly blurred face a younger Quick, full of
hope and passion. And although Quick had become gaunt over the
past months, I believed I could see in this bounteous, full visage,
the girl she once had been. But I could not be sure of it. Over the
last months, Quick had given me so much, in a way – and yet at the
same time, so little. My desire for answers had supplied me with
my own, and although they were attractive to me, they were not
necessarily true. Looking again at this life-size photograph, and
with no time left, I knew what I had to do.

In my lunch break, I sneaked up to Quick's office and took some
Skelton headed paper from her supplies, hurriedly practising
Reede's signature several times on a notepad. I typed up a brief
letter of introduction and explanation, with regards to enhanc-
ing the contents of *The Swallowed Century*, before taking a deep
breath and faking Reede's squiggle at the bottom. With the letter
in my handbag, I walked over to the main office of the Slade School
of Art on Gower Street, and asked to check their alumni records.
They barely glanced at the letter, and I spent the whole hour looking through 1935 to 1945.

No Olive Schloss had ever been registered. It felt like one of
the last remaining threads had snapped, but I refused to believe
that Olive had truly disappeared. She was in the Skelton, on those

walls, surrounded by her work – she was in Wimbledon right now, a person I was determined to pin down. I found a phone box and dialled Quick's number, praying that she would answer.

'Hello?'

'You never made it, did you?' I said.

'Odelle, is that you?' The words came out oddly, her voice slurring. She sounded frail, and my relief at finally hearing her voice soon gave way to fear.

'Quick, I've been to the Slade.'

There was silence on the other end. I went on, frustrated and desperate, my face getting hot, my heart beginning to thump. 'No Olive Schloss ever registered at the Slade. But you knew that, didn't you? Just tell me the truth.'

'The Slade?' she repeated. 'The Slade . . . why were you at the Slade?'

'Quick, the exhibition opens tomorrow. Isaac Robles is going to get your glory. I don't think you should be alone.'

'I'm not alone.' She stopped, wheezing for breath. 'I'm never alone.'

I peered through the phone box's grimy squares of glass, Londoners rushing back and forth in front of me. I felt as if I were underwater, and their bodies were not really bodies, just smudges of colour, moving across my sight.

'I'm coming to see you,' I said, surprised at how adamant I sounded, more than I'd ever dared to sound before.

I could hear Quick hesitate, thinking, the catch of breath as she stopped resisting. 'What about your work?' she said. 'They need you for the exhibition.'

Her protest was weak, and her words were everything I needed to hear. Quick needed me; she knew she did. '*You* are my work, Quick,' I said. 'Can't you see?'

'I'm not in a good way.'

'I know.'

'No – you don't understand. I'm scared. They're coming. I never meant to hurt her.'

Suddenly I felt very claustrophobic in this phone box; I wanted to get out. 'Who didn't you want to hurt?'

'I can hear them—'

'No one's coming,' I soothed, but she was unnerving me. I needed air, and her voice was so desperate. 'Don't be scared,' I said. 'Quick, are you still there? You can trust me, I promise.'

'What did you say?'

'Listen, Quick. I'll be there soon. Quick?'

The line had gone dead. Feeling sick, I pushed my way out of the phone box, and hurried to the nearest Tube.

SEPTEMBER 1936

XVIII

It was still warm by late September, the air in Arazuelo heavy with honeysuckle, the earth reddened and cracked. Lying beneath this beauteous landscape was sour matter, but it didn't feel like war; not how the Schlosses thought war was supposed to be. It was something worse, a localized, persistent terror. Italian and German bombers would fly overhead, shooting at stationary planes on airfields, at Malaga port, at petrol tanks. But there was a strange sense of limbo, an intermittent hope that all this would be tied up soon, that the Republican government would sort a resistance against these nationalist rebels and their foreign allies, who were stretching their reach across the country.

The nationalists had gained control of Old Castile, Leon, Oviedo, Alava, Navarre, Galicia, Zaragoza, the Canaries and all the Balearics, except Menorca. In the south, they had seized Cadiz, Seville, Cordoba, Granada and Huelva. Malaga was still in the Republican zone – as was Arazuelo – but nevertheless, the rebels felt very near.

Harold would drive into Malaga in order to bring back supplies. He said some shops and bars would be open, whilst others were closed, and the trains and buses would mysteriously cease and resume their timetables with no warning. Nothing was stable. No one was even wearing neckties any more, for such flourishes were taken as a sign of bourgeois tendency and might make you a target for the reds. Harold hoped the worst the Anarchists might do was steal his car, vehicles requisitioned 'for the cause', petrol siphoned off for trucks, elegant motors left to rust.

The days were bearable; the worst was the nights. The family lay awake in the finca as gunshots peppered the fields, ever nearer. Each side of the growing battle saw the other as a faceless, viral mass contaminating the body politic, requiring excision from society. Right-wing and left-wing gangs were taking the law into their own hands, removing opponents from their homes, leaving them in unmarked graves amongst the hills and groves.

In many instances, politics was the cover for personal vendetta and family feud. Most of the right-wing terror was directed against those who had influenced the violence against the priests and the factory owners back in 1934 – union leaders, prominent anti-clericals, several Republican mayors. And yet – mechanics, butchers, doctors, builders, labourers, barbers – they too were 'taken for a walk', as the phrase came to be known. And it wasn't just men. Certain women who had become teachers under the Republic were removed, as were known anarchists' wives. None of it was legal, of course, but there seemed no means of stopping it, when hate and power were in play.

As for the rogue elements on the left – despite the posters Harold had seen plastered around Malaga, imploring them to stop shaming their political and trade organizations and to cease their brutalities – they went for retired civil guards, Catholic sympathizers, people they knew to be rich, people they *believed* to be rich. Houses were looted, their property damaged – and it was this fear that often struck first into the imagination of the middle classes, rather than the chance they would be shot.

The Schlosses did not fear for themselves. They thought no one would touch them, as foreigners. They were nothing to do with all this. Death was taking place beyond their village, outside municipal authority and the sight of the people. The violence in the country – against both the body of a village and a villager's bullet-riddled corpse – was concealed, although everyone knew it was there. Because you couldn't see it, you carried on. It was odd, Olive thought, how you could live alongside this; how you could know all this was happening, and still not want to leave.

She had long ago abandoned trying to listen to the BBC to seek the facts, for it offered little more than an improbable-sounding hybrid of information from Madrid and Seville, adding it together and dividing it by London. Yet the Republican government stations were one long barrage of victory speeches and claims of triumph, which were rather undermined by actual events. Granada's frequency always crackled, not a word could be heard – and the same applied to the northern cities, whose radio waves could not penetrate the southern mountains.

The city of Malaga, however, was constantly broadcasting denials, rumours and myths; Republican calls to arms, meeting times and orders to build a new Spain, free of fascists. And on the other side, the alarming nationalist invective was a frequency in Seville. In the daytime, it would play music and personal announcements, as if there was no conflict going on at all. But by night, the insurgents would broadcast, and although there was still much bombast and warmongering in it, Olive used it to deduce the changing state of her adopted country's fortunes. She listened as Queipo de Llano, the general who had first broadcast from Seville, maintained his unrelenting bloodthirstiness, crying out that there was a cancer in Spain, a body of infidels that only death would remove.

IT WAS UNNERVING, ALL OF it; and yet there were heartening stories of people refusing to do exactly what the generals wanted. Teresa reported how a priest in the neighbouring village prevented a Falangist gang from shooting the atheists in his parish. She had also heard rumours of leftists reprimanding Anarchists for trying to burn down the local church, even hiding right-wing neighbours in their bread ovens, protecting them from certain death when the radicals turned up.

Olive, listening to these tales, could see how most people were massed in the middle. They wanted no disturbance, desperate just

to live their lives away from these demonstrations of power, talks
of purge, of brutality sprayed in blood against a whitewashed wall.
But their desire couldn't change the truth of Arazuelo's atmosphere. She would walk into the village and see people's pinched
faces, worrying who was going to defend whom when Arazuelo's
day of reckoning finally came.

ISAAC PURCHASED A RIFLE IN Malaga from a trade-union contact,
who was fond of poaching his boss's boar. He reinforced the bolt
across the cottage door, but he knew this would mean nothing to
someone determined to get him. More 'people of interest' to the
nationalist rebels had left their villages to hide out in the countryside, or join the militias run by the Communist party in Malaga.
But this wasn't far enough for Teresa. She wanted him to leave.

'I think you should go north,' she said. 'You've made too many
enemies here. You don't fit. The left won't trust you because of our
father, and the right don't trust you for not being his legitimate son.'

Isaac regarded his sister, the new severity in her face. 'You
don't fit here either, Tere,' he said.

'But you're the one who put a bullet through the Madonna.
You're the one who's spent his life teaching peasants their rights.
You're the one—'

'All right. But you think they're only going for men? You'd have
to come with me.'

'I won't leave.'

'Jesus, you're as stubborn as the Schlosses.'

'Well, we all know why they won't leave. Because of you. If you
think about it, Isa, you're endangering them too.'

The British Consulate in Malaga had sent letters out to any of His
Majesty's registered subjects it knew of in the region. Wide-eyed,
Teresa handed over the consul's letter, which was addressed to
Sarah. After a thin breakfast, bread being scarcer and the goat

milk drying up, the Schlosses discussed whether they should stay or go.

The letter informed them that warships were waiting to take them off Spanish soil into Gibraltar – and on, if they wished, to England. The threat, it said, was not from these nationalist insurgents and their foreign troops, but from those on the Spanish far left, the reds – who might soon loot these British-rented fincas, and confiscate any private property.

Olive was determined that they should stay. 'We can't just leave when it doesn't suit us. What sort of example is that?'

'*Liebling*,' said Harold. 'It's dangerous.'

'You're the one still driving into Malaga. We're foreigners. They won't come for us.'

'That's exactly why they *will* come for us,' said Harold, pointing at the letter. 'That's what the consul said.'

'Liv's right,' said Sarah. 'I don't think we should leave.'

Harold looked at his two womenfolk in bemusement. 'You *both* want to stay?'

Sarah got up and walked to the window. 'London is over for us.'

'I'm confused,' said Harold. 'Only two months ago, you were clamouring to leave.' Sarah ignored him. '*I* think,' he said, 'that we should leave if it gets any worse, but invite Isaac to come with us.'

The women turned to look at him. 'It's my duty,' said Harold. 'He's too valuable.'

'Isaac won't leave,' said Sarah. 'He'll fight.'

'What would you know about it?'

'It's obvious. He feels great loyalty to this place.'

'As do I,' said Olive, still on the sofa, reaching over to light one of their dwindling supply of cigarettes. Her parents did not stop her. 'Mr Robles isn't a coward,' she said, exhaling deeply, surveying them both. 'But if you're planning to take him, then quite frankly, you should take Teresa too.'

'Has he nearly finished this *Rufina* painting?' asked Harold. 'I keep dangling the bait for Peggy, but have not been given any news.'

'I do not know, señor,' said Teresa.

'You normally know everything, Teresa,' Sarah said.

'He's nearly finished,' said Olive. 'It won't be long.'

'When you next go to Malaga, darling,' Sarah said to Harold, 'buy a Union Jack.'

'What?'

'I want to hoist the Union Jack. So whatever bastard comes along to shoot us up, they know that we are neutral.'

'We're hardly *neutral*, Mother,' said Olive. 'Have you even looked at the newspapers?'

'You know I don't like the newspapers, Olive.'

'Unless you're in them.'

'*Liv*,' said her father, a warning in his voice.

'Well, she lives in a bubble. Our government has refused to get involved. So have the French. They're saying that defending the Spanish Republic is tantamount to a defence of Bolshevism.'

'They're worried, *liebling*,' said Harold. 'They fear revolution, that the situation here will spread to France, up and up across the Channel, into Regent Street, along the Strand and the Pennine Way.'

'Baldwin's so scared of Hitler, he won't do anything.'

'I don't think he is,' said Harold. 'The Prime Minister is buying *time* rather than German favour.'

'Either way – where does that leave you, Mr Vienna?' said Sarah. 'Better for you – for all of us – if we stay in Spain.'

Rufina and the Lion was in fact completed, and Olive hadn't painted anything since. She'd never experienced this lack of willingness to approach a canvas, and she didn't like it at all – feeling useless, and frightened by her lack of confidence. She didn't want to connect it directly to Isaac's lack of interest in her – she wanted to work independently of him, of any factor outside her own creative impulse – but it was proving impossible. She had begged Isaac to present *Rufina and the Lion* to Harold, but he wouldn't do it. 'I've got more important things to worry about,' he'd said.

'But you could just hand it over. My father's waiting. Peggy Guggenheim's waiting.'

'I do not care if the Pope is waiting,' he snapped.

Olive started to feel that *Rufina* was clogging up her mind. Its power over her had become a reflection, not just of her relationships with Isaac and Teresa, but of the political situation that was swirling around them. Fear was stoppering her. She had painted it as a purge; now she needed it gone. When Isaac wouldn't take it, Olive suggested that Teresa take the panel down to the pantry, out of her sight.

Teresa refused. 'It is too cold in there, señorita,' she said. 'It might be damaged.'

'But I can't paint anything now.'

'*Tranquila, señorita*,' said Teresa. 'It will come and go.'

'Well, it's never gone anywhere before. What if that's *it*? What if it's just been these paintings, and that's it?'

ONE EVENING IN EARLY OCTOBER, the Schlosses invited Isaac for dinner. He was quiet throughout, and afterwards Olive caught him alone, staring into the darkness of the orchard. She slipped her hand in his, but he did not take hers, his own resting there like a dead man's. She tried to cajole him again, saying that surely he could do with more money for the Republican side, and that giving Harold *Rufina and the Lion* would be the ideal way.

'The Soviets have promised us arms,' he said. 'We may lose Malaga. We may lose Madrid and half of Catalonia, but we will win the war.'

She leaned over to plant a kiss on his cheek. 'You're so brave,' she said.

He seemed not to notice her kiss at all, as he ground the cigarette under his heel, ash smearing black on the veranda. 'Teresa thinks I should go north. Our father is becoming more and more . . . loud, about those on the left. I represent something that holds him back. He's ambitious. Ambitious men do well in times like these.'

'Will he hurt you, Isa?'

'He will not get his hands dirty. Those days are over. But some-one else might.'

'Isaac, no.'

'They're bombing Malaga again. You should leave, Olive. You all should go.'

'But we *live* here.'

'Imagine if you stayed. You might never paint again, all because you wanted to be brave.'

'If I was dead, I don't suppose I'd much care. Besides, I haven't painted a thing since finishing *Rufina*.'

He turned to her in surprise. 'Is that true?'

'Yes, that's why I keep asking. I know it's selfish, Isa, I know.' She could feel a cry coming, but she swallowed it down. 'Without you I'm stuck.' He did not respond, and she turned away to the blackness of the orchard.

'You don't need me, Olive,' he said, eventually. 'You just need to pick up your brush. Why do you insist so much on involving us? Is it so that you can blame us if it goes wrong?'

'No.'

'If I had half your skill, I wouldn't care who loved me.'

She gave a dry laugh. 'That's what I thought too. But I'd rather be happy.'

'Being allowed to paint is what makes you happy. I know that about you at least.' She smiled. 'I like you, Olive,' Isaac went on. 'You are a very special girl. But you are so young to be thinking of for ever.'

Olive swallowed again, tears pricking at her eyes. 'I'm not young. You and me – why can't this be for ever?'

He waved his arm towards the darkness. 'War or no war, you were never going to stay here.'

'You don't *see*, do you?'

'What don't I see?'

'That I love you.'

'You love an idea of me.'

'It's the same thing.'

They were silent. 'I have been useful to you,' he said. 'That is all.'

'What is it, Isa? What's changed?'

He closed his eyes and shivered. 'Nothing's changed. It's always been the same.'

She pounded the veranda rail with her fist. 'You should *want* to be with me. You should—'

A muffled explosion from beyond the valley silenced them both. 'What the hell was that?' said Isaac, scanning the horizon.

'Teresa said they've started to bomb bridges again. Is it true your father is helping them?'

Isaac's eyes were so dark with anger, she moved back. 'I need to go to Malaga,' he said.

'At midnight? What use will you be now?'

'More useful than standing here.'

'So that's it, is it? Us?'

'Our ideas of what this is have always been different. You know that.'

'What am I supposed to do with that painting?'

'Give it to your father. I must deal with my own.'

'What do you mean? I won't give up on this—'

'You're mixing things up, Olive. You're frustrated you cannot paint—'

She grabbed his arms. 'I need you. I can't paint without you.'

'You painted before me.'

'Isaac, don't leave me – please.'

'Goodbye, Olive.'

'No!'

Isaac stepped down from the veranda and walked towards the orchard. He turned back to the house, his face half-illuminated by the moon. Behind her, Olive felt a presence at the kitchen door.

'Where's he going?' Sarah said.

'*Suerte*,' Isaac called over his shoulder, before slipping between the trees.

'What does that mean?' asked Sarah.

Olive could feel her tears coming, but she refused to let her mother see her cry. 'It doesn't matter.'

'Olive, tell me what he said.'

Olive turned to Sarah, struck by the expression of worry on her face. 'All it means, Mother,' she said, 'is good luck.'

XIX

A few hours after Isaac slipped away from the Schloss women and into the darkness, Don Alfonso's finca was attacked with fire and a second salvo was launched upon the church of Santa Rufina in the centre of Arazuelo. Later, people whispered that yes, they'd seen a disrobed Padre Lorenzo, running away from the flames into the village square, with a naked woman fast on his heels. Some said there hadn't been a woman at all, just the priest in a white smock, the bump of his private part visible under the cotton. Others swore on the Holy Bible there'd been a woman – a vision of Rufina herself, running from the godlessness behind her before she took flight into the air.

The only truth Arazuelo could attest to was that by dawn, the church was a shell and Don Alfonso's estate a blackened skeleton. Wood smoke hung over the air, smarting the eyes of those trying to go about their business, until the whole village fell into an uneasy stupor, knowing full well that retaliation for something like this would eventually come.

When Teresa came running through the grey dawn light, bashing on the front door of the finca, Olive knew something was very wrong.

'Isaac has done something stupid—'

'What's he done? Where is he?'

Teresa looked stricken. 'I don't know. The church is gone.'

'Gone – what do you mean, gone?'

'Fire. And my father's house also.'

'Dear God, Teresa. Come inside.'

AROUND TWO HOURS LATER, DON Alfonso appeared, his once-pristine suit now smeared with charcoal. He too banged on the finca door, and upstairs with Olive, Teresa cowered. 'It's going to be all right,' Olive whispered.

Teresa gripped her wrist. 'No, señorita. You do not understand.'

Harold let Don Alfonso in, and the man moved angrily through the hallway into the front east room. Olive crept down the stairs to peer through the crack in the door.

'You have heard what happened?' Don Alfonso said.

'I have.'

'News travels fast. It is an outrage. I could have been dead. My wife, my children – it is only because my daughter Clara is an insomniac that any of us are still here. Three of my stable grooms, an under-butler and a pot-washing boy had a part in it. I've found these men, Señor Schloss, and they are all in the jail, waiting their punishment. And do you know what they tell me? They tell me that Isaac Robles paid them for their help. Where did Isaac get the money to pay those men? It was certainly not from me. I cannot get the answers, because I cannot find my bastard son. Do you know where he is, señor?'

'No.'

'And yet you know my finca was set on fire.'

'Is he not at his cottage?'

'I sent Jorge and Gregorio there. All they found was *this*.' Don Alfonso held aloft an old copy of *Vogue*. 'Your wife's, I assume?'

A look of surprise passed over Harold's face, but he adjusted quickly back to an impression of calm. 'She gives them to Teresa.'

'My son set loose thirty of my thoroughbred horses, señor. He torched my stables. He burned down Lorenzo's church.'

'Sit down, Don Alfonso, please. These are severe accusations.'

'His own friends have turned him in. He is a devil, señor.'

'I beg to differ,' said Harold, clearly irritated now. 'Don Alfonso, your son does not have time for these games. Your son is a gifted man.'

It was Don Alfonso's turn to look surprised. 'Gifted?'

'Have you never seen his work?'

'What?'

Before Harold could explain further, Olive pushed into the room. Both men jumped and turned to her. 'Go upstairs,' said Harold in a tight voice.

'No.'

Behind Olive, Sarah appeared. 'What's going on?' she said. Her eye rested on the figure of Don Alfonso, and the colour drained from her face. 'Is he dead?' she whispered. 'Is Mr Robles dead?'

'Don't be ridiculous, Sarah,' said Harold, unable to mask the stress in his voice.

Don Alfonso inclined his head towards Sarah in a curt bow. 'Is Teresa here?' he asked her.

'Upstairs,' replied Sarah.

'*Mother*,' said Olive. 'No.'

'Please bring her to me,' said Alfonso.

'No,' said Olive. 'You can't have her.'

'Liv, don't be ridiculous,' said Harold. 'Be civilized.'

'*Civilized?*'

'Go and fetch Teresa.'

OLIVE WENT UPSTAIRS, BUT TERESA was nowhere to be seen. Olive waited, buying time, pretending to look for her, praying that Teresa had got herself somewhere safe. She moved back down with determined steps and returned to the front east room. Don Alfonso narrowed his eyes when he saw she was alone. 'Are you hiding her, señorita?' he said. 'I know you think you are her friend.'

'I'm not hiding anyone.'

He turned to Olive's parents. 'It won't be good for you, hiding them. Isaac is wanted for theft, arson, criminal damage, attempted murder—'

'For God's sake,' Harold interjected. 'We are not hiding your children.'

'They are no longer my children. You should leave here,' said Don Alfonso. 'You should go.'

'On the contrary,' replied Harold. 'I think we should protect those who do not enjoy your protection. I am beginning to understand you much better.'

Alfonso laughed. 'You foreigners, you're all the same. You think you are protecting Teresa and Isaac? They will be the ones who will have to protect you. And do you think they will? That you are under some magic shroud, that your maid and gardener love you?'

'Teresa is our maid, yes, and a bloody good one – but Isaac is not our gardener. You have no idea about what your son—'

'I know him better than you do. What will he use to defend you, señor – a saucepan? Those degenerates he consorts with are more likely to put a hoe through your heart and join up with the Reds.'

When Don Alfonso had disappeared in his motor car shortly after, Olive ran through the finca's rusty gates, down the path, into the village – by this time breathless and leg-sore – and out and up the hill again, to Isaac and Teresa's cottage. They were not there, but Jorge and Gregorio had turned the place over. God, this cottage was a spare place, sparer than Olive had remembered it to be. In her mind's eye, it had become a rustic haven, a place to think and breathe and paint. In truth, it was a place one might wish to escape.

Isaac's room contained nothing but his unmade bed and a jar of dying roses on the windowsill. Teresa's meagre belongings were scattered on her bedroom floor. Olive was surprised to see one of her old paint tubes – the grasshopper-green shade she'd used for *The Orchard*. There was a Veuve Clicquot champagne cork, and stranger things; a cut-out square of material that matched her father's pyjamas. There was a crushed packet of Harold's cigarettes, and when Olive went to shake it, several stubs had been saved inside, their ends covered in the unmistakeable rouge of her mother's lips. Lying around the floorboards were loose pages ripped from a notebook, with words and phrases written in English in a diligent, neat hand: *palaver – snaffled – crass – gosh – I'm starving – ghastly – selfish*. Alongside them were their Spanish meanings.

Olive's heart began to thump. Looking at this flotsam from her parents' lives, this notebook of the things they had probably said in careless passing – she had the chilly sensation that she didn't really know Teresa at all.

The front door banged; her skin turned to gooseflesh. No footsteps followed and she told herself it was the wind. The noise still unnerved her, and she imagined a wolf, sneaking in from the mountains. She was about to move out of Teresa's room, when she saw a photograph on the floor. It was a picture of herself and Isaac in front of *Rufina and the Lion*. Olive was smiling and Isaac, his eyebrows slightly raised, looked ready for his painter's pose. Olive had never seen this picture before, and without thinking, she rammed it deep into her pocket.

As she passed back down the corridor, she saw Isaac's original painting, propped against the wall. Teresa must have moved it back here, out of sight. The idealized faces of herself and her mother seemed to loom out, and Olive was struck again by their mannequin, monstrous blankness.

SHE WENT OUTSIDE TO LOOK at the hills. There was a wreathing pallor of smoke still in the air, the taste of the fire's aftermath. Isaac knew these hills well, better than Don Alfonso. He knew where to hide – but Teresa had not had as much time to escape. Something terrible was coming, Olive could feel it; and there was nothing she could do.

'Teresa?' she called to the land, and her own voice rebounded back. 'Teresa?' she shouted again, her panic rising. But all that Olive heard was the echo of Teresa's name, falling down the hills.

XX

It was Jorge who spotted her, disappearing into the forest on the outskirts of the village. He and Gregorio were on the hunt, but it was only by chance that Jorge had his head turned in that direction; the glimpse of a slim brown leg, the flash of a dark plait. What happened next changed Arazuelo for ever, the place that was always supposed to stay the same. The trauma of it rang out, long and ineradicable down the years to come, however hard those who witnessed it attempted silence.

Had he been any further away, Jorge would have lost her; for Teresa was swift-footed and he was much heavier. But together he and Gregorio stalked her through the trees. When Jorge shot his pistol into the air, she spun to face the direction of the sound, and Gregorio took the opportunity to grab her from behind.

She kicked and screamed, but Gregorio did not let go. 'Where is he?' Jorge shouted at her, lumbering through the bracken.

'What do you mean? Put me down.' Teresa felt as if her heart was inching its way up her body, weighing down her tongue.

'Where's your brother?'

'I don't *know*.' Jorge moved forward, pushing his face close to hers. She could smell the sour catch of old alcohol on his breath. 'Come on, Teresa, you know everything, little bird-eye. Little spy. Where's your fucking brother?'

'I don't know,' she repeated.

'Tie her to the tree,' Jorge said, but Gregorio hesitated. 'You heard me. Do it.' Gregorio didn't move.

'I don't know where he is, Jorge, I swear,' Teresa said, sensing a chance. 'You think he'd tell me? No one tells me anything—'

'Your brother set half the village on fire last night. When we catch him, he's a dead man. And you're going to help.'

He began to drag Teresa by her plait towards the tree. 'Isa's known you since you were schoolkids,' she said, gasping at the pain arcing across her skull. 'Twenty years your friend. How does your mother look you in the face?' she hissed.

'At least I've got a mother who does,' said Jorge.

'You're shaking, Gregorio,' Teresa went on at the softer man, out of her wits with fear, but scenting his discomfort.

'Jorge,' said Gregorio. 'We should take her to the station.'

'Shut it,' Jorge said.

'I mean it. I'm not tying her to this tree. Don Alfonso never said – let's put her in the truck.'

JORGE EVENTUALLY RELENTED, AND THEY put Teresa in a cell at the civil guard headquarters, and all night Teresa was silent. 'Check she hasn't done herself in,' Jorge spat. 'Like her mother before her.'

'What?' said Gregorio.

Jorge looked at his colleague. 'Don't tell me you never knew. Her mother drowned herself. Probably didn't want to hang around to bring up that piece of shit,' he added, directing his voice down the dank corridor, loud enough for Teresa to hear.

The next morning, Teresa had barely slept. She had not been wearing many clothes in the first place, and no one had offered her a blanket – but what hurt more, what made her skin palpably shiver, was that no one had come from the finca to speak for her. In the deep of the night, staring up through the bars, thinking of the cruel words Jorge had uttered, Teresa had convinced herself that any minute Olive would come, Olive would call her name, demanding that these brutish boys let her out. Teresa had to believe it, because if she didn't believe it, then the firing squad would come instead.

But Olive never came – and neither did Harold, even though he would have had more authority than his daughter. And as dawn broke, Teresa began to think, *Of course, of course, why would they come?* – and she was glad that no one could witness the pitiful embarrassment of hope.

Jorge and Gregorio came into her cell at eight o'clock in the morning, where she was sitting upright on the bed, every one of her vertebrae pressed up against the cold stone of the wall. 'Up,' said Jorge.

She stood, and he approached. 'For the last time, Teresa. Where is your brother?'

'I don't kn—'

He whacked her round the mouth and her head flew back, cracking against the wall.

'I said, where is he?'

Teresa began to scream, until Jorge punched her again and she heard Gregorio cry out before she fell unconscious. The next thing she knew, she was blindfolded, bumping up and down in the back of their truck again, the iron tang of blood and a loose tooth in her mouth.

She tried to turn her head to the open air to see if she could sense where they were going, but she was still disorientated. Her neck hurt, her skull throbbed. The blindfold had been tied so tight that it cut across her eye sockets. It smelled like sweat, someone else's blood. Was this it? Deep in her heart, in her dreams, she had feared this moment. She was going to be shot in the head, round the back of some hut, fifty kilometres away from her home. And who would miss her? Who would mourn her passing?

The truck stopped. Teresa heard the men jump out of the wagon and swing down the back flap of the truck.

'Don't shoot me. Don't shoot me,' she pleaded, hearing the crack of her own voice, surprised at this overwhelming passion to live, and how prepared she was to abase herself in order to do it. Anything, to live. 'Gregorio,' she said. 'Please. *Please*. Save me.'

But Gregorio did not speak. A hand took her arm and walked her a few steps, pushing her down onto a chair. Teresa heard footsteps moving away, crunching against what sounded like gravel. She had been placed in the direction of the sun, and she could feel it warming her face, orange and gold through the blindfold and the tender skin of her eyelids. *This is it*, she thought.

'Olive,' she whispered, 'Olive.' She kept saying the name, and the blindfold was lifted. There was silence, then the sound of a few birds as they flapped across the sky. Teresa squinted, blinking to adjust her vision to the light. To her surprise, she saw Olive standing to her right, her head haloed in gold, the buildings behind her squares of white.

'Am I dead?' Teresa said.

'No,' replied a man.

Teresa could see now that she was in the main square, on a chair placed directly in front of the charred frame of the church. The villagers had started to gather – shrinking away like a shoal of fish, as Teresa turned her head. She tried to rise from the chair towards Olive. Olive took a step towards her, her arm outstretched, but Gregorio pushed Teresa back down.

Jorge waved his pistol at the gathered villagers. 'Keep back!' he shouted, but Olive stayed forward.

'What are you going to do to her?' she shouted in Spanish. 'What are you going to do?'

'Shut up!' Jorge said, going over to the truck and pulling something from the passenger seat. He walked back to Teresa, hands on his hips, assessing her, pacing round her slowly before taking her plait in his hand, weighing it like he was a widow at market, turning his nose up at the produce. With his other hand, he lifted up a large pair of shears, the kind gardeners used to prune their plants and flowers.

'I'll be fair,' he said, his fist wrapped round the plait. 'Let's
unravel it, bit by bit. I'm going to ask you one more time about your
brother, and if you cooperate, you can keep your hair.'

TERESA HAD TURNED TO STONE, the only living thing her plait,
coiled and twitching in Jorge's fist. Her gaze was distant; her body
was there, but she was not. As Jorge undid her hair with an air
of industry, she didn't flinch or cry out – she just sat, staring into
nothingness. So still, so meditative, she looked almost complicit
in the spectacle, until you noticed her bunched fists, the knuckles
whitening through the skin.

'Don't do this,' Olive said to the men. 'She doesn't know where
he is.'

Jorge swung round to face the other girl. 'That's what she says.'

Snip went the shears, a long tendril of black hair falling to the
ground, where it lay in the dust like a snake. No one whispered,
no one even seemed to breathe. 'Señorita,' Gregorio said to Olive.
'This is not your affair.'

'Don't hurt her,' said Olive. 'You'll regret it. Does her father
know you're doing this—'

'If you don't shut up, you'll be next,' Jorge shouted, lifting the
shears again. 'Where's your brother?' he asked Teresa, and still
Teresa did not speak. Jorge began to hack the second handful
of hair.

Just say something, Tere, Olive thought. *Anything, a lie.* But
Teresa was mute, keeping her eyes on the burned-out church,
and Olive could almost feel the whisker-touch of dark hair falling
against her own neck. Teresa still did not flinch, but Olive could
see fear glimmering in her eye, buried within that blank look.

'Where is he?' came the question, again and again. And still,
Teresa was silent, so Jorge cut more of her hair, close to the line
of the skull, emerging as a clumpy, patchy thing. 'You're a furry
mushroom,' Jorge said, laughing. No one in the village joined him,
but neither did they move to stop this spectacle.

'Teresa,' Olive called. 'I'm here.'

'For all the good you've done her,' said Gregorio.

Once the bulk of Teresa's hair was gone, Jorge produced a bar-
bering razor from his pocket. 'What are you doing?' hissed Gregorio. 'She got the message.'

'I don't think so,' said Jorge, placing the blade on the top of
Teresa's head. He began to shave the remaining patchy tufts until
she was completely bald, the ancient humiliation, back to the Bible
days, the days of blood.

'This is what happens,' said Jorge, holding the razor aloft,
'when you conceal information about a wanted criminal and fail
to cooperate with the law.'

'The law?' said Olive.

The villagers remained immobile. Teresa's skull was covered
with weeping nicks where he'd cut into her skin. Jorge pulled
Teresa up out of the chair, and she moved with him like a puppet.

'Now take off your skirt and blouse,' he said.

'Stop!' shouted another woman next to Olive, and Jorge stalked
towards her.

'You next, Rosita?' he said. 'You want to look like a mushroom
too? Because I promise you can be next.' Rosita shrank away,
shaking her head, fear distorting her face.

Slowly, Teresa peeled off her skirt and blouse, revealing her
skinny legs, her underwear. Olive wanted to seize her, but she
worried that darting forward and grabbing Teresa might now
make things worse for her. Jorge seemed so pumped up, and even
though Gregorio was less sure of himself, he could be equally
dangerous.

From the truck, Gregorio fetched a smock-like dress that looked
like it had been sewn in the sixteenth century, and a bottle, the
contents of which Olive couldn't work out. He put the smock over
Teresa's head, and helped her elbows and hands through the
heavy sleeves. 'Take off your shoes, Teresa,' he said, like a parent
to a child, and when Teresa obeyed him, it was absurdly painful.

Teresa's fingers fumbled over the knot in her shoelaces. Gregorio grew impatient and sliced them in two with his flick-knife. And it seemed to be this – more than the shaving, more than the stripping – that finally unleashed Teresa's rage. Her one pair of shoes, so neatly polished despite their age, were now unbound flaps of leather lying in the dust. She cried out and fell down.

'Get up!' Jorge screamed, but she didn't move. Jorge thrust the bottle at her. 'This is what we do to traitors,' he said.

'Who's the traitor?' Teresa replied, her voice a croak.

'Do you want me to pour it down your throat myself?'

Teresa stared up at him, still refusing. 'Gregorio,' Jorge said. 'You do it.'

Gregorio was upon her before Teresa could ready herself. He pinned back her arms and drove his knee into her lower back. Pallid and sweating, he grabbed her jaw and hinged it open. 'Drink it!' he screamed. The shock of Gregorio turning on her seemed to make Teresa numb with terror, and Jorge worked the neck of the bottle into her mouth with relative ease.

'Drink it,' Gregorio hissed. 'Drink the lot.'

Opening her eyes wide, Teresa turned her head so that Gregorio was forced to meet her gaze, and she kept them open as the contents were emptied down her throat. Some of the villagers ran away at this point, the spell of violence finally broken by this horror.

When the bottle was empty, the men let Teresa go. She gagged, strands of oil falling from the corners of her mouth, pooling into the dust.

'Who knew we lived next door to the Devil?' one man near Olive whispered.

'Go home now, Teresa,' Jorge said. 'And try not to shit yourself. If we haven't found him in the next few days, expect another visit.'

Teresa rose to her feet and stumbled, and Olive pushed past the men to take her by the arm. This time, they didn't stop her. Teresa sagged against Olive's side, and the two girls staggered out of the square, the remaining villagers parting to let through this gagging, bald creature, whose bowels might go at any minute, thanks to the dosage of an entire bottle of castor oil.

No one jeered her progress – not even half-heartedly, in the presence of Jorge and Gregorio. No one said a thing, slack-mouthed in horror. They watched the girls up the dusty path, out of the village towards the finca. They kept watching, until they couldn't see them any more.

Jorge and Gregorio stepped into the truck and revved away in the opposite direction. Gradually, the square fell empty except for the dark clumps of Teresa's hair, abandoned in the gravel.

XXI

*O*live bathed Teresa and burned the filthy smock. She dressed her in her own Aran jumper and a pair of blue silk trousers that Sarah donated. Perhaps the beauty of the blue silk was to distract Teresa, but all it did was make her look incongruous; the luxury compared to the woollen jumper and her bald head. By the time Harold came back late from Malaga, Teresa had been administered two of Sarah's sleeping pills, and she was upstairs in one of the first-floor bedrooms, fast asleep.

Before she could even tell him what had happened in the town square, Harold unburdened what he'd seen in the city. He was very shaken. The roads were terrible, he said. Since the two main bridges had been destroyed, isolating the centre, no one had done anything to fix them. He called it the perverse Buddhism of the Spaniards. Letting fate flow was all very well – but not at the expense of life. For how else could one explain not mending a bridge that might help feed citizens waiting in the city, let alone the troops?

He'd parked outside and walked in on foot, and when he'd finally made it to the centre, there wasn't much food to be had. No tins at all, no cheese – no cheese! – no cake. He'd managed to find a kilo of sugar and one of weak acorn coffee, a rationed amount of salted cod, some fresh sardines, a box of cigarettes and a feeble chorizo. He said the place was becoming unrecognizable – where once there were hanging baskets were now bombed buildings, the staring faces of the recent homeless, with nowhere to live and little to eat. Although the hotels were still standing – safe enough, for they were locked at night against marauding gangs – certain parts of the city were now nothing more than a smoking shell.

'The organization's hopeless,' he said. 'It's a fucking disaster,' he spat, and his wife and daughter flinched. What was bothering Harold so much – he, who was not from this place, who could leave any moment he wanted?

He told them that the ex-pats who were staying in the city were holed up in the Regina Hotel, but the vast majority of foreigners were leaving on the second wave of destroyers the British Consulate had sent news of. He saw them down at the dock, their passports in hand, travelling trunks scattered around like a game of dominoes. English, Americans, Argentines, Germans and Chileans, some wealthy-looking Spaniards. 'They're saying the red wave will strike them, but it's Mussolini's bombers overhead,' he said. 'The sea might be the only reliable way of sourcing food from now on. I don't see, with those bridges down, how it's all going to get in.'

'We're too far from the sea here for that to be of any comfort,' Sarah snapped, picking up the sardines and chorizo and disappearing with them into the pantry. 'Did you find the flag to purchase, like I asked?' she called.

'Don't you have a clue?' he shouted back. 'The air raids, the Italian warships bombing the port? You think I'll find a Union Jack in the middle of that?'

BUT DESPITE MALAGA'S TERRORS, OLIVE believed it was Teresa who really began to unnerve her parents. Her presence was like a dark mass in the first-floor bedroom, and an atmosphere of guilt pervaded the house. Sarah did not know what to do with her, puffing perfume around the girl, bringing all the *Vogue*s and *Harper's* she might desire. On seeing these offerings, Teresa said nothing, fixing Sarah with a surly look. Sarah kept away after that, unwilling to be near such volatility. Harold lugged the gramophone up the stairs, but she played not one of his crackling jazz records.

By the third day in the finca, Teresa had contracted a fever. She lay in bed, muttering, *Bist du es? Bist du es?* over and over, as Olive dabbed her forehead and prayed a doctor might dare to come. Olive called for Sarah to help, but Sarah did not answer. Teresa's expression was fixed, her eyes clamped shut, face swollen with fatigue, her skin pale and clammy like a peeled egg.

There was no news of Isaac. Every night in the village, one of the bar owners would turn his wireless towards the hills, so that all those who might be hiding out there in the woods could keep up with the news. General Queipo de Llano, still broadcasting from Seville, told his listeners that he had fifty thousand Italian troops, three *banderas* of the Foreign Legion, and fifteen thousand North African tribesmen known as the Army of Africa, waiting to come in to Malaga. The report made Olive shiver, but she comforted herself with the idea that Isaac was somewhere near, listening too. She didn't want him to be in the north, she wanted him here.

Teresa's fever broke, and she lay on her back in silence for several more days. At night, listening to the whine of the distant bombers, Olive could hear Teresa moving up and down the corridors, a bare-footed catharsis of pacing – but what did she want? Was this a night-time vigil to call back her brother? Why, when he was the reason for her humiliation? Olive remembered Teresa's scream of rage in the town square, her look of impotence, her terror as Gregorio clutched her. She wondered if, after all this, Teresa really knew where Isaac was.

But Teresa was buried beneath the memory, by day curled up on the bed like a foetus, her face towards the wall. She called for no one. It was a trauma none of them knew how to handle. Olive would wake at dawn and stand in front of a blank canvas, unable to lift the brush. She could not escape the image of the chair in the village square, the smock stained with faeces, Teresa's head a dull white glow, her feet weaving up over the finca hallway. Fearing she might never paint a picture, nor see Isaac again, Olive was ashamed to realize that she couldn't tell which deprivation struck her deeper. *I have been useful to you*: Isaac's words resounded in her head.

As the days progressed, Olive waited for the crust of Teresa's silence to crack open. Silence like this was Harold's worst nightmare. He thought people should speak, voice their pain. He became all bluster, trying to force the issue of the prone girl lying up in one of his rooms. But Olive was sure it was coming; she could almost taste the power of Teresa's humiliation in the air, damming up the door of the spare bedroom, soon to break.

Harold said that as soon as Teresa was better and set up back in her cottage, they were going over the border into Gibraltar. As for Isaac, he had made his bed and was going to have to lie in it. Trying to sleep in her own bed in the attic, Olive could barely picture a proper pavement, a cultivated park, the slate roofs of Curzon Street and Berkeley Square wet with rain. To get to London meant leaping a metaphysical boundary as much as a country's border, and she didn't know if she could, if she even wanted to at all. London might be a different sort of suffocation. If she was truly honest with herself, Olive could admit that there was something life-affirming about living here, so close to the possibility of real death.

She began to feel responsible for Isaac's disappearance. He had been so angry when he departed through the orchard that night on the veranda, calling *good luck* before he left. How long ago it seemed now, arriving here under the thin January sun, Isaac laying his hands on that chicken. Olive remembered the provocation she felt in her own body as he broke its neck. He'd given her so much. Had she satisfied him in return? No, she did not think so. When she tried to summon the memory of his hands on her, she found that she could not.

'Do you think Isaac got away?' Sarah asked her one evening, when it was just her and Olive sitting in the front east room. Harold was in his study, Teresa still upstairs.

Olive rubbed her arms. The firewood was dwindling and they were rationing supplies. 'I don't know.'

'I'm sure he did,' Sarah said. 'I'm sure he caught a train.' Olive noted how well her mother looked, despite the meagre rations, and Teresa's trauma that was threatening to engulf them. It was as if the stressed situation had finally given Sarah a sense of purpose.

'Do you want to leave, Liv?' Sarah asked.

Olive pulled at a thread on the tatty sofa. Isaac had been right after all. They had come here and they would go again. 'No,' she said. 'This is home.'

Later that night, Olive heard a knock on her door. 'Who is it?'

Teresa shuffled forward, hovering on the threshold. She was thinner than ever, and her hair had grown a little bit, but mostly Olive was relieved to see the determined look in Teresa's eyes.

'Do you know what your father is saying?' Teresa asked.

Olive lay back on the bed. 'He says many things.'

'He talks about the fatalism of the Spaniards.'

'Ignore him.'

'What he says is not fair.'

'I know it isn't.'

'Does he think we are not trying to fight?'

'He doesn't think that. It's easy when you're an outsider to say these things.'

'It is not safe.'

'I know, Tere.'

'You should go.'

'I'm not leaving you.'

'You are not staying for me, señorita. I know why you are still here.' The girls looked at each other. 'He isn't coming back,' Teresa said.

Olive sat up in the bed. 'He might.'

Teresa laughed. It was a cracked, bitter sound. 'You of all people should open your eyes.'

'I should say they're pretty bloody open, thank you very much. More than most of the English back home.'

Teresa walked slowly into the room, running her hand over the top of *Rufina and the Lion.* 'My brother has done damage,' she said.

'To the village?'

'To this house.'

'What do you mean?'

'I would like to thank you,' Teresa said. 'For taking me away from Jorge and Gregorio.'

'I wouldn't have done anything else.'

'I have tried to fight.'

'I know.'

'But it is hard. It is like fighting yourself. And there are times I don't see why we should have to. Why should we have to fight?'

'I don't know the answer to that, Tere.'

'If you go, Olive – could I go too?'

Olive hesitated. Her father had no plans to take Teresa with them. 'Do you have papers?'

Teresa made an unconscious gesture with her hand, patting her head where the scabs were beginning to heal. 'No.'

There was a silence. 'Let me neaten that situation,' said Olive.

'What does it mean – "*neaten*"?'

Olive got off the bed and came towards her, putting her hands on the other girl's arms. 'You need a new notebook of words. Here, I won't hurt you. I'll be gentle.'

Placing Teresa on the edge of the bed, she used a razor taken from her father's dressing table, and slowly shaved away the remaining patches of hair on Teresa's head. She rubbed calamine over the cuts as Teresa sat motionless, looking out towards the window, listening to the far-off crumps of the guns in Malaga.

'This is my brother's fault,' Teresa said dully.

Olive held the razor above Teresa's head. 'Well, we've all been foolish. You could blame it on your father. And he'd blame it on the government. And they'd blame it on the last government. I don't think Isaac meant for this to happen to you.'

'Isaac thinks about the land, but forgets his doorstep,' Teresa said.

'Isaac is a good man.'

'You think so?'

'He has a conscience.'

Teresa laughed.

'You know where your brother is, don't you? I promise I won't tell anyone. I just need to know.'

Teresa turned again to the window, her shoulders sagging. 'It is better that you do not know.'

She heard a *snip*. Horrified, she turned to Olive and saw that the other girl had removed an enormous chunk of her own hair. 'What are you doing?' Teresa said, as Olive cut away another handful.

'You think I've just been playing a game down here, don't you?' Olive said.

'Stop with your hair. Stop it.'

Teresa went to grab for the razor, but Olive pointed it in her direction, as warning to keep back. She began to hack and hack at herself, tufts of her thick hazel-coloured hair floating to the floor. Teresa watched her, mesmerised. 'Now you shave my head,' Olive said.

'You are crazy.'

'No, I'm not. What do I have to do to make people take me seriously?'

'Having the same hair as me does not give you the same grief as me.'

'Teresa, just do it.'

As she delicately scraped away every last hair on Olive's head, Teresa tried to hide her tears. She could not remember the last time she had cried in front of someone. She thought about that first painting of Olive's she had swapped onto the easel, Saint Justa becoming a woman in a wheatfield. Isaac had been convinced she'd done it because of the kiss she'd witnessed against the rusty gate, that Teresa was punishing him out of jealousy, taking away his opportunity to shine. Teresa had to admit, seeing what happened between them had hurt her at the time, making her feel left out and ignored, although she couldn't exactly articulate why. But she also knew her impulse had always been something more deep-rooted, not really connected to Isaac. It was something else Teresa couldn't quite understand herself. The nearest way to describe it was as a bond she had made for herself, and Olive being rightfully rewarded.

'Tere, I'm going to ask you again. Do you know where he is?' Olive said.

Teresa almost felt the pressure of the question in her body. 'Forget Isaac,' she said. 'He does not love you in the way he should.'

'Oh, Teresa. What do you know about love?'

Teresa's brief time in the house with the Schlosses had taught her more about love and its problems than Olive could ever imagine. But she had also known, long before the arrival of the Schloss family and their overflowing hearts, that whilst everything has a consequence, nothing can simply be put down to fate. Teresa had always made her choice – to see, and stay silent. All her life before Olive, she had kept her own counsel.

But Olive, and her paintings, and her parents, had changed that stance. They had opened Teresa up, made her vulnerable to the worlds of other people. And once again, Olive was forcing her hand. Perhaps there was no good to be had in staying silent any longer. Perhaps it was time for Olive to truly see, and to free herself for ever.

'A shepherd's hut,' Teresa said.

'What?'

'Go and look for a shepherd's hut. You will find him there.'

Olive looked at her in astonishment. 'I don't believe you.'

'You'll find him. Ask my brother what it means to be in love.'

TERESA WATCHED HER DEPART, AND began to sweep away the other girl's severed hair with a mix of dread and elation. She wasn't sure exactly what Olive would find, but she had a fair idea. She noted the back of Olive's newly bared head with something bordering pride. When the reckoning came – and it was certainly going to come now – Teresa knew that they would question her character. At least they would see that she had not left a mark on her mistress. It was not possible to mend Olive's heart, but at least the girl's head was finally clear.

XXII

The plane engines over Malaga had grown quieter as Olive pounded down the hill from the finca, in the direction of the cottage. No one seemed to notice as she tiptoed out of the house. It did not occur to her there might have been no one left in the house to hear.

At dusk Arazuelo was a ghost village. The main square was empty, the shutters of the bar on the corner were up; the church was its blackened shell; the butcher was closed; the school and the offices around it blanked of life. Olive patted her pockets, feeling in one the torch she'd grabbed from the kitchen, and in the other, the cold bulk of the pistol Isaac had left with them.

She could barely allow the hope that he might still be near. Teresa, it appeared, was a locked box of secrets, until you found the right combination. Whilst everything outside her seemed quiet, Olive's thoughts cascaded with a force she found hard to control. If she could find him and bring him back, everything would be all right. Panting, she tried to regain her breath as she scanned the woods beyond, the line of the trees inkier and inkier as the last natural light disappeared into a smoky sky.

INTO THE GROWING DARKNESS OLIVE ran, switching on the torch. *Don't use a torch*, Teresa had told her. *You don't know who else is out there.*

I'm not afraid, Olive had replied – but now, out in the hills, she couldn't see a thing without it, and her adrenalin was coursing. She barely knew where she was going, but she supposed it couldn't be far. Towards the foothills, she would find him; she would, she would. *You think he's gone north?* Teresa had said. *He hasn't gone north.*

If you hate him so much, why didn't you tell the civil guard all this? Olive had asked; but she knew the answer to that already. Teresa had revealed nothing about Isaac – not to protect her brother, but to keep Olive near.

I'll be waiting, Teresa had called out, as Olive fled the attic. No one had ever said such a thing to Olive before.

THE FIRST THING SHE SAW was the sardine tin, glinting in the grass. It had clearly blown from inside the hut, and now rested several metres from where Olive stood. She switched off the torch and watched the shepherd's hut. A faint light was showing between a hewn-out window hole and a piece of flapping oilskin. Olive crept nearer. She could hear a voice, a low murmur – Isaac's voice. Teresa had not been lying to her. Her heart rose with joy to know he was here, and she ran forward.

Then she heard a woman's laugh. She recognized it. She thought she was going to choke. Her throat tightened, her tongue felt too big at the back of her mouth.

A noise, a deep sigh, another and another from inside the shepherd's hut, and finally Olive understood what Teresa had meant, what she had squirmed to say, resisting the outright truth, sending her here so she could see it for herself. She understood it, even as she couldn't bear to. And there it came again – regular, deep, and unbearable; an expression of pure pleasure. As the universe above Olive's head deepened in its darkness, she fixed her fingers on the pistol and pushed open the door.

XXIII

Sarah screamed, pushing back against the wall. '*No dis-pares!*' shouted Isaac. *Don't shoot!*

Olive lifted the lantern that was on the floor. Isaac and her mother were both naked, their limbs still intertwined. Sarah twisted her body away in panic, and Olive saw the dome of her stomach clearly risen with a child.

'Olive,' said her mother, dumb with shock. 'What's happened to your hair?'

They stared at each other. Seconds passed that felt like hours. 'Does Daddy know?' Olive eventually said, her voice a husk, the sound robotic. 'Does Daddy know?'

Sarah scrambled to sit up, clutching Isaac's coat to her chest, reaching for her trousers. 'Liv. Livvi. Put the gun down.'

Olive kept the barrel up in the direction of her mother. 'Does he know?'

'He doesn't know,' said Sarah, gasping. 'Put that down, for Christ's sake.'

'Is it yours?' Olive asked Isaac. 'Is the baby yours?'

'It's not his,' Sarah interrupted. 'It's not.'

Isaac got to his feet. 'Olive,' he said gently. 'Put the gun down. No one needs to be hurt.'

Olive felt a roaring in her ears. 'Why?' she said. 'Why?' Her question soared into the night.

'Ssssh!' Isaac hissed. 'Keep quiet.'

'You hypocrite. All that talk about going north, fighting for your country, and you're less than a mile away, with her—' Olive put her hand on her mouth, fighting back a sob.

'Livvi,' said Sarah.

'Don't you *Livvi* me. Don't fool yourself it could ever be love with her, Isaac. Is it yours? Is that baby yours?'

The look that passed between Sarah and Isaac was almost worse to Olive than discovering them. The intimacy of it, the fluency; complicity.

'How long have you – when did it start? What was wrong with me? Why couldn't I—'

Isaac began to come towards her. 'Calm down, Olive. Please. I can explain—'

As he approached, Olive fired a shot through the thatch of the roof. '*Mierda!*' he shouted. 'Shit! Do you want to get us killed? Now every gang out there will know that someone is here.'

Sarah let out a low moan and began scrabbling around in the dark for the rest of her clothes. 'I have to go. I have to go,' she kept repeating. 'He'll be back.'

'You snake,' said Olive.

Sarah looked up at her. 'I'm no snake.'

'I'd say you are. I never want to speak to you again.'

'How did you know I was here?' asked Isaac.

'How else do you think?'

Sarah groaned. Olive closed her eyes to blot out the scene before her.

'How long has Teresa known about this?' whispered Sarah.

'I don't know,' said Olive, and it was the truth. Had Teresa's silence until now been out of protection, or something else – the power of knowing what Olive did not? Had they all been laughing at her, so in love with her Boris Mon-Amour? Better to have kept Isaac a figure in a book, a man in her imagination, than the monster she had created in real life. She could hear one of the last things Teresa had said to her, up in the attic: *Ask my brother what it means to be in love.*

'Olive,' said Sarah, more in control now that she was fully dressed. 'I know it's not always been easy—'

'Oh, God. No, I don't want to hear it.'

'I never meant to hurt you.'

'And yet you always do.'

Sarah got to her feet and faced her daughter. 'Do you think you're the only one who's lonely? The only one who suffers?'

'I don't care about your loneliness. You're married. To my father.'

'And do you think it's easy, being married to him?'

'Shut up. *Shut up.*'

Isaac was in the corner, hastily putting on his clothes, his face darting between the women with an expression of misery.

'Isaac isn't yours, Olive, no more than he's mine,' Sarah said.

'He is mine – we've – what are you going to tell Daddy? He won't take you back.'

Sarah laughed. 'I never knew you were so old-fashioned.'

'Old-fashioned?'

'You know his paintings don't pay for all this, Liv. The finca, our travel, our lives. It's not a question of "taking me back". One day, Olive, you'll understand what a mess everyone makes of their life. I don't know a single couple who hasn't had their problems. Marriage is *long*, you know—'

'Stop. I don't care. When did you first seduce Isaac?'

'Darling, it was the other way round. In fact, not long after Daddy bought Isaac's first painting.'

'Just get out,' said Olive.

SARAH STARTED TO WALK OUT of the hut with all the insouciance of leaving a Mayfair restaurant, but she faltered at the dark. 'I can't see anything,' she said.

'I'm sure you know the way by now. Watch out for wolves.'

'I'll go with you,' said Isaac.

'You're not going anywhere,' said Olive, lifting the pistol in his direction.

'Olive, you're being so bloody foolish,' said Sarah.

'Just *go*.'

'I'll see you soon,' Sarah said to Isaac. 'Olive, come back when you've calmed down.'

Isaac and Olive watched as she disappeared into the night. 'You shouldn't have let her go alone like that,' Isaac said.

'I wouldn't have shot her, you know. Or you.' Olive lowered the gun and switched on the torch. In the bright white light, he looked wary. 'For God's sake, Isaac. Have you any idea what happened to your sister?'

'What happened?'

'No, I don't suppose my mother bothered to tell you. How Teresa paid the price for your heroics.'

'Do not hide things, Olive. I do not like it.'

'That's rich, coming from you.'

'What have they done to her?'

The panic on his face was genuine, so she relented, telling him about Jorge and Gregorio, the hacking of Teresa's hair, the castor oil, the midnight wanderings through the finca corridors.

His face crumpled in pain. 'But why have you no hair?' he asked.

'To make her feel better. Less alone.'

Isaac looked beyond the torch's orbit, out into the darkness. 'So she told you I was here.'

'Yes.'

'Did she tell you about the child?'

'No. Just that you'd be here.'

'Did she mention Sarah?'

'No. I asked her what she knew about love, that's all.'

They were silent for a moment.

'She is the cause of so much trouble,' he said.

'Yes. But at least now I see you for what you are. I suppose that was her intention.'

'Do you truly think my sister has always had your best interests at heart?' Isaac said. 'She is a cat, always landing on her feet.'

'You overestimate her power. You haven't seen her. And anyway, she hasn't hurt me. You have.'

'Perhaps that's true. And I am sorry for it. But you just see an idea of me that suits you. You never stop trying to create me. Your mother – how do you say? Clear-sighted. She sees me as I am. She does not want me to change.'

'Yet. But probably she doesn't have the imagination. And she's ill.'

'Is boredom an illness? She is not ill. It just suits you to say she is. Even her'

'You took advantage.'

'I did? Olive, I never promised you anything. I never told you I loved you. You heard and saw what you wanted.'

'You slept with me, Isaac. Several times.'

'Yes. And I said yes to the paintings too. We all make mistakes.'

'What are you trying to say? The more I painted, the less you liked me?'

He looked away. 'I'm trying to say that your mother – it is a different thing. It is a separate thing.'

'It isn't separate, Isaac. Her behaviour affects us all, just as my father's does – and as mine does, I suppose. Did you stay here for her?'

He hesitated. Olive closed her eyes, as if in pain. 'You think you're the first,' she said. 'She only slept with you to punish me.'

He laughed, putting his hands up to his head. 'You really are an artist, aren't you? You think it's all about you, and you never stop looking for pain. It isn't about you, Olive. You have nothing to do with this.'

'I'm going. Good luck, isn't that what you said?'

Olive turned to the darkness, in the direction her mother had descended.

'What will you do?' he asked.

'I'll go back to England. You were right. I'll find somewhere to live. Leave my parents to it. See if the art school will take me.'

'That is a good plan.'

'We'll see. Here.' Olive handed the pistol to Isaac. 'You might need this more than me.'

'And Tere?' he asked, tucking it into the back of his belt. 'Will you take her with you?'

Olive sighed. 'I don't know, Isaac. She doesn't have any papers.'

'She has had a hard time.'

'A minute ago you were saying how much trouble she was.'

'She is only sixteen.'

Olive couldn't hide her surprise. 'She said she was eighteen.'

'Well, there you are. But if Jorge decides – if my father—'

'You don't need to tell me. I was there when it happened. When you were up here.'

He put out his hand. Olive looked down at it. 'You know,' she said, 'I'm glad I painted you with a green face.'

SHE HAD MEANT IT AS a joke; she had not really meant that he was naive, or sick. It was just an assertion that she was the artist, that she would paint him in the colours that she saw fit. She wanted Isaac to see that she was grown up enough to deal with this, even though she did not feel it. He would always be the man who had changed her life. But as she had gone to take his hand and hold it, and tell him this, Isaac crumpled at her feet.

It seemed unreal to her at first, as she stared down in horror, her torch darting over the blood that was gushing out of Isaac's head, the red cascading into his eyes. And then she heard what she'd missed the first time; the muted pop of a gun firing in their direction. Two more shots ricocheted around the hills, their reports cracking the air, thinning to nothingness above the woods. She started to run.

Jorge, who had heard Olive's pistol being fired half an hour earlier, had come up to the hills to see if he could find its source, and had been watching them from a distance. He couldn't believe his luck; Isaac Robles in hiding, and his bald sister, handing him over another firearm. And the stupid girl had kept her torch on, so after shooting Isaac, he could follow her easily enough, the torchlight juddering all over the place as she stumbled down the hill.

Jorge fired three more times, watching as the torch tumbled, coming to rest like a small white moon upon the ground. He waited. Nothing moved. So close was the quality of silence that followed, so sickening that mute after-note of execution, that it seemed as if the fields were turning in on themselves, and the earth was giving way.

PART V

Rufina and the Lion

NOVEMBER 1967

18

The lifts at Goodge Street station were broken, and when I finally caught a Tube in the direction of Waterloo, it kept stopping in tunnels. In total, it took me an hour and a half to reach Quick's house after leaving the phone box outside the Slade. The front lights of her house, both upstairs and down, were blazing. She had not drawn the curtains, and I could see in the top room a white, cracked ceiling with a naked bulb, which seemed at odds with her usual cultivated aesthetic. A sharp pool of light haloed across the cornicing, a decayed grandeur to the fissures she had not sought to fill in.

Feeling deeply uneasy, I knocked on the front door and waited, and there was no answer. 'Hello?' I called through the letterbox, but the house remained silent. I deliberated – I could stop this, go home back to Clapham and my equally silent flat. But guilt kept me there; and curiosity, a need to see this through.

It was very dark as I slipped along the side fence, the last of the fallen autumn leaves crisping under my shoes. Even the lights through the side windows shone out – an electric conflagration, every light bulb burning, giving me the distinct feeling of being exposed. It was like a film set – a giant rig of dazzling sodium illumination – a wattage to attract and drown.

When I reached the garden and looked into its darkness, my

eyes could not cope with the loss of light. Every time I blinked, orange orbs slunk across my sight, fading to smaller planets which danced around the outlines of the trees. The clock tower struck eight. I was in a fable again.

What I saw when I turned back to the house, I shall never forget. Quick was sitting in the kitchen, upright on a chair. The curtains here were also drawn back, the whole place lit up. I thought I might cry out in shock. Quick had no hair. There was nothing on her head but a few dull tufts, a patched map with no coordinates. She was looking at me, and I raised my hand in greeting, but she did not react, and then I realized with horror that she was not looking at me at all – but at someone – or something – beyond me, waiting in the garden.

I heard a twig snap and my throat closed in fear as I turned to face the darkness she'd lured me to, ready to fight, ready to yell. I was sure there was a presence beyond the shrubbery, concealed behind the hanging branches of the wilderness, but nothing showed.

I whirled back to the house, ran to the kitchen door and forced my way in, desperate to get away from whatever was waiting in the garden. I was in front of her now. She was still upright, still in the chair. There was a macabre perfection to her pale skull, a look of beatitude and finality on her serene face. Her wig lay on the floor like the pelt of an animal. I had no idea she'd ever worn one.

'Quick?' I said, the horror churning in my throat.

But of course Quick did not reply, because Quick was dead.

I called the police before thinking about how this looked – the house locked, but me inside it, the kitchen door still open, my foot marks in the grass. It wasn't until the post-mortem revealed the estimated time of Quick's death, and that her bloodstream contained ten times the amount of painkillers she had been prescribed, and the coroner learned of her cancer, that the suspicion was removed from my head and it was declared an accidental death. It made me so angry, I can't tell you. That I, the only person she had come to trust, might ever be suspected of breaking into her house and killing her. I was the only one who'd ever been willing to find out Quick's true story.

AFTER CALLING THE POLICE I came back to the kitchen, and knelt down beside her, touching her body. It was still warm. Perhaps I had missed her by a matter of minutes. She had not strictly invited me that night; it was me determined that she should not be alone. But had she wanted this end? I told her I was coming over – she would know I would be the first to find her. Maybe she had wanted to be saved. I'll never know.

I looked around. The bottle of pills was in front of her, and half a bottle of gin. This didn't necessarily mean anything; she loved drinking, and she had been in pain. I could not countenance that what she'd done was deliberate.

'Police,' said a voice. I jumped, and went to the front door.

THERE WERE TWO POLICEMEN, AND they'd also brought an ambulance. I was in shock – their energy was so different as they came into the house; officious yet weary, seen-it-all-before. I was jumpy, new-born with the fear and shock. 'Who's her next of kin?' asked one of them, and I said I didn't know, but Edmund Reede was her boss – and perhaps they should call him.

Reede was still at work, the exhibition due to open the next day, and he was working to the nail. I couldn't hear his response as the policeman stood in Quick's hall, telling him what had been discovered. The call was brief. I sat in the front room, and a policeman came and placed himself opposite me. The clock ticked. He eyed me, and then I realized what he might be thinking, and I envisaged my incarceration, the Carib murderess – the outrage it might cause, the inevitability of it, of people like me.

Reede seemed to appear within minutes. He'd hared down over Waterloo Bridge in his car, and burst through the front door, *What the hell's happened, where the hell is she, what the* . . . and the words died on his mouth as he watched the paramedics carrying Quick out. She looked so tiny and frail, and I saw the shock on Reede's face, a pain that for once he had no means to control.

It was actually thanks to Reede that the police didn't arrest me there and then. They were intimidated by him. He gathered himself quickly, exuding power and authority, and their uniforms meant as little to him as they meant everything to me. He became angry when he got the whiff of their questions and attitude, and he told them that if they wanted to accuse me of anything, they could bloody well go through him. 'She was with me in the office until an hour ago,' I remember him saying.

I have to admit, I was surprised. I never thought the day would come when I would feel in debt to Edmund Reede, and I didn't really like it, because I didn't know what I would be able to give in return. We left the house together; him giving me a lift back to my flat in Clapham.

'How did she sound when you called her?' he asked, as we zoomed along Clapham Common.

'Weak.' I went to say something more, but I stopped.

He looked at me. 'What is it?'

'She was ill, Mr Reede.'

'Ill?'

'Very ill. I don't think she – had long left.'

He looked back to the road. 'Jesus Christ. She always was too good at keeping secrets. And so are you, apparently. No wonder she liked you.'

We sat in silence. I felt completely drained. I couldn't believe she'd gone, with so many of my questions left to answer.

'Mr Reede – did you know her long?' I asked eventually.

'Since she was practically a girl.'

'I'm sorry.'

I wondered what he was thinking – was he hurt that Quick hadn't told him how ill she was, or was he simply in shock and sadness that she was dead?

'I'd like you and Miss Rudge to organize the funeral,' he said.

'Of course. Does she have any family I should tell?' I asked.

'None that I know of. But you'll have a bit of time. The police won't release her body yet.'

'Why won't they? What do they think I've done?'

'Don't worry, Miss Bastien. It will all be fine.'

But I didn't see how it would be. 'Will the exhibition still go ahead?' I asked.

'Don't see we have much choice. And it's what she would have wanted.'

But half the problem, I thought, kicking off my shoes and sinking on to my bed still in my clothes, as Reede's car revved off up the road, was that none of us had ever really known what Marjorie Quick had wanted.

19

The next evening, the exhibition opened, with Quick's body still lying cold in the police morgue. I couldn't marry these two facts easily; she, dead and alone, and here, so much noise and colour, milling bodies, excitement brewing at the discovery of the new Isaac Robles.

Julie Christie walked past me, her face too good to be true. The gallery was full. I recognized her, but who were these other people? Actors, critics, lords and bankers, gold buttons forged not from battles, but casts of power. Wine being drunk like it came from their own cellars. Jagger wasn't there, much to Pamela's chagrin. Rotund cabinet ministers talked to haggard-looking old men of art as some optimist put on a blues record, the trumpet's scattered notes whirling towards the ceiling. At the unleashed sound, two men in blazers swapped glances of disdain. Where were their deft van Dycks, their easy Gainsboroughs, their plump majestic Stubbesian horses? All they had here were modernist streaks of colour, women, holding heads, women, curled amidst their shattered pots, a poised lion, third wheel in a tragic game of Renaissance saints.

A snare drum snuck into the blues, a syncopation that only just nipped my bud of bitterness. I felt utterly disorientated without Quick. She should have been there; she was going to tell me the truth. At the end of the room, the photograph of Isaac Robles and

Olive Schloss loomed, black and white and granular, the girl's face locked in what I now felt was a misplaced expression of hope. It was almost an insult that the photograph was up there. I wanted the blues to be louder, for a pair of these wine-flushed stuffed shirts to break into a jive, whirling one old tanty round till she false teeth fly.

With an inward sigh, I moved on, my wine glass a weapon. Shuffling past the growing crowd, I neared *Rufina and the Lion*, protected now by a scarlet rope, two guards flanking its sides. Reede clearly knew the special touches to make things seem official.

I noticed a thin, grey-haired man in a suit, leaning over the rope to peer at one of the painting's corners. He was very close, his nose inches from the minuscule crests of paint on the girl's severed head. He was incredibly curious; he couldn't stop looking. The left guard's feet shifted, sensible shoes of menace. I felt a surging anxiety that something bad was going to happen; but then again, the worst already had.

'It's ghoulish, Frederick,' said a woman, coming to join the man. 'It's painful.'

Behind me, the noise in the gallery lifted. As the temperature rose and the crowd grew, guests began looking through each other like open doors. A woman laughed above the swell, and it sounded like a cry for help. Why were these people here? They didn't care about Isaac Robles. They didn't care about Quick.

I felt a tug at my elbow; Pamela. 'You all right?' she said. 'Look like you've seen a ghost.'

'I think I have.'

Pamela frowned. I hadn't told her about Quick; Reede had said he wanted a lid on it until the exhibition was on its feet.

'You read too much, Dell,' Pamela said. 'Ain't no such thing as ghosts. Listen.' She looked pained. 'I broke up with Billy.'

'Oh, Pamela. I'm sorry.'

A cloud passed across her face. 'Turned out he didn't want to marry me. I gave notice on my room and everything, and then the bugger broke it off. And another girl's moving in.'

I wondered if she meant on Billy, or into her old room. I didn't ask. Instead, I said the words I never thought I'd say. 'Would you like to share with me?'

Her face opened into a smile. 'That'd be good. That'd be really good.'

'I'd like it too.'

Pamela went pink, giving me a hug before she turned away and melted into the crowd.

I FOUND LAWRIE, AND STOOD close beside him. 'My mother would never believe all this,' he said, drawing his arm in an arc across the gallery. 'She'd love it though. What a snowball. It's just got bigger and bigger.'

'Lawrie,' I whispered. 'I have to tell you. Quick's – she's dead.'

He turned to me. 'What?'

'I found her. Last night.'

'Oh, Delly. I'm so sorry. Are you all right?'

'Not really.'

'What happened?'

'I'll tell you later,' I said – for how to explain, at the launch of his exhibition, that I didn't think the paintings around this room were by Isaac Robles at all, that the real painter behind these works had died with her secret intact? Cynth had warned me to keep all my ideas about Olive Schloss and Marjorie Quick to myself, if I wanted harmony in my love life. But if this entire exhibition was predicated on a lie, that sat uneasily with my sense of creative integrity. I was struggling to work out which was more important – Lawrie's feelings, or Quick's artistic restitution. If it was me who'd painted these pictures, I'd bloody well want everyone to know.

Lawrie took my hand. 'I know she meant a lot to you.'

I hadn't thought of mine and Quick's connection in that way before – in terms of affection, or quality. Nor did I think I'd ever communicated such a sentiment. Until now, I'd treated Quick as an interesting conundrum, a diversion, both a source of inspiration and an obstacle. But Lawrie was right. She did mean a lot to me. Despite her mercurial manner, Quick had welcomed me, helped me. I liked her. And it was too late to tell her so. There was still, at the back of my mind, some niggling thought that she had wanted me for something, but that now it was too late.

'Dell, do you want to leave?'

'No, of course not. I'll be fine.'

'All right. Listen, Gerry wants you to come over for dinner. He's here, you know.'

'Really? That's good he's out and about.'

'Yes it is, I suppose. You don't have to come if you don't want to. But he's always asking after you. When he read your story in the *London Review*, he boasted to his friends he knew a writer. I think you've got a fan.'

'I'm not a writer.'

'Of course, I forgot. You're a typist.' The exasperation in his voice made me turn. 'Well really, Odelle,' he said. 'Are you going to keep on like this? Do you know how many people would give their eye-teeth to be in the *London Review*? I wouldn't waste it.'

'I'm not going to waste it,' I said. I was tired, unable to keep the hurt out of my voice. 'And it's not up to you to tell me what I should or shouldn't call myself.'

He up put his hands in surrender. 'All right. I just – you must keep writing, you know.'

I rolled my eyes. 'You sound like Cynthia. You sound like Quick. Everyone wants me to write, but they never try it themselves. If they tried it themselves they might shut up.'

He shrugged. 'Quick did you an enormous favour. And I bet if she knew you were dragging your heels—'

The last few hours finally caught up with me. 'I'm *not* dragging – don't use her – she *dead*, Lawrie. She dead. I don't – I can't – we don't all have paintings we can sell, you know. I have to do other work.'

'You're right. Of course. But sometimes I do think you need reminding how good you are.'

We stood in silence for a few minutes. I knew it was true that I had stalled again on my writing. For once, I was too caught up with actually living my life to stop and turn it into words. People like Lawrie – who never wrote a single line of prose, as far as I knew – seemed to want those who *did* to walk around with a pad and pencil hanging round their neck, jotting down the whole thing, turning it into a book for their own pleasure.

As if he knew he'd trod on tender ground, Lawrie changed the subject. 'It looks like there's a couple of people interested in buying *Rufina*,' he said.

'That's good.' I saw his rueful grin. 'Isn't it?'

'Grass greener for Rufina. Told you I was a poet. Thing is, now there's a chance I'm not going to have it any more, I'm rather reluctant.'

'Well, it's not any old painting.'

Lawrie looked across the gallery, where the colours of *Rufina and the Lion* glowed, the people crossing back and forth, intermittently obscuring our view. 'It certainly isn't. But what am I going to do with it, Dell? I don't have any money and it isn't going to feed me.'

As we looked at the painting, vanishing and reappearing again and again behind people's heads, I knew that Lawrie and I were looking at different things. In its uniqueness, I read multiple stories. Through its technical brush-strokes, I experienced metaphysical sensations. It was a one-off I should do my utmost to protect and keep in public view. I could guess at the impulses behind the artist's decisions, I could meditate on how the painting made me feel, but I understood that I would never know its truth.

But Lawrie saw something else. The new frame Reede had commissioned was a window, and the painting within was a curtain he was pushing aside. He claimed he was reluctant to sell it, but he hadn't seen the cheque yet. He didn't really want to keep hold of *Rufina* – although it was his mother's, he seemed unbound by the memories it clearly had evoked for her. And why else had he come to the Skelton in the first place? He said it was to find me, but maybe I was a bonus. For him, the painting was a thing for sale, a transitional object that would take him places. He saw in it opportunity, a chance to start again.

Reede tapped his wine glass and began to address the crowd. He stood in front of *Rufina and the Lion*, starting by taking us through the skeleton story of Isaac Robles; his importance in the early journey of art in the twentieth century, his gift cut short. He thanked the Guggenheim foundation in Venice, and built on the particular mystery of the discovery, pointing out Lawrie in the crowd, who blushed and raised his glass to appreciative applause at his good fortune for having such a painting concealed in his house, and his generosity in deciding to show it.

When Reede spoke of how Robles' work was a meditation on adversity, the people in the Skelton gallery probably thought he was talking about war and dictatorship, and the struggles many of them were old enough to have lived through and remember on a visceral level. But I just thought what Quick had said about it: *It's the subject that overwhelms. As if there's an extra layer to the painting we're not privy to, that you just can't get at.*

Rufina and the Lion moved me that night in a transcendental way; it was the conduit through which I channelled my sense of loss, of accepting I might never know the truth, but that that was the secret of art. And perhaps I wasn't alone. Because after Reede had finished speaking, I noticed how people – even the old buffers in club blazers – began to look at *Rufina* with a little more respect.

The reviews for the opening night of 'The Swallowed Century' were mixed. Some were veritably lukewarm. '*The painting is a tableau that summons death, and it is wrong to ignore it,*' was as praising as the journalist in the *Telegraph* went the next morning, before going on to speculate how much money it might fetch – '*Edmund Reede confirmed at the end of the night that* Rufina and the Lion *was going to auction.*' In *The Times*, there was an article on the star-studded event, with very little information on the artist himself. I smiled; Quick would have seen the irony in that. And when the journalist referred to the '*express symbolism*' in the paintings,

I disagreed. He was dismissing the painting as obvious, but I think there was another language in those paintings, and the only person who knew how to speak it was gone.

The *Daily Mail* asked whether the whole thing was an elaborate practical joke, that Isaac Robles should have been left where he was found, and that if this was the state of modern art, what fresh hells would we be forced to look at in the 1970s. The *Observer*, however, went in the opposite direction, congratulating Reede on refusing to rest on his laurels when it came to '*art history revisionism, forgotten painters and colour.*' It made me laugh, to think all these men had been looking at the same painting.

I felt Quick's absence through the corridors, knowing that never again would the lunch summons come, never again would the restaurant next door send up a cold bottle of their best Sancerre. Reede was not in; I wondered if he'd seen the papers, and how we would deal with it. Pamela, who'd been informed about Quick, had been sniffling in the loos, and even the empty rooms felt as if they were in mourning. I wondered whether, had Quick been there, the reviews might have taken a more praising timbre; Quick cajoling the critics, forcing them to put their egos aside and see what was in front of their noses.

And yet, if anything, the *Mail*'s diatribe helped us. There were queues forming to come in and see *Rufina*, to see if it was really a joke. But for me, it only made things worse. Why hadn't Quick spoken up? Why was she so determined to keep her life a secret?

I began to meditate on what Lawrie had said about Quick doing me an enormous favour when she sent 'The Toeless Woman' to the *London Review*, and that I shouldn't waste it. My green notebook had lain untouched for several weeks; but I just didn't know what I wanted to write about. I don't think Quick ever wanted me to feel in her debt; she had facilitated something, and was happy to do so. Nevertheless, I began to think about how I might thank her for what she'd done, in a way I hadn't managed when she was alive. The funeral was scheduled for the following week, and I decided I would use the intervening time to write her eulogy. After all, Reede had left it to me and Pamela to organize, and no one else had volunteered.

The first post came late that day; Pamela was outside dragging dolefully on a cigarette and I was covering reception. It seemed strange to me to receive post at the Skelton, but there it was; an envelope with my name on it.

If the first letter Quick had sent me was a touchstone of transformation, then this was in another realm. Although I have received many extraordinary letters since that time, the one sent to me at the Skelton still beats them all.

A law firm called Parr & Co., whose offices were in Bread Lane in the City of London, were requesting my presence on Thursday – and would I please bring my passport and some proof of address? I recall how terrified I was. If you are made to feel, repeatedly, that you do not belong in a country, despite previous assurances to the contrary, then a letter telling you to bring your identity papers will freeze your blood.

I tried to imagine how Quick would deal with this. I felt lost without her assurance, the shelter of her steel wing. If I'd called Lawrie and told him, he wouldn't understand, because he belonged. He was wrapped in a web of invisible yet unbreakable tissue, layer upon layer of it, that had begun to spin for him before he was even born, binding him in safety, giving him such a sense of security that no letter from a City lawyer would ever have scared him. His possible amusement at my nerves would only confirm my worry.

I decided to show it to Pamela instead. 'What do you think it is?' I said.

'God knows, Odelle. But it ain't nothing to worry about. If they wanted to arrest you for something, they'd just do it here.'

Pamela had a point, as ever, and so that Thursday I went. Would I have been less terrified or more had I known that I was going to hear the final will and testament of Miss Marjorie Quick? I cannot say. The choice was made; there was only ever one path, and just as in life, Quick kept me on it from beyond the grave.

PART VI

The Sticking Place

XXIV

*T*hey buried her under an olive tree in the orchard. Teresa didn't remember much about it, but she could always remember the sound of the earth being flung on top of the casket, the same earth they'd once dug together, the rainbow through the falling drops. Padre Lorenzo had left the village, so Doctor Morales led a makeshift service. Harold and Teresa stood by and watched, virtually propping each other up, and Sarah was sedated upstairs.

The doctor would not look Teresa in the eye. Did he truly believe the rumour that she'd been the one to pull the trigger? She knew what was happening in the village. Jorge, probably in a pre-emptive strike against any guilt falling on his own head, had been going around saying that he'd bet a month's wages it was Teresa who'd shot Isaac and Olive up on the hill. She'd probably wanted to punish her brother. Teresa was sure Jorge was responsible for the shootings, but had no evidence to prove it. And in times like these, the truth was no barrier to men like Jorge. She did not sleep at night, wondering what would happen to her when people started to take Jorge at his word.

And in some ways, Teresa believed that what Jorge was saying was true. She had wanted some punishment for her brother. She had been responsible for sending Olive out, so that Olive might learn the truth about the man she considered the key to her success. Teresa came to believe that Olive had died because of her, and at night, she howled the guilt into her pillow. That Harold might hear of Jorge's rumour was both Teresa's greatest worry and her dearest wish. Harold might kill her in his grief – but at least it would end her misery.

IN THE DAYS AFTER OLIVE was buried, Harold, Sarah and Teresa moved around as if underwater. Teresa felt she was choking for the lack of air. Marbella and Alhama fell to the rebels, and still the Schlosses did not move. It was not until a 500-kilo bomb killed fifty-two people in one building in Malaga, and at the Regina Hotel a girl lost both her legs on the eve of her wedding day, that the family shook the stupor off their grief.

The naval bombardment was stepping up, as were the aerial attacks. There were five warships in the waters round Fuengirola. In Malaga, they reported, there was no longer anyone in control, nobody in authority. No public services, no organization whatsoever. The militia were half-crazed, there was no electricity, no trams, no police. Madrid looked like a picnic after its air attacks, they said, compared to Malaga.

'We must leave,' Teresa told Harold. 'Please. Isaac is dead, and half of the village already think that I am guilty – how will I ever live?'

'You'll survive,' he said.

'Please, señor, I have worked hard. I am innocent.'

He looked at her. 'Are you?'

Teresa held his gaze. 'Señor. I have always kept your secret.'

She watched the comprehension dawning on Harold's face, keeping her own expression neutral, although her heart was thumping. She had no choice. 'Señor,' she went on, 'would your wife keep you in money if she knew about the German?'

'WE'RE TAKING TERESA OUT OF Spain,' Harold said to his wife, the very next day. 'It is the least we can do. She will go on Olive's papers.'

'Fine,' Sarah said, unwilling to catch Teresa's eye. Teresa knew full well that Sarah had her own good reasons to wish her far away, but Teresa held Sarah's secret too, and so the Englishwoman said nothing.

It was a cold afternoon when they left. They were a strange reconfiguration, the most fractured trio on that ship – and that was saying something. There was no glamour in departure to echo the way that they'd arrived; the sky a sheet of changing greys, the sea beyond unending. The noise of the rusty chains loosening from the quay at Malaga caused in Teresa a monstrous sort of happiness. For under her sense of relief that she was leaving, she felt already the pulse of guilt. She had paid her escape with Olive's blood.

Her own expression was mirrored in the faces of the other passengers, as the land began to diminish and thin. It was a bitter miracle. They'd done it; they'd got away, but at the same time they hadn't, of course they hadn't. Teresa knew that part of her would never be able to leave.

SHE HAD NEVER BEEN ON a ship; she'd only ever known the land. Harold said the vessel was called a *destroyer*. Teresa thought of her ruined notebook, of how blackly apt an English noun could be. She gripped the rail, resisting the desire to jump, to plunge into the churning waters. It was so many colours, the sea; mud and milk, slate and leaf, and bronze when the light caught the crest of a wave – and at times, where it was still settled beyond, where the bows had not carved through it, a purer blue. Teresa realized that over the months, she'd come to understand how many colours there were that she had never noticed. She wanted the wind to whip her face, to sting and numb her, but it wasn't happening. No force of nature could erase her.

SHE THOUGHT AGAIN ABOUT THE morning they found Olive. Harold still didn't know why Olive had gone out into the darkness the night before. In his grief to flee, to get out of this hellhole, his daughter dead, he didn't stop to wonder why Olive might have been out there in the first place. He didn't consider that other members of his family might also be looking for love, for some purpose or salvation in another person. But when that morning had dawned, and Olive didn't come down to breakfast, Sarah and Teresa looked at one another, and assumed between them that silence on this matter would be better. So it remained.

The initial, mild discomfort of that morning had turned to horror, as Harold, realizing his daughter was missing, had taken the car out and found her body on the hillside. An hour later the women heard his motor again, the clang of the gate as he clipped it with the car, Olive's body lolling on the back seat. Harold staggered towards the women, his daughter in his arms. *I'm taking her with us*, he'd said, his voice oddly dull, as if he were miles away, speaking down the tunnel of his own body. At the sight of her dead child, Sarah had broken down.

Now, trying to recall all this, forcing herself to face it in order to carry on – Teresa could only remember fragments of these moments. It was the physical that stuck with her; the thud of her knees sinking to the ground, the taste of the cheap acorn coffee coming up her throat as she vomited onto the flagstones. The touch of Olive's body. White-skinned but bluish, stiff and bloodstained, three gunshot wounds visible through her jumper.

'She called this place home,' Sarah had said, slurring, hours later, the three of them sitting in the front east room. Harold was drunk, Sarah was on some pill or other. It was a living nightmare. They had placed Olive's body in the kitchen, the coldest part of the house, at the back. 'We must bury her here,' Sarah whispered, haggard with grief.

'What happened to my brother?' Teresa asked. Sarah covered her face with her hands.

'Jorge came for him,' said Harold. 'I only carried Olive.'

'Jorge?' said Teresa. 'Where did he take him?'

'I don't know.'

When both Sarah and Harold had passed out – Sarah on the sofa and Harold upright in the armchair, his whisky tumbler beginning to slip – Teresa set the glass on the floor and tiptoed down the corridor. She imagined Jorge, slinging her brother's body somewhere in the woods, a shallow grave perhaps, no means of ever finding him again. She had to lean against the wall, ramming her hand into her mouth to stop herself from screaming.

OLIVE DIDN'T LOOK LIKE OLIVE any more. Mottled, eyes closed, mouth slightly ajar. Her teeth were visible, which made her look even more vulnerable. Teresa reached out to touch Olive's arm, feeling how solid it was, now the blood no longer flowed. She touched Olive's head, and felt dead herself – a dead person living, a ghost with flesh on her bones. She saw something sticking from the pocket of Olive's skirt. It was the photograph from Isaac's set; Olive and Isaac standing in front of *Rufina and the Lion* in the attic.

I promise you on my life, she said to Olive in Spanish, putting the photograph in her own pocket, *I will not let this go unpunished*.

But even as she spoke, a quiet voice within Teresa told her already how hard it would be to avenge their deaths. How can you battle with a shadow in your own village square? This was the worst of it; that in the face of this senseless waste, Teresa was powerless. There was nothing she could do to bring them back. The only thing she could keep alive was memory.

THE NEXT DAY, SARAH HAD come up to the attic as Teresa was finishing her packing. All Olive's paints and sketchbooks were stowed away. All that was left was *Rufina and the Lion*, propped against the wall.

'Is that it?' Sarah had asked. 'The next one?'

'Yes.'

Sarah stood in front of it, saying nothing, drinking it in. Then she turned to Teresa, fixed her eyes on her, and said, 'Teresa, what's Isaac's painting doing up here?'

'Olive – was looking after it.'

'Why?'

'I don't know.'

Sarah turned back to the painting. 'I see.' She walked towards it and placed her hand on its edge. 'Well I'll be damned if that Guggenheim woman gets it,' she said, her voice breaking. 'This is for me.'

'No, no, señora, it must go to the Guggenheim gallery.'

Sarah whirled on her. 'Are you telling me what to do? This is the last thing I have—'

'Señora,' Teresa pleaded.

Sarah narrowed her eyes. 'What's that in your hand?'

'Nothing,' said Teresa, putting the photograph behind her back.

'Show me.'

Sarah grabbed the photograph. On seeing Isaac and her daughter, captured in what looked like a moment of happiness, she put a hand to her mouth and turned away, dragging *Rufina and the Lion* with her along the floor.

Teresa called down the stairs. 'I think Isaac's body is in the wood. Will you help me bury it—'

'Shut up,' said Sarah. She stopped, but did not turn round. Her hand came up and touched her straggly curls, and Teresa saw that she was trembling. 'I can't,' she whispered. 'I can't help.' She stumbled down the stairs.

To see the painting disappear with Sarah felt to Teresa as if her own strength was leaking away. But she could hardly wrench Olive's painting out of Sarah's hands. If she wanted to leave for England, for now at least there was nothing she could do.

TERESA TRIED TO PUSH THESE memories away, placing her chin on the handrail as the ship gained speed through the water. She wondered what Sarah was going to do with the painting and the photograph. The painting was in the hull, right now. Idly, she considered sneaking down and putting it into her own trunk. But it was too risky; she had to keep a low profile. The photograph would be easier to lift with light fingers – it was probably in Sarah's purse. Was it that Sarah had wanted an image of Isaac, or of Olive? It was hard to tell, but either way, Sarah had clutched that photograph like a talisman. She was vaguely aware of other passengers behind her on deck, taking a walk before night fell.

'Hello,' said a man, breaking into her thoughts.

Teresa flinched, her gaze fixed on the horizon as she tugged the woollen hat she was using to cover her short fuzz of hair. She didn't want to talk.

'Bloody shame, isn't it,' he went on.

He was English; young and upright. Teresa saw his fingers on the rail; black hairs sprouting on each one. 'Not good at all,' he said. 'I should have stayed, but I couldn't. We had to close the consulate.'

Teresa turned: he had blue eyes and a stern face. He looked like something out of an adventure book. He was frowning, almost talking to himself. She noticed the shadows of sleeplessness on his face, but he was the one to ask her if she was quite well.

'I am, yes, thank you,' Teresa replied, in her best English. She looked over her shoulder. Harold and Sarah had not emerged from their berths. She didn't want them to see her talking to anyone, but she wondered if they would by this point even care. Sarah had been insistent on going back to London, but Harold wanted to pick up the thread with Peggy Guggenheim in Paris. They were going to separate; Teresa could see it, even if they couldn't. Olive was a shadow between them, a touchstone of guilt, recrimination and pain.

'Why couldn't you stay?' she asked him.

'The bombs. That, and other parts of Europe requiring our attention. But still.' He cleared his throat. 'Don't think it's right.'

'No.'

'What's your name?' he asked.

She said nothing, and there was amusement on his tired face. 'I see,' he went on. 'Like that, is it? I detect an accent though. Do you speak Spanish?'

'Yes.'

Teresa could tell he was intrigued by her. In the satchel she had not let go of since leaving the finca, she had Olive's admission letter from the Slade, and a telegram from Peggy Guggenheim expressing her impatience for the next Isaac Robles. Given that Harold had kept hold of her identity documents, these flimsy bits of paper were all Teresa had left. She touched the satchel, her guard down with tiredness, her mind hopping too quickly to hold her nerve. Picturing being thrown off the side of the boat for her failed impersonation, she gripped the rail harder.

'Any other languages I should know about?' the man asked, passing her his hip-flask, which she drank from, hesitantly. She told him she knew a bit of German and at this, he became even more intrigued. 'Where are you going?' he asked.

'England.'

'Nowhere more specific?'

'London. Curzon Street.'

'Very nice. Family there?'

'Parents.'

'I see,' he said, but he did not look convinced, and Teresa felt herself collapsing within. 'And what are you going to do when you get there?' he pushed.

Teresa suspected that Harold and Sarah, for their separate reasons, would be glad to see the back of her. They'd done enough, bringing her out of Spain to protect their respective secrets, using their daughter's name to do so. Teresa knew she was already a nuisance they'd rather forget. She wasn't sure how far she'd be able to push her luck.

'I don't know what I am going to do next,' she said to the man, thinking there was no harm in fusing a true statement in the middle of her evasions.

'I might be able to help you. If you're willing to help me.'

'How?' she asked. Behind his head, the coast of Spain had by now completely disappeared.

'Come to this address,' he said. 'Whenever you can. A Monday is best.'

Teresa took the small card he was proffering, and read the words *Foreign Office, Whitehall, London*. She didn't know what that was, or how to get there, but she worried that if she confessed to this man, he would take his offer away. She tried to assess him; was it her body he wanted? It didn't seem so, but then, she knew by now how false the English could be, how good they were at saying the opposite of what they really meant.

He picked up on her hesitation. 'I promise, it's quite all right.'

Teresa turned back to watch the horizon. She pictured Olive's *Rufina*, the girl and her severed head and her lion, buried deep in the ship. *A girl has died*, she thought, *because I tried to save her*. She looked down at the water, remembering the promise she had whispered to Olive's body. 'Whitehall,' she repeated to the man. 'Best on a Monday.'

He smiled again. 'Excellent. I hope to see you there.'

Teresa heard his footsteps receding. She ran her fingers over the card. It was cream-coloured, and it had weight to it, a touch of authority. She flipped it over. There was nothing on it but a name: *Edmund Reede*. She repeated the strange words under her breath, before slipping the offering into her satchel. While she could not envisage what this Whitehall was, nor what Mr Edmund Reede might do for her, she knew that there was nothing left behind that would make her turn back.

The other passengers had retired. It was very cold by now. The sun began to disappear, but Teresa stayed on deck. Even when she could no longer feel her limbs, even after the night had claimed the horizon, she waited. She watched the blackness, watched the stars, as the destroyer carved its passage to England's shores.

Afterword

20

I recognized Quick's lawyer immediately. He was the thin man in the suit I'd seen at the gallery on the opening night of 'The Swallowed Century', staring closely at *Rufina and the Lion*. He was called Frederick Parr, and without much ado, he welcomed me into his office and handed me a thick folder, tied at the side with a red ribbon. My hand shook slightly; the breath was tight in my throat. I wanted to ask him how he'd come to be in the gallery that night – whether it was Quick who had invited him, and why, but I was too intimidated, and the weight of the folder in my hands seemed to keep my mouth closed.

'It was Miss Quick's request that no one read that but you,' Parr said.

'Thank you.' I fumbled the folder into my bag and began to exit the office, relieved that our transaction was over.

'That's not the only reason you're here,' he went on. 'Please, come and sit down, Miss Bastien.'

I obliged, walking across his dark green carpet, lowering myself into the large wooden chair in front of his desk. Parr stalked round this wide piece of furniture before settling himself opposite me. The air between us thickened. I saw why Quick might have employed him for such disbursements, for he remained unmoved by my obvious nerves. Parr suited her purposes entirely. He was a sphinx; his job to execute her wishes and nothing else. He looked down at the document on his desk. 'Miss Bastien,' he said, pressing his spindly fingers together to make a temple. 'Marjorie named you in her will.'

I heard these words, and although I understood them, I could not grasp their implication. 'I'm sorry?'

Parr blinked, impassive as a lizard. Outside, below us, the city traffic honked and beeped. 'She had a cottage, in Wimbledon,' he said.

'Yes.'

'She bequeathed it to you. In perpetuity.'

I MUST, AT SOME POINT, have left the offices in Bread Street and walked back to St Paul's Tube station. I imagine the walk was slow, that my heart felt odd. Quick had left me her cottage. I had signed some papers. It was overwhelming. When, *when* had she made such a decision? And why me? It was an inheritance the like of which I would never have imagined.

I must have clutched her folder tight. At least here was a solid thing – a gesture embodied in paper that I might better understand. Perhaps the answers to all my questions were in here. I was probably terrified that I might be mugged, and I must have sat on the train all the way to Clapham Common, refusing to open it in public. It burned my lap, but I needed to be alone, in quiet, when I finally read it.

I managed to get off at my stop, and was barely up the stairs and through the flat door before I tore the ribbon and began to read. *Dear Odelle, This is a long story*, it began, and I sat up till midnight reading it. I forgot to eat, my neck was stiff, but I didn't care. Here was everything Quick had ever wanted me to know, but couldn't find the words to tell me to my face. People, places, evenings spent under the vast Andalusian skies. Her story was bigger and brighter than anything my own imagination would have pictured. And as I finished it, my eyes red and shrunken with tiredness, my head pounding, I realized something else. Here, also, was everything that Olive Schloss had never wanted the world to know.

This folder was the evidence of Quick's perpetual, honourable silence over *Rufina and the Lion*, which conflicted with her anxiety to pass on the story of Olive Schloss before it was too late. For most of the time I knew Quick, she had been in crisis. Her centre could no longer hold. It must have been an astounding trigger to see that photograph of Olive and her brother, and the painting of *Rufina*, all those years later, to understand better than anyone what it represented – and to watch it be commodified, re-moulded, attributed to Isaac, yet again.

As Teresa Robles, she knew Olive had wanted to remain anonymous. As Quick, she felt the injustice in that. Nothing had been resolved between these two selves. This pressure, and the memory of what happened in those last days in Spain, coupled with the powerful pain relief she was on, no doubt exacerbated Quick's hallucinatory states and her general inability to put it all to rest. What she left for me to read in the folder explained why her behaviour had wheeled between solicitous and elusive. Teresa had cracked open; the reappearance of the painting had proved too much.

I still do not know if her death was accidental. Most of the time, I believe that it was not. She realized she would never find the words to speak the trauma of Olive's last days. And one might argue, that in the face of such aggressive cancer she saw that she could at least control her end, leaving the folder for me to find through her lawyer. I think often of Teresa's notebook of English; discarded by Jorge, discovered again by Olive, and then, in that folder, by me. It seems that she – like myself – always found the written word an easier means through which to understand the world.

She left no specific instructions with Parr as to what I was supposed to do with this folder. So for years, I did nothing. In fact, until now, I never told anyone what I read, that cold November night under my bedsheets. I didn't even speak to Reede about it, although I wish I had.

In the folder, Quick didn't detail exactly what happened when she arrived in England, but she must have taken up Reede's offer to meet him in Whitehall. I imagine that with her languages, and

Reede's connections in the Foreign Office, she would have been useful to Britain as the world groaned its way to war. There were quite a few Nazis in Spain by the early '40s. And in its way, I'm sure that Britain – and Reede – was useful to her too. Gratitude comes in strange shapes. A beautiful cottage on Wimbledon common, for example.

I BECAME AS GOOD AS Teresa at keeping people's secrets. I never told Lawrie that Quick was possibly his aunt, an aunt he'd met several times without realizing their true connection. I didn't want to set something in motion that I could never conclusively prove, I suppose, and besides, Quick was dead. It might have made it worse for him, knowing there had been family left behind, but everything being too late. In the folder, Quick mentioned Sarah's *affair* with Isaac, but not a pregnancy. *I* knew Sarah Schloss was Lawrie's mother, that she was pregnant when she came back to England, because Lawrie told me that himself. But it is arguable – given the time frame – that Teresa, and therefore Quick, had not known that Sarah was pregnant when she was having her affair with Isaac. Quick would not necessarily have made the connection between Lawrie and her brother.

This leaves unexplained, of course, why Quick had the Scotts' address in her telephone book, and her interest in the question of Lawrie's mother. It could have been due to her own investigations over Lawrie's possession of the painting, before the cancer was too much. But sometimes, I wonder. Did Quick look at Lawrie and see her brother's face, echoed there? Or did she see Harold Schloss's features imprinted in his son? Or did she think nothing of it at all? Whatever it was, she always seemed unenthusiastic that Lawrie was my boyfriend.

One only need look again at the photo of Isaac Robles to see similarities between him and Lawrie – but Harold had dark hair too. Lawrie's paternity remained a question mark. I do sometimes wonder if Lawrie knew this, too – given how vague his mother always was to him about his father. And yet, I will always remember how he requested from Reede a copy of that photograph of Isaac Robles.

SOME PEOPLE WILL THINK THAT my silence all these years was wrong. After all, the rare times that an Isaac Robles comes onto the market, it sells for astronomical sums. Olive Schloss deserved her artist's triumph, Lawrie deserved to know the whole story – but is there ever such a thing as a whole story, or an artist's triumph, a right way to look through the glass? It all depends where the light falls. Teresa Robles witnessed the benefits of working anonymously, and as I read Olive's story, so did I. As far as I can tell, she certainly enjoyed the pseudonym. The work, for her, was everything.

Rufina now hangs, of all places, in the National Gallery in Trafalgar Square, beyond those huge lions where once I saw Cynth waiting, dressed in her new sheepskin coat. After several years in a private collection, it went back into auction, and was purchased by the nation as part of the gallery's drive to acquire more twentieth-century art. There was fierce competition from the Prado in Madrid, and I expect Reede was grimly satisfied that they didn't get it. He never forgot the time they wouldn't lend him that Goya. The photograph was returned to the Prado. How it got there in the first place is a mystery; I can only suppose that Sarah returned it to Spain's national gallery, in a mistaken attempt to keep their interest in Isaac Robles alive.

IT WAS A STRANGE TIME, after Quick died. The exhibition was considered a success by the Skelton, and Reede was pleased with the attention and income it generated. Gerry did sell Sarah's house, so Lawrie lost his home, just as I found mine. The sale of *Rufina and the Lion* severed Lawrie's ties to his mother's past, to Gerry; all of it. Or at least, he probably hoped it did, for art rarely obeys human desire. I expect such a painting left its imprint, even when he couldn't see it. With *Rufina* sold, Lawrie used some of the funds to go on a trip to

America. He invited me, but I stayed in London, because I wanted to be in Quick's house, to keep working at the Skelton.

In the end, Lawrie didn't come back.

I'd like to say that the elasticity of youth meant the skin stretched easy. He would call from New York every week, to tell me he missed me, why didn't I come over – but I was where I wanted to be, and the fact was, I did not miss Lawrie as much as I might have missed my work. He had told me to keep writing, so I did. I would have preferred not to have to choose between writing and loving; because for me, they were often the same thing.

It was a time of new experiences, without the benefit of the old to mitigate the after-effects. My life was a beanstalk and I was Jack, and the foliage was shooting up and up, abundant, impressive, at such speed that I could barely cling on. I loved and I lost love; I found new creativity and a sense of belonging. And something deeper happened, something darker, which we have all gone through – and if we have not, it is waiting for us – the indelible moment when we realize we are alone.

Perhaps I didn't have to choose. Perhaps that was a dichotomy I set up myself. Regardless; the phone calls became more sporadic, and then they stopped.

ON THE DAY I WENT to Quick's cottage with the keys, I took both Cynth and Pamela with me. The place was much as it had been that night the ambulance men carried Quick out on the stretcher. There was the faint smell of her Eau Sauvage in the air. It was cold. The heating had been off and it was nearly December. I expected the face of her cat to appear at the kitchen door, but he had fled.

We went from room to room. It is not a large cottage. There are four rooms upstairs – three bedrooms, and a bathroom that freezes your skin in the winter months due to the inappropriately huge single-glazed window and tiles everywhere. Quick didn't have much. Simple beds, attractive rugs, cracked ceilings. In the room I assumed was hers, she had a small table wedged under the window, which overlooked her garden. On the table was a type-writer, the same she had used to write the contents of the folder. I stared down at the machine. It felt like it was staring back at me.

Every day since, I have tried to put that typewriter to good use.

ON THE OCCASIONS I AM asked to look back and reflect on my own books, I realize it has been my lifetime's purpose to try and understand what happened when I started working with Marjorie Quick. It started with me writing her eulogy, and has gone on from there. The preoccupations, the timbre, the shape of my writing have hinged on that short period of my life. My writing is the constant reconfiguration of how I myself was once reconfigured.

I often visited the gallery, specifically to see *Rufina and the Lion*, to stand with the public and admire its enduring power. What Teresa intended all those years ago, had, in its own way, come true. And yet more recently, as I have watched the sisters, I know that behind those eyes and underneath those brushstrokes there is another story, a story that is now partly mine. One woman, her body buried by the roots of an olive tree. Another, fleeing and facing unknown waters. Then me.

The rediscovery of *Rufina and the Lion* in 1967 was bound up with my own awakenings: my understanding of Quick, Cynth and her baby, my affair with Lawrie, a growing confidence in my own writing. That painting set delayed time bombs, which carried on exploding – sometimes gently, sometimes with perturbing force – as the decades rolled on.

And last year, a question began to press inside me, as persistent as a lion who sets his sight upon you and will not let you go. For years I had enjoyed the girls' hidden truth, this extra privilege, this miraculous secret of a nineteen-year-old, painting in the attic of her father's rented house in Spain. And I wondered: might someone look at Rufina, at me, and believe such things? A new curiosity, rather than my hard-earned confidence, became the fuel to write.

Although any collective answer to my question remains to be seen, personally I feel quite certain of it. Because if there's one thing I've learned, it's this: in the end, a piece of art only succeeds when its creator – to paraphrase Olive Schloss – possesses the belief that brings it into being.

Odelle Bastien

Wimbledon, 2002

BIBLIOGRAPHY

ART

Berger, John – *About Looking* (Writers' and Readers' Publishing Co-op, 1980)

Bernier, Rosamond – *Matisse, Picasso, Miró – As I Knew Them* (Sinclair Stevenson, 1991)

Bernier, Rosamond – *Some of My Lives* (Farrar, Straus & Giroux, 2011)

Chadwick, Whitney – *Women, Art and Society* (Thames & Hudson, Fifth Edition 2012)

Guggenheim, Peggy – *Out of This Century: Confessions of An Art Addict* (Deutsch, 1980)

Hook, Philip – *Breakfast at Sotheby's* (Penguin, 2013)

Mancoff, Debra N. – *Danger! Women Artists At Work* (Merrell, 2012)

LONDON

Reed, Jane – *Girl About Town: How to Live in London – And Love It!* (Tandem, 1965)

SPAIN AND THE SPANISH CIVIL WAR

Barker, Richard – *Skeletons in the Closet, Skeletons in the Ground: Repression, Victimization and Humiliation in a Small Andalusian Town – The Human Consequences of the Spanish Civil War* (Sussex Academic Press, 2012)

Buckley, Henry – *The Life and Death of the Spanish Republic: A Witness to the Spanish Civil War* (I.B. Tauris, 2014)

Casanova, Julián – *A Short History of the Spanish Civil War* (I.B. Tauris, 2012)

García Lorca, Federico – *Romancero Gitano* (1928)

Graham, Helen – *The War and Its Shadow: Spain's Civil War in Europe's Long Twentieth Century* (Sussex Academic Press, 2012)

Koestler, Arthur – *Dialogue with Death* (1942)

Lee, Laurie – *A Moment of War* (Viking, 1991)

Lee, Laurie – *As I Walked Out One Midsummer Morning* (1969)

Preston, Paul – *The Spanish Holocaust* (HarperPress, 2011)

Woolsey, Gamel – *Death's Other Kingdom* (1939)

TRINIDAD AND THE CARIBBEAN EXPERIENCE IN BRITAIN

Braithwaite, Lloyd – *Colonial West Indian Students in Britain* (UWI Press, 2001)

Chamberlain, Mary – *Narratives of Exile and Return* (St Martin's Press, 1997)

Dathorne, O.R. – *Dumplings in the Soup* (Cassell, 1963)

Hinds, Donald – *Journey to an Illusion: The West Indian in Britain* (Heinemann, 1966)

James, C.L.R. – *Black Jacobins* (Martin, Secker & Warburg, 1938)

Lamming, George – *The Pleasures of Exile* (Michael Joseph, 1960)

Miller, Kei (ed.) – *New Caribbean Poetry; An Anthology* (Carcanet, 2007)

Mittelholzer, Edgar – *With A Carib Eye* (Secker & Warburg, 1958)

Naipaul, V.S. – *Miguel Street* (Deutsch, 1959)

Schwarz, Bill – *West Indian Intellectuals in Britain* (MUP, 2003)

Selvon, Sam – *The Lonely Londoners* (Alan Wingate, 1956)

Stuart, Andrea – *Sugar in the Blood* (Portobello, 2012)

Tajfel, Henri and John Dawson – *Disappointed Guests* (OUP, 1965)

Radio

Radio 4 (2015): *Raising the Bar: 100 Years of Black British Theatre and Screen*, presented by Lenny Henry – particularly episode 2, *Caribbean Voices* – writers and actors from the Caribbean coming to work in London

Film

The Stuart Hall Project (dir. John Akomfrah, 2013) – Key domestic and international historical events feature West Indian migration to the UK, the Suez Crisis, the Hungarian Uprising, the birth of youth counterculture, the Civil Rights movement and the Vietnam War, and Hall's mixed experiences with 'Britishness' as a post-war immigrant

London – The Modern Babylon (dir. Julien Temple, 2012)

Fighting for King and Empire: Britain's Caribbean Heroes (BBC4 documentary, producers: Marc Wadsworth and Deborah Hobson of The-Latest.com, first aired May 2015, based on the documentary, *Divided By Race, United By War And Peace*, also made by The-Latest.Com)

ACKNOWLEDGMENTS

Thank you to:

Francesca Main, Megan Lynch and Jennifer Lambert, who made this possible

Juliet Mushens, who saw me through

Sasha Raskin and Sarah Manning, who brought up the rear

Professor Mary Chamberlain, who gave her time and opened my eyes a bit wider

Colin McKenzie, who lent his erudition on matters of art

Professor Patricia Mohammed at the University of the West Indies, Trinidad, who generously advised on Odelle and Cynthia's language

Gail Bradley, who diligently scoured the script

Any inaccuricies in these matters are, of course, my own.

Also to:

Alice O'Reilly, Teasel Scott and my family; in less obvious, but equally important ways, you helped me write this novel

and

Pip Carter, for everything